D1349178

# UNHOLY LOVE

*Also by Meg Hutchinson*

ABEL'S DAUGHTER

FOR THE SAKE OF HER CHILD

A HANDFUL OF SILVER

NO PLACE OF ANGELS

A PROMISE GIVEN

BITTER SEED

PIT BANK WENCH

CHILD OF SIN

NO PLACE FOR A WOMAN

THE JUDAS TOUCH

PEPPERCORN WOMAN

*Writing as Margaret Astbury*

THE HITCH HIKER

THE SEAL

# UNHOLY LOVE

## Meg Hutchinson

Hodder & Stoughton

Copyright © 2002 by Meg Hutchinson

First published in 2002 by Hodder and Stoughton
A division of Hodder Headline

The right of Meg Hutchinson to be identified as the Author of
the Work has been asserted by her in accordance with the
Copyright, Designs and Patents Act 1988.

10 9 8 7 6 5 4 3 2 1

A CIP catalogue record for this title
is available from the British Library.

ISBN 0 340 81817 4

Typeset by Hewer Text Ltd, Edinburgh
Printed and bound in Great Britain by
Mackays of Chatham PLC, Chatham, Kent

Hodder and Stoughton
A division of Hodder Headline
338 Euston Road
London NW1 3BH

To those 'glassmen' of Sunderland Glass Museum, in recognition of their kind co-operation in demonstrating the processes involved in the making of glassware, and for allowing me the pleasure of blowing a piece for myself, an unforgettable moment. But especially my thanks go to David Mulligan for his patience in answering what must have been for him my many and tedious questions.

# Chapter One

'You robbed me of my son!'

Archer Cranley's eyes folded in on themselves, rage spitting between narrow slits.

'You robbed me of the one thing I held dear in life . . . your jealousy and your spite robbed me. And now you turn that spite against your own mother, now she is the one you would see dead . . .'

'That's not true! Father, you know that is not true.'

'Do I?' Archer flashed. 'Then who else killed the boy, who else eh? Answer me that. There was only the two of you there by that mill-race, two of you and no other. It was you wandered off towards that mill knowing your younger brother would follow: you who threw a dandelion into the water, telling him to do the same; then when he did you pushed him, pushed him into those swirling waters and watched as he was caught by the wheel: watched his little body being turned round and round . . .'

'No . . . I wouldn't . . .'

'Oh, but you would!' Archer Cranley's eyes widened a fraction, satisfaction gleaming deep beneath the rage. 'And you would do the same again, you *are* doing the same again. Oh this time you can't push the one who stands in your way into a mill stream, but that won't stop you will it, Philip? You know other ways, ways infinitely more subtle, ways such as torture of the mind. That be what you're using against your mother, driving her so far out of her mind that in the end she'll kill herself; that way no blame can be attached to you. But death by her own hand or not, we'll both know the truth. Murder be murder however you dress it up.'

His fine-boned face devoid of colour, Philip Cranley stared at the man stood opposite. All of his life, as far back as memory could reach, there had been no love in this man. Not once in all of those memories was there one of being taken into that man's arms or seeing him smiling. Not one smile that said 'I'm proud of you' and certainly never one that said 'You are my child and I love you.'

The pain of the thoughts lancing sharply across an already heavy heart Philip answered quietly, 'I would rather die myself than harm my mother in any way.'

'Fine words!' the older man snarled. 'But then they come easy to you. What do they call it . . . a honeyed tongue . . . but we both know it has a sting at the end. You want your mother dead, dead so you can come into your inheritance the sooner. Greed, Philip, greed . . . that is the tool of the devil and you know well how to use it. Greed and pride, that is the true legacy of Nathan Briant, it was the very blood and bone of his existence and now it is yours; and you will honour it, live up to it in every way he did, even if that means sacrificing your own mother.'

'I did not ask for my grandfather's legacy . . . I would much prefer not to have it.'

'You would much prefer . . . you bloody hypocrite!' Archer Cranley's fist hit the leather-topped desk hard. 'Would you say that if you were of an age to give it all up? No! No, you would not. Words, that's all it be, words you use to hide behind, them and your mother's skirts. But now you can be doing without the skirts, you be feeling your feet; how long before the hindrance of a mother and a father become too much, how long, eh Philip . . . how long before we both be thrown into a mill-race?'

Why was it always like this? Philip watched the anger blazing in those ferret-like eyes, the thin lips turned so far in on themselves as to have almost disappeared. Why did their every meeting, their every conversation turn almost at once to Nathan Briant's Will?

'How long before you turn your mother and me onto the streets?' Archer Cranley's mean mouth snapped like a trap. 'Don't be frightened to say it, Philip, if ever you intend to be your own man then start now; or should I say it for you, should I tell your mother to pack her bags and we'll leave at once?'

Knowing that the unhappiness that haunted every day could not be hidden Philip turned away, gazing out through a tall window. Away in the distance the cone of the glassworks rose to brush against the sky. If only that Will had been worded differently, if only everything had not been left to Nathan Briant's daughter to do with as she wished, then none of this animosity, this resentment would exist; but then how long might Hannah Cranley have existed? Being sole owner of the glass-works, the only one ever to have complete dominion over it, seemed to be a consummate obsession with Archer Cranley, the only passion, the only true love of his life. There could be no telling what lengths he may have gone to in order to fulfil his dream. May have gone to? Staring out at the cone, tall and black against the evening sky, Philip felt the twist of churning stomach nerves. Or would still go to!

Was it not enough to rob his own child of its identity, to take a daughter's name, changing it as he had so long ago and forbidding its use ever again? In the eyes of the world it was not the son of Archer Cranley who had died in that accident but his daughter: yes, Philippa was dead to everyone and in her place stood Philip. The secret had been guarded well, the blossoming shape of womanhood hidden beneath a man's clothing . . . but for how much longer could she live a lie that must have her act the role of a son? Would Archer

Cranley forgo his own desires once the full terms of that Will were reached?

'You know it will never come to that.' She spoke quietly, hoping the raw feelings did not show in the words. 'I would never turn Mother or yourself from this house.'

'Hah!' Archer Cranley laughed, a dry cynical laugh that stayed in his throat. 'You say that now but later you'll sing a different song . . .'

'I mean what I say.' She swung around, her blue eyes veiling their pain. 'This house will always belong to Mother . . .'

'Yes, to your mother . . . to Nathan Briant's precious daughter!' Archer Cranley's knuckles cracked under the pressure of being pressed against the desk top. 'And me . . . what do I get? A bloody paid hand! Oh, Briant thought it out so very well; a paid hand I was and a paid hand I would be until you came of age and then it would be out with Archer Cranley altogether. That was the way her father took his revenge; he couldn't kick my arse from his door, not if he wanted to hold on to his daughter's love, so he kicked it this way, by making sure naught save a pittance of his money ever came to me, and in a few months even that will go. It will be all yours, Philip, yours alone, yours to finish what Nathan Briant could not.'

As if only now realising the full significance of what was said Philip, as she knew she must always think of herself, felt a strange calm settle in place of pain.

'Yes, it will all be mine, mine to do with as I wish.'

Across the desk Archer Cranley's ferret eyes sparked a sudden fear. He had let his bile rise too high, showed the feelings that had eaten away at him for years, that still ate away at him. Had he gone too far to smooth things over? There were so few weeks left . . . the plan he had would work but he must curb the hate that burned in him, the resentment that bit like acid in his soul.

Lowering slowly into the leather chair set at the desk he let his head sink to his chest, his voice holding a tremble.

'I shouldn't have spoken that way, Philip, it's just that I be so worried. I've followed the terms of your grandfather's Will, holding the glassworks together for the sake of your mother and for you, keeping it going 'til you were of the age to take it upon yourself. That being so, my working as manager of Briant Bottle and Glass, I had neither time nor opportunity to create a business of my own, to build a secure financial background for my family. The money I have been paid all these years was sufficient only for the needs of your mother, the continual care of her health; there was never anything left to save and when my position at the works comes to an end . . .'

Letting the last come out on a juddering breath he lifted both hands to cover his face.

Was that the real underlying cause of so much friction between them, was that the source of the anger and unhappiness, the all-pervading misery that hung continually over this house? She looked at the man slumped at the desk, his dark hair glinting silver where it showed between the fingers spread across his temples. Or was there more . . . more than had ever been told?

Watching him now Philippa could not push away the thought, could not deny the feeling that this was no show of remorse nor of worry for the welfare of his wife but a farce played out to cover his own tracks. And if there was more? Then it could remain untold, remain Archer Cranley's secret to hold, as he so dearly held the wish to own Briant Bottle and Glass.

'If I could have renounced my inheritance I would have done so years ago.' Her words drifted quietly over the bent head. 'If I could have signed it away whilst still a child then I would have done so gladly, but the law forbade that. However, in a few weeks my childhood will be over and the law will no longer be a restriction on my actions. Very shortly now I shall be twenty-one years old and seen by law to be proficient at handling my own affairs. As you say, Father, the whole of my grandfather's property will then become mine including this house, mine to do with as I see fit. When that time comes I will sign the entire estate, works and all, over to Mother and to you. It will belong to you, Father, every stick and stone of it. Briant Bottle and Glass will become Cranley Bottle and Glass. I want no part of it!'

Hearing the study door close quietly Archer Cranley lifted his head, his thin mouth parted in a smile. Nathan Briant had taken every step to avoid any such happening, to prevent Briant Glass ever becoming Cranley Glass; at least he had thought he had taken every step, but Archer Cranley knew a sidestep . . . The smile widened like the mouth of a serpent preparing to take its prey. Yes, he knew a different step, and it was one he would take.

A few weeks more, a few weeks of the misery that had stalked a lifetime. Philippa Cranley looked up from the columns of figures filling a page of a black-bound ledger. Soon it would be over, this house and all it held could be left behind. But could it? Beyond the window heavy-headed roses nodded on long, slender stems. Hannah Cranley's favourite flower. Hannah, the one person who had ever shown love, ever had any time for the slight, perpetually frightened child, a woman who seemed no less afraid; how could she be left behind, left to the terrifying mood swings and temper of Archer Cranley? They could of course go together. She tapped the pen against tight lips. Would Archer allow that, would he be satisfied with the Bottle and Glass and let his wife go free? From the garden full-blown roses swung their beautiful heads as if rejecting the unspoken words. No, he would not let her leave; he would not let either of them leave. There must be no danger of anyone outside of this house learning of Archer Cranley's true feeling for his wife and child, no whisper of the extent of that man's cruelty.

The sound of sharp footsteps crossing the highly polished floor of the hall brought her back to the ledger. Edna Cranley was never far away, always hovering in the vicinity, her darting button eyes missing not the smallest detail; watching, always watching.

Hearing the door of the study open, Philippa ran the nib of the pen slowly down the length of neatly entered figures. Behind her Edna Cranley drew a long, almost vindictive breath. The pretence of having any feeling of tenderness for her had long since fallen away, and she knew it. But then she had never shown tenderness for anyone, not even her own brother. She had ruled this house for years, answering only to Archer Cranley, using her brother's wife and child as a means to vent her spite and frustration.

Keeping the pen to the figures Philippa ignored the figure watching from the doorway. Edna disliked her brother's family as much as he himself did; the question was why had she stayed here, why did she stay now? She had asked that same thing as a ten-year-old.

Pretending to insert a figure at the base of the column Philippa turned the page, repeating the process as before; but instead of numbers she saw a young child dressed in grey knickerbockers and sombre dark jacket, wheat-coloured hair plastered flat to the small head, a pale upturned face staring back as the question was asked.

Her fingers tight about the pen, Philippa saw again the closing of that thin vicious mouth, the raising of a long bony-fingered hand . . . the pen slipped across the page as the blow crashed down onto the child's face.

Why had Archer Cranley allowed such treatment of a child, why did he keep that woman in the house?

Throwing the pen down as the door closed behind her aunt, Philippa stared out of the window. There were questions to be asked. Nathan Briant's legacy would be signed over to Archer Cranley but not before answers had been given.

From the mantel above the fireplace a small marble clock sounded the hour of four. There was no echo of footsteps; only silence, heavy and living, hovered like some waiting beast over the house. Edna Cranley could be standing at the other side of that door, waiting to catch her leaving. It would not be the first time she had done that, it had been a particular trait of hers to lurk behind closed doors, a long-fingered claw fastening onto a child's collar, demanding to know its every move.

But childhood had passed into youth and now that too was almost passed, yet still Edna Cranley dominated every move. Pushing the chair away Philippa listened to the throb of silence. Edna would be in her room, but inner sense said she would not be sleeping; the child she had so bullied had wondered if the woman ever slept, the same thought often coming to mind even now.

Leaving the room, each footfall deliberately softened, her senses flaring like some burglar intent upon crime, she walked up the stairs and along the corridor to the room that should have been shared by Archer Cranley and his wife, but Archer Cranley spent no night in that large bed.

One hand resting on the handle, she listened again to the enveloping quiet, the brooding silence that dared any sound to break it. There was none from inside the room. A quick glance showing the landing corridor to be empty, her lungs holding a tight breath, she stepped inside.

Heavy curtains drawn across the half circle of a wide bay window held back the soft afternoon sunlight, leaving the bedroom shrouded in deep shadow. The atmosphere inside the room was warm and cloying. Philippa breathed, feeling a surge of anger rise at the familiar aroma. Laudanum! Edna Cranley had given her sister-in-law a dose of laudanum!

Drawing the curtains a little aside, allowing the light from the window to rest on the drawn face so pale the tracery of veins showed beneath an almost translucent skin, Philippa felt the anger change to despair. Hannah Cranley looked so frail and weak it seemed she might not live through those next few months. But she had to live!

8

Her fingers bunched into fists. Without Hannah what would it all have been worth, without her what would the future be worth? The future of Archer Cranley would become that which he had always wanted, always desired; that to which he had sacrificed a woman's happiness and a child's life; he would be sole master of Briant Bottle and Glass. And Edna Cranley, what would her future be, what prize had she demanded for the years given as her brother's housekeeper and wardress to his wife and child? She was not a woman to do anything out of the goodness of her heart, there was no charity there, no pity in that icy soul. Whatever the reason for her leaving her parents' home to live with her brother there had to be a payment, but when was that payment to be made?

'What are you doing here?'

Philippa turned sharply. There had been no sound, no disturbance of the stillness had heralded the approach of that woman.

'I came to see my mother.'

In the half-light Edna Cranley's pencil-line mouth folded in on itself, her button eyes glittering.

'You know your mother always sleeps in the afternoon.'

Beneath the sardonic words Philippa recognised the challenge, and anger ripped the answer from her: 'That is not surprising, seeing the amount of laudanum you feed her!'

'She needs it.' Edna Cranley's ferret eyes, so like her brother's, darted to the green glass bottle stood on the bedside table.

'Does she!' Philippa answered coldly. 'Does my mother really need so much opiate, or is it you, Aunt . . . you and my father, is it the two of you need my mother's silence, the silence that drug brings?'

'She has to have laudanum!' Edna's little eyes flashed, 'Her turns . . .'

'Oh yes, my mother's "turns".' Philippa stared sceptically at the narrow-featured face, the twitch of the thin mouth. 'The "turns" she has suffered since I was born, the "turns" only you or my father have ever witnessed. Tell me, Aunt, why is it I do not see her suffering one, have *never* seen her suffer one?'

'Because I have always taken good care you shouldn't, I've always guarded you against that.'

'Taken good care.' Glancing at the sleeping figure Philippa felt every nerve tingle. 'Oh yes, Aunt, you have done that all right! But just who were you guarding, me or my father and yourself?'

Clasped across her brown skirts Edna Cranley's hands twisted together but her eyes remained fastened on that young face, her reply a venomous hiss: 'What does that mean?'

Philippa's glance returned to the thin, sharp, drawn features of the woman who for so long had darkened life, dislike of her rising hot and thick.

'It means what it says. Was the fact that not once as a child was I ever allowed to be alone with my mother, because I was being somehow safeguarded? Or, now that I have almost reached adulthood, is she forever sleeping whenever I get to see her because I still need to be guarded . . . or because you and my father are afraid of what I might hear, afraid now I am old enough to understand that my mother might tell me what it is you both want hidden? Is that the real cause behind the use of this?'

A swipe of one hand sent the bottle skimming across the room.

'Is that the reason my mother is kept a virtual prisoner in her own home? But that will not go on for much longer. I don't know what it is you want from my father but I know what it is he wants from me, and if he is ever to be the owner of Briant Bottle and Glass then you will leave this house the day I reach my twenty-first birthday and my mother will be given into my care, never to see Archer Cranley again.'

Among the sifted shadows Edna Cranley's eyes glowed with the vicious light of uncertain sanity.

'That day will never dawn,' she breathed, her lipless mouth

drawing back in an animal snarl. 'The only way you and her will ever be free of Archer Cranley is to leave this house in a coffin.' The eyes glittered more brightly. 'And I will help to lift you into it.'

# Chapter Two

You have kept your secret long enough, and so have I. Unless you want the whole town to know what it is you keep so well hidden you will be at the bandstand in Farley Park at 5 o'clock on Sunday afternoon of this week. Make no mistake this is not a joke, ignore it and by Monday it will be common knowledge.

*. . . what it is you keep so well hidden . . .*

Archer Cranley stared at the letter delivered by hand a few minutes ago, that one line dancing before his eyes. Who else could know . . . who could possibly have found out?

He stared at the letter again. It was unsigned and the hand was one he did not recognise.

Edna? No, his sister had too much to lose to go opening her mouth to anybody. Hannah, then? No, not her either, she rarely left the house and if she did then Edna was with her every moment. Visitors . . . they had soon stopped calling once they found out they were not welcome.

So who had written this letter?

Reading it through once more he tore it savagely into shreds, flinging it to the back of the fire and watching the flames snatch it with hungry tongues.

Some bugger who thought to make money out of him,

somebody who thought to blackmail him. Whoever it was penned the letter had not asked for money but a man with two blind eyes could see that was the intent.

Archer's thin lips whitened. If it were Simeon Beasley had let his tongue flap . . . but he wouldn't be fool enough, he was in this thing as deep as himself.

Edna said the letter had been delivered by a child who claimed he had been given a penny to bring it. He did not know the man who paid him nor was he given a name, he was told simply to deliver the letter.

'I am about to take Hannah's tea tray upstairs, will you be coming up to see her?' Edna Cranley looked at the taut face of her brother as he strode from the study.

'No.' It snapped out as he brushed past grabbing his tall silk hat and cane from an ornate coat stand.

'Is something wrong . . . did that letter bring bad news?'

'It brought nothing you needs know about, you tend to your business and leave me to tend to mine!'

Slamming the door behind him he stood a moment, drawing in a lungful of air. Somebody thought to rob Archer Cranley. Somebody was in for a very rude awakening!

Leaving the trap in the yard he walked in the direction of Phoenix Street. Swan Village was not so far from Farley Park and it would not be thought unusual for a man to take a late afternoon stroll.

Forcing his footsteps to remain casual he walked on, crossing over Hadley Bridge and on down Ryder's Green Road, raising his hat politely to the women or touching it with the tip of his cane to the men who passed by.

The entrance to Farley Park lay in Whitehall Lane. Archer turned to his right, passing a row of tall four-storeyed houses strung like costly beads along its edge, each trying to outdo the other with fancy porticoes and high-reaching windows. Pit owners and ironmasters all putting their money into bricks and mortar, each seeking to better the next. He laughed silently.

He would soon be doing the same, he would have his bricks and mortar and they would house the finest furniture; but not here, not in Swan Village nor Greets Green. Archer Cranley would have a home fit for a lord and it would be in some place where every breath you took was not laden with the filth of coal mines and ironworks.

Turning into the park through intricately wrought iron gates he had no eye for the tall pointed cypresses, the wide-spreading Lebanon cedars or the long dropping clusters of golden laburnum that edged the well-kept grounds, their tracery of leaves a perfect foil for the flower-beds that spread an exquisite tapestry of colour beneath their branches.

Following the path as it wound its way towards the bandstand placed at the heart of this small oasis of green, Archer's mind stayed with the letter he had burned.

*You have kept your secret long enough . . . Make no mistake this is not a joke.*

His hand tightening about the cane he tried to keep the anger from his face, nodding pleasantly to the polite greetings of other strollers in the park. Oh, he would make no mistake. Whoever had written that letter would find Archer Cranley made no mistakes!

Standing for a moment, he ran a sharp eye over the audience. There was no face familiar to him. While applause marked appreciation of the finale of *Pirates of Penzance*, he took one of the two seats remaining empty.

'I do so enjoy the works of Mr Gilbert and Mr Sullivan. They make such pleasant listening, do you not agree?'

Forcing a smile he glanced at the woman sat next to him. Dressed in sugar-pink moiré silk that rustled as she clapped long-gloved hands, she smiled beneath a concoction of feathers and roses. 'Indeed, ma'am, most entertaining.'

Was this the one had summoned him? Surely not. Archer removed his top hat, resting it on his knee. Surely a woman wouldn't dare . . .

'Especially the pirates, they really are most delicious, I find pirates quite fascinating.'

'So do I . . . as long as they are only a figment of their composer's imagination.'

The feathers of the hat trembling beneath the breath of a light summer breeze the woman giggled, turning her attention to the blue-and-gold-clad bandsmen as the conductor tapped his baton.

If it were she who had written the letter why not say so. Not moving his head he swivelled a glance sideways at the woman speaking now to the man sat on her other side. Were they both in this together?

'It don't be them you've come to see, Mr Cranley.'

The words were spoken in an undertone only just heard beneath the rousing notes of a military march.

Keeping his eyes to the front, every muscle of his body tautening, Archer made no reply.

'I knows you got my letter, Mr Cranley, I made sure o' that. I watched the lad hand it in at the door, your wife was it . . . the woman who took it from him? But no that would be your sister, for your wife 'as fair hair, don't she?'

Who the hell was this man . . . how had he got his information? Archer remained silent.

'Don't want to answer? Well, that's all right just so long as you listens . . .'

A clash of cymbals and roll of drums bringing the march to its climax the man stopped speaking then, as the applause greeting the softer, more delicate strains of 'The Blue Danube' masked his words, he said quietly, 'I meant what I said in my letter. I knows all about your little secret and if you wants it to remain secret then you be going to 'ave to pay. I ain't a greedy man, Mr Cranley, not like some. Five 'undred pounds be all I'm asking, five 'undred to keep your secret safe; now don't you calls that reasonable?'

Five hundred! That would only be the first of it. This type of scum clung like a leech to its victim, sucking at it 'til there was no more left to suck; pay and he would be back . . . again and again.

His lips so tight they hardly moved, his eyes still on the musicians, Archer tried to sound if not dismissive then at least derisive.

'What is this so-called secret I am supposed to hide?'

Alongside him the man smiled.

'Do you really need to be reminded?'

'As I thought.' Archer lifted the top hat from where it rested on his knee. 'A catchpenny trying his luck at blackmail. Approach me or my home again and I'll inform the constabulary!'

'You must do as you think fit, Mr Cranley, but afore you goes informing anybody, think on this: two can talk to the constables and I think they'll be more than a mite interested in that son o' your'n.'

With his fingers tight about the cane Archer remained absolutely still.

'I guessed that would 'ave you thinking twice . . . !'

The man clapped as the strains of music died away. Keeping his voice so low as not to be heard by any other than Archer he went on, 'If your second thoughts be the price is fair then I will expect you and the money tomorrow night at nine. William Bailey's in Whitehall Lane.'

He rose, touching his hat to the woman in the flower-strewn bonnet. Then as the band struck up again he smiled at Archer.

'Oh, and don't think to bring the police nor no one else with you, I don't be alone in this and we wouldn't want anything 'appening to your family . . . or to *you*. I make myself clear, Mr Cranley?'

'You make yourself clear. But I will not be seen in that beer house.'

'Too many folk to see the great Archer Cranley do business with the likes of me?'

Glancing at the cheap clothes, the edges of jacket sleeves

worn almost threadbare, the shirt boiled to a shadow, shoes of which polish could not disguise the age, Archer nodded.

'Exactly that!' Then as the other man drew a hiss of breath he looked into the narrow jaundiced face. 'You want that money you will get it beneath Ryder's Bridge or you can forget it!'

Rising to his feet Archer tipped his hat to the woman smiling beneath the heavily flowered bonnet then, pushing past the other man, strode quickly towards the park gate.

He would come. His sort were not easily deterred, not that he had tried to deter him, it was best the man be paid. And be paid he would.

Leaving the park he smiled at couples strolling past. Oh yes, be paid he would.

Five hundred pounds!

His stride as leisurely as before, Archer Cranley made his way back to Swan Village. Approaching Rowley House he felt the echoes of distaste he always felt for this house, this town. But it would not be this way for much longer, a few weeks more then he would shake the dust of Greets Green and all that went with it from his feet!

Letting himself in at the front door he went quickly to his room, the false look of all being well sliding instantly from his face.

Five hundred pounds! And then what? That bastard would not let matters rest there; money tasted sweet and like all things pleasurable it could become addictive.

But he had waited too long for his reward to allow anyone to snatch it from him; spent too much of his life in this hell-hole of a Black Country to share what by right should be his alone. Would be his alone!

Too much time! Stripping away coat and shirt he stared at the figure reflected in the long dressing mirror. At fifty-six years old he was still fit, still virile. There would be time yet to enjoy life, time to beget another son, time to do all he had longed to do but could not. Soon Nathan Briant's Will would no longer bind him, and Nathan Briant's daughter would no longer be a weight on his coat-tails.

Slipping out of his trousers Archer dropped them to the floor before smiling at his reflection.

Yes, very soon Hannah would no longer be an impediment, any influence she could have had would be gone for ever . . . just as her child's would be.

Hearing the tread of footsteps pass the dining room, the sharp snap of the front door closing, Philippa breathed more easily. There would be no more confrontation tonight, Archer Cranley would not return to his home or his own bed before the early hours.

'Have you had all you want?'

'Yes, thank you.'

Philippa avoided the coal-black eyes of Archer Cranley's sister. It made no difference how long the man was absent from this house for Edna Cranley's eyes saw every movement, her ears heard every word and all was reported back to him in the minutest detail.

'There be apple pie fresh baked.'

Philippa's head shook quickly. 'Thank you, but I have eaten enough. I will go and finish the books.'

A mouthful of food then haring off like a cat with a banger tied to its tail! But for how long? Edna glanced at the half-eaten meal.

'You should leave that 'til morning, keeping at it leads to tiredness and tiredness leads to mistakes.'

She wasn't really interested in probable tiredness nor yet a mistake in those figures, let Archer worry about that; but as long as Philippa was awake she too must be awake. Picking up the dishes and setting them on a tray, Edna looked at the slight figure. Hair the colour of wheat, the fine-boned face with its sky-blue eyes turned from her. The child of Hannah Cranley was handsome. For a moment she felt a pang of regret for the past years . . . she could have loved this child, if only . . . But the past was the past. Edna choked back any trace of compassion. And the future? She stacked the plates neatly on the tray. The future would happen and she would make no move to alter its way.

'You should be away to your bed.' She lifted the tray.

'I must finish the books.' Philippa replaced the napkin on the table. 'I have to ensure they are correct if Father is to be satisfied.'

No account book would satisfy Archer Cranley, no matter how well kept. Edna watched the slight figure rise from the chair. Archer wouldn't be satisfied until he alone was all that was left of Nathan Briant's family.

'How has Mother been today?'

Knowing her true feelings of anger would show in her face, Edna turned towards the serving table set along one wall of the dining room. How could she tell the truth, tell how her sister-in-law had been slapped by her husband and herself. There was already suspicion in that young face.

'Your mother lay down all afternoon and then took with a headache a while ago; I settled her for the night. You best let her sleep.'

'Has she had one of her turns?' Philippa's voice was level.

Her turns! Edna Cranley felt her blood flush rapidly. That was another of Cranley's lies; telling folk his wife flung herself about when her 'illness' came upon her, that she bruised herself against doors and furniture, when all the while it was his fists and hers did the marking.

'It were not a bad one.' She had to answer but the lie slipped easily from her tongue. 'She bumped her cheek on the bedpost so I put her to bed. She will be well enough by the morning.'

'I think I should go to see her.'

'And do what?' Edna answered quickly. 'Wake her up! What

good will that do? You do like I say and leave her be, time enough tomorrow for you to sit with her.'

'You will tell her I asked after her, that I wanted to call in on her?'

'Course I will.' Edna met the question with a nod. 'Now you get yourself off afore that father of your'n be back wanting to know why you be dallying here 'stead of being at the books or else in your bed.'

Walking towards the door, Philippa turned. 'It's strange isn't it, Aunt, all the years my mother has been ill, all the turns she has suffered and I have never seen her in one. I find that difficult to understand.'

'We must thank the good Lord for that.' Edna made a pretence of checking the stacked dishes, giving herself a moment for the truth to die from her eyes. It was no improvement in health kept Hannah Cranley free of her 'turns' when anyone else was present, that was yet one more result of her husband's sly ways. He never raised a hand to her in the sight of others, leaving that to the privacy of his wife's bedroom. Only he and his sister knew the source of Hannah's bruising and the reasons for it.

'Yes, we should be thankful.' Philippa turned away towards the study. 'But I still find it strange.'

Sat at the broad-topped desk, the hiss of the gasolier and the soft ticking of the mantel clock the only sound, she let the pen fall idle.

There had been a strangeness in Edna's voice. Her Christian name was preferable to the title 'aunt' and slipped easily into all thoughts of the thin sour woman. Her voice had always held a fleck of something that to a child had seemed akin to anxiety when speaking of her sister-in-law, but now seemed to hold a deeper, more pronouned trace, a trace of fear.

But why should Edna feel fear? What was it could give rise to that?

Philippa picked up the pen, twirling it absently.

Was there some threat to her? If so, it could certainly not

originate with her sister-in-law. So if not Hannah Cranley, then what of her husband? Could he be threatening his sister, did he have some sort of hold over her that he used to his own advantage . . . and why that fear only when speaking of the woman she had been brought to this house to nurse?

'*I still find it strange.*'

The words spoken in the dining room returned clearly and with them came an icy touch of trepidation. Those so-called 'turns' had always held a depth of worry all the way through childhood. Never witnessing them, never understanding them, forever turned away when asking about them, being told it would be too distressing or that it was not fitting for a child to see its mother in such a disturbing situation.

But childhood was over. The excuse Edna had always given was no longer valid.

Throwing the pen aside Philippa strode determinedly from the room, crossing the hall and reaching the landing corridor atop the stairs as Edna came from the kitchen. Calling sharply she followed, almost tripping over her full skirts.

Inside Hannah's bedroom Philippa lit the oil lamp stood on a table beneath the window, then carrying it across to the bed she stood looking down at the pale sleeping face. She looked so fragile, like some flower the sun never smiled upon, one so delicate the faintest sigh of the wind would destroy it for ever. But it was no wind would destroy Hannah Cranley, laudanum was doing that.

'You shouldn't be here, you'll wake your mother.'

Edna puffed into the room as Philippa bent to kiss the still figure.

'No, no I won't.' She straightened. 'You have given her too much laudanum for that, or was the drug given to prevent her saying how she got these?'

Edna caught her breath, holding it as the lamp was held closer to her sister-in-law's face and showed the purple bruises.

'Your mother had a turn,' she said tightly. 'A particularly nasty one. She became more violent and had to be restrained.'

'Restrained!' Philippa turned, a slow scathing stare finding the eyes that glittered like jet at the light's edge. 'And how did you do that, Aunt, was it laudanum or was it this?'

Edna's fingers fidgeted with her skirts, grabbing and loosing the fabric as the lamp was lowered, showing the bruising more clearly.

'Was it the drug you used to restrain my mother or was it your fist!'

The blue eyes so like Hannah's held her own and for a moment Edna felt a touch of panic. Philippa Cranley was no longer the child she had bullied, the child she had beaten until the small body had been covered with the marks of her cruelty. She could no longer take a stick to that back or strike her hand to that mouth, but a hand could be taken to her . . .

'I would never strike your mother!' Fear throwing the lie from her mouth, she took a step backwards.

Philippa's glance remained steady, remained filled with dislike and contempt.

'Like you never struck a young child. Like you never beat it and left it to cry itself to sleep in the dark! Is that what has happened here, Aunt? Has my mother been left to cry herself to sleep in the darkness after she was slapped into submission?'

'No! How can you think such a thing!'

'Because I know you, Aunt, and I know my father. You are both cast in the same mould. Greed sours your hearts and pride corrupts your souls, they are the gift of Cranley blood and the only legacy either of you will ever have. Yesterday I told my father he could have the Briant inheritance. Now I tell you: he will never get it. You have both made my mother's life and mine a misery, but no more. The moment I reach my majority you will go from this house and in the meantime you might think on this: one more mark on my mother's face, one more sign of "restraint" and you will answer for it. Now get out and leave me with my mother.'

She had known this day would come. Her fingers still twisting with shock, Edna stood in her own room. She had warned Archer years ago that one day the worm would turn, that Philippa would take a stand, but Archer would have none of it. The child was a weakling, an inept milksop afraid of its own shadow. Hannah Cranley's child would never dare speak out of turn let alone cross him.

'So how will you feel when I tell you, Archer?' she breathed. 'How will you feel when I tell you that weakling has found its strength, that it knows now how to deal with Archer Cranley?'

Caught by the pale glow from the lamp Edna Cranley's face had turned a sickly shade of white as she heard the words.

Anger still trembling in every nerve Philippa unbuttoned the black vest, slipping it beneath the jacket then hanging it in the wardrobe that stood against the wall beside the window.

The thought of a possible share in the Briant fortune was the only loyalty that had kept her in this house, the only faith she held to. But whatever the promise made to her by Archer Cranley would not be kept and the god she worshipped would prove an empty god. Edna Cranley would get not one penny.

Removing shirt and undergarments she washed with water already in the large bowl that sat on the washstand. Why had life turned out like this, why so much hatred?

'*You robbed me of my son!*'

With her eyelids pressed hard into the towel, Philippa felt the sharp pain those words always brought. Thrown so often as never to be forgotten, the sting of them never lessened.

They had been children, no more than four and six years old!

Pressing her face into the towel afforded no respite.

They had been playing beside the brook that led to the mill-wheel, that was what Archer Cranley said. But why did she have no memory of that day? Surely something so terrible as a drowning would linger even in a child's mind.

'*You were too young to remember.*'

Those were Edna Cranley's words whenever the question had been asked. Then she had snapped that Hannah must not be reminded of it, before bustling the bewildered child back to the schoolroom.

Stephen had been that other child's name. A child without a face. Lowering the towel Philippa stared into the long cheval mirror. A child her memory could not produce, yet one that stayed forever on the brink of consciousness; a young boy murdered from spite and jealousy.

But another child, one almost as young could not be so long held to blame, one life destroyed because another had been lost! Yet Archer Cranley could not forget, neither would he forgive. The child left to him was inferior, a second choice that was no choice at all.

Folding the towel over the rail of the washstand she stared once more into the mirror.

Archer Cranley had been robbed of the son he loved, a son who had held all of his dreams, who had centred every wish. And this was the result.

Reaching for the nightshirt draped across the bed she held it for a moment before slipping it over soft curves.

One body for another! Fate had laughed long and loud.

And it was still laughing.

# Chapter Three

Returned from the park Archer Cranley washed and dressed in fresh clothing. Tying a pale grey silk cravat about his throat he stared once more at the reflection in the dressing mirror.

Yes he was still fit and yes he was still virile. He touched a finger to the cravat, appreciating the feel of the expensive silk.

Tonight he would prove that virility, and tomorrow?

He smoothed the lapel of his jacket, seating it a little more perfectly over the grey-silk figured waistcoat.

Tomorrow he would prove that Archer Cranley was no man to be played with.

Closing the door of his bedroom he walked quickly past his wife's room. He had no wish to listen to more of her maudling. One visit a day was too much, and he made it only to ensure she knew exactly the rules she had to follow.

Leaving the house in the same silence as he had entered it he strode across the open pasture that separated Rowlay House from those bordering Phoenix Street. Hailing a hansom and asking to be driven to the railway station he leaned back against the leather-covered upholstery. Tomorrow he would pay his would-be blackmailer. He would pay the man in full.

Alighting at the station he purchased a ticket to Dudley Port. 'Nice evenin', Mr Cranley.'

The ticket office attendant smiled pleasantly, pushing the pink ticket over the small counter.

'Very nice,' Archer nodded, 'we are going to have a warm summer, I think.'

''Tis to be 'oped so, sir, it does a body good to feel the sun on 'is back.'

Murmuring agreement Archer took the ticket, slipping it into his pocket as he walked onto the platform. A little further along the platform the engine steamed and belched, sending speckles of soot floating into the air.

Stepping into the first-class carriage he handed a coin to the one porter the station boasted, who was holding the door open for him. Checking his pocket watch as the grateful porter touched his cap then closed the carriage door, he sat down just as, with another huge belch of steam, the engine juddered and the wheels began to turn. He had timed his arrival to perfection as always.

A warm summer maybe. He smiled to himself. But there was one man would not feel the sun on his back.

Alone in the comfortable compartment he watched the passing fields, crops spreading a green carpet on both sides, their only mar the few buildings that were the Rattlechain and Stour Valley brickworks. These were the only sores on the landscape but how long before they became an infestation, how far into the new century before the whole of West Bromwich was one huge industrial quagmire?

But that would be of no consequence to him. He would be gone from this town. Greets Green and Swan Village would not even be a memory, he would wipe his mind clear of it all.

Dudley Port was quiet as he walked from the tiny station. They were pious folk here. Everyone who could walk would be in chapel or church and those that couldn't would be indoors, the Good Book in their hands, praying their lives would take a better turn. Archer smiled sardonically to himself. The only turn that would relieve their lot was the one that led into the graveyard.

Buying a bunch of flowers from an old woman sat at the entrance to the grounds of the chapel that stood some little way from the station, he caught the sympathetic stares of several women garbed in mourning clothes, their heads bobbing like a clutch of black hens. Touching his hat to them as they reached the chapel door he heard them murmur as he walked towards the gravestones dotted beneath wide-spreading trees. There would be no thought given to a man visiting the resting place of a loved one.

Choosing a stone set beneath the furthest corner of the low wall enclosing the small cemetery, he waited for the first hymn to rise into the quiet evening. There was no one left outside the chapel, no other person hurrying in at the last minute.

Absolutely certain there was no one to observe, he dropped the flowers onto the grave then stepped over the wall, making quickly for the house some ten yards away.

'You be expected, sir, if you would wait upstairs.'

Handing coat and cane to a young woman, whose frilly white apron over a blue cambric dress matched her frilled cap set on flaming red hair, he turned towards the stairs.

Lit by oil lamps dotted sparingly in a tiny hall and along the narrow landing, the house breathed its ancient breath in draughty gasps that echoed strangely from the dank walls.

Archer suppressed a shudder of distaste. If you wanted your entertainment where no one else knew of it then there could be little choice of venue.

Entering a room that over the months had become familiar to him, he carried the solitary lamp closer to the bed set beneath the only window. Holding it close he turned back the sheets. He might have little choice of where to take his particular brand of amusement but he would at least ensure the sheets were clean.

Placing the lamp on the bedside table he turned as the door opened quietly.

With his breath catching between his teeth, Archer stared at the small figure outlined by the gleam of fire lit fresh in the heavy cast-iron grate.

Grey flannel knickerbockers and long socks topped brightly polished boots. Black waist-length jacket, its breast pocket emblazoned by a gold-edged badge, lay open against a white shirt, the narrow heavily starched collar enclosing a gold-and-black tie knotted at the throat, while a black cap resting just above the ears sported a smaller version of the coat badge.

'You wished to see me, sir?'

The slight figure bowed from the waist.

'I did not *want* to see you, Povey, but your behaviour of late dictates that I must.'

Crossing the room to stand before the fireplace Archer rested his hand behind his back, a glare sweeping the figure standing with head abjectly lowered.

'Do you deny your behaviour is lacking?'

'No, sir.'

The answer barely disturbed the air hanging damply between them.

'Are you then deserving of punishment?'

The figure shuffled both feet.

'Well!' Archer's voice rose fractionally. 'Are you deserving of punishment?'

'Y—yes, sir.'

Caught in the firelight's dancing beam Archer's eyes seemed to glow, and the breath caught noisily in his throat throbbed as if from pleasure.

'What was that? Speak up, boy!'

With the answer trembling on shaking lips, the figure took a nervous step backwards.

'I . . . I said yes, sir.'

For several seconds neither of them moved. The only sound the young boy's rapid breathing. Archer glanced about the shadowed room, a feeling of excitement beginning to tug low in his stomach.

'Then you must ask for it,' he purred, 'ask for punishment.'

'Please, sir . . .'

'I said *ask* boy!'

The boy whimpered softly, the whole of his slight frame shaking visibly.

'I . . . I beg for pardon, sir.'

'You beg for pardon, Povey.' Archer's thin lips rolled back in a brutish smile. 'That is the wrong word. It was not pardon I told you to ask for, it was punishment. Now you *must* beg, boy, beg for that punishment.'

The whimper louder, almost a definite cry, the lad's legs buckled beneath him. Eyes wide with fear, face ghostly pale in the light of flickering flames, mouth trembling, he looked at the older man stood with legs spread before the hearth.

'I b— I beg you, sir, please punish my bad behaviour.'

Finding it difficult to control the excitement growing in his stomach Archer swallowed hard.

'Stand!' He waited for the lad to rise. 'Cap and tawse!'

Going to the cupboard, almost invisible where the deepest shadows merged, the boy took out a silk-tasselled mortarboard and a bone-handled whip, its plaited cord ending in five small metal balls, each having several sharp spikes.

'There.' Archer pointed to the bed then, as the objects were laid on it, said thickly, 'Prepare me.'

His arms loose at this sides he made no attempt to help as the jacket was slipped from his shoulders, the tiny pearl buttons of his shirt were slowly undone and both were followed to a fireside chair by a spotless undervest.

Waves of excitement rolling like surf in his loins, he bit back a gasp of breath at the touch of slender hands trailing down his chest.

Infinitely more slowly than freeing the buttons on his shirt, the lad released trouser buttons, rolling them through long fingers, teasing each in an interminable foreplay, his hands following languorously over hard flesh as the last garments dropped to the ground.

With firelight dancing over his naked limbs, excitement surging hot and fierce in every vein, Archer looked at the figure knelt at his feet.

Glancing upwards, the young eyes gleamed among the shadows, the tip of a tongue pushing between parted lips as those soft hands began to move.

As they began stroking over his legs, pressing sensuously over his thighs, the exquisite movement an intoxication inflaming his blood, driving his senses before it like a tide, Archer felt his whole body burn, then the hands closed over his buttocks, a new strength in them pulling him forward towards the peeping tongue.

'Punish me please, sir.' Hushed as a prayer, the words touched against his fevered brain, their plea tantalising and provocative while the moist tongue flicked over hard aroused flesh, dragging a gasp from his open mouth, sending Archer's body jerking backwards in an arc.

'Punish me –' the voice an infection in his blood, Archer pulled in a ragged breath as the fingers slid from his buttocks to cup the hard mound between his parted legs '– punish me –' soft lips brushed the jerking flesh '– punish me with this.'

'The bed.' Croaking the reply, Archer forced himself to break from the delight that threatened to engulf him. Turning his back to the boy he said shakily, 'Prepare yourself for punishment.'

Impatience a sweet torment, he listened to the quiet sounds coming from behind him, the soft swish of falling garments, the slight creak of bed springs, then when all was quiet once more he turned.

Light spilling from the lamp played over the form lying face-down on the bed, bare legs and bottom gilded by the pale translucent gleam.

The breath tight in his throat, he picked up the mortarboard and set it on his head. Taking up the whip he cradled the bone handle in one palm.

'You have been a naughty boy, is that not true, Povey?' With his mouth pressed against the covers the boy's answer was muffled.

'Bad behaviour deserves stiff punishment.'

A quiet cry rising from the bed was fuel to the flame of rampant emotion as Archer flipped the whip, the cut of it whistling around the room.

'How many strokes shall we give today, boy? How many times shall we allow the cat to claw that soft little bottom of yours . . . three . . . ten?'

He flicked the whip again, slicing it in the air above the semi-naked form, smiling as another whimper echoed the sound of plaited leather.

'Do you cry for mercy?' The whip hung motionless in the shadows. 'Is that what you beg for now?'

Face-down among the covers the small head nodded.

'So!' The whip arced downwards, one metal tip glancing across soft flesh, turning whimpers to a sharper cry of pain. Yellow light catching his eyes gave them a demonic glow as Archer laughed softly in his throat. 'You plead for mercy now. What would you have me do . . . what mercy should I give?'

Below him the slender buttocks lifted slightly, the movement sending wave after hedonistic wave of fire burning in the base of his stomach. Throwing the whip aside he climbed onto the bed, straddling the still form, spreading the legs wide.

Beneath him the boy's flesh was soft and pliant. The smell of cheap perfume invading nostrils and senses, Archer drew a quivering breath then drove deep into him.

This was his pleasure . . . this was the one thing brought him that pure enjoyment . . . this was what Nathan Briant's money would buy over and over again.

A low cry of pain broke the silence but served only to increase the sensual volcanic tremors wracking Archer's body. Slipping one hand beneath the head he cupped the small chin.

But how much of that money would remain after . . .

Through the haze that wrapped his brain he saw the narrow jaundiced face of the man he had met at the bandstand.

There would be none, that blackmailer would take it all.

He drove harder into the yielding softness, mixed passions of anger and desire lending a new degree of hardness to his flesh.

He would lose it all unless . . .

Pressing one arm heavily across the narrow shoulder he gasped, his upper body rearing back into an arc, his hand pulling the boy's chin upwards.

Archer Cranley would not be the one to lose!

Taking a moment for his brain to clear he climbed from the bed, reaching automatically for his clothes as he threw off the mortarboard.

Dressed for the street he fished in his pocket, drawing out a five-shilling piece. It was more than Povey would make in three nights but then to get what he wanted he must pay.

'The same time next week. Be sure you take a bath on Sunday afternoon, and remember I require fresh sheets.'

Glancing at the still figure, Archer frowned. Povey was usually up and counting the takings before he was dressed.

'I said remember . . .'

Leaning over the bed he slapped a hand to the side of the boy's head. The blow dislodged the cap and a veil of vivid red hair fell, half-covering the face that lolled at an awkward angle.

'Povey!' He grasped a shoulder, twisting the figure onto its back, then stared at the wide-open eyes and grotesquely twisted chin.

Ripping open the shirt he touched a hand to a spot between the pointed breasts, then snatched it away. There was no heartbeat. Sally Povey was dead!

But how? Forcing back the bile that rose to his throat Archer went over the events of minutes ago.

He had been thinking of that scum in the park. One arm had been across the girl's shoulder, the other hand beneath her chin . . . the moment of climax! Archer drew a quivering breath. At

34

that moment he had jerked, snapping her head upwards. At that moment he had broken her neck!

Panic sweeping through him, he rushed to the door then, as it opened to his hand, he hesitated. Leaving her there sprawled on the bed was begging an investigation. He closed the door, turning the key in the lock.

Nobody knew he was here. He breathed deeply, calming his racing nerves. But it could only prove safer to be provident.

Gathering the whip and mortarboard he replaced them in the cupboard. Then quickly stripping the body, he hung coat and cap beside them, placing folded shirt and knickerbockers on a shelf above the brightly polished shoes.

Everything neatly in place he looked at the naked girl, her head twisted on her neck. Regardless of what he had done to make it appear otherwise, it was still only too clear she had been murdered and that would mean a police inquiry. But they would find nothing to connect her with him. The killing of a common prostitute; it could be any one of her many clients.

But the police were not all fools, they might dig and dig and who knew what they might uncover. But he had tidied things away, left no trace of his being here. He glanced about the shadowed room. There was nothing out of the ordinary. He swallowed hard.

Nothing other than a corpse on the bed!

There had to be something, some way of disguising the truth.

Beyond the window the clock in the tower of the church chimed the quarter hour. There was not much time. Archer felt the sweat wet on the palms of his hands.

In fifteen minutes he had to be back in that graveyard, there to mingle with departing worshippers, covering his tracks the way he always did.

But he could not leave the body to be found as it was, the risk was too great.

Moisture gathering into droplets that oozed from his brow down over both cheeks, he turned off the lamp. The fainter light of the fire must serve for what he had to do, he could take no risk of being seen through paper-thin curtains.

Snatching the sheet from beneath the inert body, he tore the whole into wide strips. Knotting them together he looped one end about the broken neck, drawing it close about the throat. Taking the other end he fastened it to the iron bedstead.

Blinking perspiration from his eyes he peered cautiously through the window, breath wheezing gratefully from his lungs as he saw it looked straight onto the cemetery, the headstones rising like fingers of the dead struggling to break free beneath the covering darkness. There would be nobody lurking there.

Raising the sash he listened to the silence. Satisfied he was watched by nothing but shadow he lifted the body from the bed, lowering it carefully from the window. Giving one last look about the room he walked downstairs. Taking hat and gloves he let himself out of the house, a cold smile touching his mouth.

Sally Povey had committed suicide!

# Chapter Four

'Philip said that?' Archer Cranley stared at his sister. 'You are sure those were the words?'

*'Yesterday I told my father he could have the Briant inheritance. Now I tell you: he will never get it.'*

Edna repeated the words Philip had flung at her the night before.

'I told you, Archer. I warned you one day the tables would be turned . . .'

'Nothing has been turned!' Archer Cranley's eyes glittered viciously.' And nothing is going to be turned. I've waited too long to be denied now, that business will be mine, with or without that signature.'

'But how . . . should a refusal—'

'Refusal?' His thin lips folding into obscurity Archer stared, ferret eyes sharp and bright as ever. 'Being a sister of mine you should know I never accept refusal. I didn't accept yours, did I?'

'Mine was no real refusal,' Edna snapped back. 'But this one . . . this will be real enough. Philip meant what was said, meant every word; you would never get Briant's property.'

'So Philip meant those words, but what gave rise to them, what happened to spark that anger? You haven't told me that.'

'It . . . it was in Hannah's bedroom—'

'Hannah's bedroom!' Archer Cranley's face darkened like a

thunder cloud. 'I told you Philip was never to go there unless I was present.'

'I was seeing to the supper dishes and Philip was in the study. The books had to be finished and up to your standard before the morning. It wasn't until I came out of the kitchen that I saw the door of Hannah's room was open, and that was when I guessed what had happened.'

It was not exactly as it had occurred but Edna had no intention of testing her brother's anger with too accurate a description.

'Philip was already beside the bed when I got there and holding a lamp, the light from it showed the bruises on her face.'

His hand already bunched into a first Archer raised it above his head, teeth clenched together.

'I've told you,' he snarled, 'told you 'til- I'm sick of telling, keep your fists to yourself.'

'And you keep yours the same way, least when it be me you be talking to.' Edna did not flinch. 'It were your hand did the damage, but strike me and I'll tell it all to Philip, tell what it is you be guilty of.'

'Shut your bloody mouth!' Archer's eyes flashed a warning but his hand lowered, the fingers uncurling. 'You be as guilty as me, remember that before you threaten again, for sister or no, I would make sure you paid every bit as much as me.'

'I'm sure you would.' Edna smiled sarcastically. 'But I've got nothing much to lose apart from the little you promised.'

'Then if you want it as much now as when you agreed to it you will keep your mouth shut.'

'A promise is a promise, eh, brother dear!'

The bitch was as sour as ever, was it any wonder no man had ever wanted her. Archer sank heavily into the chair behind the desk. But he had to put up with her for the next few weeks, suffer her sharp tongue and acid face until his plans were realised and the Bottle and Glass was his.

'Hannah . . . you be certain sure she was asleep?'

The sudden flame of her nerves subsiding, Edna nodded. Archer could beat his wife but he could not afford to beat his sister; nor would he be able to cheat her of what he had promised, though the intention to do so was powerful in him. Archer had a great deal still to learn about his sister . . . a very great deal!

'Certain sure, I gave her enough laudanum to put a horse to sleep.'

'Be careful with that stuff.' He looked up sharply. 'We don't want her going before time be ready.'

Her eyebrows lifting, Edna stared contemptuously at the man whose greed had driven him to such lengths and would drive him further yet; and she would watch him as he went . . . and be waiting at the end.

'It was your idea she be given laudanum.' She smiled acridly. 'You told the doctor she was not sleeping, that the pain of her mind kept her awake sobbing throughout the night; but we both know that wasn't true, don't we, Archer? We both know it was you didn't want your wife to know how you spent those nights . . . or who with.'

Fury a venom in his small jet-coloured eyes, Archer drew a slow breath as he looked at the long narrow face, every feature tight as a drum, greying hair parted at the centre of her forehead and wound in plaits around her ears. Had she ever been pretty . . . had he ever liked her?

'I've warned you too many times, Edna –' beneath the quiet tone threat throbbed loud and clear '– take note this be the last. What I do in or out of my own house be my own business, keep your tongue still if you want to keep it!'

'Except this don't be your house!' Edna's reply was crisp. 'It be your wife's house and after that it be Philip's. Now I warn you, Archer, I don't be no paid skivvy to tremble every time you sets foot in the house and I be no fool neither. I've taken steps to guard my back for I know you too well for trust. I watched you grow up, remember; watched your devious ways and your mindless cruelty.

But p'raps I shouldn't term it mindless for you were ever aware of what you did, weren't you Archer? Whether it were torturing a helpless animal or blackmailing the couples you spied on in the meadows. Oh yes, I know my brother well and he should know me. But so there will be no doubt, I will explain. Everything you have done, everything you hope to do has been set down in writing; you do to me what you intend to do with Hannah and her child and the whole lot will come out. You will be exposed as a thief and a murderer. How will that go down with your fancy lady friends!'

Sat behind the desk Archer Cranley curved his mean-lipped mouth in a vicious smile, the cold malignity in his eyes lending an almost satanic look to his dark narrow features.

'Have you ever asked yourself why Richard Stanton hanged himself?' The laugh in his voice embellished the evil that enfolded him, draping itself like a cloak about his body. 'It was because he couldn't face up to the prospect of marrying you. Death was preferable to being tied for life to a plain-faced, sour-bellied spiteful woman whose only joy in life was seeing others suffer. You were that way as a girl and you are that way now. You will always be that way, Edna, a vicious scheming bitch nobody likes and nobody should trust. He knew what you were, what you would become.'

'Unlike Hannah . . . unlike the woman you intend to kill!' Edna Cranley's face suddenly matched the evil of her brother's. 'We are of a kind, you and I. Blood of my blood, Archer . . .' she laughed softly. 'We were both spawned of the devil and both follow willingly in his footsteps.'

Turning away she paused at the door, the words she laughed back at him soft as black silk.

'Blood of my blood, Archer, blood of my blood!'


'Why should I not be allowed to see my mother?' Philippa Cranley faced the man tracing a finger down a row of neatly columned figures.

'Who says you are not allowed?' Archer Cranley did not raise his head.

'The door to Mother's room was locked, it has been that way the last several times I have been to see her. Why is that, Father, if not to keep me out?'

Checking the column again Archer took time before answering.

'The way you say it makes it appear you feel it is only yourself kept from your mother's room.'

'That is exactly what I feel!' Philippa's irate answer cracked across the quiet room.

'Why?' Archer Cranley turned a page of the heavy ledger.

'Why! I have told you why! Each time I try to see my mother I find her door locked and I demand to know the reason.'

'Demand!' One finger halfway down the page, Archer looked up. 'You demand! Are you forgetting, Philip, you are not yet master in this house.'

'I'm sorry, Father, but—'

'Have you also forgotten' – the interruption was cold and deliberate – 'that although she be your mother, Hannah Cranley is my wife, that who she does or does not see be for me to choose, and that the same will apply even after you come into your inheritance. This house will one day belong to you but Hannah Cranley will always belong to me!'

'Is that a threat, Father? Are you saying I might not be allowed to see my mother again?'

Closing the ledger Archer pushed it a little way across the desk, one hand resting possessively on its black-bound cover.

'I have only reminded you of the position: you as the child, myself as the husband. How you interpret my words is up to you.'

'They need no interpretation, Father, I understand them perfectly.' Philippa regarded the seated figure with an even stare. 'I am to see my mother only when and if it pleases you. Then I must accept that, but you must accept this: I have seen my mother's bruises . . .'

'They be due to her throwing herself about, her turns sometimes be violent.'

'I don't believe that, Father.' A shake of the head added force to her rejection. 'I've also noted the laudanum your sister feeds her, the almost perpetual stupor the effects of it leave behind. My mother does not have the strength left in her to throw herself around, in fact I doubt she ever did. I think the 'turns' you say she suffers are no more than figments of your imagination; in other words lies, Father. I think you and your sister have lied for years so you could keep your hands on the business . . . and it so nearly paid off, Briant Bottle and Glass was so nearly yours. But now I tell you what I told my mother's gaoler: you will *never* get it.'

'One moment!' Archer's voice was quite calm, halting Philippa at the door of the study. 'I have listened to you, now you will listen to me. The doctor who prescribed laudanum for your mother prescribed something else. He advised she be put into a sanatorium for the mentally disturbed. In other words, Philip, that she be locked away in an insane asylum . . . for her own safety, you understand. Up until now I have refused but all it will take is one word, just one, Philip, and your mother will be put away for ever. Oh –' he smiled vindictively '– and while the subject of your mother's failing mental abilities are being discussed let me say that your own have also been brought to the attention of the doctor. His prognosis . . . ?' The smile widened, folding away the almost invisible lips. 'What is in the mother often comes out in the child. So you see, Philip, it is not only your mother I will be forced to lock away, it is you, too. True, I will not get your grandfather's business but then a man can't have everything, not in this life.' The smile still on his face he stood up. 'Now, shall we both go and see your mother, maybe this time her door will be unlocked and while you are there you can tell her your news.'

'News?' Philippa's brow furrowed.

Coming to the door Archer stood with one hand on the door-knob, his black ferret eyes cold and malign as before.

'Yes, the news I have not told you yet. I have arranged for you to go into the glassworks, to gain a working knowledge of the business your grandfather bequeathed to you. You start there today.'

You start today . . . Archer Cranley followed the slight figure up the wide staircase . . . and in a month you will be finished. It is a shame silica dust is so deadly!

You thought your precious works would never come to me, that Archer Cranley would never amount to anything more than a bloody employee, and so did your grandchild. But you were wrong, Nathan, you were both wrong . . . so very wrong!

With these thoughts riding through his mind Archer Cranley stared at the road ahead of the horse-drawn trap.

True, I've had to bide my time, to wait for the right chance but that waiting be over now; in a few short weeks everything you once owned will belong to me. You couldn't ever have guessed, Nathan, never have dreamed the way it will be; but then, astute a businessman as you were, clever as you thought yourself, you were no match for Archer Cranley. Sly was what my sister called me, sly and devious, the spawn of the devil. But he takes care of his own. He showed me the way to defeat you all those years ago and he is showing me again now. You will have lost, Nathan, and I will have won. What good will your safeguards have proved then, how beneficial will they be to your daughter and her child? Watch, Nathan, watch from wherever your scheming soul rests; watch, learn and grieve!

Satisfaction warm as a heated bottle against his chest he glanced at the slight figure seated beside him, then felt it cool as he studied the fine-boned face, the pale wheat-coloured hair, both hallmarks of the Briants. Why could it not have been this one that died? Why could he not have kept the dark-haired sturdy boy, the stronger son, the child that would have grown to the pattern of the father, with the father's will and drive? But there would be another. He was still virile, he would father another son, one that would grow to carry forward the dream, to serve and hold anything he desired, one with the same craving for power. And the one beside him now, the child of Hannah's body that Will dictated . . . that one would be long gone to the grave.

As his satisfaction returned, he switched his glance back to the road that curved away in front of the trotting horse.

'You say the figures for the month be good, how good is good?'

The question could and up 'til now had been asked at home. Philippa Cranley kept a firm glance on the passing hedgerows. So why this sudden change, and why so suddenly had the decision been taken regarding a working knowledge of the process of glass-making? A decision so sudden as to leave no time for the purchase of suitable clothing.

'The works produced a further four hundred and fifty bottles and eight hundred more drinking glasses last month than they did the month before.'

Archer digested the answer in silence. Four hundred and fifty at seven pence a bottle, and eight hundred glasses at three pence a glass. His quick brain juggled the numbers. That came to twenty three pounds, two shilling and sixpence.

Satisfaction warmed to a flood that flowed rapidly through every vein. The extra money brought in was from his idea, it had been him seen the way to increase the production. Reckon to that the money saved by sacking six men paid at twenty shilling a week and replacing them with others willing to do the job for no more than ten shilling a week, that made another three pounds.

Gratification an aphrodisiac to his innermost heart he breathed deeply, allowing a smile to flit quickly across his mouth.

Altogether that came to a total of twenty-six pounds and half a crown clear profit on the month and little more outlay apart from the cost of the materials. It paid to sack men and take on lads at only half of the wage. The smile flicked again. It made them that were kept on work twice as hard lest they be the next down the road. What had worked once would work again; and then there were the women, them that worked the packing sheds. Why pay a woman ten bob a week when a wench of seven and eight need be paid no more than two? Yes, the women would be next to go!

'The extra output —' he glanced again at Philippa '— it didn't mean extra labour, did it?'

Contempt thick in the reply Philippa stared resolutely at the passing fields: 'No extra hands were taken on. All was done as you ordered, the workforce remains the same as before. The extra production came about as a result of the men working longer hours. But it can't go on, the men are near to breaking point, you have to allow them more rest or—'

'Can't go on!' Archer Cranley slapped the reins viciously over the mare's rump. 'You don't be owner of that works yet and until you are I will be the one to say what can and what can't go on. The fact that them extra bottles and glasses were made be proof that they could be, proof that them men ain't been working nowhere near their full capacity. You have to learn that capacity, and learn it soon, if the works be going to continue to prosper; forget it for a single moment, give them workmen one chance of seeing you ain't ahead of them and you can kiss the business goodbye, for they'll be only too happy to sit on their idle arses from dawn to dusk then carry home their tins on a Saturday night with a grin as wide as the Tame Brook itself. If I hadn't learned sharp as I did there would have been nothing left by now. Remember you will be running a business not a bloody philanthropic society!'

A business. Philippa felt a coldness that reached deep inside. A business that already felt like a millstone about the neck. One that would gladly have been given away but must now be kept.

Briant Bottle and Glass was all that stood between Hannah Cranley and an insane asylum.

'What about the silica?' Archer refused to relinquish the warm glow of self-satisfaction. 'How did that go?'

It was all that interested the man. Profit and how to make more of it. Philippa's sense of coldness deepened and with it the feeling of dislike. To dislike one's own father! The realisation had once brought guilt and with it an attempt to fight off the dislike, but gradually the attempt had failed. There had been no love to die, there had never been any love to survive! Archer Cranley had never felt tenderness for his own child!

Not breaking the stare that fixed on the fields giving up their harvest to the scythes of sweating men, she answered stonily, 'Reduced by five shilling a ton.'

'Hah!' Archer's satisfaction beamed. 'I warrant that made Boswell's eyes water. When it came down to it he knew it had to be my terms or none at all, he knew what I buy from him I can buy from another easy enough but there be no other glassworks in Greets Green for him to sell to.'

His smugness a small fire inside him, Archer urged the horse on. Next month silica would be reduced by ten shilling a ton.

Preoccupied with the thought of extra profit already made and extra yet to come, Archer drove the rest of the journey in silence.

Climbing from the trap as it drew to a halt in the works' yard, Philippa's head swam as she stretched it backwards, the only way sight could travel the height of the huge smoke-blackened brick building reaching, like a gigantic inverted cone, a hundred feet into the air. There had often been a glimpse of it rising in the distance, dwarfing the belching smokestacks of West Bromwich iron foundries and the winding engines of the coal mines that infested the area, pockmarking the land like black pustules. But to stand beneath it, to see at first-hand the sheer size of it!

Blood swirling like a whirlpool snatched at the senses and Philippa swayed.

'Steady, lad.' A hand gripped one elbow. 'It don't do to go staring upward like that, it'll 'ave you flat on your back afore you knows what be 'appening.'

'Don't stand there gawping like a ninny, glass don't make itself!'

Following behind as Archer strode away, Philippa felt the inquisitive eyes of young lads shovelling sand into large wheel-barrows. Nodding knowingly to each other as the pair passed they grimaced behind the back of the slight figure dressed in charcoal-grey coat and vest, pale hair brushing the collar of a crisply starched white shirt, a figure almost running to keep up with the deliberately lengthy stride of the older man they knew to be their employer.

'You be starting here today.' Elbowing aside a young girl carrying several large deep-bottomed wicker baskets, sending her sprawling on the rough setts of the yard, Archer strode on.

'Do you hear!' Asking the question for the second time he glanced irritably behind him to where Philippa was helping the girl to her feet.

'What the bloody hell do you think you are doing!' The demand rang about the yard, bouncing from the sheer walls of the cone, echoing from the low-roofed brick sheds.

'The girl had a slight accident, Father. I was helping her to her feet.'

It had been no accident. Archer Cranley had deliberately pushed the girl from his path like so much rubbish. Handing the girl her baskets Philippa smiled at the frightened face. How old was the child, eight . . . nine?

'When you've finished playing bloody Sir Lancelot p'raps we can get on, I've got other things to do than watch you ponce about!'

'The child might have been injured, Father.'

Archer caught the glances shooting between the sand boys; they were young but they were nobody's fools and they had caught the reprimand beneath those words.

Anger like grit between his teeth he breathed sharply. 'We can't have young girls running the risk of injury can we, Philip? You!' He strafed the trembling child with a glare. 'You get your tin, you be finished here.'

'No, Father.' Philippa's hand grasped the girl's thin arm as she cried out. 'She was doing no harm, you cannot sack her.'

Lads filling wheelbarrows with sand and silica bent quickly over their shovels but Archer knew they strained to hear his reply. For the first time since his taking old Briant's place somebody had dared to oppose what he said.

'Sorry, Mr Cranley, sir, I were in the cone, I've only just 'ad the word you be 'ere.'

Archer did not look at the man who came rushing up wiping blackened hands along the sides of dusty scorch-marked trousers as he ran.

'The girl,' Archer said, 'does she have family working here?'

Samuel Platt frowned, his glance taking in Philip's hand on the child's arm, the cold fury on his employer's face. Christ what 'ad the wench done?

'Ar, Mr Cranley.' He nodded.

'How many?'

Glancing at the girl's tears tracing clean lines through the dust clinging to her face, the works' chargehand swallowed hard.

'There be the father and two lads in the cone, a lad loading silica meks three, then there be the mother and two wenches in the packin' shed and this one fetches baskets, that meks—'

'I know how bloody many that meks, I learned how to count,' Archer snapped. 'Get them out here.'

'Be there summat wrong, Mr Cranley?'

His flat cap, covered in a layer of thick grey-black dust of silica, snatched from his head and held in his hands, a middle-aged man glanced anxiously at his assembled family then at Archer.

'My son thinks your child runs the risk of being injured here at the works, therefore I have given her her tin, and you –' he smiled malevolently at Philip '– you lot get your tins, we can't have the girl separated from her family, now can we?'

'Mr Cranley, please . . . I d'ain't mean to get in your way, please don't give we the sack. Tell 'im, mister,' the girl looked up at Philippa, her face a mask of tragedy, 'tell 'im I d'ain't mean it.'

'Father, the girl—'

'Platt! See them off the premises, and you –' he glared once more at Philippa '– p'raps you'll think twice afore questioning any other decision of mine.'

Knowing that to argue, especially here in public would only make matters worse, Philippa stood silent, watching the family troop away. Would they find employment elsewhere, the men and boys might be given something in the coal pits but what of the woman and her daughters?

'He be starting today.' Archer Cranley turned across the yard as the chargehand came hurrying back. 'He is to learn all there be to learn about the making of glass, the mix, the pressing, blowing and annealing. He will work the same hours any other man here works and you will see to it that by the time a month be passed he'll have as much knowledge of glass as any one of them.' Turning to stare at the workman who had stopped the respect- able few yards behind, he barked, 'Did you hear that?' Twisting his cap between his fingers, the man nodded.

'Ar, Mr Cranley,' the man protested, 'there be more to the mekin' of glass than you thinks, it can't all be learned in a month.'

Half-turned away Archer Cranley stood still for fully ten seconds, drawing in a long hissing breath. Ferret eyes glistening, thin lips folded inwards, the small Edwardian beard accentuating the length of his narrow face, full eyebrows drawing into one straight black line, he turned with a slow long-drawn-out movement.

'What I think be what I want,' he ground out, holding on to each word as if reluctant to part with it. 'It also better be what I get or you can take your bloody tin same as they've just done.' He flicked his head towards the group disappearing through the wide gateway. 'You might find somebody else to take you on, though I doubt it. Folk in these parts be like shit in a cow field . . . thick on the ground . . . and not enough jobs to take up half of them; there'll be many a man only too glad to say yes to your job. You follow what I'm saying?'

His eyes on the cap being slowly mangled between nervous fingers, the chargehand nodded.

'Then I say it again. Today he begins to learn the ins and outs of the glass-making. He will need to know more about a bottle than that you can drink from it or piss into it if he hopes one day to run a business that will be his, a business that will go down the drain soon enough lessen a man knows it like his own hand. Now, do you teach him or does that job . . . and yours . . . go to some other man?'

'I . . . I'll see to it, Mr Cranley.' The chargehand ran his hands again along the sides of his trousers, his eyes flicking worriedly to the younger man. 'It . . . it'll be as you say.'

'See that it is!' Archer turned on his way. 'See that it is!'

Striding on towards the small brick-built office that stood to the side of the glassworks, affording sight of all who came and went beside housing the one works' clerk, Archer smiled to himself. He had said this business would one day belong to the pathetic figure trailing his steps, but that day would never dawn. A few weeks of breathing in silica would set the wheels of death in motion for Philip Cranley, and then . . .

'No need for you to come in here.' At the door to the office he turned. 'You know all you need to know as far as book-keeping be concerned; you might as well start on learning the practical side of the business right now.'

'But my clothes!' Philippa Cranley touched a long-fingered hand to the fine alpaca cloth of her coat.

'What about your clothes?'

It was coldly asked and Philippa winced at the sneer embellishing the question. Like everything ever asked of Archer Cranley it had been met with sarcasm.

'I . . . they will get covered with dust.'

'And that be unacceptable to you, eh!' Glancing at the chargehand still stood several paces from him, Archer bawled, 'Bugger off 'til I calls for you!' Then stepping close to Philippa, looking down at the face that barely reached his shoulder, he murmured through set teeth, 'There be too much of the bloody fancy pants left in you yet but we will work that out of you; working the glass will make a man of you and that is what your mother wants . . . a son who is a man not a bloody flossie dressed up in a fancy jacket.

'I knows the style of clothes you've worn some fifteen years have never wiped the knowing of what you were born from your mind, but now let my warning be clear: you will be Philip Cranley, a man not only in dress but in mind and in soul. You will eat, drink, sleep and breathe as PHILIP Cranley. From this minute on use that name even in your thoughts, for one mistake will see you and your precious mother locked away for life. Remember, I said one month and that month be already started.'

A sharp jerk of his head his only signal for the workman to return, Archer walked into the office and slammed the door at his back.

*'From this minute on use that name even in your thoughts . . .'*

Following after the workman Philippa knew that was what she must do. From now on, even in the most secret of her thoughts, she could be only Philip.

# Chapter Five

Should he withdraw five hundred pounds?

With the glassworks left behind, Archer returned to the problem he had yet to deal with.

Should he take that money with him when he met that man tonight? It was a large sum, large enough to arouse the bank manager's curiosity, even though he dare not put that curiosity into words. But the risk would be there should questions be asked . . . though they would not be, he would take as much care to cover his tracks with this one as he had with the business of Sally Povey.

There had been no report in the morning newspapers of her being discovered, but then it was a little soon for that.

Holding the reins loosely in his hands he kept the mare to a trot, guiding the trap past the bank stood on the corner of William Street. He would not be withdrawing any five hundred pounds, he would not be withdrawing any amount to give away!

It was an annoyance that demand coming now but it was no disaster. That thorn was easily removed from his flesh, and right now he had bigger problems on his mind.

Deaf to the shouts and calls of wagoners and the coarse language of women shoppers barely missed by heavy iron-rimmed wheels he reached the junction that led towards the bridge crossing the canal.

Philip had reneged on his word to sign the glassworks to him, had threatened to turn him from the house without a penny. Christ, what had Edna been thinking of, the stupid cow! Hadn't he said never to let Philip see Hannah without he himself being there!

His mouth tightening, Archer flicked the rein irritably.

He had meant to wait a little longer before dealing with the problem of Philip but that threat meant bringing matters forward; as he said, an annoyance but no disaster. Still it was as well to remember time was moving fast and with each day the chances of becoming the sole owner of the glassworks became slimmer.

If only his first child had lived. If only that accident had never happened. But it had and with it had died his dream.

He clucked impatiently to the horse, the blare of a steam horn from ironworks set alongside the canal causing it to shy.

*. . . on the death of the said male heir . . . in the event of the death of . . . Hannah Cranley . . .*

The words of that Will came quickly as they always did, taking advantage of every unguarded moment to plague his mind, breaching the defences he had set around it.

Well, the child he had; one who would say and do what Archer Cranley instructed. As for his wife he could have taken the step years ago, the step that would rid him of her, one he would do right now and willingly were it not for the terms laid down by Nathan Briant; terms that left him to always play second fiddle.

But he would not occupy that position for very much longer!

Guiding the trap over Ryder's Bridge he glanced down into the lock slowly filling with water, then to the narrow boat moored beside the towpath waiting to be lowered to the next level.

Briant had appointed an executor to his Will. Almost at once Archer's thoughts returned to the topic ever close to the surface of his mind. Appointed him to watch over the affairs of his daughter and her offspring, to keep a close eye on the actions of the son-in-law he detested.

'But you didn't choose very well, did you, Briant; you did not choose very well at all.' He murmured the words quietly, relishing each one. 'That is, you did not choose well for Hannah, but for me you could not have chosen better. How I wish you knew, Nathan, how I wish you knew what Simeon Beasley truly was, how easily he was persuaded my way was better than yours.'

It had not taken long to get the measure of Simeon Beasley and as the years progressed he had come to know him very well, his little foibles . . . his particular fancies. No, there would be no interference from that quarter, and if things went to plan there would be none from Philip either. There would be no takeover, no removal of power from his hands and no sell-off of the business . . . at least until Archer Cranley decided there would be.

And there would be no query regarding Hannah's death!

Hannah's death! He hugged the thought to himself. That was already decided, the only question being how. She was already quite ill, that much showed in her face and in her doctor's bills. Yes, Hannah would be disposed of but it had to be done slowly, it must not pre-date Philip's coming of age. As long as Hannah lived she could be used as a pawn to hold Philip in check and, when the moment was ripe, to force the signing away of every penny of that inheritance.

Following Ryder's Green Road he glanced at the densely packed line of small, dreary, smoke-blackened houses that bordered it like a dark mourning ribbon, each huddled on its neighbour, close as coals in a sack. His mouth thinned into a sneer as children's voices lifted in a hymn of praise floated from one of the several chapels interspersed among the houses.

Bloody chapels and Sunday schools! He flicked the rein sharply. What good had they done the folk of Greets Green, what had all their psalm-singing and knee-bending brought them? Nothing but a life of hardship and poverty, a lifetime of labour that wouldn't leave them with enough to give a man a decent burial.

But that was not all Greets Green would give Archer Cranley. He called softly to the mare, urging her on. He meant to have all this place could give, and then some. With the Bottle and Glass safely in his hands he would leave the smoke and grime of the Black Country behind. With no one to monitor how he spent the profits of the business he would live the life he ought to have lived these twenty-odd years; he would have a house worthy of a prosperous industrialist, have all he had ever dreamed of having and that would include a second wife, a woman both beautiful and young enough to give him the strong son he needed; one to replace the child that would so quickly follow Hannah to the grave.

With the thought warm inside him, the smile he had allowed himself on leaving Philip at that factory returned to curve his thin mouth.

Yes, Archer Cranley would have it all, everything he deserved.

Turning the trap to the right he guided it along Tasker Street. Reaching Hemming's Dining Rooms he gave the trap into the care of an ostler.

Glancing about him he held back the feeling of distaste. This establishment was good enough for the businessmen of West Bromwich, even of Birmingham, but not good enough for Archer Cranley. Soon he would shake the dust of those towns from his feet. He would be free of the terms of that Will, free of the shackles Nathan Briant had so expertly forged.

Seated at a table set discreetly in a corner Archer watched his guest over the rim of his wine glass. Simeon Beasley was a man who liked his food but he was one who liked his entertainment more; especially if that entertainment were of the right sort and paid for by someone else.

Refilling the other man's half-empty glass with the full-bodied claret, he almost smiled. Today's hospitality would require no money from Beasley but then neither would it come free.

'So, you say Hannah is getting no better?' Simeon Beasley dabbed his lips with the white linen serviette. 'That be a pity, she is a fine woman, a fine woman. You must find it very worrying.'

'I do.' Archer stared into the deep red depths of his glass. 'Especially with the boy not yet having come of age.'

'Ah yes.' Beasley leaned back in his chair, his glance keen with anticipation. 'The grandfather's Will. Should Hannah not live until the boy reaches twenty-one then . . .'

'Then the lot goes to some bloody charity!' Archer's glass came to rest on the table as he looked across to his guest. 'Should that happen we will both feel the pinch. I will lose a comfortable home and you, you will lose the very generous financial "gifts" you've been getting for nigh on twenty years; quite a loss to both of us, wouldn't you say?'

'Advice needs to be paid for.' Beasley smiled. 'Nowt comes for free, Cranley, 'specially when it be of the best.'

Lack of interference needs to be paid for! Archer thought acridly. It had cost a pretty packet to keep Beasley from dipping his nose into the business but this was the last he intended to pay.

'Always the best.' He tried to keep his tone amiable. 'And now it appears I must once again ask for your help.'

'Ask away.' Beasley rolled claret around his tongue before swallowing noisily.

'It is about my wife's health.' Archer lowered his voice though the buzz of conversation of other diners already over-shadowed it. 'It has deteriorated rapidly over this last few months, especially her . . . her mental health; I would rather not elaborate, the subject is entirely too painful.'

'Of course, of course.' Beasley nodded.

Watching the bright button eyes in that flushed heavy face

and reading the greed behind them, Archer felt a tingle of pleasure. Beasley's golden goose was about to become infertile!

'The fact of the matter is this, should my wife . . . should Hannah die—' He swallowed hard, at the same time allowing his fingers to grip the stem of the wine glass dramatically, his knuckles standing out white and hard.

'That would be painful to us all.' Beasley nodded sympathetically. 'But there is the boy, he will be taking on the running of the business in a very short while, he will take that pressure at least from your shoulders; so, sad as is the condition of your wife's health, thankfully it can have no serious repercussions upon that.'

Aware of the sarcasm behind the little speech Archer kept his glance on his wine glass. Simeon Beasley could make his snide remarks but he wouldn't have the last laugh.

'One would think not,' he answered quietly.

'But not you, eh Cranley? You thinks different.'

Archer twisted the stem of the glass between his fingers. 'It is more what I hope rather than what I think, though how far I might rely on hope is a hazardous guess.'

Accepting a dessert of strawberry meringue, smothering it with freshly whipped cream, Beasley waited while Archer waved the trolley away and ordered instead two large Cognacs.

'I can't say I'm with you, Cranley,' he said when they were once more free of attentive dining-room staff. 'I don't follow what you say at all.'

'How could you?' Archer shook his head, hoping the effect was one of near-heartbreak. 'It was my one wish no one would know, that which I prayed would never come to pass; but I see now I must face up to the truth, horrible as it is.'

'The truth? What truth?' Pastry fork halfway to his mouth, Beasley frowned the question. 'What on earth are you talking about, man?'

'My son,' Archer whispered, 'I fear my son will soon be unable to administer any business; I fear he is suffering from the same malady as his mother.'

'Cranley . . . I'm so sorry.' Simeon Beasley let the fork clatter noisily onto the china dish, but already the greed in his eyes had turned to speculation. 'How long . . . I mean how do you know?'

'For the last ten years.' Archer drew a craggy breath. 'I thought at first I was mistaken, prayed I was mistaken, but things got slowly worse; sometimes he would become violent, throwing himself around the room until he had to be restrained for his own safety. That was the reason for his being kept close to the house. But now he demands to be given a position inside the glassworks. I tried not to give in to that demand but I fear I have to in order to keep him and his mother on an even keel.'

'But is that wise? A glassworks is no place for a . . . well, it ain't no nursery.'

'I know.' Archer nodded. 'But it was either agree to his demand or see him go over the edge completely and that would kill Hannah for sure, so I agreed. You understand, I had to. But I gave Platt strict instructions never to let Philip out of his sight, not for an instant. Do you think I did wrong?'

'Seeing the circumstances, I don't see you had any other choice.' Beasley took up the fork once more, filling his mouth with cream-topped meringue.

'Then you would advise I let him stay on at the works?'

'If that be the only way of curbing his . . . of holding the lad's mind together, then yes. I say leave him to get on with it.'

'But it could be a danger for himself and for the men he will be working with.' Archer took the brandies, saying no more until the wine waiter had passed beyond hearing. 'What do I do about them?'

Licking the last trace of cream from the back of his fork Simeon Beasley took up his own brandy glass, inspecting the rich colour reflecting the light.

'You do nothing.' He smiled over the rim of the heavy cut-glass goblet. 'They be paid to work the glass not to question their paymaster. Who you sets to work alongside of 'em be none of their business.'

Resting his glass on the snow-white linen cloth covering the table Archer Cranley hid the smile that hovered in his small beady eyes, saying anxiously, 'But molten glass be a hazardous thing, a man could be seriously burned!'

'He could.' Beasley swallowed a generous amount of brandy, his eyelids blinking rapidly as the fire of it bit the back of his throat. 'But then a man could be out of a job and his family on the streets, that be a bloody 'azardous thing an' all, jobs don't grow on trees not that there be many o' them neither, not in Greets Green. But if it makes you feel the better then tell 'em, tell them men your lad's brain ain't all it should be, tell 'em and give 'em the chance to go or to stay. But think of the stir the news will cause in West Bromwich; do you want that, Cranley?'

No, he did not want that. Archer continued to gaze at the cloth. The less that was known of affairs at Rowlay House the better. He would stick to the plan he had decided upon, not that he had ever intended deviating from it. His seeming anxiety for the welfare of those workmen was nothing but a charade, and that included the welfare of Briant's grandchild.

'Look, Cranley, I knows this might sound 'ard but have you given thought to having Philip . . . well to having him put in a 'ome somewhere?'

'A mental institution!' Archer shuddered then took a long sip of brandy, his eyes closed as if shutting out the thought. 'God Almighty, I can't . . . ! I can't lock away my own child.'

'If it be as you says then you might have to.'

Raising a hand Beasley summoned the wine waiter, ordering two more brandies. Once the drinks were delivered he looked at the man sat opposite.

'You say Philip is growing more violent every day, more demanding. As the strength of them fits increases there's bound to come the moment that sister o' your'n won't be strong enough to 'andle it, and if you should be away from the house that could lead to God knows what. Think of it, Cranley, think of the harm could be done to your womenfolk! You have to face it, man. Heartbreaking as it be for you, you must consider an institution.'

Lifting the glass Archer stared for several seconds at the golden liquid, seeming to draw comfort from its depths. Beasley had tasted the bait, now would he take the hook?

'What you say is sound advice, as always, and I thank you for it.' He breathed a slow, defeated breath. 'It will of course have to be acted upon; I did not want to see that but now I know I must. It will be hard enough for Hannah and me but it be the folk at the glassworks will come off worst.'

' 'Ow do you make that out?'

Archer gave a slow shake of the head, his face as he lifted it filled with sympathy.

'You heard the terms of Briant's Will. The male child must be married before reaching the age of majority or the whole lot is sold off. Where will those men and women be then, will the charity that benefits see to their wellbeing? I have my doubts, Beasley . . . I have my doubts.'

'The old man's Will?' Simeon Beasley blinked as the strong liquor slid past his throat. 'It did not, as I remember, specify which charity the proceeds of a sale would go to.'

'That's not surprising.' Archer's voice hardened. 'Briant wouldn't give a blind man a light. That clause was inserted to spite me but still he couldn't bring himself to name who it was his money were to be given to, he left the choosing of that to Hannah.'

His podgy face flushed from the effects of brandy, his eyes re-lit with new greed, Simeon Beasley smiled.

'Then there's your answer, Cranley. Get your wife to sign a paper making everything that was hers over to charity –' he smiled more widely '– a charity of your own choosing and one which will benefit only two people.'

'Two?' Archer asked the question, a frown furrowing his forehead.

As if washed away by a cloth Simeon Beasley's smile vanished and when he spoke it was with cold precision.

'Two, Cranley . . . you and me.'

It had gone well. Climbing into the trap Archer tossed a coin to the ostler holding a hand to the horse's bridle.

Beasley had gone for it hook, line and sinker. So far as he knew, Philip was as ripe for the madhouse as Hannah was. But Hannah would never get there.

His hand light on the rein he let the animal move at its own pace, habit guiding its steps towards Ryder's Bridge.

Beasley was a fool too blinded by his own greed to see beyond the end of his nose. But then, like everything else that had cropped up to keep Archer Cranley from what he wanted, Beasley could be cut down. There would be no equal division, no fifty-fifty sharing. To the victor went the spoils and Archer Cranley would be the victor.

It could not be avoided having the man at his back all these years, being executor of Briant's Will had dictated that. So cautious, Nathan, Archer smiled to himself; but not quite cautious enough. The man you chose to safeguard your precious business is interested only in the handouts he has been getting and that he sees to get in the future. Simeon Beasley was easily bought, Father-in-law, and he will be as easily gotten rid of as your daughter!

With a chuckle rising to his throat he urged the horse to a gentle trot.

But first things first. He had an appointment with a black-mailer, an appointment he would keep.

# Chapter Six

'You be kin to the master?'

The man Archer Cranley had appointed as tutor coughed, the noise of it like pebbles rattling together in his chest.

Glancing at the face covered with a film of grey dust which mixed with sweat and filled the lines etched so deeply into the skin they seemed drawn with charcoal, Philippa felt a rush of sympathy. Was this what the making of glass did to men, caused them to age long before their time, filled their lungs with the dust of silica until one cough-free breath was a luxury?

Catching the enquiring glance that met the failure to answer, Philippa nodded. 'Yes, I am . . . I am Archer Cranley's son.'

Snatching off the filthy cap that had been replaced only after his employer had entered the works' office, the man's eyes darkened with anxiety.

'Eh, sir, I asks your pardon. I d'ain't know.'

'There is no need to apologise.' She smiled. 'How were you to know? I have not been here before and my father made no introductions.'

'No more you 'aven't, sir.' The man shook his head but no relaxation showed in his face. 'Nor 'as your father done more than walk through the place a couple of times, that were why I said there be more to making glass than he knowed. I meant no disrespect but then there be more to it than can be learned proper in many a month, let alone one.'

'But one is all we have.' Philippa glanced towards a low arched doorway giving onto the works. 'And we had better make a start on using it before we both hear more.'

'Ar, sir, reckon you be right.' The man's eyes swivelled towards the office, then back to Philippa. 'Archer Cranley don't take kindly to men using their tongue 'stead of their 'ands. It be this way, sir, though I'll not tell you to be mindful of your clothes for you'll not protect them once inside of that cone.'

'Pay no mind to my clothes.' Philippa's rare smile deepened. 'They are going to be the very last of my worries for the next month at least; and if I am to be one of the hands then I do not think the others will take kindly to my being called sir. Here I am no more than Philip Cranley, apprentice to the glass.'

'That be easy said but what if the master should 'ear a man using your given name? Mebbe 'e wouldn't tek kindly to that.'

Speaking over his shoulder as the flat cap was replaced, Samuel Platt led the way to the huge cone-shaped building.

Following him, Philippa swallowed the acrid taste of oxides and silica dust already coating lips and tongue.

His given name! The using of that would not offend Archer Cranley. Did he truly believe the aim of placing his only child in this place was not obvious? Did he not intend that 'glassman's lung', the disease that killed so many people involved in that trade, would place Briant Bottle and Glass permanently in his own hands? But then would not Philip Cranley's death, by whatever means, be preferable to the life lived now?

'I think a general look around be best for to start, then we'll set you to the packing, that be wrapping the glass that be ready for dispatch and setting it in baskets such as the little wench carried. No sense in destroying what 'as no need to be destroyed.'

The chargehand glanced at Philippa's well-tailored jacket and trousers, clothes that five years of his wages would not buy.

'Tomorrow be time enough for the doing of anything else,

besides, it will afford you time for the gettin' of summat a sight less costly to wear in these works, for the fact be they'll be little use for wearing anywheres else after a day or two of 'andling molten glass.'

He could have said that the immaculately clean fingernails would not emerge the same, or the soft white skin of the shapely hands, but that observation remained closed away in his mind. Archer Cranley's lad would seem to have more to worry over than the effect of dirt on his hands.

'Every man and lad works shifts,' he went on, 'that be six hours on and six hours off all through, both day and night.'

'They work at night also?'

Following the other man into the cone Philippa gasped, the heat of twelve furnaces grouped in a circle beneath the rising stack striking with an almost physical blow.

'Ar.' The chargehand nodded affirmatively. 'The furnaces 'ave to be kept stoked, they can't never be allowed to die out for it teks too long a time to fire 'em up again; teks several full days to build up the kind of temperatures needed to melt glass and them would be the days gaffer were making no profit and men were unable to feed their families.'

'But what of Sundays, surely Sunday is not included?'

Taking the end of a rag muffler tied about his neck the man passed it across his mouth and cheeks, wiping away droplets of sweat gathering like tiny crystal beads.

'Ar, Sunday be a day of rest. That be what the good Lord said, only I reckon he forgot to tell certain folk of it.'

Folk like Archer Cranley. Philippa touched a finger to the inside of the stiff collar rapidly becoming a vice about the throat. He had thoughts for the welfare of none but himself and profit was the only god he worshipped, the one deity whose word he obeyed.

'Each group operates its own "chair".' Samuel Platt continued his explanation, tactfully ignoring the rapidly rising discomfort of the young man beside him. 'The top bloke be the Blower, then there be the Bit Gatherers, they brings the molten glass to 'im, they be followed by the Taker In who carries the finished article to the lehr to be annealed. If a "chair" be making bigger things such as jugs and tankards then it 'as what be called a Workman, 'e does the shaping and the shearing.'

Continuing to talk the man led the way slowly around the floor of the cone-shaped building, pausing at each of the open-arched workshops that flanked it, further explaining the duties of men scurrying back and forth between the bank of furnaces and the men whose cheeks swelled out like balloons as they blew down a long tube-like implement; their trapped breath was caught by the blob of molten glass attached to the opposite end and enlarged it to fill the cavity of a mould. But though Philippa listened, the words did not intrude on thought. Men here worked six-hour shifts through the day and the night, with six hour intervals between! That meant that men and even young boys worked eighty-four hours a week. Eighty-four hours in heat that could be matched only by the fires of hell . . . and every hour spent breathing in the dust of sand and oxides!

'It'll tek a while to sink in.' The man turned, catching the look of incredulity on the face of the newest apprentice and entirely misunderstanding the cause. 'But you'll learn, we all do given time.'

A shout from one of the adjacent alcoves that housed a chair rang out, echoing again and again as it was drawn up along the great chimney, and a young lad, heavy wooden clogs rapping over the uneven setts of the floor, ran towards a furnace, the long blowpipe with its blob of half-shaped glass held out like a lance before him.

Philippa watched the glass being thrust into the red-hot maw of the furnace, the boy twisting the pipe as the mass reheated, then racing with it back to the Blower. These men had a lifetime to learn, a lifetime that must of necessity be given either to the making of glass or the mining of coal, for Greets Green offered little else; could one be worse than the other?

And what of the life Archer Cranley dictated for his own child, ordered by him as he ordered that of his workers? What difference was there between them? Theirs was a penance, Philippa Cranley's was a sacrifice!

'The packing be done over the yard.'

The soles of her leather boots slipping on the uneven setts, Philippa's balance faltered and would have given way altogether had not a passing Bit Gatherer paused to hold out a steadying hand.

'Ya must pay 'eed to the floor, sir.' A lad no more than fourteen years of age held her arm with a strength which years of carrying the heavy blowpipe gave him. 'Water from the cracking off turns the dust to sludge and that be fair slippery under foot.'

'Thank you. I will remember.'

Satisfied Philip was once more steady on his feet the lad's glance travelled to where his Blower stood waiting for the molten glass. At a brief nod he turned back, thrusting the rod with its molten glass into a small side furnace that was used to reheat glass that had cooled before the shaping was finished, the tiny aperture Philippa's guide called a Glory Hole.

'I apologise for disrupting your work.' Her voice seemed to have no sound against the roar of the ducts that fed heat into the bank of furnaces. Stood in his own alcove the Blower made no attempt to reply but the eyes that met and held Philippa's seemed filled with a thousand silent words.

'It be this way, sir . . .'

'The name is Phil— Philip.' The words answered the appointed apprentice master but as the watching eyes of the Blower turned away Philippa felt strangely as if they both knew they had been meant for him.

Dodging the scurrying Bit Gatherers and feeling the stares of men who were employed in every alcove to service the chair like so many worker bees attending their queen, she followed Samuel Platt out of the further end of the cone and into a low building, its shadows hardly relieved by the one window whose panes were almost totally obscured by coat upon coat of the fine grey dust that found every niche and every cranny.

'You best start in 'ere. This be the packing shed. Over there be sawdust and the crates be along yonder wall. Be sure to seat the glass in plenty of straw and wood shavings for every broken piece be paid for outta your wage. Young Ginny 'ere will show you the ropes, oh and be sure and count what it is you pack and 'ow many; I'll be in when the shift ends to tek your numbers.'

Staring about the brick-built shed Philippa shivered, and not only from the coolness so sharply felt after the fierce heat of the cone but also from the sheer dreariness of the place. A long bench covered with sawdust and paper together with an assortment of bottles and glasses was set against the one wall that boasted a window, but more light was given by the several holes in the roof.

'If I was you I would tek off that jacket and roll back them shirt sleeves. Leave 'em as they be and you'll look like a chimbley sweep in no time; but then ya'll end up lookin' like one anyway.' The girl swept a deprecating look. 'Were a daft idea coming to work in clothes like that, I don't know what ya thought ya was coming into but it ain't no palace and it ain't no place for the wearing of fancy togs!'

'Nor is it any place for a wench to go talking to a man in that way, Ginny Morton. Your mother gets to 'ear of your cheek and you'll be teking yourself a smacked arse to bed. Now see to your task for I'll be wanting your numbers an' all and they'd better be the usual or you'll be follerin' the Turner family outta the gate.'

'The Turner family?' Philippa asked as the young girl, her face growing a warm shade of pink beneath its covering of wood dust, turned back to her work. 'Would those be the ones given their tins just now?'

Samuel Platt nodded, his glance following the girl's deft fingers.

'Ar that be the Turners, God 'elp 'em. They made little enough working in the glass but at least it put a crumb into them

68

babbies' mouths, but now –' he shook his head '– there be precious little work anywheres 'cept p'raps the pit and the new laws says wenches and women can no longer serve underground so it looks like the workhouse for them right enough.'

Giving one more stern glance to the girl the chargehand turned away.

The workhouse! As a child Philippa had heard Edna Cranley relate tales of people unfortunate enough to be assigned to that institution, of men and of women who had hanged themselves sooner than be sent there.

'Mr Platt.'

Turning at the call, Samuel Platt hesitated inside the doorway.

'What is it, lad?'

Crossing to him Philippa spoke quietly, not wishing the girl to hear.

'My father, you said he rarely walks through the cone.'

'That be true, so rare as to be nigh on never.'

'And the packing sheds?'

'The same, but why—'

'Mr Platt,' Philippa interrupted quickly, 'going by what you say then my father would not necessarily know should the Turners be reinstated.'

''Re in what?' Samuel Platt's brow furrowed, adding to the tracery of lines etching his face.

Glancing towards the girl whose ears were likely straining like greyhounds on a leash, Philippa drew the man outside the shed.

'Mr Platt,' she began again, 'what I meant was this. If my father so rarely visits the works then it is a possibility he will not recognise many of the people employed here other than yourself . . .'

''E would know the Blowers.'

'Was Mr Turner a Blower?'

'No.' The chargehand's frown deepened. 'Ike Turner were no Blower, 'e were a Bit Gatherer; look, lad, what do this be leadin' up to?'

'It is leading to this.' Philippa paused, waiting for a woman carrying a pile of wicker baskets to pass beyond hearing. 'Could not the Turners be given back their jobs?'

'What . . . 'ere in the glass!'

'Yes. Here in the glass.'

'Eh, lad, you don't know what you be asking. Should Archer Cranley find out then 'e would kick my arse so far off this ground it would tek me a week to walk 'ome.'

'But he doesn't have to find out, and if he does then you say it was done on my instruction.'

Lifting his dust-soaked cap the chargehand scratched his scalp with one finger.

'Your instruction . . . I don't know . . . the gaffer ain't one to look kindly on his order being flouted, no nor changed neither.'

'But that family.' Her eyes dark with concern, Philippa pressed again. 'You said yourself there was no work for them here in Greets Green.'

'No more there is.' Platt lowered his cap, pulling the peak low on his forehead. 'And none for me should Archer Cranley get wind of what I be doing . . . but, but then the workhouse be no place for babbies nor for the women that bore 'em.'

'So you will give them back their jobs?'

'And risk gettin' my arse kicked?' Samuel Platt's smile broke, clearing the frown. 'Ar, lad, I'll do that . . . I never was one to balk at 'aving to walk a ways.'

Thanking him Philippa returned to the packing bench, drawing a loud breath of relief.

'What were that all about?'

Taking up a bottle and copying the girl's quick movement, Philippa settled it firmly in the straw-lined crate.

No day over eight years old, stick-thin, with hair that hung like brown pencils over her shoulders, a ragged dress already well clear of ankles lost in boots many sizes too big, handling bottle and paper with a dexterity that said this was not her first year spent working at this bench, the girl watched her with bright inquisitive eyes.

'Nothing.' Philippa placed another bottle in the wooden crate.

'What ya means to say is keep ya nose out, Ginny Morton!' the youngster snorted. 'Well all ya needs to do is say it.'

It should not have to be said. Philippa hid the smile working its way mouthwards. But there was no intrusion meant, it was a natural way with children; they asked without thinking.

'You have a pretty nose, Ginny . . .'

'Ya think so . . . ya really think my nose be pretty?' The child blushed but this time it was from pleasure. 'Me mom allus says it be as long as a heliphant's trunk, 'er says that's what comes of puttin' it where it don't be wanted.'

'Have you ever seen an elephant?'

'Never.' The girl shook her head. 'But me mom says as 'ow they be big clumsy creatures wi' no sense.'

Philippa's smile broke out. 'I have no wish to contradict your mother, Ginny, but elephants are not without sense, neither are they clumsy though they do have very long noses.'

'Longer than this?' She spread her thin arms sideways.

'Yes, Ginny.' Philippa laughed. 'Much longer than that. But it is very sensitive, it can pick up the smallest of things.'

'Things small as . . . small as a 'azelnut?'

'As small as a hazelnut.'

'And they don't be clumsy?'

'No, they are not clumsy, they move their feet very carefully, especially so when stepping over people.'

'Steppin' over people!' Ginny's mouth fell open. 'You means they sometimes walks on folk, treads on 'em?'

'Not *on* them Ginny, *over* them. They can move so carefully as not to touch a man as they step over him.'

'Strewth!' Opening her eyes wide with wonder Ginny stared upwards, her hands idle on the bench. ''Ave you seen a heliphant . . . a real live one?'

'Hmm.' Philippa nodded.

'And you've seen 'em do that, walk over a man wi'out treadin' on 'im?'

'Without touching a hair of his head.'

'Strewth!' she exclaimed again. 'Me mom will never believe that . . . you ain't coddin' me, am ya?'

Resting a wrapped bottle on the bench Philippa smiled into the upturned face. 'I am not trying to fool you, Ginny. I have seen it for myself. I was sometimes taken to the circus as a child, I saw elephants do many tricks.'

'A body can teach 'em tricks . . . then they ain't stupid?'

'Far from it. Elephants are very intelligent. Their trainers say that once they meet you they never forget; so if you meet with an elephant be sure to treat it kindly just in case you meet it a second time.'

'Don't see no likelihood of that.' Her face clouding, the child turned back to the work on the bench. 'There ain't never no money in our 'ouse to go spendin' on circuses. I don't reckon Ginny Morton will ever get to seein' no heliphant.'

'Perhaps one day you will. But until then would a picture of one do?'

'You ain't got no picture.' Born of disappointment the words shot out.

'I do have a picture,' Philippa answered gently, understanding the bitterness beneath the child's reply. 'I have a book full of animals from all over the world, even elephants. I could bring it for you if you want to see it.'

'Strewth!' She stared, a mixture of wonder and delight potent in her brown eyes. 'You means it?'

'Tomorrow.' Philippa's smile deepened. 'I will bring it for you tomorrow.'

'I 'eard old Platty call you Philip . . . be that your name?'

Philippa nodded. Maybe it would always be her name.

'Can I call ya by your name or do I calls ya mister?'

'I prefer Phil— Philip will do fine.'

Standing idle a moment longer the girl glanced at the hands on the bench, their whiteness already marred by ink rubbed off newspaper, the nails so clean minutes ago now filthy with sawdust, and the earlier smile broke over her thin face.

'Well then, Philip, I tell you the advice I give ya afore. Tek that fancy jacket off lessen ya wants it to look like one a chimbley sweep wouldn't be teken for a corpse in.'

Philippa held up both arms, surveying the sawdust already covering them in a fine dust cloud.

'I see what you mean. But I was given no idea I was to be set to working here today otherwise I would have obtained more suitable clothing.'

'Summat else ya should get be a different way o' talking. The folk at Briant Glass don't trust that 'igh falutin' way o' speaking . . . it smacks too much of gaffers and gentry and they 'arbours no love for any of that kind.'

'Then you will have to teach me, Ginny.'

'Me teach you? Gerroff wi' ya!' She laughed, the sound echoing off damp-grimed walls. 'Me mom says the best way a body as to learn anything be to listen well an' watch close. That be the way *you'll* 'ave to learn.'

Taking the bottle Philippa put deliberately in her hand she set about the tedious process once more, but her questions were by no means done.

'What do you be meaning when you be saying ya didn't know ya was to be set on today?'

'Just that.' Philippa's own hands became still. 'I thought I was being brought here on a visit, simply to be shown around the works.'

' 'Stead of which ya was dumped, huh! That be a smart 'ow do you do.'

Turning to the bench, her hands already busily packing bottles, she talked on, her tone a clear implication she did not believe what she had heard.

'Bet that was a surprise. Ain't it nearer the truth to say ya got kicked out of ya other job?'

'Perhaps that might be nearer the truth, certainly it was changed very quickly.'

Layering wrapped bottles into a crate the girl scooped handfuls of sawdust, spreading it thickly over and between them.

'That why you got yourself all done up like a dandy?' She glanced up, her hands filled with the powdery dust. 'You 'oping to get old Cranley's job? Huh, wouldn't we all like that! Bet 'e don't work no eighty hours a week, no nor even one in a dirty 'ole like the glassworks; 'e gets folk like we to do that and pays pennies for the doing; but you won't even get pennies if Sam Platt comes back and finds you ain't started.' Dragging the crate away from the bench and across the uneven floor to stand with several others near a door at the further end of the building she stood regarding the slight well-dressed figure.

'Just what job did you 'ave afore you landed this one? It must 'ave been a bit of all right if you could afford clothes like that to work in. Eh . . . ya wasn't Mrs Cranley's little darlin' was ya?'

Her laugh ringing again from the brickwork the girl returned to the bench, shuffling her feet in order not to lose the oversized boots. Glancing at Philippa she positioned an empty basket beside the workbench.

'Well, don't be tight-mouthed, ya can't 'elp being sacked, I don't suppose ya chose it. What was this job you 'ad that paid a fortune?'

Removing the dark coat and rolling back shirt sleeves Philippa took up bottle and paper.

'I kept the account books for Mr Cranley.'

''Ere you didn't go on the fiddle, did ya?' The girl's eyes widened. 'Is that 'ow come you can dress so fancy?'

Philippa wrapped a bottle, laying it on the bed of sawdust. 'I hardly think I would have been given any job by Archer Cranley had I embezzled money, even one in the glassworks.'

'No, ya be right.' She nodded. 'Old Cranley would 'ave 'ad you down the line that fast folk wouldn't have seen your arse for

74

dust. 'E must 'ave had some reason, I mean for not getting rid of ya altogether, but why put you 'ere?'

Philippa's smile was tight. 'He thinks I am, as he put it, "'too much the fancy pants". The glassworks will knock that out of me.'

'You ain't, am ya?' The wide eyes stretched wider. 'Funny, I mean; on the turn? Christ, the men 'ere'll laugh you into your grave if that be the case!'

'On the turn?' Philippa straightened from scooping sawdust over a layer of glassware.

'Yes.' The child's glance never wavered. 'You know . . . preferences, like . . . you would rather go to bed wi' a man than wi' a woman? That be it, don't it!' She laughed triumphantly as Philippa's colour rose. 'Old man Cranley fancied you and you told 'im what 'e could do with his fancies so 'e stuck you 'ere to get his own back, so 'e could watch you suffer.' The laugh dying on her lips, the girl's eyes darkened. ''E be a bad one is Cranley but one day the devil will whistle and that swine will dance a different jig.'

Reaching for another bottle Philippa answered quietly, 'I was not placed here for either of those reasons but I think he will enjoy seeing me suffer.'

'Then why don't you leave?' The girl's fingers moved swiftly as she spoke. 'You don't be like the rest of the men old Cranley sets to working. If you can do that accounting thing like you says then you 'as to 'ave learning so you could do a damn sight better than to tek work in the silica, for that be naught but a death trap.'

That was the very reason for being put here. Philippa worked in silence. The death of his only child would leave Archer Cranley's way clear. But leaving was out of the question. It was not only the child's life was in danger but the mother's also.

Remembering the drawn face, unhappy even in sleep, her hands tightened. Hannah Cranley's life would not be given a second thought if she were left alone with her husband and sister-in-law. No, there could be no question of leaving Greets Green while Hannah lived.

'You go to Sam Platt and tell 'im you be leaving, then sling your 'ook afore Cranley finds out what you be at.' The girl set the last bottle in the crate then covered the whole with a generous layer of sawdust. 'Find yourself some other work that'll give you a living, for anything be better than working for Cranley, that slave driver would see a body into its coffin and come a second time to pinch the nails.'

'It is not that easy . . .'

Philippa's answering smile was wry.

'. . . you see, Archer Cranley is my father.'


There were no fresh bruises on that tired face. The threat made to Archer Cranley and his sister had worked in some measure at least.

Philippa smiled into the tired eyes that must once have been a sparkling vibrant blue but now held the shadows of misery.

'How do you feel today, Mother?'

A faint smile touching her mouth Hannah gathered the work-stained hands between her own, lifting them to her lips.

'The same as I always feel when you are here . . . well. You make me feel well, my dearest, but what is this?' She held the hands at arms' length, looking first at the flesh rubbed sore and red, then at the soiled jacket and trousers.

'Forgive me, Mother.' Philippa smiled apologetically. 'I was too eager to see you . . . I should first have bathed and changed my clothes.'

'But why are they so dirty?' Hannah frowned. 'I never saw you in such a state not even when you were a child.'

'I am far from that now, Mother.'

Across the room Archer Cranley caught the glance lifted briefly to him. Understanding the double meaning he clenched his teeth, suppressing the anger it aroused. The gosling was feeling its feet, the gander must needs strike soon if it was not to be the one ousted from the nest.

'I have been visiting the works.' Philippa smiled again at the pale face, the tired eyes ringed about with shadows. 'Father allowed me to see inside the cone.'

'Should you have done that, Archer? The cone is so very dangerous.'

'Not if you know what you're doing.' Archer Cranley's face tightened, the criticism adding to the anger beginning to bubble beneath the false smile. 'You worry too much, my dear. After all the lad has to learn the business sooner or later, and besides which I gave him into the care of Samuel Platt, no man be better qualified to see to his safety than that one.'

'I asked Father if I could stay.' Philippa smoothed the roughening surface. 'But I did not remain long in the cone, it was too hot; then I found the work of the packing and dispatch so interesting I'm afraid I lost track of the time.'

'Well, you are home now.' Hannah kissed both hands again, pressing her lips against the torn skin. 'Off you go to wash then have supper. Philip –' she stared intently, holding on as Philippa made to rise, her faded eyes suddenly alive with feeling '– take care, my dearest, and remember . . . I love you, I've *always* loved you.'

She could not have said it more clearly.

Stepping out of soiled clothes, leaving them in a heap on the floor of the bathroom, Philippa climbed into the deep cast-iron bath, the one concession to comfort Archer had allowed into a house unchanged for years.

'*I've* always *loved you.*'

The word emphasised so clearly said what her mother had so often said in the past, that Stephen's death was an accident, the action of a child too young to know its consequences. The love she held had never been diminished, never scarred and never withdrawn; the love she held for her older child was unconditional. Unlike her husband, Hannah Cranley was able if not to forget then at least to not ruin another young life with the continual pointing of the finger of blame.

But her sanity had remained precariously balanced on a fine line. Both husband and sister-in-law had stressed the need for the charade they had devised, a fiasco her child had been irrevocably drawn into. It had had to be played, must still be played if that sanity were to be kept.

But what a charade!

Philippa lifted the sponge, squeezing warm water over tired eyes.

What a terrible price to pay!

*'Tell 'im you be leaving, then sling your 'ook.'*

The remembered words rang dully.

So easily said. But they could not be carried out. Hannah Cranley would never be deserted. As long as she lived the deception must go on: Philippa Cranley must live life as a man.

# Chapter Seven

Archer Cranley laid aside the evening edition of the *Express and Star*. He had scanned the newspaper carefully, finding a report of local prostitute Sally Povey being found hanged from her own bedpost. Foul play was not suspected.

It was as he thought, the police were satisfied the woman had committed suicide. But he must continue to turn up at that chapel for a few weeks, to drop it off all at once might arouse suspicion.

Glancing up as his sister entered the dining room he felt the sour taste of dislike taint his tongue. He had never felt anything other than dislike for her, he thought, watching her come to stand at the other end of the heavy mahogany table, her thin mouth tight, a nose thin and sharp as a razor and eyes like a marauding blackbird's. No, Edna had never been what you might call pretty and with her sharp acid tongue she would die as she had lived, an old maid; for it would take a desperate man or a very well-paid one to bed her!

'There be something unusual in Hannah.'

Even her voice scratched the senses. A glede under a door sounded sweeter.

Controlling his irritation at being disturbed, he sat with one hand resting on the newspaper. Edna would not have the pleasure of reading this over her secret glasses of port wine.

Poor Edna, even now she did not realise that nothing she ever did was hidden from her brother.

'Something unusual!' He raised his brows enquiringly.

'She refuses to take her medicine.'

'Perhaps she is not quite ready for it.' Taking the watch from the pocket of his waistcoat he glanced at it before slipping it back. 'Does it have to be given at this hour?'

Edna's narrow features seemed to close in on themselves, her lips seeking obscurity.

'No, it don't have to be given at this hour,' she mimicked sarcastically. 'That is if you be prepared to sit with her 'til the hour do be right for it to be given, for I won't. I put up with her all day long, it's me has to do that which you finds irksome.'

The hand resting on the newspaper curled tightly.

'A well-paid duty, Edna, let's not forget that.'

'A *promised* well-paid duty,' Edna flashed back.

His control stretched to the limit Archer rose slowly to his feet, the newspaper gripped in his hand.

'You know the situation as well as I do,' he said, crossing to stand before the fireplace, 'you knew it when you came to live in this house. A comfortable home with a settlement at the end was what you agreed.'

'It was what we *both* agreed.' Edna's bird-like eyes glinted. 'Let's not forget that, Archer; that is what we both agreed.'

'Yes, it was mutual,' he answered quietly. 'But now I put another proposition to you. You may leave now, this very evening, with a third of what was originally offered . . .'

'A third!' Edna's caustic laugh was cut off as Archer continued.

'. . . but I would advise caution before making your decision, Edna, for though you may believe otherwise I tell you frankly that even with that money you'll find no man will take you on, not even as his whore!'

Her breath hissing between clenched teeth, Edna's hands curved like talons, digging into her skirts.

'God damn you, Archer!' she glared. 'God damn you to hell!'

'Why bother asking for something that has already been done? He damned me when Nathan Briant drew up that Will and He damned you when Richard Stanton turned his back on you. What was it you said, Edna . . . blood of my blood? Well, what's in the blood comes out of it!' He slammed the newspaper into the fire, his thin mouth curving into a cold smile as he watched the flames curl about it. 'We'll go to hell together, sister dear . . . we'll go to hell together!'

Eyes gleaming with a passion that held her mouth in an iron line, Edna turned from the room. His victory bringing no solace, Archer followed. Hell was already with him and it would be with him so long as he was in this house.

Close behind his sister he entered his wife's bedroom, the irritation he had felt downstairs returning in full measure. If only it could be done now . . . but it couldn't. He must wait awhile yet.

'Edna tells me you refuse to take your medicine.'

Hannah's faded blue eyes lifted. He had given her no greeting, asked no question as to her wellbeing. But then since when had he done either? Archer Cranley suffered her presence here only because it suited him . . . and he would suffer it only so long as it continued to do so.

'I want to see my child, Archer, I want to see Philip.'

Stood beside her brother Edna clasped her hands together over her skirts.

'I've told her, Philip is not in the house.'

'Why?' The speed of Hannah's retort taking them by surprise, the two glanced at each other.

'He does not have to be in the house every minute,' Archer answered sharply.

'Nor out of it every minute.' Hannah looked steadily at the man her father had so disliked. 'But it seems that is the situation, for every time I ask I am told Philip is not at home. Why, Archer? I want to know why!'

'I've told you—'

'So you have, Edna, and should I wish you to answer me again then I will direct my question to you, meantime I am speaking to my husband.'

The very unexpectedness of her sister-in-law's reply causing her mouth to slacken, Edna stared at the pale drawn face then with a snort stormed from the room, the door slamming at her back.

Ignoring Edna's display of temper, her own features calm, her voice quiet, Hannah held her gaze steady.

'I want to know, Archer. Why is it I see less and less of Philip every day?'

'It be mostly late when the lad gets home and you be settled for the night.'

'Why is Philip late home each night?' Hannah's glance suddenly sharpened. 'Tell me, Archer, is Philip working in the glass?'

Why all these question now? Where had Hannah found the courage to ask them? Beneath the irritation a flicker of concern trickled along Archer's nerves. Was the laudanum ceasing to have effect? No, it couldn't be that, she was given too strong a dose to fight that off, unless Edna had been leaving the room before seeing the stuff swallowed, in which case it could be going out of the window. But Edna was too careful for that, so just what was the cause of the change in Hannah?

Displeasure masking dilemma Archer slapped a hand noisily against his thigh. 'Yes, Philip is working in the glass and before you say more, understand this. There be precious few weeks left afore that business be taken out of my hands, before it becomes Philip's for good; that be the reason for the decision to take on the job of learning the trade, a decision made not by me but by himself: that be the reason you sees little of him.'

Twisting a ribbon of her nightgown about one finger, the only sign of the true tumult inside her, Hannah answered, 'I don't believe you, Archer. I don't believe the decision or the choice was Philip's.'

'Then don't bloody believe it!' His temper mounting, he kicked viciously at the leg of a chair. 'Believe what you like.'

Though slightly unsteady on her legs, Hannah retrieved the toppled chair, standing with a hand on it as she righted it.

'It is what I don't like that I believe. You have put Philip in that glassworks for one reason only; I know that reason, Archer, and I warn you . . .'

His face darkening, the short pointed beard seeming to lengthen the narrow features, he drew a short noisy breath, his hand lashing out to catch across that calm face.

'You don't warn me!' He took a step towards the reeling figure, striking again as he spat, 'You won't ever warn me!' Standing over Hannah where she sprawled on the floor his lips drew back in a snarl.

'Listen to me one more time, Hannah. My word is law in this house, it will be questioned by no one . . . you understand, Hannah . . . no one!'

With blood trickling from her mouth, Hannah looked at the man standing over her, a man with murder in his eyes. She had so feared him in the past but now that fear was gone, all she felt for him now was contempt. But for Philip she felt a strange dread. The business would not be given if Archer Cranley could find a way of holding on to it.

Touching a hand to the warm wetness oozing down her chin, Hannah smiled.

'As you say, in this house your word is law. But only for a few weeks more, then the rule of law will be broken. You will no longer be master of Rowlay.'

The laudanum had taken her looks and sapped her energy but it had not robbed her completely of her senses.

His look one of loathing he turned away, going to stand beneath the window, its heavy curtains drawn against the night sky.

Drawing several long breaths he calmed the fury riding him like a banshee. Behind him, Hannah lifted herself to a chair.

'While we are discussing Rowlay —' he turned to face the woman dabbing blood from her mouth '— it might be as well to recall the terms of your father's Will. The heir will be married by the age of twenty-one or Rowlay House will be sold along with everything else, and Philip is not yet married.'

'I am glad my father made the Will he did, glad he made it impossible for you to keep anything that was his, glad you will have no more control.'

'But I won't lose control of everything that was his . . .'

Soft and silky-smooth, the words creamed from smiling lips.

'. . . you forget, my dear, you are my wife. It is my responsibility to see to your welfare and should that welfare mean locking you away in an insane asylum—'

Watching the shrug of his shoulders Hannah smiled widely, wincing at the sting of already swollen lips.

'You have threatened that too many times for it to frighten me, Archer.'

'Have I?' Smooth as before the interruption came softly, its quietness adding to the threat it carried. 'Then maybe this will return that fear. Today I spoke with Simeon Beasley . . . you remember him don't you, your father's executor? It was my sad duty to tell him of Philip's condition.'

Hannah's nerves jarred, the strange dread of moments ago increasing to a drumbeat in her temples.

'I had to tell him of the deterioration of Philip's mental capacities which would very shortly leave me no alternative but to have him, like yourself, confined to the asylum.'

With her hand pressed hard against her mouth, Hannah was mindless of the pain of broken lips as she stared horror-struck at the smiling face.

'I see I have your attention, Hannah, that's good, for there is something else I have to tell you.'

Crossing the room he opened the door quietly, standing for several seconds to glance both ways along the landing to ensure his sister was not eavesdropping, then returned to a chair drawn close to Hannah's.

'Yes, my dear, there is something else I have to tell you.'


Walking from the packing shed, its air heavy with the dust of wood shavings and straw, Philippa drew a long cooling breath, wiping the drip of perspiration on the strip of cloth Samuel Platt had said should be tied around the throat.

As she glanced in the direction of a rough wooden bench set beneath the wall of the packing shed, the tiredness in every limb suddenly struck home. Almost gasping at having to force muscles to move yet again, she staggered to the seat.

How did these people keep working at such a pace? With her eyes closed against the throb of aching limbs, head resting on the wall at the back of the bench, her thoughts ran on unchecked. Boys no more than ten years old, men six and seven times that ran to the rhythm of their chairs, each forced to keep going for should there be a shortfall in the glass they produced then the job would be snatched away and no care given as to how they would manage to survive. What a dreadful way to have to live. But that way would go on so long as Archer Cranley was in charge.

'I ain't seen you afore . . . be you started 'ere long?'

Opening her eyes, Philippa blinked, the brightness of the afternoon keeping the face of the man who spoke in relative darkness.

'Not very long.'

'I thought that much.' The man silhouetted against the sunlight nodded. 'You be in the shed?'

'Yes.' She did not want conversation, only rest.

'It be 'ard work in there, old Cranley works 'is men like 'osses, they be good for nuthin' after a few years workin' forrim; but it be that or the work'ouse for most, for there be precious little else in these parts. You live in Greets Green, do ya?'

Her answer was a shake of the head. Couldn't the man see there was no desire for talk?

'Where do ya come from then?'

The man pursued his questioning, ignoring the tired movement.

'Like I says, I ain't see you around 'ere afore today an' I gets to see most folk as lives in the Green.'

If the question was answered the man might go away, spoil no more of the chance to enjoy the few precious hours free of the works.

'That is because I do not live in Greets Green.' She drew a near-exhausted breath. 'My home is in Swan Village.'

'Swan Village!' Surprise registered loud in his voice, and the man dropped to the bench beside her. 'That don't be the place the like of glassmen comes from.'

Pointedly replacing the rag muffler, Philippa knotted it but the man took no notice. Eyes a little closed against a burst of sunlight, he looked closer at the tired face, a handsome face in spite of the weariness drawn across it.

'There be little in Swan Village apart from the Cranley place,' he went on, his keen glance taking in the slim body, the hair soft and pale beneath the coating of dust. 'Is that where you was afore?'

Not wanting to be rude but at the same time not wishing for company she gave a brief nod.

'So you was workin' over at Cranley's 'ouse, doin' what, I wonder . . .'

Her eyes closed in the hope of warding the man off, but Philippa jerked them open again as the man shuffled closer on the bench.

'. . . or was it what you didn't do had Cranley pack you off to the glass?' Oily smooth, a smile spread across the dirt-ingrained face. 'Do that be it, was it Cranley wanted to play games but you wasn't interested, be that the reason you bin stuck in the cone?'

'Why don't you mind your own business?'

Arms folded across her thin chest, Ginny Morton stared at the man sat next to Philippa.

'An' if you can't, why not put your questions to old Cranley? I be sure 'e would answer 'em all, every one wi' a kick of 'is boot against your arse!'

'Why you cheeky young bugger!' The man shot to his feet, dirty hands already reaching for the girl. 'I'll put my boot to your arse and kick the bloody old buck outta ya!'

'No, you will not.' Her aches and pains forgotten, Philippa's moves were quicker. She caught the man's collar, hauling him backwards so he stumbled back onto the bench.

'Leave the old sod go!' Ginny's head tossed in defiance . 'I ain't frightened of 'im, 'e be nuthin' but a nosy old git; it needs somebody to tell 'im.'

Her eyes accustomed now to the clear light of afternoon, Philippa caught sight of the stooped shoulders of a thin figure coughing its way across the yard. Samuel Platt would not take kindly to the girl wasting her time chatting, regardless of its cause.

'Then I will tell him, you go back to your work.'

'Not afore I kicks the bloody cheek out of 'er!'

Breaking free from Philippa's hold the man lunged at Ginny who skipped easily out of reach of the blow.

'Any kickin' to be done on these grounds and I'll 'ave the doin' of it!'

'Then ya can start wi' the wench.'

Long years of coming and going from the huge bottle-shaped building leaving him immune to the sudden changes in light, the chargehand's faded eyes never blinked as he came to the bench.

'I'll thank you not to tell me what I needs to do or who to be doin' it to, Thad Grinley. I suggest you sees to the loadin' of your wagon then bring the cash for them bottles to the office. I'll be there to see to the payin' of it.'

'Do that be it?' Thad Grinley's dirt-lined features seemed to swell with rage. 'Do that be all you going to do? That wench insulted me.'

'She was acting on my behalf,' Philippa interjected as Ginny shot a frightened glance at Samuel Platt.

''Er was shootin' 'er mouth off, that's what 'er were doin'.' Grinley straightened his dust-caked jacket. ''Er just strolls over and starts throwin' words where they wasn't necessary, an' summat better be done or I teks my custom elsewhere!'

'Ain't nowhere else meks bottles.' Her tongue quicker than her wits Ginny clamped a hand to her mouth.

'Y'see, Platt. Even now 'er can't keep 'er tongue atwixt 'er lips. I say ya needs put your foot under that one!'

Yellowed eyes glinting with anger, the chargehand shifted his glance from the girl whose face told him she knew she had made one mistake too many. Looking at Grinley he spoke sharply.

'An' I say again, you look to your job an' leave me look to mine. If you wants them bottles then take 'em now or leave wi'out 'em.'

The ultimatum delivered he waited until Grinley was halfway to the packing shed, then turned to Philippa.

'I don't want to know what 'appened but this I say for your own benefit: give Grinley a wide berth. He don't be the most savoury of characters and certainly 'e ain't a man whose company I would advise. Now get you off to your meal and rest for you'll be on again at six o'clock. And you –' his glance switched to the girl already on her way back to the shed '– I've warned you of usin' your tongue where it don't be called for. Get your tin, you be finished!'

Stood beside a low-backed cart drawn up to the doorway of the packing shed, Thad Grinley gave a satisfied smile. Platt knew all right. He knew that should the wench get away scot-free then Archer Cranley would hear of it, hear it along with the cancellation of the monthly order of five hundred assorted bottles . . . and that would be the skids under Platt's feet.

'Mr Platt, please . . . I d'ain't mean no 'arm!'

Grinley's smile widened at the cry. Serve the cocky little

bugger right, the workhouse would prove a good place for her, they would stand no cheek in that place.

'I don't want to 'ear, Ginny!' Samuel Platt coughed, the rattle of it loud in his chest. 'Get your money and go, I've spent enough time listenin' to you.'

'Then perhaps you had best listen to me.'

Facing the cart, Thad Grinley pricked his ears. There was a quiet authority in that voice, an authority that might make listening a profitable venture.

'Ginny will not collect her tin . . .'

Grinley's smile gave way to a frown. Who the hell was the man to talk to Platt as he was? Had his guess been right after all, was the pretty boy old man Cranley's plaything, put here to teach him which side of his bread was buttered? His interest heightened, he strained to every word.

'. . . she will not lose her employment; she was simply trying to help me.'

'But, Mister Philip, Grinley is a valuable customer, should the gaffer find out—'

*Mister* Philip. Well, well! Grinley's smile returned. The handsome lad must be well in favour with Cranley.

'He will find out . . . from me.' Philippa's voice floated clear across the yard. 'As he will find out you were the one given your tin should my words go unheeded. You do understand me, Mr Platt?'

Oh he'll understand all right, and so do I. Grinley watched the last heavy crate loaded onto the cart. There was only one answer to how come that lad could dish orders out to Platt, that answer being he was Archer Cranley's personal arse warmer, his own handsome little bedfellow.

Making pretence of adjusting the harness draped over the heavy carthorse, he listened as avidly as before, his brain already calculating the profit to be gained from what had already been heard.

'But I've 'ad cause to warn the wench a few times . . .' Samuel Platt stuttered between coughs.

'And this will be the last, is that not so, Ginny?'

'Ar.' Ginny took a couple of nervous steps backwards. 'Ar, it is, Mister Philip. I . . . I won't poke me nose no more . . . honest I won't.'

'Ginny,' Philippa watched the tension pulling at the pale features. 'Mr Platt has responsibility for the behaviour of the workers at Briant Glass and that includes you. From now on you will keep your promise to hold your tongue; if you break your word once more then his decisions will not be overridden.'

'I understands, Mr Philip.' Bobbing a curtsey, Ginny fled back to the shed paying no heed to the smiling Grinley.

'I apologise for my action, Mr Platt.'

As the flash of patched skirts disappeared into the packing shed, Philippa turned to the chargehand.

'I know I should not have countermanded your orders,' she said quietly, 'but I could not see Ginny dismissed for trying to help me. I will tell Mr Cranley what has taken place and you are not to worry, there will be no comeback on you.'

'That be good of you, Mr Philip.' The old man lifted his dust-encrusted cap, scratching a finger to his scalp. 'But this I 'ave to say. Next to Archer Cranley I be teken to be gaffer 'ere an' it might prove best for it to remain to be seen that way. I don't mean no disrespect, lad, but one gaffer be all a place can tek an' still work 'armonious, like; let some folk find out who you truly be an' well . . .' he lifted his thin shoulders expressively, '. . . they'll play both ends against the middle an' not give a bugger who gets throttled by the knot.'

Watching the stooped shoulders stoop even further as the man coughed his way to where Thad Grinley still fiddled with his horse's harness, Philippa dropped to the wooden seat.

Play both ends against the middle. That was what Samuel Platt had said. She stared into the sunlight streaming onto the cobbled ground, wishing its glow would swallow the heart-crushing shadows that followed the thought. That was what Archer Cranley did with such cruelty and ease. He played child against mother, not caring for either, his only thought being for himself and what he could gain.

And there was nothing could be done!

Rising from the seat she headed towards the gate.

There was nothing could be done!


His sister had not been on the landing.

Archer Cranley took the chair drawn close to Hannah's.

Edna had not been *seen* out there on the landing but that was no certainty she had not been hiding, ready to come and listen at Hannah's door. He glanced towards it, ears strained for any sound. Edna Cranley was not a woman to let anything past her sharp nose.

'There was something you had to tell me?'

Hannah held a delicate lace-edged handkerchief to her mouth. Watching the trickle of blood stain crimson patches into it Archer felt no remorse. The pale-faced, wasted woman he turned his attention to meant nothing; she had never meant anything to him other than a means to her father's money.

'Yes, there is something else. Simeon Beasley agreed that the safest place for Philip is an asylum for the insane. He proposes I have him committed at once before he harms you and Edna.'

'That is not true!' Hannah gasped. 'Simeon would not make such a horrible proposal . . . you are lying!'

'Oh no?' Archer's thin mouth curved cruelly. 'Simeon Beasley will do anything for a price; but should you still not believe then perhaps you had better see the letter signed by him.'

Handing her a sheet of paper from his pocket he sat in silence, watching hands and lips tremble as she read the contents.

'You see, my dear –' he snatched the letter, placing it back in the pocket of his coat '– Philip is as good as locked away right now.'

Her faded eyes brightened by the wash of tears, Hannah shook her head.

'That . . . that letter means nothing. You have to have the doctor's agreement.'

'Oh! Oh, I'm sorry, my dear.' He drew an unsealed envelope from the same pocket. Taking out the sheet of notepaper he unfolded it, holding it out for her to read. 'How remiss of me, forgetting to show you this!'

Despair flooding through her, Hannah read the letter condemning her child to a life behind locked doors, then the signature: P. D. Barton. Physician.

'What do you want, Archer?' she whispered. 'What more do you want?'

'Only what should have been mine twenty years ago.' He replaced the envelope in his pocket. 'But in order for Philip to sign over the business it must first be inherited, and that will not happen unless he is married.'

For a moment real happiness glistened behind the veil of tears clouding Hannah's eyes.

'Then you still lose, and I'm glad.' Hannah paused, hating having to use the only name allowed her. 'I would rather Philip never had a penny of my father's money than it be signed to you; for, like you say, Philip is not married therefore the lot goes to charity.'

'You cannot really think I would allow that to happen.' Caught by the lamp set beside the bed Archer's close-set eyes gleamed with a feral brightness. 'Arrangements are already in hand. Philip is to be married.'

'Married!' The handkerchief dropped from Hannah's hand. Stunned, she stared at the man smiling behind vicious eyes. 'To . . . to whom . . . when . . . why, why was I not told?'

'To whom?' He flicked a hand dismissively. 'That does not really matter. But I thought Joseph Lacy's daughter would serve the purpose as good as any other. As for when? Within the month. Why were you not told? Because it does not concern you!'

'Joseph Lacy's daughter!' Her voice cracking with desperation, Hannah reached for her husband's hand. 'You can't mean it, Archer, you can't . . . please, I beg you.'

Shaking off her hand he rose, his glance cold and impervious.

'Oh, but I do mean it, Hannah. Philip will wed the Lacy girl, and if you want to keep your precious child free of that institution you will do and say exactly what I tell you, the first thing being the making of a new Will.'

Fetching writing materials from a small bureau set to one side of the room he came to stand over her.

'We must take the precaution of seeing that your father's wishes are carried out; after all, should Philip not inherit then there would need to be a named charity.'

'I have named a charity.'

'So you have.' Archer set paper and pen before her on a small mahogany table. 'But it is not the charity I prefer.'

'But . . .' Hannah looked up quickly. '. . . the choice was to be mine.'

'And now it is mine.' Picking up the pen he placed it between her fingers, squeezing hard. 'Write, Hannah, write as I tell you or I promise you will regret your refusal.'

As the pen scratched on paper, Archer glanced about the shadowed room comparing it in his imagination to the splendid rooms he would have when the whole of Nathan Briant's legacy was his.

'The name?' He had smiled as Hannah asked the question. 'The charity will be set up under the title of Cranley House, Home for Destitute Women.'

Watching the words being written he drew a deep, satisfied breath. It was an unnecessary safeguard but it would allay any suspicions Simeon Beasley might otherwise have.

'Also,' he went on as the scratching of the pen ceased, 'you will revoke the bequest you made to Philip, instead the residue of the sum your father gave you, together with your mother's jewellery, will come to me.'

As the finished document was snatched from her hand, Hannah made a last desperate attempt.

'That paper will not be held to be legal, it has not been witnessed.'

'A triviality!' Archer laughed. 'Don't let it worry you, a gold sovereign signs anything.'

'Was it money got that letter of incarceration signed?'

'Of course.' Blowing on the paper, ensuring the ink was dry, he folded it then slipped it alongside the envelope in his pocket.

'Then you still lose, Archer.' Hannah's smile was weary. 'With Philip locked away the charity will take everything.'

'I always said you were stupid, my dear . . . so very stupid. Philip will be locked away, that is true, but he will be alive . . . *alive*, Hannah; "a male child, born of her body" your father said, he did not say that male had to be of sound mind. So, you see, either way I cannot lose.'

Clearing away any evidence of writing he crossed to the bed, taking up a small glass from the night table beside it. Holding it so the light of the lamp outlined the contents he noted the amount of liquid contained in it.

Edna had already measured the generous night dose. Glancing at the level again he slipped the cork from the bottle his sister had not put away. The cold smile returned to touch thin spiteful lips. Picking up the bottle he added several drops of the colourless liquid to the glass.

Hannah must not be left in any condition to talk of what had just taken place in this room, she must be too far under the influence of laudanum to do anything but sleep.

'Now, my dear, take your medicine.' He held the glass to Hannah.

'No!' She turned her head away. 'I don't want it, I told Edna I don't need it.'

Maybe she did not. Archer's lips turned inward but he needed the surety the drug would bring, the surety that he would not be disturbed again tonight. He glanced at the figured mantel clock, its dial just discernible in the dancing firelight. Quarter to eight.

He had spent too much time here, now he had other matters to take care of.

Stepping to Hannah's side he twisted the fingers of one hand in her hair, snatching her head hard back on her neck and throwing the contents of the glass into her mouth as she gasped from pain; then, jerking her to her feet, still grasping her hair, marched her to the bed and flung her face-down on to it.

'You always were too stupid to learn.' He looked dispassionately at the sobbing figure. 'But that proved to be an asset . . . to me.'

Turning away his eye caught the medicine bottle, the heavy, ridged glass of it glinting greenly beneath the lamp. Snatching it up he smiled coldly at Hannah.

'We must not put danger in your way, must we, my dear. You must not be tempted to end it all . . . at least not until you have seen your darling Philip safely married!'

And a marriage would take place; what did it matter that bride and groom were of the same gender? He smiled to himself as he left the room. A marriage followed almost immediately by a tragic 'heart attack', the means of which were hidden in his room; and with his beloved son dying in this house, Archer Cranley's secret would be kept!

# Chapter Eight

He had told Hannah that Philip was to marry Joseph Lacy's daughter and it would be as he said; Lacy did not know of it yet, but it would be as he said. For now, though, there was a more pressing engagement to be kept.

Going to his own room Archer glanced testily at the ormolu clock above the fireplace. Damn Hannah and her irritating ways, it was already near enough eight, which meant he must hurry. Deciding against changing the dark jacket and trousers he had worn during the day he crossed to the cupboard he kept locked. Reaching a hand to the ornamental carved ledge that ran around the top of it, his fingers found a small key.

How often had Edna used this key? He smiled acidly. The poor fool. He knew she regularly inspected the locked cupboard, but that was what she was meant to do; it kept her sharp nose from being poked in other places.

Unlocking the doors he drew them open, the smile remaining on his thin mouth as he looked at the contents so neatly in place, not one of them relaying the fact his sister's fingers had been at work; but all she would find here were those things he wanted her to find, letters whose contents appeared important but were not. Bank correspondence that said nothing of the private accounts he held in several, the brandy flask that led her to believe that he drank heavily in the privacy of his room. Edna would gloat over all of these, congratulating her cleverness whenever she found something new, but she would never find the true secret of this room.

Taking out the flask he placed it on the night table, first spreading his handkerchief beneath it; then, turning to the bed, he removed the pillows. Reaching deep below the feather-filled mattress he ran his fingertips lightly over the carving, counting up three leaves of the beautiful design from the lowest edge of the headboard.

No one knew the secret of this bed, not even Hannah. He had commissioned it specially after . . .

Archer's lips drew back in a silent snarl.

Nathan Briant had laughed as he made that wedding gift, laughed as it was opened before the assembled guests.

Pressing a finger to the woodwork, he straightened.

Nathan Briant had made a fool of his new son-in-law but the real fool had been himself. This bed had been made while he and Hannah had been on honeymoon, made to a very specific design.

Carrying a chair from the fireside, he stood it close beside the bed. Though five feet ten, he could not reach the heavy wooden canopy. Climbing onto the chair, he reached over it. No, Edna would never find this. There had been no sound in the room, no gentle swish that would tell of a panel sliding open, no give-away sign that the roof canopy was hollow at one end.

Fingers closing over the soft cloth, the silent snarl became a hiss. Briant had not yet paid enough for his insult.

Beside the cloth his fingers touched a small box. Taking both from their hiding place, he set them beside the brandy flask.

'Such a joke, Nathan,' he murmured, staring at the cloth, 'and not yet paid in full, but it will be, just as that other joker has to pay.'

Taking up the small box he gazed for a few seconds at the intricate design worked in vibrant glowing colours. Bilston enamels were very beautiful and some, like snakes, were colourful but deadly.

Twisting off the lid he smiled. Colourful but very, very deadly!

The bed had not been all he had acquired in those first months of marriage. He glanced again at the cloth. 'Your little joke was a blessing in disguise, Nathan,' he smiled, 'a blessing of the devil.'

Setting the box beside the brandy flask, taking care it too stood well onto the handkerchief, he tore a corner from the flap of an envelope he had in a pocket of his coat.

Sally Povey had committed suicide . . .

Dipping the scrap of paper into the box and scooping a little of the white powder it held, he trickled it slowly into the flask.

. . . what would be the verdict on his blackmailer?

Slipping the tightly corked flask into his coat pocket he touched a hand to the folded cloth.

'A blessing in disguise, Nathan.' He laughed softly. 'I really should have thanked you. Had it not been for your wedding gift I might never have bought that Ricin. From seeds of the castor oil plant, that chemist told me. Bride's Row. How very apt!'

Archer saw again the dirty little houses of Bilston huddled between collieries and ironworks. It was there he had bought his own gift, a present for his bride, but it had not been given. Not yet.

'Be very careful,' the old man had warned, ' 'tis to be used only as fertiliser, same as it be on the allotments along of Proud's Lane. I always tells the men as works 'em, this stuff be lethal, two millionths of a man's body weight will kill, that makes it twice as poisonous as cobra venom; so just you take care how you uses it, sir.'

Oh, I'll be careful. Unfolding the cloth Archer slipped the contents beside the flask in his pocket. He would be very careful.

With everything cleared away, the panel of the bed closed, the chair replaced at the fireside, he threw handkerchief and scrap of paper into the fire and watched until the last vestige burned to ash. There would be nothing for Edna to find . . .

except the missing flask! Relocking the cupboard he dropped the key into the pocket of his waistcoat.


Years of listening had Edna's ears keen. Pressed now to the door of her bedroom she caught the click that said Archer had left Hannah. No doubt the woman had swallowed the laudanum . . . after a little persuasion. But why had he not gone downstairs?

She had listened for the familiar creak of the stair but it had not come. Why had he not returned to the study? She glanced at the cheap enamel clock. Not yet eight o'clock. The evenings he was home were always spent in the study, so why not this evening?

Her curiosity deepening, she listened hard, every fibre probing the silence. Slanting another glance at the clock she saw the pointer had moved. Eight fifteen. Surely Archer had not retired for the night.

It was then the muted creak of the stair answered her thoughts. Going quickly out into the corridor she stood on the top step, watching the figure reach for his cane.

Where was he going . . . and why?

'Will you not be staying in tonight?'

Archer looked towards the stairs, dislike raising the hackles on his neck. She would be in his room the moment he was gone, but she would find nothing she hadn't seen before. One hand brushing against the pocket that held the flask, he shook his head.

'No. I should have mentioned earlier, I am meeting Simeon Beasley, we will have a meal at Hemming's Dining Rooms.'

And what else? Edna watched the front door close behind her brother. Beasley had never struck her as a man who was satisfied with only a meal to go to bed with . . . did Archer have the same appetite?

Returning to her own room she stared at the bed, feeling the tremor at the base of her stomach, a tremor all these empty years had not stilled.

They should not have been years spent alone, and would not have been but for Hannah Briant. She had been the one who had taken Richard, she who had caused those long aching nights spent in an empty bed. Richard . . . Edna's fingers twisted together . . . he had not stopped loving her, he had not . . . he had not! He would have married her, they would have made a home together far from West Bromwich, far from Hannah Briant.

A dry sob breaking through the barrier of set lips, Edna crossed to the bed, one hand stroking the pillow.

He would have slept beside her every night, taken her in his arms, covered her with his body, the warmth of his flesh on hers. But instead Richard Stanton lay in a suicide's grave.

Staring at the smooth white pillow Edna saw again the face of the man promised her in marriage. The strong handsome features cold and unmoving in death. She had made a promise as the bare wooden coffin had been closed over him. Made a promise as it had been lowered down a ladder placed against an upstairs window then passed over the garden wall. Made a promise as it was lowered into an unmarked grave without the benediction of church, beyond the blessing of sanctified ground.

Fingers moving across the pillow touched the phantom face.

I promised I would make her pay, take the light from her life as she took mine from me. A life for a life, my dearest, a life for a life!

The picture cleared from her mind but took none of the emptiness from her soul. She had taken a lifetime of vengeance on Hannah Briant, but that lifetime was not yet over . . . and Edna Cranley's vengeance was not yet done.


Almost across the empty heathland that separated Rowlay House from the small back-to-back buildings that edged the lower end of Phoenix Street, Archer Cranley halted. He had met no one, seen no one, but that would not be so once he got closer to that meeting place, for men came and went endlessly from the many beer houses set around the wharves and basins of the canal, as well as the workers of the collieries and ironworks.

With his hand touching the pocket that held the articles brought from his bedroom, the sneering laugh of Nathan Briant echoed in his memory.

'*That be the only wedding present you be worthy of . . .*'

Archer's fingers jerked convulsively.

'*. . . an' it be the only bugger you'll get from Nathan Briant.*'

Pulling the rag muffler from his pocket he tied it about his throat, following it with the flat cap which he pulled low over his forehead.

The badge of the lesser man! Nathan Briant had made it plain that a common workman he was and a common workman he would remain.

'*That be all you be worth . . . and it be all you'll get.*'

'Not all, Nathan.' Archer's whispered words met the mocking laugh. 'Not all by any means.'

The silver knob of the cane hidden in the palm of one hand, he walked on. Nathan Briant's wedding gift was truly a blessing in disguise, for dressed as he was who in the shadows would distinguish him from any other worker changing shift?

'Lookin' for a good time?'

Hardly had he reached Phoenix Street than a woman stepped from a doorway. Pulling aside the shawl that draped her shoulders she pushed almost naked breasts suggestively upwards.

'Maisie Carter knows 'ow to provide it.'

'Can't say as 'ow I wouldn't sooner be 'avin' them in me 'ands than a shovel,' Archer laughed, careful to answer in the rough dialect peculiar to the Black Country, 'but I signs five minutes from now or gets me tin.'

'Won't tek ya that long to gerrit up, not wi' Maisie to show ya 'ow.' The woman laughed coarsely. 'Ya won't need no five minutes.'

'To pay a tanner for anythin' less be money chucked away an' a collier's pay don't stretch to that. But keep these warm 'til Saturday night an' ya can earn a couple o' tanners.'

Hiding his repugnance, Archer touched a hand to the bloated mounds spilling from the low-cut blouse, his own laugh mingling with that coming loudly from the over-painted mouth.

'Mek sure ya comes to Maisie if ya wants to come in a big way . . .' The prostitute hooted again, calling after his departing figure, '— For a shilling ya'll want a lot an' as you sees, Maisie Carter 'as a lot.'

There could easily be more women like that one between him and Ryder's Bridge. Archer increased his pace. Damn Hannah! Had it not been for her tantrum he could have gone by way of Great Bridge Street, taking Henry Street right down to Ryder's Bridge. But by the time he had left the house it was already too late for that.

But perhaps this was, after all, the better way. In flat cap and muffler he blended faceless among the men working the narrow boats moored at the wharves.

Ahead of him tall brick-built warehouses rose black against the silvered ribbon of the canal, and from the other side of the lock the sound of voices carried from the Eight Locks public house. He had not thought of that beer house when demanding that the place of meeting be Ryder's Bridge . . . but then the whole thing would be over in minutes. Reassurance adding zest to his step he hurried the last few yards, glancing both ways before walking down the slight incline to the towpath.

Beneath the bridge, he had told that man. Archer stared into the black void spanning the water. That had been a mistake, there could well be several others waiting in the shelter of that darkness.

'It be all right, Cranley . . . yes, I knows it be you despite the get-up!'

Archer started at the sound.

'There don't be nobody along o' me; I don't intend to share that money, not with nobody.'

Stepping from the lee of the bridge just as the moon sailed from a bank of cloud and added an anaemic sheen to his narrow, jaundiced face, the man from the park smiled.

'Could be we stand less chance of bein' seen if we does our business under here.'

'Agreed.' Archer's fingers closed more tightly about the cane. 'But I prefer the transaction be carried out out here.'

'Meks no odds to me.' The narrow shoulders lifted in a shrug. ''Twas you specified under the bridge.'

'And now I am saying we do it here on the towpath.'

The same smile curving his mouth, the man came forward, moonlight reflecting close-set eyes that gleamed like yellow flame.

'You frightened of being set on? I'd be a fool to let that 'appen, now wouldn't I? We wants to remain friends, Cranley, for who knows? We might meet again . . . in the future.'

It was there, as he knew it would be, the threat that this demand would not be the last.

'Five hundred pounds, wasn't it?'

Archer watched the smile widen on the pallid face. There would be no future meetings with this man, for him these moments were all of his future.

'That was the sum agreed. You 'ave brought it, I 'ope.' Watching Archer's face as he made no answer, the man's smile vanished. 'It would be a mistake to think you can fob me off, Cranley, a very grave mistake for as I said in the park the constabulary would be interested . . .'

'I have the money.' Taking an envelope from an inner pocket of his jacket Archer held it out.

'Sealed!' The man took it, tapping it against his fingers. 'I trust it 'olds what you says it 'olds; wouldn't be very smart if it didn't, not with what I knows.'

It was a gamble, a risk the man would not open that envelope and look at the contents here and now, but risk-taking was not new to Archer Cranley.

Keeping his voice free of the anger bubbling inside him, he gave a casual lift of the hand.

'An agreement is an agreement, but you have only to count it.'

Taking a corner of the envelope between his fingers, the man tore it across. With the blood pounding in his head, Archer kept a steady glance on those brilliant eyes, but his fingers tightened still further about the cane. That envelope held nothing but neatly cut pieces of newspaper.

'No.' His smile returning, the other man slipped the envelope into his pocket. 'I'll save that pleasure 'til I gets 'ome. But as you says, Mr Cranley, an agreement be an agreement and gents should seal a bargain with a drink. What say we seal this'n over at the Eight Locks?'

That was the very last thing Archer wanted. Disguise or not he could not afford to be seen in that beer house, to gamble against the chance some man might recognise him. Facing up to risks was one thing, running out to meet them was another.

'Thank you, but I have an appointment.' He half turned and then, as if on second thought, he turned back. 'But I agree gentlemen should seal an agreement pleasantly over a drink. Perhaps we could still do that.'

Reaching into his pocket he withdrew the brandy flask. Removing the cork he smiled, offering the drink with a hand that showed no flicker of a tremble.

The yellow eyes glinted as the man took the flask.

Drink it! Archer willed silently. Drink it, you bastard . . . drink it!

Lifting the flask, the man hesitated. Stretched to the full, Archer's nerves sang.

With the flask beneath his nostrils, his yellowed face high-lighted by the pale glow of the moon, the other man breathed the bouquet of brandy.

Fingers gripping the cane, Archer continued to smile. Only feet away the man lowered the flask, he wasn't going to drink! Archer's nerves throbbed.

'Here's to business.' A laugh in his throat, the man touched the neck of the flask to his lips then tipped it high into his mouth.

Archer bent over the still form. He had watched it swallow several mouthfuls of the poisoned brandy. Twice as deadly as cobra venom, that old chemist had said of it. He knew nothing of the actions of that venom but one thing was certain, it could take effect no more quickly than that Ricin. The man had writhed in agony only seconds, pain taking his breath so he could not cry out. Then it had been over. Two blows of the silver knob of the cane and all sound had ceased.

Taking the envelope from the jacket pocket Archer straightened. Towpath and bridge were deserted. Grabbing the limp shoulders, he hauled the figure the few feet to the edge of the lock.

Letting it lie a moment he looked down at it. Then, placing one foot on it, laughed softly.

'Here's to business!'

The laugh quiet in his throat, he kicked the still body over the edge of the lock.

'Here's to business!' he repeated as the body hit the water far below.

# Chapter Nine

'*He will work the same hours as any other man.*'

Limbs aching intolerably Philippa walked across the yard towards the packing shed. Six hours, had it truly been that long? It seemed less than six minutes since she had left the glassworks. She'd been here nearly a week and was yet to get used to the working conditions.

Edna Cranley had met her in the hall, standing with hands crossed over her skirts, her long narrow features seeming to grow even longer as her mouth firmed to a thin line.

'Your mother is sleeping, I think it best she be left alone, you can see her another time.'

There had been no softness in the words, no assurance that all was well. Instead it had been sharp, almost a challenge that her decision could be questioned.

But tiredness had overcome any such challenge. Weariness had made it too difficult to do anything but accept.

'*Work the same hours as any other man.*'

The thought returned, mixing with the ringing of boots on the close-laid setts.

But would it be as Archer Cranley had dictated? Would Philip Cranley manage to keep going as others at Briant Glass kept going, day after endless day without respite other than a few hours that seemed to be gone before the eyes were closed?

But they did do it; boys as well as men laboured in that cone
. . . and what labour it was. Fetching and carrying at a run,
balancing great blobs of molten glass on the end of a long rod,
with never a moment between; and the youngest of them,
children not yet put into the cone, they were worked as hard,
set to filling wheelbarrow after wheelbarrow with silica and lime.

'I been waitin' of you comin'.'

The thoughts driven abruptly away, Philippa looked at the
figure that stepped from the shadowed lee of the packing shed.
Flat cap pulled low on the forehead, jacket collar turned up over
a rag muffler that did not quite conceal the lack of a shirt, the
man spoke quickly, his words running into each other.

'I be Ike Turner and me and mine wants to say thank you for
what you done for we when you got Sam Platt to tek we back on
at the glass. We knows it was you for young Ginny told it so to
the missis an' we won't forget but will say God bless you for
evermore.'

Watching the figure scurry away Philippa wondered at the
gratitude of the man. He had given thanks for being returned to
an employment that was nothing short of a punishment. But
what was the alternative? Ike Turner and Philip Cranley . . .
neither had a choice.

'Shift be changin' in five minutes, lad.'

Samuel Platt stood in the entrance of the great cone-shaped
building, his mode of dress the same as that of Ike Turner, rag
muffler tucked into collarless shirt, a flat cap pulled low over his
brow.

'You don't be goin' into the packing.'

Not going into the packing shed? Philippa frowned. Had
Archer Cranley issued fresh orders?

'There be no more to be learned in the sheds.' Samuel Platt's
cough rattled like loose stones.

'You'll be goin' into the cone.'

Philippa's gaze ran over the huge building rising like a black
mountain whose summit was lost in night's dark, swallowing

embrace. It looked disconcerting enough from the outside but that first day's brief tour had shown the inside had all the attributes of a torture chamber.

'Come along o' me.' Platt coughed the words between short wheezing breaths. 'I be puttin' you along o' Josh Fairley's chair, follow me an' I'll see you settled in.'

No further in than the threshold, Philippa felt the searing breath-snatching heat of the ring of furnaces. It was worse than memory said, the force of it seeming to melt skin from flesh, to scorch the lungs.

'It be bad first off . . .'

Samuel Platt lifted his voice to carry over the noise of air being sucked into the gigantic chimney.

'. . . but a man gets used to it.'

Supposing a man did not die of suffocation! Trying not to breathe but forced to, Philippa gagged on the hot fume-filled air.

Leading the way around the cone, Platt coughed again.

'Oh, by the way, young Ginny asked would I thank you for the lendin' o' that book. The wench returned it spick and span and as clean as you brought it, but I made sure just to be on the safe side. It be in the office waitin' of you finishin'.'

Giving an answering nod to the greeting of men as each alcove was passed, she remembered the reverence with which the young girl had received the book she had brought. First Ginny had gazed at it held out to her, then running to the pump in the yard had held both hands under the freezing cold water until her fingers had turned blue. Next she had taken a piece of white cloth from the pocket of her patched skirt. Then and only then had she touched the book, laying it carefully in the cloth, newly washed against the possibility it might hold the promised treasure, and at the end of her shift had carried it home, held wonderingly to her thin chest. Philippa smiled at the picture that memory evoked. The crown jewels of England could not have been more hallowed or held in greater esteem.

'I thought I made it clear to Ginny —' she paused, allowing a man balancing glasses on a plank of wood to pass between them '– the book was a gift to her. Would you tell her so again, please.'

Glancing critically at the lump of molten glass held on the end of a pole as it was carried past, Samuel Platt resumed his steady walk.

'You be sure o' that, lad?' he asked. 'A book such as that must be worth a copper or two, p'raps you should think a mite longer afore you decides to go givin' it away.'

'I wish Ginny to have it . . . please tell her that for me.'

Samuel Platt gave a brief smile that hid what was in his heart. Archer Cranley and Philip Cranley, the father and the son; alike in name, but worlds apart in nature. He had worked with the lad nobbut a day but that were long enough to know he was as different to his father as chalk was to cheese.

'The little wench'll treasure it . . .' he coughed again, 'that much I can tell you. That book be just about the first thing in 'er life 'er ever had give to 'er alone. It be a kindness not forgot, not 'til 'er be old and laid away in 'er box.'

'Which will be many years from now, I hope.'

'You can 'ope, lad.' Samuel Platt wheezed, drawing hot air into his throat in noisy gulps. 'We can all 'ope though it be my reckonin' it'll do no good for them as works the glass, for the silica and the oxides rot the lungs and poverty rots the soul.'

He paused to look intently at Philippa. 'It be no business o' mine and I knows it, but I will speak. You be a fine lad, made of a different metal to him that fathered you. You 'ave a heart and a conscience where Archer Cranley 'as none, you 'ave a feelin' for the folk that works alongside of you and we all waits for the day your grandfather's word be fulfilled and the Glass be given over to you. But for your own sake I tell you: get out of it now, the cone be no place for you.'

Stepping aside for a Bit Gatherer to run past balancing his pole with its lump of glowing molten glass, Philippa smiled briefly.

'You don't understand. I have to stay for the sake of . . . you don't understand.'

His keen stare catching the look of sadness that flitted over the pale drawn face, Samuel Platt answered quietly, 'I understand, lad, I understand more than you might think. So stay in the glass 'til it comes into your 'ands. But tek care, that day be a ways off yet and I be thinkin' there be them as might not wish for you to see it.'

Waiting for no reply the chargehand walked on, leading the way into an alcove where a man stood tying a leather apron about his middle to protect moleskin trousers, the top half of his body adorned only by a rag tied about his throat.

'This be Josh Fairley, you be with 'im. This be a fast chair but Josh be a fair man; do your job is all 'e asks, but shirk it and you'll feel his boot.'

A nod of the head his only reply, the tall figure continued to prepare for work. At a loss what to do, Philippa stared. With the leather apron secured, the man introduced as Josh Fairley glanced at her.

'You get eight shilling a week starting wage and any bottle you drop is paid for out of that. We work fast and you keep up or go to another chair. Is that satisfactory to you?'

'Ready when you be, Josh.'

A second man dressed much the same as the first took up a long metal rod.

Nodding assent, Josh continued to look at Philippa. 'Have you been told what it is you are to do?'

'No.' She slid a glance to the crude wooden chair and the assortment of tools laid on a bench that ran alongside.

'Well, you won't be sitting in that, not for a while yet at least.' Josh Fairley smiled, showing strong white teeth. 'You will be what we call the "Taker In". You will carry whatever is made to the lehr.'

'To the what?'

Glancing at the man returning with the molten glass, Josh gave a shake of his head.

'Shove it back in the furnace, Zeke.' Then to Philippa he said, 'It will be quicker to show you than try to explain. The finished article is cracked off the blowing iron then carried to this end of the lehr.' Walking quickly to what looked like a long open-ended tunnel, he pointed. 'The glass then passes very slowly through to the other end, by which time it is sufficiently cooled.'

'But the lehr, as you call it, is heated.'

'Yes, but not anywhere near furnace temperature. It has to be heated to prevent the glass cooling too quickly, if it did it would become strained and in most cases it would crack. The lehr is hot enough to prevent that, yet not hot enough to keep the glass viscous.'

Seeing Philippa's puzzled frown he smiled again. 'Don't try to take everything in at once, it will come gradually. All you need to do is set the glass in this end and the "Shrower" will take it out at the other and inspect it for any faults.'

'And if it proves faulty do I bring it back to you?'

'No.' Josh Fairley was already striding back to the alcove. 'It is broken up for cullet and used for re-melting. But that is the end of the lesson for today, we have a living to earn.'

# Chapter Ten

Every muscle screaming its own protest of pain, Philippa wiped a handkerchief already black with dust over sweat-soaked skin. It was the end of a six-hour shift. At last the constant fetching and carrying to and from that lehr could stop.

It had been almost a month from first being set to work in the glass, three weeks since transfer from packing shed to cone where every waking moment was spent almost at a run, of answering shouts that seemed to rain down from every quarter, of apologising for fingers that seemed to be forever thumbs; and still the process of making glass was relatively unlearned.

Returning the handkerchief to the pocket of moleskin trousers purchased for this work and already pockmarked by a thousand tiny burns, she walked from the cone into the works' yard. Alongside the huge building the packing shed stood out black against the dark of midnight. At least the younger children did not work through the night.

The night air was cold, sharp as needles against face and hands fresh from the heat of furnaces, painful in lungs that for hours on end breathed the air of hell. But cold as it was she breathed deeply, tasting the taint of smoke lingering from foundries that were the lifeblood of Greets Green.

But that blood was poisoned by avarice, drained by the greed of men such as Archer Cranley, men who paid a pittance for a week of sweated labour; men who had no thought for those who toiled in their foundries, throwing them aside the moment they weakened, giving them their tins in order to employ eight- and nine-year-old children at a fraction of a man's wage.

Boys and girls doing a man's work! She sank onto the bench set alongside the packing shop, eyes closing wearily. Children who would work out their lives at the furnace and at the end would have nothing but a bent back and a bitter heart to show for it.

'You should get yourself along home, lad.'

Her eyelids reluctant to move, Philippa took a moment before looking at the man who had come to stand beside the bench.

'You need to take proper rest, dozing on that bench will do you no good; it's a bed you need to sleep in.'

'Yes.' She moved stiffly. 'I know you are right, of course, but by the time I get home and thoroughly washed the greater part of my shift break is gone, add to that the time taken to return here and it is cut in half.'

'It be a fair trawl right enough.' Joshua Fairley nodded, the night breeze lifting his hair playfully. 'But it be as I say, sleeping on that bench will leave you worse than taking no sleep at all. You'll wake with every bone singing its own song and not one having words you'll want to listen to.'

'Every bone is aching already, Mr Fairley.'

Dressed with a million stars the night sky drew a canopy of darkness that held the earth in silence. It never failed to entrance Joshua and he stared at it now. But tonight the beauty of it did not bind his breath, did not take his soul as it so often did; yet still his chest felt bound by unseen chains. It had been that way from the lad being put to his chair. At first he had denied the fact but eventually he had been forced to recognise it. Philip Cranley somehow affected him. He had tried to ignore him but extra careful as he was to treat him no differently to the way he treated other men he worked with, still there was an undefinable something, a sort of current, a live thing that shot through him whenever he met the lad's eyes.

'No other way it would be.' Joshua smoothed a hand over hair that rose again immediately. 'Six hours in the cone be enough to make any lad's bones ache.'

Any lad. Philippa drew in a breath of air, the coolness of it stinging overheated lungs. What Joshua Fairley had not said was especially a lad like you, a lad used to a more gentle way of life, one not used to manual labour.

Outlined against the shadows Joshua Fairley passed his own soiled neck cloth over his face, an indiscreet moon revealing the lighter mark where black dust was wiped away.

Despite the weariness Philippa could not resist a smile. They must both look like zebras. The multi-holed moleskin trousers spotted with lighter-brown scorch marks, neck cloth striped with sweat and dust, faces black with silica, the eyes glinting through a white mask; it would be an amusing costume for a fancy-dress ball . . . except this was the dance of life!

The thought washed away the smile, leaving the same anger she had felt from first coming to the glassworks. Men ought not to have to toil like this, being used like pack animals and many of them housed no better.

'Sit you there awhile.' Joshua let the neck cloth fall back into place, the ends resting on his bare chest. 'Give yourself a minute then get off home to that mother of yours, she'll be wanting to know you are all right.'

There it was again. Philippa stood up. The implication of difference, that Hannah would be waiting up for her while other mothers might not.

'I hope my mother is being sensible enough to be in her bed, Mr Fairley. I see no point in both of us being abroad at midnight.'

'Give me a moment to get my jacket and I'll walk with you.'

Joshua turned back into the cone. The son of the glassmaster was respectful. Unlike his father he treated a man like a man and not like a pile of silica to be walked all over it and paid no heed. Archer Cranley could no more bring himself to address one of his workmen as mister than he could fly in the air. This lad was a gentleman, while his father was . . . He checked the thought, not allowing the words he wanted to use to take form even in his mind.

But why had Archer Cranley set his son to working in the cone, why had he placed him in the works at all?

Joshua shrugged into his jacket, dragging the rough cloth over skin still damp with perspiration.

Anybody with sense could see the lad were not cut out for labouring in the heat of those furnaces, breathing in the dust that rotted the lungs of stronger men than him. Cranley himself had never done a day in the cone, he avoided even walking through it unless the need were dire. So why set his own son to work in it?

Joshua walked back into the night, the question joined by another: why had the lad's mother allowed it? Unlike most other families in Greets Green they were not desperate for the lad's wage. But then there could be no telling a man like Archer Cranley what to do, not with his business and not with his son. Perhaps it was the same in the Cranley household as here. A tight mouth was a man's best way of behaving if he wanted to keep his place at Briant Bottle and Glass, maybe it was the same way in that house.

'Which way do you take?'

Reaching the gate he glanced at the figure barely level with his shoulder.

Philippa pointed to where the canal stretched like a silver arrow.

'You follow the canal!' Joshua could not explain the sudden feeling that gripped him, a feeling of resentment and anxiety, of anger and fear all broiling together, bringing a cold touch to his spine.

'It is the more direct route.'

'And the most dangerous!' The words burst like an explosion

on the silence. 'You . . . a lad shouldn't be alone on the towpath at night. Come up against a man with the ale inside him and . . . well, it could turn into a situation you would rather not face. You'd far better take the way of Charles Street then Great Bridge Road, it is a further way round but it avoids the towpaths.'

Great Bridge Road then almost the length of Phoenix Street before turning off for Swan Village! Under cover of darkness Philippa smiled.

'To go the way you suggest, Mr Fairley, would leave me no time at all for sleep.'

'Going by way of the canal could see you sleeping for ever!' Joshua snapped.

'In that case perhaps I should stay here, a little sleep on that bench has to be better than no sleep at all, which is what I will have if I do not go home by way of the towpath.'

It was fact what the lad said, he'd get precious little time in bed going the way of the road; but walking alongside the locks was not a thing to be done in the dark, slip into one of them even in daylight and there was precious little chance of being hauled out alive.

'I appreciate your concern, Mr Fairley.' A few yards beyond the gate she paused. 'But you do not need to worry about me.'

The words pricking like a barb in his mind Joshua Fairley stopped dead in his tracks.

'*You do not need to worry about me.*'

That one vital word summed up what had been inside him since first setting eyes on Philip Cranley. Worry! He worried the work of the cone was too much for him, worried that he was here at the works at all . . . but much more worried he would be taken away!

It was ridiculous! Joshua ridiculed himself. To worry over a lad . . . a lad he had never even seen until a few weeks ago.

Ridiculous! But if the feeling that plagued him was not worry, then what was it? What did he feel for Philip Cranley?

'That bench is no place to spend what's left of the night,' Joshua answered sharply, using irritation to cover confusion.

Turning to face him, moonlight tracing dust-streaked features, Philippa allowed the inner smile to show.

'Then just what do you suggest, Mr Fairley?'

'We can follow Charles Street down to Hadley Bridge, that is the nearest crossing point—'

'We? I did not know you went that way home.'

'There's a lot you don't know.' Joshua peeled off his jacket, placing it around her shoulders. 'Including the fact that if you stripped to the waist while in the cone you wouldn't shiver from cold when you came out of it. Now I say we get a move on afore the shift is ready to start again.'

Why had he gone out of his way to see the boy home, why had he not denied his own route home lay in the same direction?

Walking back across Swan Village heath Joshua went over each question. Why had he acted so?

The lad was nothing to him . . . nothing! Staring into darkness filtered intermittently by the pale gleam of the moon, Joshua found that like the questions that had plagued him for days the answers were no answer at all.


The evening had gone well. He had followed his established practice of taking a Wednesday evening meal in Hemmings Dining Rooms, except this time he had taken a little more than his usual care in selecting from the wine list. He had been in the mood for celebration, and why not? After all, no one could point the finger of suspicion at Archer Cranley, no one could suspect him of murder. Handing the cabby a coin, he replied to the man's goodnight then turned toward the house.

It had been several hours before that body had been found, long enough for all trace of poison to be washed from the mouth.

Letting himself in Archer went quickly to his room.

Even if it hadn't been, the chances of anyone suspecting the death was caused by anything more than a man the worse for drink falling into that lock were remote to say the least. It happened too often for it to be thought of as anything other than an unfortunate accident. Back in his room he had removed the brandy flask from his jacket pocket and placed it in the cupboard. That too would arouse no suspicion. Exactly the same as the one he had thrown into a part of the canal well away from the lock at Ryder's Bridge, this had been purchased from a tobacconist in West Bromwich High Street and filled with brandy at Hemming's.

Going into his dressing room he changed outdoor clothes for nightshirt.

Having the flask refilled was something he took care to do regularly, so there would be no speculation on that score; and should it emerge the fellow had been poisoned then it was certain the identity of the poison would remain unknown.

'*I knows of no other man 'avin' dealin' with this.*'

The old man had chattered on making no attempt to ask the name of its purchaser or his reasons for buying so deadly a poison.

'*An' that be to the good, for tis lethal stuff.*'

That had been more than twenty years ago. Archer climbed into bed. Ten of those years he had kept a discreet eye on that chemist but then the man had died and without family to carry on the business the shop had closed and, shortly after, had been totally demolished.

No chemist, no record, no shop!

Archer breathed a satisfied sigh.

That blackmailer was dead and there was absolutely no way suspicion could point to him. He had taken the fly out of the ointment, now he could concentrate on more important things.

As he stared up at the canopy the wording of his father-in-law's Will flicked into his mind . . . words he knew by heart.

To my daughter Hannah Mary Cranley, née Briant, the sum of five thousand pounds with my heartfelt sympathies she did not recognise the type of man she chose for a husband before it was too late. Also, Rowlay House for her lifetime and the holding in trust of the business known as Briant Bottle and Glass until such time as a male child, born of her body, shall reach the age of twenty-one years, by which time he shall be married.

Born of her body! Archer's mouth tightened. Nathan Briant had taken no chances.

Should any male heir born of Hannah Cranley, née Briant, fail to marry or on the death of the said male heir before reaching the age of inheritance then Rowlay House and the business known as Briant Bottle and Glass will be sold and together with all monies appertaining will be donated to a charity of my daughter's choosing.

Well, that circumstance had been neatly circumvented. Archer felt the warmth of self-satisfaction seep along his veins, relaxing the tension around his mouth. 'Charity begins at home, Nathan,' he whispered, 'and that is where yours will stay.'

To any female child . . .

The words continued to run like a tide washing everything else from his mind. Closing his eyes Archer gave them free run.

. . . born of Hannah Cranley, I leave you to the care of a father whose place it is to provide for you as I have provided for mine. And finally to my son-in-law Archer Cranley the position of manager of Briant Bottle and Glass with a salary of eight hundred pounds a year which sum will not be increased or supplemented from that business. In the event of the death of his wife Hannah Cranley before her male heir reaches majority Archer Cranley will cease in his employment as manager of Briant Bottle and Glass and will quit Rowlay House.

Everything so neatly sewn up! Turning off the lamp Archer continued to stare at the fire-lit shadows flickering like grey ghosts about the room. The memory of Nathan Briant was like a ghost, haunting his mind constantly, reminding him of . . .

Of what, Nathan? Archer closed his eyes, the smile of satisfaction returning to his mouth. Of what I had hoped to get . . . of what you so cleverly placed beyond my reach? But I have a long reach, Nathan, and for all your clever thinking you have lost. In a few weeks everything you tried so hard to deny me will be mine.

How does failure feel, Nathan? He laughed silently.

How does failure feel?

Naomi Fairley held the half-burned candle closer to the face of a battered tin clock. Josh's shift had finished over an hour ago. Pulling the worn woollen shawl closer about her, warding off the pre-dawn chill striking through a cotton nightgown that had seen almost as many days as herself, she set the candle on the mantel then bent to the fire and poked the spark of life into sleeping embers.

Josh was never late. She glanced again at the clock. Had there been an accident . . . molten glass . . . ? No, they would have sent for her before this. Forcing herself to think sensibly, not to give way to morbid thought, she swung the bracket over the fire, setting the kettle to boil. If anything had gone wrong with a melt, had the mix somehow been wrong or the temperature of the furnace fallen then the whole process would have to be done over again and Joshua was not one to leave the works until he saw for himself the job was right.

He was a good son. Naomi glanced towards the darkened window. He had had to become a man overnight. Eight years old when his father died, his lungs eaten away by silica; a child still he had taken employment with Archer Cranley, and like his father before him he would work himself to death in the glass. She had pleaded as he reached manhood, pleaded he leave her and Greets Green and find himself a place where the air was clean as the

Lord had made it, but for all her pleading Joshua would have none of it.

'Keep him safe, Lord.' The quit words mixed with shadows that folded about them, storing them away in silent darkness. Standing before the fire, her hands clasped together on her chest, Naomi bent her head in silent prayer.

'You should be in your bed, Mother. How many times do I have to tell you I can see to myself at this shift end?'

Adding thanks to her prayer Naomi turned, her lined face showing a smile in the candlelight.

'And I've told you 'til I be wearied from the telling, it be a woman's place to see the man fed and comfortable, no matter what time his shift be finishing; now you be a man, Joshua Fairley, and there can be none deny the fact, but old as you be, and as big, you ain't yet the height my hand can't reach.'

'You wouldn't beat your only child! You couldn't be so cruel . . . could you?'

Catching her up in his arms, a laugh echoing deep in his throat, Joshua swung her in a circle.

'Set me down!' Naomi pretended indignation while the proof of her son's strength was a pleasure in her veins.

'Only if you promise to go to bed.'

'I promise . . . now put me to my feet.'

Reaching for the oil lamp as he set her down Naomi held the candle to the wick, then as yellow light spilled into the tiny room she blew out the candle flame.

'You promised to go to your bed!' Joshua frowned as his mother reached a pot of rabbit stew from the oven.

'I did.' Naomi nodded, pale light glinting on the few gold strands remaining among her grey hair. 'But I never made no promise as to when. Now take the bowl into the scullery and wash the dust from your hands and face then come take your meal, I'll have more than time for sleeping while you be away in the glass.'

There would be time for sleeping. Joshua took the bowl of

water his mother always put to warm in the hearth, carrying it into the scullery. But she would not. She would do as she had always done, work her hours away in the house then in helping others of Greets Green. How he wished it were possible to give her a better life, to take her away from the poverty of this place, but she would never agree. As a lad he had tried to persuade her but she had simply shaken her head, her voice soft as she told him she could never leave his father; and as the years of his growing had gone on he had come to realise, if not to understand, the depth of love that held his mother. She would never leave Greets Green and he would never abandon her.

'Was something wrong with the glass?' Naomi filled two mugs with scalding tea as her son came to the table.

Joshua took a mouthful of the stew. He did not want to answer, feeling suddenly that he wanted to hold to himself the reason for his lateness home, but his mother deserved an answer and deserved that answer to be the truth.

'There was nothing wrong with the glass.' He broke the thick slice of home-baked bread set beside his plate. 'I . . . I walked a lad to his home.'

Sat opposite, Naomi frowned. Why did a lad need to be walked home? Even the youngest walked from that works alone. Holding the thought inside her she sipped at her tea.

He had given his mother a truthful answer. Joshua took another spoonful of stew, chewing the tender meat slowly. There was no need to say more. Yet he had never withheld anything from his mother. It lay uneasy on the surface of his mind. Keeping his glance on his plate he added, 'The lad is new to the glass, I . . . I felt he needed help.'

New to the glass. Unaccountably Naomi's nerves jarred. Why should that have her son walk him home and what was it had Joshua's mouth tighten at mention of him?

'The lad weren't burned?' Her question was swift and filled with genuine concern. She had seen the terrible wounds molten glass left behind.

'No, Mother, he wasn't burned.' Joshua spooned the stew slowly. 'I just thought it too much of a distance for a lad to walk alone at midnight, the towpath be none too safe at night.'

New to the glass. Her fingers tight about the thick platter mug, Naomi let the words linger in her mind. How new was new? Was the day just gone the first that lad had spent at the works, the first time he had trod the way of the towpath or had he truly walked that way before?

Gripping the heavy mug so tight her fingers ached, Naomi could not still the judder that throbbed again along her nerves.

If, as it seemed most likely, the lad as every other lad in Greets Green were used to walking the towpath by night as well as by day, why now did Joshua think it necessary to walk him home? Was it thoughts of the possible danger of that towpath had her own nerves jangling . . . or was it some other fear?

'The lad be new to the works, you says.' She held the mug level with her mouth, her eyes searching her son's face above the rim. 'So surely he's made no enemy there already, one that would have him feared of walking alone.'

Laying his spoon on the empty plate Joshua pushed it away. His mother's question held more than enquiry as to a lad's safety.

'He has made no enemy, Mother, rather the opposite. The men have taken to him quite well.'

Clearing away the dishes, leaving them in the scullery until the light of morning would see them washed clean, Naomi took a taper from the jam jar kept for the purpose in the hearth. Thrusting it between the bars of the grate she watched it spurt into life then held the flame to the candle on the mantel.

There was more to this business than Joshua wished to tell, something instinct told her he wanted held secret to himself.

'Get to your rest, son.'

She smiled but there was no smile in her heart. Touching her lips to the unruly hair that had taken its colour from her own she felt the touch of new fear ripple in her soul. A fear too dark and terrible to face but one she knew would haunt her in the dark hours ahead.

At the door that gave on to the bare narrow stairs she looked back at the figure sat staring into the fire.

'It be right you should be friendly towards them as you works with,' she said quietly, 'right to be a friend to any lad but let it be a friendship of the mind, don't let it become a friendship of the heart.'

# Chapter Eleven

'I shall meet with him tomorrow. You will accompany me in place of Hannah.'

'Won't that appear somewhat strange?'

Edna Cranley watched her brother across the supper table.

'Why should it?' Archer continued eating.

'I just thought Joseph Lacy might wonder why it is Philip's aunt and not his mother was present at a meeting that discussed a possible marriage between their children.'

'I have already met with Joseph Lacy. He knows of Hannah's temporary indisposition.'

And how long was 'temporary' to last? Edna laid down her knife and fork. How long before Hannah Cranley's indisposition became mortal?

'You will talk to the girl, assure her that she will be a well-loved member of our household.'

'Have you taken Philip there?'

'Taken Philip!' Archer frowned. 'To what end?'

She was being fobbed off. Just what was her brother trying to hide? Exasperatedly, Edna placed her serviette beside her plate.

'To meet the girl, of course!'

Touching his mouth with a crisply laundered square of linen, Archer lifted a bland look.

'Why?'

'Why?' Edna's vexation mounted. 'I would have thought that obvious even to you!'

'What difference will that make?'

Exasperation curving into a sneer, Edna laughed.

'It will make a difference between a welcome marriage and no marriage at all.'

Reaching for his wine glass Archer took a sip of claret, rolling it appreciatively around his tongue before swallowing.

'I fail to follow your reasoning, Edna.'

'No, you do not!' Edna snapped, her patience gone. 'You follow it very well. Just what have you agreed with Joseph Lacy?'

Behind hooded lids Archer's eyes glinted.

'I'll tell you what were agreed. That them two would be wed regardless of the difference between them.'

'Joseph Lacy agreed to that?'

Taking up his glass Archer turned it in his fingers, watching the darts of light shimmer in its ruby depths.

'He agreed . . . after some persuasion, the transfer of the glass business to his bank, together with a small consideration for himself to offset having to replace a housekeeper.'

Everything could be bought and sold! Edna met the glint of those ferret eyes. That had been Archer's creed even as a child, and as a man it had not varied. What did not suit Archer Cranley could be changed . . . or destroyed. But one way or the other Edna Cranley must profit. Letting the last thought lie warm in her heart she watched her brother refill his glass.

'And if Philip does not agree?'

Across the table Archer Cranley's narrow features seemed to draw together and the glint deep in his coal-black eyes was one of warning.

'Philip will do as I say, and so will you, sister . . . if you know what's good for you! You will accompany me to the Lacy house, you will assure them that Hannah is merely feeling unwell – a touch of the influenza – and you will speak gently to the girl.'

Archer could be most unpleasant when crossed but the years

had long since wiped away Edna's fear of him; she knew too much for him to threaten her now. Holding his eyes with her own, she laughed softly.

'The same old trick, Archer; throw your weight around and frighten off any opposition. How many times must I repeat myself? I am not afraid of you, I do what you say only if it suits me . . . so suit me, Archer, or get someone else to go with you to the Lacy house!'

Five minutes later Archer sat in the study, the faint sounds of his sister clearing the evening meal reaching through the quiet room.

A thousand pounds! The avaricious bitch had demanded another thousand pounds to agree to hold her silence. She could have demanded ten and he would have agreed. Beneath the smouldering anger, a smile flickered. He would agree to any sum he did not intend to pay.

And Edna's silence? Soon, very soon, she would be in no position to break that. The silence of death is eternal.

He leaned back in his chair, the flickering smile strengthening.

The silence of death is eternal.

He liked the phrase. Maybe he would have it carved on Edna's headstone.


'I ain't after sellin' glass bottles.'

'It be as well for I ain't in the market for 'em.'

Thad Grinley watched the man he had come to see. Face and body wreathed with fat, thinning hair drifting to one side like pale grey mist, a permanent perspiration giving a greasy look to anaemic skin, Simeon Beasley stroked a hand over a strong young thigh.

'I knows that well.' Thad Grinley swallowed hard as the podgy fingers moved in a bronze-cropped crotch.

'Then why come 'ere, spoiling a man's afternoon rest?'

Rest! Thad would have laughed except his own jerking crotch held his throat tight.

'Cos I 'ave summat else to sell.'

Thad watched young fingers play over the fat cheek, lifting the chin, greeting the slack mouth with a moist inviting tongue. Christ, what he wouldn't give for an hour of that!

Moving upwards from the crotch, Simeon Beasley's plump fingers stroked slowly over the naked body perched on his knee, his mouth open to the probing tongue.

The demand at the base of his own stomach becoming more insistent, Thad tried to look away. A few more minutes of this and his own personal volcano would spew.

'It be summat I thinks you'll find pleasurable.'

'Glass don't pleasure me none.' The slack mouth closed over soft lips, sucking them deep into itself.

'This don't be glass. And neither do this!' Thad writhed, clenching his fingers inside his trouser pockets.

'Say what it be you come for, I don't 'ave all day.'

Neither did he! Thad felt the jerk of hardened flesh as the naked figure slid to its knees, pressing its face between the podgy thighs.

'I come to make you an offer . . . one you'll like.'

The breathy words not lost on him Simeon Beasley pressed the bronze-haired head closer against his paunch, his bead-like eyes on Thad.

'Be it second-hand?'

Watching the naked figure rise to its feet, slender legs reaching up to a taut bottom, soft rounded hips beneath a trim waist, Thad Grinley had to literally push the answer between dry lips.

'It . . . it be brand-new, I'd . . . I'd stake money on it.'

'Ahhh money!' Beasley traced a hand over the tight bottom. 'And how much money are you looking to get for your brand-new find?'

'Five more than the last time.'

'Five pounds more.' Beasley's slack mouth tightened. 'You be gettin' greedy.'

'This one be worth it, it be real pretty . . . you likes pretty things.'

Easing forward in the chair Beasley drew the naked figure close, touching his lips to the gleaming bronze crotch. With his eyes glued to the spectacle Thad Grinley tried to hold the gasp that escaped his own mouth. Much more of this and he would be walking home in wet trousers.

'Pretty you says?' Beasley called as Thad turned to leave. 'Pretty as this?'

One surprising deft move of the podgy hand had the naked figure turned to face Thad, while Beasley's bright bird eyes smiled at the other man's hands gripping inside pockets.

'Prettier.' Thad swallowed painfully. 'An' younger, young an' new, just the way you likes 'em.'

'You 'ear that?' Beasley's hand rested on the firm buttocks. 'Grinley 'as one younger and prettier, so he says. P'raps I should 'ave a talk with Mr Grinley, but don't you go leavin', you wait in there.'

Smiling as the naked figure half-turned to him, a painted mouth drawn to a pout, he trailed a hand over the flat stomach.

'Now, now, don't you go sulking, and don't go playing with this . . .' Bringing the trailing hand to the bronze crotch he smoothed the knuckles beneath hard flesh, fondling the tight swollen tip. '. . . I'll do that meself.'

Slapping the smooth bottom he waved the figure away, flicking a hand towards Grinley as the naked man disappeared into another room.

'He'll keep but that won't, not unless you leaves it alone.' The corpulent frame jiggled as he laughed. 'So tell me about this new find an' then you can go play games wi' yourself 'til you goes cock-eyed.'

Hating the other man's guts but knowing it must not show if the hoped-for sum was to be forthcoming Grinley took his hands from his pockets.

'It be one I ain't seen afore but I knows you'll like it for, as I said, it be young and pretty . . . and you likes pretty boys.'

He was interested, the cash was as good as in his pocket. Grinley kept the smile from his face as those fat-enfolded eyes probed his.

'Ain't none so pretty as I'd pay twenty-five pounds for.'

The urge that had held his body now drained away completely, and Thad Grinley's brain moved with its usual speed. Twenty quid were not a sum to be gambled with, but then why turn away at the first hurdle?

'None as you've 'ad so far.' Thad turned away, the rest of his words floating over his shoulder. 'But there ain't one of 'em can 'old a candle to what I 'ave now; still, the offer were made an' refused and the next one I takes it to—'

'Wait!'

His back to the other man Thad grinned. Twenty-five pounds . . . not bad for a few hours' work.

'This new one,' Beasley went on, 'where does it be from?'

Wiping the grin from his mouth Thad turned a straight face to the man spilling from the chair.

'Couldn't say, but it don't be local to Greets Green or I'd 'ave seen it long since.'

'The name then . . . what be the name?'

This could be tricky. Thad thought quickly. Beasley liked to be certain any new trinket he bought wouldn't be missed or, worse still, be searched for. If it 'adn't been for that mouthy bitch . . . the quicker somebody done for that one the better, he might even do for her hisself.

'It be Mason, the name be Mason,' he answered glibly, 'an' there be no Masons in Greets Green.'

'You be sure it ain't second-'and? I don't take to being sold another man's leavings.'

You don't tek to 'aving any other man's leavings! Thad's steady glance hid the scorn of his thoughts. Simeon Beasley would snatch the tart from any man's plate if he thought he could get away with it; old or new it made little difference so long as the tasting was a pleasure to his palate.

'I be sure.' He nodded. 'Just as sure as I be the one you was fondlin' just now be showin' the cracks; but if you ain't in the market for a new ride . . . or be it as the price be out of your range . . .'

'Who says the price be outta my range!'

Beneath the mist-thin hair the bloated face flushed an angry red, folds of flesh rippling like waves as he pushed to his feet.

If he pushed too hard then the money was gone. Thaddeus Grinley tried to gauge the thoughts he knew were spinning behind those bird-like eyes. There weren't too many with the tastes of Simeon Beasley, and certainly none willing to shell out twenty-five quid on goods unseen.

Taking a handkerchief from the peacock-blue velvet jacket meant to disguise the grossness of his body, yet somehow adding to it, Beasley dabbed at the moisture swathing his brow.

'Twenty-five.' He wiped the handkerchief over his cheeks. 'You gets ten now, the rest on delivery, an' Grinley . . . it better be all you claims it to be.'

Folding the two white five-pound notes into an inner pocket of his own frayed jacket, Grinley smiled.

'It will be; but then should it 'appen as you think I been lyin' to you then you can allus 'ave your money back.'

'Oh no!' Simeon Beasley's heavy jowls shook as his head swung slowly back and forth on his bull-like neck. 'I couldn't do that, Grinley, for your wife would be needin' every penny of it. You see it would tek all of that twenty-five pounds to pay for folk to look for the missing pieces so that dirty little body o' yourn could lie together in one coffin!'

Leaving the gracious red-brick house stood in solitary splendour of far-reaching lawns that gave on to gorse-strewn open heath, Grinley drew in a deep breath, the fresh smoke-free air washing into his lungs. Harville's Hawthorne was a longer step to walk from Greets Green than he preferred but here he would be unrecognised.

The ten pounds snug against his breast, he glanced back at the large house, its high windows gleaming like jewels in the sunlight.

Simeon Beasley's father had built that house; toiled every day of fifty years to pay for bricks and land, a legacy to leave to his son. And Simeon? Far from building on his father's achievements he was squandering the lot, satisfying his abnormal sexual desires.

But one man's misfortune was another man's fortune!

Grinley smiled as he walked to the bend of Dial Lane then branched right, following the canal towards Brickhouse Bridge.

Thaddeus Grinley might not make a fortune out of Simeon Beasley . . . but he would certainly take a good share!


The heath had looked so beautiful dotted with the vivid colours of wild flowers set among the greenery of gorse and heather. Philippa smiled at the freshly picked posy laid on the bedroom table. Scarlet corn poppies bent their gorgeous heads shyly to grey green leaves while the tiny purple heartsease peeped up at stately white campion. Like jewels fit for a queen, but no queen so deserving as Hannah Cranley.

'Lunch be waiting.'

Edna's voice rattled like gravel thrown against the bedroom door. Glancing again at the posy picked on the way home, Philippa reached for a clean shirt.

'Them be for your mother I take it.'

Edna ran a disparaging look over the flowers as Philippa stepped into the corridor that ran past the several bedrooms.

'I thought I would see her before taking lunch.'

Tightly plaited hair coiled about her ears seemed to hold the narrow features in a vice.

'What you thought be different to what your father wants. He said to tell you to join him in the study.'

'I will see my mother first. Tell my father I will be with him shortly.'

Edna's face had always held a vinegary look but now it turned positively acid.

'You don't give me orders, Philip Cranley, I be no more your runabout than I be your father's.'

'Then what are you, Aunt?' Philip's answer cracked along the quiet corridor. 'Just what role do you play in this house . . . apart from being my mother's gaoler, that is?'

Stumbling back against the wall as Philippa brushed past her, Edna's mouth snapped rat-trap tight.

'A more important one than you think!' she whispered, watching the figure walking downstairs. 'Far more important than either the child or the mother, as you'll find out soon enough.'

'I had thought to see Mother before having lunch.' Philippa stared at the man seated behind the heavy desk.

'Consideration as always, Philip, your mother would appreciate that.'

'Then why ask me to come here first?'

Finishing the article he was reading Archer folded the newspaper, laying it aside before looking up. It had been as he expected, the body pulled from that lock had been identified as being too far gone in drink to note where he was walking.

'Why?' He glanced at the posy held in Philippa's hand. 'Because I have a matter I wish to inform you of before you see your mother.'

Inform me of! Philippa felt the coldness of it. Something to be told, to be ordered; but then it had never been the way of Archer Cranley to discuss anything with his own child.

Leaning back in the leather-bound chair Archer watched the nuances of emotion glide across the pale tired-looking face. The glassworks was not taking toll fast enough, but that did not matter now.

With his hands locked together across his chest, he said, 'I have arranged for you to be married.'

'Married!' she gasped.

'That is what I said.' Archer nodded.

'You have arranged a marriage for me without even consulting me?'

'But why would I consult you?' Archer answered coolly. 'You are a minor and as such you will do as I say.'

'No.' Philippa brought a hand down on the desk. 'For years I have done as you have said, followed the rules set down by you, lived out the lies you invented because you said should Mother ever realise the truth of that accident it would be the final straw, the one last blow that would send her over the edge into madness; but I don't believe that any more, Father. I don't believe my mother's mind is unbalanced: what I do believe is that you have lied . . . lied to suit yourself ever since my brother's death. But this I will not envisage, this time I will not do as you say. The lies are over, Father, and so is the fiasco!'

Taking a key from his waistcoat pocket Archer unlocked a central drawer of the desk. Taking out an envelope he laid it in front of her.

'So you think I have lied concerning your mother's mental condition, that what I have done for so long has been not to keep her from passing the brink of madness but to satisfy some weird fancy of my own? Really, Philip, I credited you with more sense than that! However, you must do as you see fit of course, but before you make any rash decision I suggest you read the contents of that envelope. After all, it is easy to be sorry after the event, but sorry would not have your mother released from an asylum for the insane. I assure you she would be locked away for the remainder of her life.'

Taking the single page from the envelope and scanning the words quickly, Philippa raised astounded eyes.

'You wouldn't . . . not your own wife!'

'Not me, Philip . . . you. You are the one will condemn your mother to a living hell unless you agree to what I propose.'

'Why do that, why not let me take my mother and leave? I take back what I said about your never getting the business, I will sign it over to you now if you just let Mother go.'

'I be sure you would, Philip.' Folding the letter Archer replaced it in the envelope, locking both away in the drawer. 'I be sure you would but you see it isn't as simple as that. You have to inherit before you can sign away—'

'I know that, but in less than a month I will be of age.'

'True.' Archer acknowledged the interruption. 'But that don't be all of what Nathan Briant required if you were to have his fortune. You see, Philip, what you don't know is you have to be wed by your twenty-first birthday or lose the lot . . . that would be an inconvenience to us but for your mother it would be a tragedy.'

An insane asylum! Philippa's face blanched paler than before. There was no need to ask herself if Archer Cranley would adhere to his word, the answer was written clear in his eyes.

'You say you have already arranged a marriage?'

It wasn't quite true as yet, but there would be no refusal. Archer nodded once more.

'To whom?' she asked quietly. 'Who am I to marry?'

Dropping the key into the pocket he had taken it from, Archer looked up.

'Davinia Lacy . . .'

The cold smile of a serpent touching his thin lips he patted the pocket that held the key.

'. . . the daughter of Joseph Lacy.'

A look of pure disbelief crossed Philippa's face.

'You can't mean that, Father . . . you can't mean that!'

A soft laugh slithering from his throat, Archer Cranley came from behind the desk.

'Oh but I do, Philip,' he creamed. 'Oh, but I do!'

# Chapter Twelve

He had killed her first-born. Hannah Cranley held a wet cloth to her swollen mouth. He had been responsible although he had denied it, had called her mad for saying so. He had called her mad ever since. That had proved an easy path for him, a simple way to carry on the evil that plagued their lives. He had spread the word among their few acquaintances that the death of her son had unbalanced her mind, that her doctors recommended she be taken into a private nursing home away from the constant reminding of that terrible day. Yet with the same slyness, the same pretence of grief at losing his wife as well as his son, he had told them he could not face doing that and instead had brought them to this house with only his sister to run it.

But how could she ever forget, daily seeing the face of the man who had killed her boy as surely as if plunging a knife into him? Nor did he want her to forget, for while she remembered the fate of her first child she would remain aware of the evil that hung over the second, that hung like the black plague over all of their lives, an evil that prevented any interference with Archer Cranley's actions.

But how to stop him? Wincing as she lifted the cloth from her mouth Hannah looked into the mirror at the purpling bruise surrounding the split in her lip. Archer covered his tracks well. Who would believe it was his blows and those of his sister rather than her own supposed frequent lapses into madness that had her body covered in similar marks?

'Get out of that frock and those stays!'

Edna Cranley snatched the cloth, throwing it savagely into the bowl stood on the washstand.

'I don't want—'

Edna's thin hand rose, catching the other woman viciously across the face.

'It don't be a case of what *you* want. Now get out of that frock afore I rip it off you!'

Hannah rose unsteadily to her feet, her fingers shaking as she struggled with tiny silk-covered buttons. If only her father were alive. He would take her and Philip away from here, away from Archer Cranley; he would see that Philip . . .

'I said, get it off!' Edna's hand grasped the dress, pulling it sharply, the buttons flying in several directions.

'There was no need to do that.'

'There was every need!' Edna Cranley's spite curved her thin mouth, the caricature of a smile only making her plain face more unattractive. 'That is what Archer will be told. Another of your "turns", another little bout of the madness that is eating your brain, had you tearing off your clothes. I tried not to hurt you but in your thrashing you hit your face against the bedpost, it left this mark against your temple.' Closing her hand into a fist she brought it hard down, striking Hannah a second time. 'Now unless you want more of the same you will get out of those clothes and sharp!'

Tears spreading a line along lashes curled around dark-ringed eyes Hannah Cranley stepped out of the heavy grosgrain gown. Yes, her father would have forgiven what she had done, he would have taken her back, protected her and Philip. But he was no longer here and there was no one else she could rely upon, no other person she could turn to for help, none who would fight the evil that was destroying her, destroying her child.

'You should have listened to your father.' Edna snatched at

the tightly laced corset, pulling the long strings apart. 'He knew Archer had no love for you, he knew what you were letting yourself in for, but you wouldn't listen. Archer Cranley was in love with you, that is what you thought, isn't it? But Archer never loved anybody but himself.'

'And you?' Hannah glanced at her sister-in-law. 'Does he love you?'

Gathering up the garments as Hannah climbed into a cambric nightgown, Edna's face hardened. 'No.' She shook her head. 'Archer did not bring me here out of brotherly love, he brought me here to see his secret was kept; as long as I stayed he was safe . . .'

Hannah's faded eyes lifted to coal-black ones. Too unhappy to smile she felt only pity at the quick dart of fear that sprang to them as she asked, 'And once the need for secrecy is over what then, Edna . . . what will happen to you then? Will you be allowed to share your brother's house or will he turn on you as he has turned on his wife? Perhaps we should both have left while there was still a chance.'

'You think I've been a fool, don't you?' Edna laughed scathingly. 'You think I was being a fool, as you were. That was what Archer thought as well, at least until I put him right. There will be no need for me to share a house with him. We have a bargain, my brother and I, one that will keep me in comfort for the rest of my days, and one I will see that he keeps.'

'As he kept his vow to love and cherish the girl he married.' Hannah sank to the bed, lying back against the pillows.

'The girl he married was a fool!' Edna stood beside the bed, a small medicine glass in one hand, a heavily ridged green-glass bottle in the other. 'His sister is not.'

Maybe she might have left Archer. Left alone, Hannah stared into the shadows that had become the pattern of her life. But what would have come out of that? He was not a man to let control slip from his fingers and that was what she and Philip meant to him, control of her father's business. There was no love left between them, that had died with her son and Archer felt no affection for the child remaining to them.

Lying on the huge lace-edged pillows she glanced at the medicine glass Edna had placed beside her bed. There was peace in the dark pit the laudanum opened to her senses.

Edna had come to stay immediately following the accident and she had moved with them to Greets Green, supposedly to care for Hannah and the remaining child. No servant had been allowed to come with them and none taken on here at this house, Edna alone seeing to the running of it; and it soon became obvious that his sister was to be an additional tool of Archer Cranley's cruelty.

Edna Cranley! The woman was as omnipresent as the Lord. Nowhere in the house or out of it was there any getting away from that woman's sight, even Philip's education had been conducted with those bright blackbird eyes watching the tutor's every move. She had tried to help her child, to gain freedom from those watching eyes but Archer had soon warned that he would have the child sent away and never brought home again. That had been enough for her. Hannah felt the tears trickle down her cheeks. To lose both of her children, not to see either dear little face again had been too much to risk so she had stopped her efforts to ease that lonely childhood.

Did Philip blame her, did that loneliness and oppression seem a fault on her part, was it thought she too was incapable of love?

In the shadows of her room, curtains drawn against the light, Hannah felt the warm tears against her skin.

And when she was no longer in this house? What would become of Philip then? Her life at least had afforded protection against Archer's greed, protected their child, but how long would that life go on, how much time was left to her?

Clouds of mist swirling in her brain Hannah clutched at the bedcover, trying to fight back the need for that drug. She had prayed God the day of her going would be a long way off but pathways must always find their end and soon now her own would end.

'You have always been my stay, my support,' the words fluttered faintly on lips that hardly moved, 'you have been my only help in life and I ask you to help me now. Give me the strength, Lord, the strength to help my child, the strength to save what Archer Cranley seeks to destroy.'

Outside the bedroom Edna Cranley pressed an ear to the door, listening intently. There was no sound, no movement. The laudanum did its work quickly now. Her thin mouth relaxing she turned away along the corridor, her footsteps soundless on the thick carpet. The dose she had given would keep her sister-in-law asleep for the most part of the day.

There would not be many more weeks of having to live in this house, of being subject to her brother's dictates. She had accepted the offer he had made so many years ago not fully realising the extent of time having to elapse before payment was made.

Dark skirts swishing about her ankles she stepped quickly along the corridor.

Only until my wife recovers, Archer had told her; then he had taken care that to the outside world at least it seemed she had never recovered. But now even he could not hold off Hannah Cranley's release. There was more than the marks of blows upon her face, more than the mark of Archer Cranley's mental torture. The finger of death had written its seal on those drawn features.

Did Archer know?

At the door of her room Edna stood still, her fingers curled into the fabric of her skirts, her mouth suddenly tight as it had been in that bedroom, a flicker of guilt running cold along her spine.

For years he had inflicted torment on the quiet woman lying in that bed and she too had mistreated her, used her to help ease . . .

She must not think of that. Running both hands over her

plain worsted skirt Edna swallowed hard. She had to hold herself together, more so now than ever for Archer Cranley could smell weakness a mile off and once detected . . .

Drawing in a full breath she walked steadily into her bedroom. Did Archer know?

The question flicked once more across her brain as she slipped out of the dull brown skirt.

Whether he knew it already, or whether the news of it was yet to come to him, he would only revel in the pleasure of hearing it.

Taking a fine-velour black suit from the wardrobe she laid it on the bed, staring at the rich smooth fabric.

Archer Cranley *wanted* his wife's death. Her usefulness to him was almost at an end. And his child? Yes, her brother wanted death there also. He wanted them both gone, neither of them must be allowed ever to become a threat to his ambition; only with the death of both would he lie peaceful in his bed.

And what of the threat of his sister?

The flick of fear that had traced her spine pricked cold and sharp at every nerve. Filial love? Despite her fear Edna almost smiled. Archer had never been endowed with that. No, her brother cared for none but himself, he would sacrifice his sister as readily as he had his wife.

Her fingers moving swiftly, she unbuttoned the plain cotton blouse. Replacing it with lace-edged white chiffon she reached for the black skirt. Edna Cranley must watch out for herself! She too knew enough of Nathan Briant's Will to have realised long ago the reasons for her brother's actions, actions that had brought his wife to the brink of suicide, that inflicted misery on her and on her child, and would lead him further yet.

It was an evil thing he had perpetrated all these years, a dark and terrible evil, and there was more yet to come.

He had come home late from his shift again last night. Naomi Fairley watched her son walk away from the tight clutch of tiny houses that fronted the graveyard. Churchyard Row was well named, the damp that rose summer and winter from the ground saw most folk early into their grave.

But it was not the damp or the smell of open sewers that plagued her now, it was her son. He had changed from the son her knew to one that in some ways could be almost a stranger. A few weeks since he would spend the midday shift break talking with her, telling her of happenings in the glass, of lads getting their ears boxed for dawdling and little wenches in tears when cold bit their fingers or when their pay had been docked for dropping a glass or a bottle.

But now Josh spoke of none of that. In fact he hardly spoke at all without her pulling words out of him. Sometimes he would sit through an entire meal and say nothing during the eating of it; then having finished he would go to his room to sleep.

Watching his tall figure turn the corner into Lower Church Lane Naomi went slowly back into the house.

He went to his room to sleep but her knew he didn't sleep. The creaking of the floorboards spoke fluent words.

Taking up her knitting she carried it to the chair drawn against the light of the window.

It had begun, the pacing up and down, the tossing and turning in his bed, from the night he had seen that lad to his home. Why had he seen it as binding on him to do that?

She stabbed the knitting pin hard into a stitch.

Why was he still doing it? Lads walked the heath hereabouts from the time of loosing their mother's skirts, they knew every disused coal pit, every mine shaft as well as they knew their own hands, so why not this one? Were it a blindness of the eyes?

As she pulled sharply at the wool the ball fell from her lap, rolling away across the floor. Thoughts filling her mind, Naomi ignored it.

There was no blindness of that lad's eyes whoever he might be, the only blindness was in Josh! But what had caused it? He was usually so sensible, so level-headed; even in early childhood he could tell right from wrong, spot a lie or a troublemaker afore other folk even guessed at things amiss. So why not now? For there was something amiss in all of this.

Josh must know that!

Naomi let the knitting rest on her lap, staring unseeing at the thick wooden needles.

He was deliberately closing his eyes to it, deliberately allowing himself to be fooled.

Were it a wench stealing his sleep, a wench keeping him awake nights, then her would have smiled and slept sound in her own bed for lying sleepless over a pretty wench were natural to a man; but the one plaguing her son's mind, snatching his rest from him, were no wench!

Her had asked Josh, of course her had, asked why a lad needed a man to walk him home of a night, but Josh brushed her questions aside, drawing into himself when her tried too hard. Whatever were eating away at him he were not prepared to talk of it.

But that in itself said that Josh as well as herself thought what he was doing was not right.

Going out of his way in the darkness of night to be with a lad, a stony silence when asked who it was and why did he need someone to walk the heath with him, tossing and turning in his bed when a body should be sleeping.

There could be only one reason, one cause that turned a man upside down on himself and that reason were well known to her. A man must needs love a woman for such to happen, to love or else to think himself in love.

But there was no woman in her son's life. At twenty-six years of age he had spoken tenderly of no wench, there was no shyness in his laugh or tremble in his voice when he spoke to the girls of the village. It had often given her cause for thought but set no rise to worry, many men were wise enough to wait until they were sure before leading a wench to the altar.

But was it wisdom had held Joshua?

The fear that stalked her nights and walked with her through her days stabbed its evil sharp against her heart.

It could be no other . . . it *must* be no other!

Her knitting falling unheeded to the floor, Naomi pressed trembling fingers to her mouth.

The dread that lay so heavy inside her could have no substance, no truth.

Tears sliding over her cheeks, her words a whisper, Naomi Fairley prayed. 'Lord, let what I be thinking be not so, let the fears that grip my heart be groundless, let not my son be caught in the web of Satan to walk in the ways of his wickedness.'

Her prayer was central to her life. Naomi lowered her hands. When anything untoward had occurred then her hand had been placed alongside that of the Lord. She wiped the tears with one hand. Her had faced whatever it was had to be faced, whether it were a girl unwed but carrying a child, or disease in the village, her had let nothing turn her aside; her had listened to the words of Keziah Silk, administered her potions and salves made from God's own plants and herbs.

Keziah Silk! The name brought her senses together sharply. The woman had other skills apart from the use of herbs, her was wise in the ways of people, of the ills that were not always of the body.

Leaving wool and needles where they had fallen Naomi reached for her shawl. This time it was her own son be stood in need of help; God grant that need be not arising from the cause her feared, but either way her must be knowing.

Draping the shawl about her head she hurried from the house.

Nobody in Greets Green knowed the truth of Keziah Silk's birth nor of the man that planted her seed but didn't wait of its harvesting. Naomi walked on, pausing only briefly to pass the time of day with an old man sat smoking a stained clay pipe as he sat in the warmth of the sun, or a woman too far gone with child to drag coal bogies from the pit head or lift the heavy baskets of glass at the glassworks.

Long ago there had been rumours concerning the wench that gave her life, rumours that spoke of night-time visits to the heath, of the son of the owner of Blacklake colliery being sent on a long-lasting tour of foreign parts while a maid was seen away from the house with no more than a shawl to wrap herself in.

Rumours! Naomi crossed the bridge that spanned the railway. But right or wrong the wench that had been allowed to bear and raise her child in a small cottage on the edge of John's Lane Farm had never acknowledged them, never spoken of the father, and if Keziah herself had been told the identity before her mother's death she in turn kept that same silence.

Bastard-born! Naomi drew her shawl tight as if in an effort to shut out the thoughts that kept returning. But born of a union that was natural, a union not worthy of Sodom!

Picking her way across the tram line that ran the length of Horsley Road, she glanced towards the heavy rumbling vehicle as its steam horn bellowed its passing.

Nasty, noisy things . . . unnatural to God's world! Naomi shuddered, there seemed to be many things unnatural in these times.

A few yards along the busy road the tram clanged to a halt and Naomi saw several women clamber down the stair. Ordinarily she would have welcomed company, but not today . . . not today.

Turning away from Gough's buildings, the straggle of houses that edged one side of the road, she hurried in the direction of the vicarage; once in John's Lane there would be less chance of meeting up with anyone.

How to tell Keziah? Naomi's steps slowed. How did a body tell of such a fear, a fear that numbed the soul?

Over the hedge a cow called mournfully for its stolen calf.

Would her son be taken as that calf had been taken . . . without a mother's smile, a mother's blessing? Would her own heart bleed in the night as that poor creature's had bled? To lose a son to a wench were most times a blessing, and so it could have been with her; Joshua's wife could have been the daughter that was never granted to her and Isaac.

Isaac! What would all of this have done to Isaac? For the first time Naomi found herself glad to be a widow.

What will it do to Joshua? It seemed her husband's voice asked the question and it brought her faltering steps to a standstill. The folk of Greets Green nodded and talked but then let things fade; like others of their sort they had enough to cope with just keeping themselves alive, but this . . . this would not be let fade. And what of Joshua's feeling for her, what if he found his own mother had spoken against him?

'But I don't be against you, Joshua . . .'

With pain in her heart, Naomi lifted her head high on her neck and cried aloud.

'. . . I don't be against you, I be against the evil that is reaching out for you. I love you, Joshua, you are the one reason I have to be living.'

In the field beyond the hedge the cow stared, its huge sorrow-filled eyes asking the question Naomi's soul asked.

How can I save my child?

# Chapter Thirteen

Dressed in the jet-embroidered velour suit bought so long ago Edna set a matching bonnet over hair liberally strewn with grey. Lines laid down by lonely years marked a face he had seen as smooth and young. Richard Stanton had loved her then, loved her not Hannah Briant!

Lifting gloved hands she held the black tulle veil, hatred blazing bitter fire in her eyes.

Staring into the mirror she saw again the handsome face, its features seeming carved from marble, a single red rose laid between cold dead fingers. Her rose. Her last gift to the man she had loved, a gift that carried with it the soul of Edna Cranley.

'She caused your death,' Edna whispered to the shades of yesterday. 'She, Hannah Briant, took you from me. But she did not love you as I did, as I do still. She took my life as well as yours but I have made her pay, my dearest, pay dearly, and there are payments yet to be made.'

An icy smile twisting her thin mouth she lowered the veil then took the jet-encrusted pochette from the shelf of her wardrobe. Looping its strings over her wrist she walked to Hannah's room, the smile fading as she listened at the door. Her sister-in-law would sleep long into the afternoon, and Archer? Archer was having lunch with Beasley.

Philip? Hearing no sound from inside the room she turned

towards the stairs. Too many times of trudging away the midday shift break only to find his mother sleeping or indisposed he had decided not to make the journey home.

Stepping into the warm sunshine Edna shrugged. Philip could spend his shift breaks in hell for all it bothered her.

The quiet creak of the stair telling her Edna had given up listening at her door, Hannah opened her eyes. Pushing from the bed, steadying herself against the bedpost as her senses swam, she crossed to the window. Opening the heavy velvet drapes a mere crack she watched the black-gowned figure walk away from the house.

She had prayed Edna would follow her normal routine of visiting Richard Stanton's grave; prayed yesterday each time she managed to empty the medicine glass onto the floor beneath her bed, and this morning into the vase that held the flowers Philip had brought her.

Her eyes were accustomed to the shadows she spent so much of her life in and Hannah dressed as quickly as shaking fingers would allow. She must go quickly. This would be the one chance she was ever likely to have.

Taffeta petticoats rustling beneath grey wool dress and matching frogged day coat, Hannah breathed the soft scents of the garden. How she would love just to sit there as she had once sat in the gardens of that other house, to watch her children tumble and play around her feet. But she would never see that again, never see her children together in this life; Archer Cranley had taken that joy from her, just as he would take that which was left. He would destroy Philip's life as he had destroyed hers.

The thought lending strength to her legs Hannah turned in the direction of Phoenix Street. She must find a way to help her child, a way to save Philip.

Her strength waning rapidly, Hannah glanced at the square tower of the old church rising over the distant fields. What if Edna had returned to find her gone . . . ? But even if she had, there was not much more she and her brother could make her suffer. The Lord would not refuse a plea laid before Him.

It was a sin. A sin against the Lord!

Hannah Cranley walked slowly along the nave of the church. On either side, set at intervals in the grey stone walls, high pointed windows flaunted streamers of colour through ancient stained glass, while before her along the aisle dust motes danced never endingly in golden shafts of sunlight.

He could not do it. He must not do it!

With her skirts whispering against black and white tiles set in huge diamond-shaped patterns she made her way slowly between rows of polished wood pews lined with scarlet kneeling pads, each row finished with a small carved wooden cross.

Coming to the chancel steps she stood with head bowed, her eyes on the scarlet carpet.

He must not do it. She must not let him.

Lifting her gaze she stared in front of her to where the high altar, draped in white and dressed with gold, stood beneath the east window, the tall cross at its heart spurting darts of brilliant light into the shadows.

Dropping a deep curtsey she crossed her breast, her lips moving in silent unison.

It was a sin. A sin that had gone on for eighteen years and she had watched it grow, watched the layers of deceit grow thicker, the web of lies become more and more entangled, drawing them all deeper and deeper into its evil heart.

Lies spun from lies, threads of steel that held them bound to itself, gradually becoming bonds she could not break.

Her eyes on the gleaming cross, she dropped her hand to her side. He had drained every last drop of pleasure from their lives, stifled it, killed it as surely as he had killed . . .

A sob falling from her lips, Hannah moved into the front-row pew that had been her usual Sunday seat. All around the shadows seemed to whisper, to conspire together, condemning as they always had, offering no relief for the torment that pulled inside her.

Palms together in her lap, she bent her head. How many times had she prayed like this, how many times had she asked that the wrong be righted, that the evil that had clouded her life be somehow removed? But that prayer had received no answer, the release she asked for never coming.

Her Amen whispered, her breast crossed again she lifted her head, taking her gaze to the carpeted steps. One at each side, the life-sized statues of Christ and His mother regarded her with pity in their painted eyes.

'It is a sin against you.' Hannah met the gaze of the plaster faces. 'And a sin against my child.'

Sunlight striking a window sent a shaft of beams playing over the gold-crowned head of the statue of the Virgin, giving a radiance that shimmered in the cool dimness, bringing an almost living tenderness to the gently smiling mouth.

'Maybe it will not matter this once offering my prayers to you rather than to your son.'

Hannah's words came quietly, just a breath that rested on the silence. Living eyes locked with painted ones, she continued softly.

'You knew what it was to be a mother. You knew what it was to carry a child, to feel it move and grow inside you, a part of you for nine long months. To give birth in pain and suffering as I did. You knew the joy of holding the child in your arms as I knew that joy. you fed your son from your breast as I fed mine. You too watched your son grow, felt the agony as you watched him die, the same agony I felt as I held my dead son. The heart within you kept on beating but the flame of your own life went out as the spark of his faded.'

Tears wetting her cheeks Hannah gazed up at the plaster features, the half-light seeming to move the painted lips in sorrowful agreement.

'I know.' Hannah's own lips barely moved as she whispered. 'I know, for that is how it was with me. He was so young, no more than six years old, the child I would have died to save. But it was he the evil of pride destroyed, as it was the evil of men killed your son.'

Her hands coming together, fingers twining with the force of pain that never left her, Hannah lifted them towards the statue, her voice throbbing with tears.

'Take my son into your arms, Holy Mother. Comfort him as I so often did, whisper your love when he cries in the night, for my voice can no longer reach him. Comfort him, for my arms can no longer hold him, protect him, most blessed of women. Protect him, for I could not.'

Her head lowering to her chest Hannah's eyes closed but her lips continued her whispered prayer.

'Protect him, sweet mother of Christ, and protect the child that remains, for I cannot. I have not the strength of will to fight the evil that took the life of my son, an evil that will destroy us all!'


'Where have you been?'

Archer Cranley stared at his wife seated uneasily in a winged armchair that swamped her thin figure. His wife! Discontent rose powerfully in him. Christ, what was he married to! How much longer would he be tied to that?

'I . . . I have been to the church.'

Hannah Cranley's head remained bowed, her fingers twisting the wool skirt of her dress with quick nervous movements. Archer had returned home sooner than had been expected and now his temper was following the pattern it always did if she asked to go anywhere alone; only this time she had not asked, she had left the house without his permission.

'Church! You have been to church!'

His laugh rang across the quiet bedroom, causing Hannah to tremble. She had always feared the mocking sneer of his laughter more than the shouting; mocking her had never seemed to clear the anger from his blood, only the use of his fists did that and one was never used without the other.

'So you went to church!' He repeated, his voice sour. 'What bloody good do you think that will do!'

Hannah gripped her fingers together but tight as she held them she could not stop them shaking.

'I went because it . . . it helps me feel . . .'

'Feel what!'

Lashing out viciously with his foot he kicked at a small round-topped footstool, sending it crashing against the heavy ornate brass fender that enclosed the hearth.

'Useful?'

The word was barked at her but it was cold and heavy with contempt and Hannah felt the fear of it travel her spine.

'Since when have you been of any use? You dried up after that child was born. You could have no more, what use is a woman who can bear no child! No, you have been no use to me for nigh on twenty years, but that don't be the reason you sit in that church for hours on end. More holy than thou, that is the way it makes you feel. You sit listening to that bloody claptrap and all it does is give you ideas, but they be ideas you best let lie. I be the one you need listen to; and listen well for I tell you, one more whine out of you, one more complaint and I'll have you put where nobody will listen, nobody will place any importance on the ravings of a mad woman.'

For a single moment Hannah recalled the gentle smile on that plaster face. She had to try, try before it was too late. Her fingers twined tightly, twisting into her skirts, and she held the fear of him in her throat.

'And that will make you feel safer, will it, Archer?'

The uncharacteristic poise stopped him in his tracks, and eyes already hard with anger took on the temper of steel as she lifted her head to stare at him.

'Having me locked away from the sight of the world may hide the evil you do, it may keep your terrible secret from the eyes of men but you cannot hide it from the eyes of God. He sees what you do, Archer, He sees and one day He will call you to answer for it.'

'God . . . pah!' His back to the fireplace, legs planted apart, Archer laughed. 'What God? The one that took the life of your son . . . the life of a child . . . am I supposed to be afraid of Him?'

Her own secret deep inside her Hannah continued to stare at the man she had once loved and so quickly learned to fear. He had so easily duped her with his professed passion, but he had not duped her father and that had been the bane of Archer Cranley's life. Her father had placed a limit on the son-in-law he neither liked nor trusted and now the son-in-law could see that limit ending, the power he had long wielded in this house being wiped away.

If her child did not marry within the time called for by the Will then Archer would no longer be master of Briant Bottle and Glass or of Rowlay House. He would no longer be in a position to dominate, his rule of cruelty would be ended, and the child left to them, the one he had hated ever since that dreadful day, would be free of his yoke.

And herself? What of Archer Cranley's cruelty to her? Hannah almost smiled at the thought.

She also would soon be free of his spite, of his blows. She would not suffer for very much longer.

'You would do well to fear the Lord.' She spoke again, softly. 'For He will not be derided nor will He be blind to your lies. The Lord did not take the life of my son, Archer, you did that. Your stupid pride killed one of my children and your greed has all but destroyed the other. But God will not be mocked. Remember His is the vengeance, Archer, and it is a vengeance that will not be thwarted. One day you will be brought to account and the evil that drives you will condemn you, you will be made to pay.'

'So this God you keep calling on, the one you ask for the help that never comes, He is going to send me a bill, is He?' Archer laughed loudly. 'Well, I hope He don't add up the figures too soon for I haven't finished yet and I wouldn't want Him to reckon Himself short.'

'You are the one should not reckon Him short.' Hannah rose, the thinness of her body undisguised by the heavy folds of her gown. 'What you are planning to do is wicked, it is an offence against God and against man and most of all it is an offence against your own child, one you have abused almost from birth. But this is too much, I cannot allow—'

With one stride Archer Cranley was beside his wife, his narrow features drawn with anger, his raised hand coming down in a vicious slap that sent her reeling back into the chair.

'You cannot allow!' he breathed, teeth closed together. 'You cannot allow! Listen to me, woman, you will do as I tell you, same as you have always done. You will say nothing, do nothing unless it is on my instruction. What I choose to do or not to do with my child be my concern and nothing to do with you or that mewling God of yours!' Leaning over her, bringing his face closer to hers while the back of the chair refused to let her draw any further from him, he pulled in a slow breath, warning gleaming like hot coals in his eyes. 'Do you understand?' he asked, his tone one of quiet venom. 'Do you understand?'

A sob her answer, he straightened, feeling dislike thick and acid in his throat. Being married to a pious sow was bad enough but when that sow could produce no other litter . . .

Returning to stand before the fireplace he stared into the room, anger and revulsion mixing his blood to poison. Why had it happened to him, what had he done to deserve such? A child he had loved taken from him. A wife he had never loved draped about his shoulders like a necklace of stone! And it was a necklace had been measured to fit; one he could not easily remove. Her father had known. He had realised the man who asked for his daughter, who had inveigled her into believing he loved her deeply, had held no real love for her. He had recognised the true polarity of Archer Cranley's feeling, knowing it was money and the greed for it that had motivated his proposal of marriage.

Looking at her now huddled in the chair, hands to her face,

he felt the long years of frustration drum a bitter beat in his pulses. Nathan Briant had allowed him to feel the power of that money, to know the headiness it could give, but the money itself he had not given. He had taken steps to safeguard all that his daughter would inherit. Briant Bottle and Glass was to be hers only *until such time as a male child, born of her body, shall reach the age of twenty-one years.*

Archer remembered the words of the Will in their entirety. He had said them over to himself until they had become engraved across his soul. Her father's business would be his to administer with an executor. Should there be no son, then on the death of his daughter business and house were to be sold and the proceeds, together with every last penny bound up in that business, were to go to charity.

Charity! Archer's pulses beat savagely. Since when had Nathan Briant had a single charitable bone in his body? No, it was not charity that man had in mind but vengeance. Nathan's own revenge was what the selling of Briant Bottle and Glass would serve: revenge on his daughter for taking Cranley as a husband, and on Cranley himself for his ill-conceived greed.

And he, Archer Cranley, had been trapped by it, held by words that might have been forged from iron. It had been devised cunningly. Briant had thought well and long. Should his daughter die before the said son then the estate in its entirety would revert to the sole administration of the executor until the boy reached the age written.

Archer felt cold hate tighten the muscles of his body, jerking him like a puppet on strings. The necklace had been locked tight but that did not mean the lock could not be picked.

Swallowing the distaste that filled his mouth whenever he looked at the thin pale figure of his wife he strode to the bedroom door. Throwing it open he shouted, 'I know you be bloody listening. Tell Philip I want to see him . . . now.'

'Philip is not home.' Dressed once more in her usual brown

skirts Edna Cranley strode into the room, her mouth drawn tight.

'Not at home!' Archer swung to face her. 'What do you mean, he don't be home? It's only half-past four, he won't be gone back to the works yet.'

'He did not come home for his break—'

'Didn't come back!' Archer barked. 'Why the bloody hell not?'

'It is a long walk, he said he would take his meal on the heath.'

Edna glanced at the scarlet weal spread across Hannah's cheek, then at her brother. What had happened to drive him into this latest temper?

'I left word the figures for the month were to be gone over while he was home this afternoon.'

'Well, he didn't come home!' Edna's eyes returned her brother's fire.

'I told Philip there was no need to come home at midday.' Hannah's voice shook as she spoke. 'Philip makes that journey so as to spend time with me but I am hardly ever awake, so I thought . . .'

Laced with contempt Archer's glance swept over the trembling figure.

'You thought!' he ground. 'You don't have that need for to think; by Christ, if wit were shit you'd be constipated!'

'I . . . I'm sorry.' Hannah dropped her head.

'Sorry!' The words like gravel in his throat, Archer's hand curled into fists. 'That's all you ever be. But then you don't be as sorry as me, sorry I be saddled with a wife that be worse than useless and a child . . . a child that should have died in place of the other!'

'And where were you when I came home?' Archer swung his glance to the watching Edna. 'Not in this room where you should be!'

Edna's look was contemptuous. 'Everybody has to piddle, Archer, even you.'

'But you weren't just off to piddle!' Archer barked again. 'You was off to see your long-lost love, leaving Hannah alone in the house.'

'I visit Richard's grave every week,' Edna replied coldly. 'Why should this week be any different?'

'Why! I'll tell you why. Cos every other week you don't go out until you see that laudanum has done its work, but this time you didn't, did you . . . did you?'

'I saw her into her nightgown and abed . . .'

'You didn't see her asleep!' Archer kicked viciously at the leg of Hannah's chair.

'So maybe I didn't. Why the fuss?'

His nostrils widening as he drew a calming breath, he stared at his sister. The bitch was a thorn in his side . . . a thorn he would soon extract.

'The fuss, Edna, is this.' He breathed again deeply. 'Hannah thought to take herself out, my wife has been to church.'

'That's nonsense.' Edna flicked a hand dismissively. 'What makes you think she has been out of the house? If it is because of her dress then let me tell you she often dresses herself once she wakes.'

'Only this time she didn't sleep. You didn't wait to see her swallow that potion. Look at her shoes. It rained little over an hour ago, the heath is muddy when it rains.'

What had she done with that laudanum? Edna glanced at her sister-in-law's boots, boots caked with mud.

'Yes, Edna, she has been out –' eyes heavy with threat glared at her '– and you had better do as she says she has done, you had better pray, Edna, pray that church is the only place she has been.'

The door closing behind Edna he rounded again on Hannah.

'I won't tell you again,' he breathed. 'Interfere with my orders just one more time and it will be your last action in this house. Tomorrow afternoon Philip will work on those figures.'

Stepping close he brought a hand smashing down on the arm of her chair. 'What I say will be done *will* be done, by both of you!'

Drawing a lace-edged handkerchief from the pocket of her dress Hannah stared at the square of flimsy lawn.

'When the work you set is finished, can Philip and I sit in the garden?'

'No, you bloody well can't!' He swung away, kicking angrily at the fender. 'Were it left to you he would be as soft as muck.'

'Were it left to me Philip would be allowed—'

'Shut your mouth!' Small ferret-bright eyes blazing, mean lips rolling inwards, leaving no sign of their existence, nostrils flared with rage, Archer Cranley spun round to face his wife. 'Shut your bloody mouth!'

His voice dropping to a hiss, hands balling into fists, he stared at the woman he resented to a point of hatred.

'Never say that, you hear? Never *ever* say that, for if you do I swear I'll kill you, you *and* your bloody child! You will do better to say nothing at all, for every time you open your mouth you irritate me!'

Drawing the soft cloth of the handkerchief through her fingers Hannah Cranley looked up at the man she had married twenty-five years before. Would she have stayed with him given any choice? But choice had been denied her. Married to him she had become the property of Archer Cranley, her life his to direct as he desired, just as the life of their child was his to order, his to destroy.

The tie had been made and now it was a tie she could not break, the tie of love for her child. Archer had destroyed her life. The thought rang in her mind. Cruelty and arrogance had been his weapons, the weapons he would go on using unless . . . A spark that had not shown in her sad eyes for many years flickered slowly into life.

'No, Archer,' she said quietly. 'It is not the words *I* speak which irritate you, it is the words my father wrote. You see his business slipping from your grasp. Soon the time set will be up and you will no longer have charge of Briant Bottle and Glass. No doubt had my father not made the proviso of that business reverting to the care of his executor should I die before that due limit then my time would have been up long ago. A little thing like a woman's life would never be allowed to stand in your way, would it?'

Her eyes steady, fear of him showing only in the short nervous breaths that jerked from her throat, Hannah watched the fury mount like red flags to his face. She knew the risk she was taking, the physical pain of the beating that would follow, the mental torture of his threats against the child. They had always been the tactics Archer Cranley used, the method of drowning her every attempt to alter his plans. The pain of the former she could stand but his threats against Philip, the thought of what might happen . . .

That had always stayed her hand. Hannah drew a long deep breath. But now time was too short, Archer would do the evil thing that was present in his mind, do it and damn her child to purgatory unless . . .

Holding her breath for a trembling moment she went on, 'For twenty-five years you have been the power at that glass-works, men have run to your beck and call. My father knew that was all you really cared for, position and a sense of power. But to get it you had to take me, and it seems he also thought me of only finite worth. Twenty-one years of worth. But in a short time now you will lose that power, you will be little more than you were when my father tied you to me. You bargained with the devil, Archer, now he must be paid!'

'Yes, you would have died!' The hiss was low and threatening as a cobra's. 'You would have died and I would have had a son worthy to be called a man instead of that worthless, puerile . . .'

'Worthless?' The spark still alight in her eyes, Hannah continued to stare at him. 'Surely not. You have found a way our child can be of great worth . . . to you! But take care, Archer, your intentions have not yet been realised, what you have so carefully planned has not yet taken place.'

'But it will!' He stepped towards her, his face twisted with rage, his fist large and hard against her mouth. 'By Christ, it will, or neither of you will see another day!'

# Chapter Fourteen

'Look, lad, you can't go on like this, best let me tell that father o' your'n so.'

Leaning against the wall of the packing shed Philippa closed both eyes against light that after the gloom of the cone grabbed a person's eyeballs.

'He'll see you ain't meant for labour such as this.'

'No.' Squinting in the strong daylight she looked at the face of the works' chargehand, seeing his creased brow furrowed deeper with concern. 'I just need to rest then I will be all right.'

'You won't be all right.' Samuel Platt shook his head. 'You be near to all out, anybody can see as much; you go on as you be doin' and you be like to kill yourself.'

There would be no sadness in that, except for Hannah Cranley no one would mourn. The thought bitter, Philippa wiped the dust-crusted neck cloth over brow and cheeks.

'You had my father's order, Mr Platt, I would work the same hours as any other man here.'

'But you ain't like any other man 'ere! Men 'ere 'ave shifted for theirselves since leavin' the cradle, they was baptised with 'ard work and cut their teeth on labour. Graftin' be mother's milk to this lot, but you . . . you ain't never 'ad to graft for nothing, you ain't never knowed no 'ard work.'

Pushing back his dusty flat cap Samuel Platt stroked a hand over his hair.

'Your father, he don't be realisin' the strength that be needed to work the cone six hours at a stretch, if he did then he'd 'ave you out of it double quick.'

Refastening the neck cloth, pushing the ends beneath her cotton shirt, Philippa sat upright.

'My father is of the belief that in order to run this works properly I must first learn the process of glass-making, every aspect of it. To do that I have to work as other men here do, the same shifts, the same hours; in your own words, Mr Platt, I have to graft.'

Samuel Platt watched the chafed hands knotting the neck cloth, tired half-alive movements of sheer weariness. He was right in what he said, this lad were not fashioned for labour such as this.

'Do your father also 'old the belief that a dead man can run a glassworks? I begs your pardon for speaking out of turn but seein' as it be half-said then I'll go on to speak the rest. This work in the cone, it ain't for you, you must mek your father see that; I can guide and teach all there be to know about the mekin' of glass without you killing yourself in the learning.'

The killing would be the thing most acceptable to Archer Cranley. Philippa shook her head.

'Please understand. I must do as my father thinks best.'

Replacing his cap, pulling it low over his forehead, Samuel Platt glared at the girl come to stand at the entrance to the packing shed.

'Little wenches with big ears often gets 'em smacked, Ginny Morton, but this you can listen to: get back to the bench and tend to your job afore I rattles your tin.'

'A body needs a breath of air!' The girl tossed brown hair flecked with wood shavings.

'A body can get all it needs walking across the 'eath, you can fill your lungs while you be lookin' for another job.'

Meeting the chargehand's glare the girl's thin face broke into a cheeky grin. 'Just winding your spring, Mr Platt.'

'Ar, well, one day you'll overwind and it'll snap.'

Watching the girl wave to Philip the old man allowed his glare to soften as she turned back into the shed.

'Young Ginny'll be a bit of a handful come the time for marryin', the man that takes her to his bed won't 'ave things all his own way.'

'Ginny is a lovely girl and has a lively mind, it is a pity she has to work so hard.'

'Ar, it be a pity, it be a pity we all has to work so hard but at least we was born to it, not like yourself. The hardest thing you've ever been called upon to do is push a pen over a paper, that be right, don't it?'

'Yes.' Philippa nodded, hiding the lie.

'Then 'ow does you expect to do all as others 'ere do? It can't be done . . . not without you payin' the penalty.'

Standing up she tried not to show the pain of aching muscles. 'Then I shall have to pay it, Mr Platt, but I thank you for your concern.'

Thank me for my concern. Samuel Platt walked back into the cone, the blast of hot air almost unnoticed against his lined face. A few more months in this place and Archer Cranley's son would be in no position to thank anybody; Archer Cranley's son would be dead.

'Be you takin' your dinner on the 'eath?'

Philippa turned as Ginny's face appeared round the edge of the packing-shed doorway. Seeing the quick glance towards where the chargehand had gone the girl laughed. 'You don't want to take much notice of old vinegar face, his bark be worse than his bite.'

'You should not test him too far, Ginny, he is in charge here and he could sack you.'

'Gimme me tin! He wouldn't do that.'

'Maybe not but it could prove beneficial not to tempt him.'

'Don't know what that word means,' the girl giggled, her brown eyes gleaming, 'but if you be sayin' it be best not to yank his chain too often then I says you be right, but it be 'ard not to, it be the only bit o' pleasure to be had in this place.'

'An' you knows what preacher Jeffries says about bits o' pleasure, young Ginny, they 'as to be paid for.'

Looking at the men leaving the cone Ginny's answer was quick as her smile.

'That be sins o' the flesh he talks of . . . and Lord, don't he talk! Half of Sunday every week harpin' about sins o' the flesh. Old Mother Bates says he be like a babby blarting for a stick o' suck it can't 'ave.'

'I don't know about a baby cryin' for a twist of barley sugar but I knows a wench who'll be cryin' for her job if Platt cops her canting.'

'Oooh!' Ginny loosed a long breath. 'You be as bad as old Platt you does, Ben 'Arvey: begrudgin' a wench a little chat.'

'You 'as a little chat too many times in a day.' Ben Harvey's grin faded. 'Just take care, Ginny, your mother can scarce do without the coppers you takes 'ome.'

Turning her smile to Philippa the young girl winked. 'Seems everybody 'ere wants to keep we apart so we'll just 'ave to do as always and meet on the 'eath at midnight.'

'That wench be askin' for trouble!' Ben Harvey shook his head despairingly as Ginny returned to her bench, but his grey eyes laughed. 'And it be my bet it be the lad as falls for her will be the one as finds it.'

'I think he will find it worth it.'

'Won't be much use him blartin' if he don't,' another of the men answered Philippa. 'You lies in the bed you meks for yourself unless you wants the 'eat of hell fire 'neath your backside, least so preacher Jeffries says; but like Old Mother Bates I reckons he'd be willin' to risk the flames to 'ave his bed warmed by a pretty wench.'

'Don't go talkin' o' beds and pretty wenches, it don't bide well with a bloke who has a full shift ahead of him.'

'Thinking be all you can do even at the shift end, you can do bugger all *but* think 'til that missis of your'n has given birth! The sins of the flesh, Jake, they prick as 'ard whether you be glassman or preacher.'

Shrugging jacket over bare shoulders Jake Speke joined in the good-natured laughter.

'If you ain't for going 'ome to your meal then why not come 'ave a tankard in the Boat?'

'Boat?' Philippa looked puzzled.

'He means The Narrow Boat.' Jake Speke retied the cloth circling his throat.

'The ale house across the lock there, it be a pleasanter place to eat than in the yard here.'

Following the line Ben Harvey pointed, Philippa hesitated. The heath with its fresh air and solitude seemed infinitely more desirable.

'Ar come along 'o we, a pint of Bill Thomas's best'll set you up for the evenin' shift, you'll work like a hoss after a drop o' brew.'

'We work like hosses as it is.'

Casting a grin at Ben's answer Jake Speke nodded. 'That be right, we does. So I reckons we should count our blessings for hosses get only water to drink.'

Caught up by the men's good nature Philippa could find no way to refuse. Disguising regret behind a smile she followed across the wide oak beam that spanned the lock, trying not to look into the shiny black waters far below. Earliest memories of childhood had featured dark swirling waters, waters that reached for the body of a child, drawing it down beneath the surface, and though the waters in the lock were still and placid they evoked the same nightmare.

Stepping into the tiny bar room of the canal-side inn, the fog of tobacco smoke a cloud above the dozen or so heads, the air thick with the smell of beer, she felt the retch of dislike, but even this was preferable to the dreams that had risen like phantoms from that lock.

'You chooses your company well these days, Harvey . . .'

Conversation in the bar stilled as the voice rose above it.

'. . . and we all knows why. What were given to one can be as easy took from another.'

Placing a sixpenny piece on the counter Ben Harvey took up two frothing tankards, handing one to Jake, the other to Philippa. Turning to pick up the third he looked to where a heavily built man stood a few paces from him, beetle brows scowling over deep-set eyes.

'I always chose my company well, Jukes, that be why you was never among 'em.'

'Oh ar, all o' the glass knows there be no love lost atween we two, same as they all knows an arse-licker when they sees one!'

Ben Harvey's hand tightened on the handle of the tankard.

'And that be what they be seein' now?'

'When they looks at you then that be exactly what they be seein'!' Ned Jukes smirked. 'You, your nose so far up the arse of the gaffer's brat it be 'ard to tell what colour boots you be wearin'.'

'Oh!' Ben glanced at the floor. 'Since you can't see 'em, Ned, then I'll tell you. I be wearin' black boots, 'ere see for yourself.' Jabbing one foot forward he brought it hard against the other man's shin, then as Jukes bent over in pain he grabbed the head beneath its grimy cap, forcing it upright. 'Still can't see the colour? Then let me help you, this'll wipe the shit from your eyes!'

Lifting the tankard he threw the contents full in the twisted face before pushing the heavy figure away.

Dashing the ale from his eyes Ned Jukes threw himself forwards but Ben had already stepped aside.

'That be enough o' that!' The landlord slapped a deadly looking club against the counter.

Breathing heavily, fists opening and closing, Ned Jukes stared at Ben. 'I be going to break your bloody back!'

'Then you does it outside.' The landlord brought the club down expressively, setting tankards rattling.

'You 'ave to go back to the glass, Harvey,' Jukes glared, 'and on the way mek sure your eyes be well peeled, for Ned Jukes will be waitin' on you an' that bloody nancy boy you an' others 'ave teken a shine to; better keep his nose out of it else he be like to find we don't all grovel like Turner.'

'I give the lad my thanks, Ned, it were no more'n right I should after what he done for me and mine.'

'What he done for you and your'n were done for nobody but hisself.' Jukes swung on the man who spoke. 'He 'ad to get hisself accepted . . . what better way forrim and his father to work it than one to give a bloke his tin and the other to 'and it back again? They be playin' a clever 'and do that pair, but it seems none sees the stakes 'cept Ned Jukes.'

'My father had nothing to do with Mr Turner and his family being reinstated.' Philippa's retort was sharp.

'That be what you says 'ere in front of everybody but I'll tek any man's wager it don't be what you says once you be back in that fancy 'ouse along with Cranley.'

'It is the truth—'

'And I for one believes it.' One arm preventing Philippa advancing further towards the ale-soaked Jukes, Ben Harvey's mouth tightened.

'Well you would, seein' as where your nose has been planted since his comin' into the glass.' Jukes snorted. 'We all knows you be lookin' after your own interest whilst you be satisfyin' his.'

'I said that be enough!' Lifting the flap of the counter the landlord stepped through. 'I don't care where you brawl but you don't do it in my 'ouse. Now unless you wants a taste of what I can give with this 'ere club you'll drink your ale quiet like.'

'Remember, 'Arvey, I'll be waitin' for you.'

'What on earth was all that about?' Philippa watched the thick-set figure lurch through the smoke-filled doorway.

'It be an old tale, Mr Cranley—'

'Philip.' Smiling, Philippa turned to the man whose job had been saved. 'Please, the name is Philip.'

'It be an old tale . . . Philip.' Turner nodded, his own smile awkward. 'Ben there 'as a sister that Jukes's eye dropped on but the wench 'ad little liking forrim. Well, to cut the fat from the meat, Ben catched 'im trying to force the wench and . . . let's just say Jukes won't go tryin' no such again, not with Ben's sister anyways; but the 'iding he took ain't never been forgot and Jukes don't be a man to forgive.'

'He could be right, though.' A man standing at the bar sucked on the stem of a yellowed clay pipe. 'About it being a put-up job you being given your tin then 'aving it 'anded back to you like it was. It bears thinking on.' He sucked the pipe again then spat into a brass spittoon. 'Was it the lad's doing and the lad's alone?'

'How do you mean?' Jake Speke took a long pull at his tankard, wiping the back of a hand over his mouth.

'Seems to mek sense, Jake. Ask yourself, if Archer Cranley's son 'olds any true influence 'ow come he be slaving in the cone along wi' the rest? Stands to reason, a bloke wi' any love for 'is lad ain't like to set 'im skivvying six hours on an' six hours off, day an' night.'

The ale in the tankard untouched Philippa set it back on the bar counter. If only they knew! But they never would, for the business of Archer Cranley's feelings for his child were not to be the subject of discussion.

'My father's reasons for setting me to work at the Bottle and Glass are, I would have thought, obvious. As you yourselves set your children to learning the trade that provides their living, so my father has done for me. If you or any other man at the works believes otherwise then that is their prerogative.'

'There be a way to find out which way the wind be blowin'.' Ben Harvey looked from his tankard to the man sucking on his clay pipe. 'Next time old man Cranley be at the works you go ask 'im, then we'd all know the answer.'

Saliva catching in his throat, the other man choked. 'Ask . . . ask old Cranley? Like bloody hell, I will. That'd be the door for me an' you knows it!'

Draining his tankard Ben set it down, signalling for the publican to refill it.

'P'raps it be well if the lad 'ere be put to learn the glass an' nothing more or there might be one or two men collected their tins by this time –' he looked full at the man chewing the pipe stem '– and others set to go the same way . . . and I don't just mean Jukes.'

The pipe moving agitatedly between whiskers heavy with silica dust the man looked anxiously at Philippa, Ben Harvey's message clearly understood.

'Eh, lad, I d'ain't mean . . .'

'You were simply voicing your opinion, we all have the right to do that.' Philippa smiled.

'We 'as the right true enough.' Ben lifted the refilled tankard. 'But when a man's livin' depends on another it sometimes pays to keep that right under your cap.'

Clearly feeling he had spoken out of turn the man looked again at Philippa.

'Like I says, I d'ain't mean no 'arm, lad. Will you tek a tankard just to show there be no 'ard feelings?'

To refuse would be seen as harbouring those very feelings. Disguising reluctance by widening her smile, Philippa accepted.

His own drink finished hurriedly the man tapped the smouldering ash from the bowl of the clay pipe. 'Mustn't stop any longer, the missis'll 'ave the meal on the table an' her'll play merry 'ell if I be late.'

Setting the empty pipe once more between his teeth he knotted the rag about his neck and, with a word to the landlord, was gone.

'Don't let what Caleb said turn you from your ale.' Jake

pressed the first tankard back into Philippa's hand then slapped a coin on the counter, calling for three more of the same.

Her stomach turning at the thought of having to drink more beer, she knew that to refuse would be to offend. It was a mistake to have come, but to be accepted as one of these men meant behaving as they did.

Forcing the liquid past a throat that closed at the very thought was almost impossible and it took every atom of will to hold it down.

'Your round tomorrow . . .'

Ben laid his tankard on the counter as he looked at the figure they all took to be a lad.

'. . . best not tek another tankard or Jake'll sleep past the start of the next shift.'

'Be you sayin' I can't tek my ale?' Jake grinned. 'I can drink you on your back any day of the week, Ben 'Arvey, and still do a good day's work after it.'

Nodding to the landlord Ben led the way out into the clear air. 'Don't be the day that be in question, Jake, it be the night; a few tankards of Bill Thomas's best leaves many a man good for nowt but his bed.'

Stepping onto the heavy beam that operated the lock gates Jake walked across with the casual ease of a man who had used this method of crossing over the canal almost from the time he could walk.

'Ar, but I don't be any man,' he laughed. 'I be Jake Speke, an' therein lies the difference.'

'Reckon that be a good enough explanation.'

Ben stepped onto the narrow ledge of the gates, balancing with the same ease. Behind him Philippa faltered, the mixture of tobacco fumes and ale making her head reel.

'I said I'd be waitin' for you, 'Arvey!'

The shout rang over the water. Philippa's eyes blurred as they lifted. Across the lock a figure waved a short thick branch.

'I said it, d'ain't I, 'Arvey? An' here I be.'

Halfway across the huge gates whose ropes formed an improvised bridge, Harvey came to a standstill while from the other end Jukes grinned savagely.

'Well come on, 'Arvey —' the branch waved again '— where be your bravado now . . . you don't be scared, do you?'

A yard or two from the grinning Jukes, Jake Speke was apologetic.

'I never seen 'im, Ben, there were no sign of 'im when I crossed, he must 'ave been hidin' behind a clump of gorse; but stop you there, I'll soon do for this bastard.'

With her head swimming, Philippa tried to still the ground that swirled with every breath.

'A bloke wi' his brains spread on the ground don't be in no position to do for nobody!'

Her eyes following the shout Philippa blinked, frowning as a figure seemed to sail through the air.

Across the canal Jukes had turned as Jake bent to pick up a stump of branch, bringing his own weapon crashing down on the other man's head, sending him sprawling sidewards.

'You next,' he laughed harshly, already stood once more at the further side of the lock gates, 'you next an' then your little playmate.'

There was no way past Jukes other than a trek along the towpath to Ryder's Green Bridge and no way out of that lock should he fall into it! Ben glanced at the oily waters some fourteen feet below. Placid but deadly they swallowed the light. Once in that he would be a gonner long before he was fished out.

'Well, what you be waitin' on?' Jukes swung the branch, the cut of it whistling through the air.

Even should he walk to the bridge Jukes would shadow him from the other side and he would still have to get past that branch.

Reasoning the situation in his mind Ben cast around for a means of fighting back.

A raucous laugh greeting the move, Jukes bellowed again. 'I asked you, 'Arvey . . . what you be waitin' on?'

'He be waiting for you to move, Jukes, and so am I!' Unseen by the men concentrating on Jukes, Joshua Fairley walked across the stretch of heath.

Shouts and figures dancing together, drawing senses into their own whirligig, Philippa swayed with them.

Turning at the voice that had not spoken until now, Ron Jukes sneered. 'You be waitin' to pass do you, Josh Fairley? Then you just gonna 'ave to wait.'

'I have no mind to wait.'

'You 'ear that, 'Arvey?' Glancing to where Ben had stepped onto the operating beam, Jukes grinned, the branch clutched in his hand waving ominously. 'You 'ear that? Josh Fairley be wantin' to be across the cut; you be in 'is way.'

Looking past the figure stood on the beam Josh saw Philippa sway. The bloody fools . . . they'd got the lad worse for drink. Mouth tightening, he brought his glance back to the sneering face. 'It's not Harvey that's in my way, it's you . . . I ask you to step aside.'

'I don't give a bugger what you asks!' Jukes roared. 'I'll shift when I be ready to shift, not when some arsehole says for me to do it.'

Across the ribbon of water he saw Philippa stumble towards the beam, any moment she would step onto it . . . or miss and drop into the lock. Not wanting to look away from the swaying figure but knowing Jukes would not move of his own accord, Josh tensed.

'Not *some* arsehole, Jukes,' he breathed, 'THIS arsehole!'

Moving like greased lightening he shot forwards, tackling Jukes to the ground. Almost as quickly the other two were with him, pinning the struggling figure beneath them.

'Listen to me!' One hand gripping the chin of the spluttering Jukes, Josh glared into the maddened eyes. 'You and me had a set-to once before and you didn't come out of it any too well as I remember, so listen carefully: if you and me have one more set-to then you won't come out of it at all!'

Grabbing the dropped branch Josh flung it away.

'Christ Almighty! Josh, look at that!'

Following the direction of Ben's glance Josh caught his breath.

Halfway across the heavy beam Philippa Cranley's foot slipped over the edge.

# Chapter Fifteen

Halfway along John's Lane Naomi turned onto the rutted cart track that led to the farm. There had been no other body passed her since coming off the Horsley Road and no man working the fields or pastures bordering her path, but nor had there been sight of Keziah Silk.

'Let her be to 'ome,' Naomi whispered quietly to herself.

Set in front of the tiny cottage a mass of flowers bent and swayed, a dancing breeze ruffling gorgeously coloured petals and cool-green leaves. Keziah's garden had the ordering of no hand, each plant taking its choosing where it would grow, but it was always beautiful.

Standing with a hand on the gate that hung drunkenly from one hinge Naomi let her gaze wander over the cacophony of colour.

Stately peach-petalled delphiniums lorded it over brilliant spikes of snapdragon; heavy-headed opium poppies spread grey-green leaves to touch the pixie-hat blooms of aquilegia with a superior hand; while purple clematis and full-bodied white roses spread voluptuously around the door, draping themselves beneath thatched eaves.

But there was more than simply wild beauty here in this patch of ground wrested from the heath. Here Keziah grew many herbs and plants whose uses or dangers had long been lost to the women working the glass or the coal pits; but their benefits were remembered and many a foot trod the path that led to this door.

'I been a waitin' of your coming, Naomi Fairley.'

Quiet as the voice was, it startled Naomi. Fingers clutching the top bar of the gate she looked round. Stood between tall bushes of mulberry and elder Keziah Silk's small figure was almost lost among her plants.

Naomi felt the woman's eyes on her, saw the glance that skimmed her taut fingers. Keziah Silk was old but her senses were sharp.

'You'll need to bide for to ask your question.'

Keziah stepped forward. Shoulders bent from years spent gathering plants, skirts wide and black, she looked like some huge hooded bird. Adding a handful of marigold flowers to the assortment already in the trug she carried, she glanced again at the woman stood at the gate.

'A sup of tea helps with the asking, thought it don't always be of help in the swallerin' of the answer. Will you be taking that tea, Naomi Fairley?'

It was more than an invitation to take a cup of tea, it was a warning that what she was about to ask may not receive the answer she looked for. But she had come this far. Naomi pushed the gate aside, the creak of rusted hinges loud on the quiet afternoon. She would not forgo the asking now.

Following the older woman into the tiny sun-filled kitchen she waited while the trug was placed in the scullery.

'Will I brew the tea?'

Keziah Silk's bright eyes rested for a moment on the tired-looking face. 'I be able yet to brew my own pot.'

It would have been easier having something to occupy her fingers if not her mind, Naomi thought, watching the bent figure lift kettle to teapot; something to stop her mind travelling the path whose only end was one of more worry, of more not knowing.

Tiny pink glass beads dangled from a linen cover set over a pretty china jug, tinkling against its sides as it was placed on the table between them. Adding milk to her cup then waiting until the other woman was settled at the rickety table, she said, 'I be wanting to ask—'

Lifting her cup, Keziah's sharp glance softened. 'I knows what it is you be wanting to ask, and I tell you there be no pill will ease the soreness from your heart and I have no potion that will rid your soul of the worm that be nibbling it.'

'I did not come for pills or potions.'

'I knows that, too.' Keziah nodded. 'Same as I knows you came here seeking the Tarot, seeking to be told of your son. But you have sought the cards afore, you be familiar with the ways of them, they speaks of one that lays their hand and will tell of no other. A man's business be his own . . .'

'Not when it be worrying a mother to the grave!'

Taking several sups of tea Keziah set her cup down. 'You knows the ways,' she answered quietly.

'Yes.' Naomi nodded, regretting her outburst. 'But I be near my wits' end with the thought that be in my mind day and night, the thought of my lad and . . .'

'Say no word of that to me.' Keziah's look sharpened again. 'If you still be of a mind I will spread the Tarot but it will answer only that which is for your knowing; and remember, seek not to fool the cards for they won't be fooled.'

Seeing her visitor's nod she went to the ancient dresser, taking a box from one drawer. Laying a pack of cards face-down on the table she looked at Naomi.

'Lay your hand to them and ask in the silence of your heart what it is you be here to ask.'

Touching the cards Naomi closed her eyes, the whole of her soul yearning to be given the comfort she sought.

'Divide them,' Keziah instructed as she looked up once more.

Following the ritual she separated the large cards into three groups then gathered them up again, central group first then right hand to left hand before spreading the whole, fan shaped, across the table.

Slowly, her shaking hand hesitating over each move, she drew ten, pushing them, still face-down, towards Keziah.

The selection made the old woman gathered the remaining cards to one side.

'The question be asked, the answer be sought.'

Speaking as much to the ten cards as to the woman sat opposite whose tense fingers were clutched together, she turned the first six cards, placing them in the form of a cross, laying the final four, faces to the table, in a vertical column to the right.

Through the small-paned window sunlight touched the grey head with gold and Naomi felt her breath catch. It was as if something else touched the woman, something that drew her into itself, whose own whispered voice began to speak.

'This be the centre of your questioning.' One finger rested on a card portraying a man wearing a crown and holding a sceptre. 'You know the one it tells of, he be honest and conscientious.' She moved the finger. 'But this speaks of you. You fear a trap, a tempting that will be too strong, you fear a profane love, an unholy love.'

Her throat tightening yet more, Naomi stared at the cards as if mesmerised. How could pieces of paper tell Keziah what she had not dared tell to herself?

'You see the future as this card shows.' She touched the picture of a tower struck by lightening. 'You see it as holding misery and that will be so, for as the next tells, your heart dwells on scandal and disgrace.'

Caught as Keziah was in that strangeness that had held her at its centre, Naomi was uncertain whether the choking gasp of her own breath reached her, whether it told of the bands of fear squeezing her heart at the words that seemed to hold nothing of which she hoped, as the woman turned the second of the four cards that remained with their faces hidden. The devil! Naomi's nails bit into her palms. The card of evil!

'There be shock for you and a ravaging of the heart,' the quiet voice went on. 'You will know pain. You will be in bondage to your own fears; insecurity and disquiet of the mind will plague the days that lie ahead.'

Was there to be no hope? Watching the turning of the final card Naomi felt the world crashing about her. She had come seeking reassurance, some thread however fine that would lead her to knowing her son was not crossing the line which marked that which was unacceptable to heaven, taking part in that which should not be between men.

Turning the card Keziah let her hand fall onto it as if to hide the figure of the skeleton wielding a scythe.

Lifting a hand to her mouth, Naomi pressed her knuckles hard against her lips, stifling back a cry. It was the card of death.

Across the table Keziah lifted her head and for a single moment a blaze of sunlight seemed to shine from her face, a radiance that wiped away all signs of age, exchanging them for a clear beauty. Then, as quickly, it faded and she looked again at that last card, her voice when she spoke as quiet as before.

'There will be a parting, a passing of what be. You'll look into the very face of fear and despair will claim your soul. There be change, it stands close, change that will take that you cherish most—'

'Stop!' Thrusting out a hand Naomi swept the cards together. 'I can't hear no more, Keziah, I can't.'

Gathering the pack together and returning them to the box, Keziah shoved them quickly back inside the drawer, glancing towards the window as she pushed it shut. There were those who would see a body gaoled for reading the cards.

'I couldn't be altering what the Tarot said.' Keziah looked sympathetically at the woman sat twisting her fingers in and out of each other. 'I knows it weren't what you be wanting to hear but I can only tell what be there and you should have heard to the end.'

Naomi sniffed back her tears. 'I knows that well, Keziah, but there be just so much a body can stand. My Joshua be all I has in life and if he goes wrong—'

'Say no more of the lad!' Keziah interrupted sharply. 'His business be not for my ears lessen he bring it here hisself. I knows it be 'ard for you, wench, watching him walk in the ways of his choosing. But this I can tell you: take your heartbreak to the Lord, ask His help in your troubles. He'll not turn His back to you nor keep His hand from you. Pray to Him, Naomi, and He will keep evil from your door.'

Pray! Hurrying back along the narrow farm track, Naomi pulled her knitted shawl about her head. Wasn't that what she had been doing these weeks past?

Tears she had held now spilled softly down her cheeks. The sins of the flesh! They had ever been a man's downfall . . . and her son was to be no different!


'God Almighty, Josh, he be goin' over!'

Jake Speke glanced towards the canal as Ben Harvey pointed but Josh was already on his feet. Quicker than he had ever moved before he hurled himself onto the broad beam with which the lock gates were opened and closed. Ahead of him, as if in slow motion, the arms of the toppling figure stretched wide and the white face turned up to him, a terrible sadness in the blue eyes.

Not hearing his own desperate cry, Josh threw himself across the intervening space. Reaching for a flailing arm it seemed his own body was held by a force stronger than himself, that seemed to keep him suspended, floating slowly in mid-air. Still a distance from him the white face smiled as the figure fell sidewards over the edge of the lock. His second cry soundless in his own ears, Josh dived forwards, his body sprawling heavily across the beam, the breath knocked from his lungs, his arms jerked almost free of their sockets as one hand closed over the beam's low iron rail, the other fastening about the wrist of the falling figure.

'Hold him, Josh . . . for God's sake hold him!'

The struggling Jukes forgotten, Ben Harvey raced across the beam. Jumping to one side of Josh, dropping flat on his stomach, he grabbed the dangling figure. 'I be with you, Josh, ready when you be.'

'Now.' Josh loosed a relieved breath. 'Get him out now.'

Pulling together they dragged the still figure slowly onto the beam, grinning at each other as it lay safely slumped across it.

'That were a near thing an' no mistake.'

'Too near, Ben, much too near.' The answer came on a ragged breath. 'Let's get him onto the towpath.'

Loosing the hand rail Josh rose to his feet. Balancing the unconscious figure between them the two men inched slowly across the yawning black void of the lock.

'Where the 'ell was you, Speke?'

Holding the slim figure against him, Josh smiled grimly. 'He was there, but seems Ned Jukes has been at his old tricks.'

'The bastard!' Ben swore loudly as he looked at his friend lying motionless on the grass verging the narrow towpath. 'I'll do for that swine, just see if I don't!'

Laying Philippa gently on the ground Josh cautioned, 'Best not move him, he's bleeding badly. One of us needs to go back to the works for help, Jake is going to need a stretcher.'

'I'll go, you still be winded from chucking yourself onto that beam. Is there anything else?'

Glancing up at Ben, Josh nodded. 'Tell Sam Platt there's been an accident with Phil— with the lad, that he should be sent home.'

'I'll tell him.' Ben was already sprinting in the direction of the glassworks, 'and I'll tell 'im there be another bugger going to meet wi' an accident once I finds 'im!'

Ben's running figure now almost out of sight, Josh sank to his knees, a weight heavy as a lead shroud enveloping the whole of him. Slipping off his jacket he rolled it into a pillow, setting it beneath Jake's head, but his mind was on the other man. Philip, he could so easily have fallen into the lock, so easily have been sucked beneath those dark waters.

Shuddering at the thought Josh stared at the still face,

translucent lids closed over eyes that had been filled with an unspeakable sadness.

'Philip,' he whispered drawing the slight figure into his arms, the touch of it against his bare chest sending rivers of flames along every vein. 'Philip, I thought you gone.'

His brain saying to lay the boy down, that the emotions burning through him were wrong, Josh's arms tightened. This was what he wanted each time he walked the lad to Rowlay House, each time their glances met in the cone. It was wrong, God help him he knew it was wrong! But this was the only chance he would ever get to feel that body against his.

Why had this happened to him? Never in his life had he felt this way, not for any girl and certainly not for another man. He had tried to fight it, fight off the thoughts that crept with him into sleep; he always woke with a feeling of guilt for the dreams that came unbidden yet somehow welcome. He had told himself of the heartbreak his mother would suffer should she ever know of the feeling he harboured for Philip Cranley; but she would never know, no one would ever know. But for this one moment he could live those dreams, hold the one that beckoned in the hours of sleep, the one that in the privacy of his heart smiled back the tenderness he felt.

His nerves jarring, Josh stared out across the heath. It was true. He felt more for Philip Cranley than any man should feel for another. He was in love with Philip Cranley! But the whole thing was ludicrous, madness! A sweet madness that was poison to a man's soul. Nothing could come of it, nothing but the mockery of the men he worked with, a turning away of the folk he had lived among, their disgust and recriminations making outcasts of him and his mother.

Sodom! A picture of the chapel minister launching into his favourite sermon filled Josh's mind. *Men who followed after the ways of evil would perish in the flames of the Lord's wrath! He would wipe away the scourge of the unclean.*

But what was in his heart did not feel unclean, did not feel evil; it felt right, felt as if every part of him sang of its pureness. With Philip Cranley in his arms Joshua Fairley's world was bathed in light. And what of Philip's life? The thought brought a coldness in its wake. What of the mockery and derision, the scorn and finger-pointing that would be turned upon him? The lad did not deserve that. Not by any word or action had he shown anything but the most ordinary of friendship, his smile or word being no more than he showed to any other man in the cone. He had not asked for such feeling, for such a love.

Touching a hand to the wheat-coloured hair, shining despite a film of silica dust, Josh felt the heart inside of him shrivel. Philip Cranley had not asked for his love and he would never speak of it. The lad he held in his arms would soon be his employer, as far above him as was possible in Greets Green. Drowned in that lock or here safe in his arms, Philip Cranley was lost to him.

The thought tearing the soul from him, Josh touched his lips to the pale face.

'Now that be what I calls real touchin'. It fair pulls at a man's 'eart. But it don't be your 'eart that one pulls, do it, Fairley? We both knows what bit it is as young Cranley plays on, or should I say plays with?'

His head lifting sharply, Josh glanced across the canal. Stood on the opposite side of the lock Ned Jukes grinned.

# Chapter Sixteen

'What the bloody hell brought you being in that beer house!'

His narrow features flushed with the heat of anger, Archer Cranley brought a fist hard down on the wide-topped desk.

'I was invited.' Philippa's head throbbed with the after-effects of ale.

'You was invited!' Archer sneered, not bothering to lower his tone. 'I suppose you was invited to throw yourself into that lock an' all.'

'I slipped, Father. The beam was greasy.'

'You slipped right enough; but it were no grease that took your balance, it were ale, you were drunk!'

'No, Father.' She winced at the pain throbbing at each temple.

'Don't bloody tell me no!' Archer thundered, staring at the face that still held no colour. 'You was drunk as a fiddler's bitch! Sam Platt had to have you carried into this house.'

Philippa drew a deep breath, fighting the nausea that rose again and again. 'I am sorry, Father, I did not think—'

'That be the trouble with everybody in this house!' Archer turned from the desk, kicking at a chair as he strode to the fireplace. 'I be the only one with any brain, I needs to do the thinking for all of you.'

'It will not happen again. I shall apologise to Mr Platt for the trouble I caused him.'

'Too bloody true it won't happen again!' The words shot like bullets from the thin lips. 'An' you'll do no apologising to any man as works for me; not that Platt, nor them you stood drinking yourself stupid with works for me any more.'

'What do you mean?' Philippa's head jerked round despite the sharp ripple of pain.

His black ferret eyes gleaming, Archer met the question with a cold smile. 'I means what I've said. Platt and the others be finished in the glass, they had their tins this afternoon.'

Sacked! She stared unbelievingly at the man straddling the hearth. He had taken away the living of those men with no more concern than breaking a dead flower from its stalk, men who had acted out of naught but friendship.

'Why? Why did you sack them?'

Coming bluntly, accusation underlying every syllable, it took Archer by surprise.

'Why?' he echoed, recovering his bullish attitude. 'Cos I bloody well felt like it that's why.'

Not to be put off by the flash of anger that had not left her father's mouth or eyes Philippa replied, 'Did you give them their tins because of me?'

'Because of you . . . because you couldn't hold your ale and had to be hauled out of that lock! It be nearer the truth to say I sacked 'em cos they *did* haul you out. Had they left you to drown as your brother drowned then I'd have given twenty sovereigns apiece. Now go get changed into some decent clothes, we have a visit to make to Joseph Lacy.'

So there had been no change of plan. Philippa continued to stare at the narrow features, the mouth drawn tight. The distress in Hannah's face when the subject of marriage with Davinia Lacy had been broached had been evident; but with her husband's threat, one Philippa knew he would not hesitate to carry out, it had been useless to argue.

'Don't sit there like a mawkin, I said for you to change your clothes!'

Maybe there was nothing for it but to meet with the Lacys, though there was something could be done for Samuel Platt, Jake Speke and Ben Harvey. Ignoring the steady beat of pain behind her eyes she gave a quick shake of the head. 'No, Father, I have no wish to meet Joseph Lacy.'

'What?' Archer's maddened roar swept around the room. 'What do you mean?'

Behind the façade of ease Philippa almost laughed. But, hiding the smile, she deliberately repeated the words Archer had flung only moments ago.

'I mean what I've said. I have no wish to meet with Joseph Lacy.'

As his eyes folded back beneath half-closed lids, Archer Cranley's mouth took on a vicious twist. 'You have no bloody wish . . .'

'Correct, Father.' Philippa remained calm. 'Neither, for that matter, have I any inclination to meet with his daughter.'

'Inclination!' Archer's little eyes seemed to grow smaller. 'Who the bloody hell cares whether you has inclinations or not!'

'You, Father,' she answered quietly. 'Or at least you should if you wish that meeting ever to take place.'

Watching the shades of temper chase across the tightly drawn face Philippa recognised the danger of that ultimatum. The future of two people hung in the balance. Yes, Archer Cranley would condemn wife and child to an institution, if not to achieve the goal he sought, then for revenge.

'What does that mean?'

'It's really quite simple. You reinstate those men or you tell Joseph Lacy the deal you have cooked up between you is off.'

'Do you realise what you be saying, what I can do to you . . . to your mother?'

Archer's words slithered between set teeth, his black eyes

spitting venom, and for a moment Philippa's resolve faltered but as a look of triumph glittered the hesitation faded.

'I realise very well, just as I realise that once you have what you want my mother will still not be safe from your spite; as for myself, I ceased to care long ago.'

'That be easy said.' Archer laughed caustically. 'But once you sees inside of an asylum you'll wish you'd said different.'

Rising from the chair she nodded. 'Most probably you are correct yet again, Father, but then it will be too late for both of us. I will have lost my freedom and you will have lost my inheritance, and all for the sake of the jobs of those three men. Is it worth it, Father . . . is it?'

Anger working his mouth Archer wrestled with the desire to strike out at the figure facing him defiantly. It was a stance being taken too often. If he could just implement that letter now, have them both shut away! But what had been said was fact; lock Philip away now and the business could never be his, the signature of a man considered mentally incapable . . . !

Turning his back hid the look of chagrin but could not erase the anger from Archer's tone. 'I'll get word to Platt, he can set the others on again.'

'Thank you, Father.' Philippa walked from the study. At least those men had been helped; but Hannah Cranley, how could the cloud that darkened her life be removed?

They could go away together. Philippa scooped cold water over a throbbing brow. They could slip away one night when Archer was away from the house. And go where? Money had always been meticulously kept from Philip Cranley and there was no journey could be taken or lodging given without payment; the workhouse was the only place for the destitute. The workhouse! As she lifted a dripping face to the mirror it seemed the crystal drops fell like tears. Not there! Never there! Hannah Cranley would not end her days in that place. But to avoid it was to consent to that marriage, to go through with Archer Cranley's devious proposals. Yet there had to be a way, there *must* be a way to circumvent the malignity of that man.

Dressed in crisply starched white shirt and dark trousers she passed a comb through wheaten hair that brushed the collar of a grey alpaca jacket.

There had to be a way. But until that way were found the sinister dance of evil must go on.

'Samuel Platt given his tin!' Astounded by what her son had told her Naomi Fairley stared.

'Him and two others.' Josh nodded. 'Jake Speke and Ben Harvey, all three sacked for getting the lad home drunk.'

'Be that all it was?'

'What other reason can there be?' Josh looked up at his mother stood with the kettle in her hands. 'They've always given a good day's work.'

'That nobody can argue with, but to get the lad drunk, they should 'ave had more sense; it be no wonder Cranley sacked 'em, the cone be no place for a lad with a stomach full of Bill Thomas's ale.'

The cone was no place for Philip at any time. Josh dropped his glance, knowing the thought must show in his eyes.

'I agree they shouldn't have taken him but it wasn't done with the intent of having him the worse for drink.'

Returning the kettle to the bracket, Naomi stared at the glowing coals beneath it. 'How many of us have intent for much that happens in life; and how many times do we wish it never had, yet never do anything to rectify it?'

Sharp as an arrowhead the softly spoken words pricked at Josh's conscience. He had never intended the feeling he held for Philip Cranley, the whole thing was guilt to his soul, yet what had he done to rectify that guilt? Nothing, he had done nothing! He could have told his mother . . . he could tell her now, she would understand, even be glad should he leave Greets Green.

Yet still that force which was stronger than himself kept locked its invisible chains.

' 'Tis the wives of them men I feels for, it'll be no easy thing keeping bread in the mouths of their babes. As for Bella Platt, it be naught but the herb woman's potions keeps her alive but they'll 'ave no strength against her man's losing his job . . . Ehh!' She turned, her head shaking slowly. 'It were a bad day when Cranley's lad come to the cone.'

'This is none of Philip's doing, it is not his fault.' The words were out before he could stop them. Too late, Josh saw the understanding and the pain, the sadness and the anger well deep in his mother's eyes.

'And your feelings, Josh, your feelings for him, feelings that be wrong, ones any man be shamed to 'ave, be they none of Philip Cranley's doing, be they none of his fault?'

There had been no need to tell his mother. Josh dropped his head into his hands. She had guessed. But how long had she known, and who else had guessed his secret? His voice holding all the anguish of guilt, he answered quietly, 'Philip knows nothing of how I feel nor has he ever shown anything but ordinary friendship for me.'

'Then end it, end it now!' Setting the pot she held on the table Naomi wrapped her arms about her son. 'End it afore it becomes too strong. It may be the lad don't 'ave feelings for you or could be he ain't showed 'em yet, but either way you be in peril of following after the devil, he will use that which torments you to drag you on, to destroy you, ar and the Cranley lad an' all should this get abroad.'

Taking the hands that cradled him Josh pressed them to his mouth. 'It won't get abroad, Mother, no one but you will ever know.'

'Then you'll leave Greets Green, make a new start some-wheres else?'

Leave Greets Green! The very words were a lance in his heart. But the pain of it did not come from the thought of leaving this house or the only life he knew, it came from the thought of never again seeing that pale gentle smile or those deeply blue eyes with their haunted, almost helpless, look, of never again seeing Philip Cranley.

Still holding the worn hands between his own Josh met his mother's pleading gaze. 'No.' He shook his head again. 'To go leaving Greets Green would be to take this feeling with me. I would live with it for the rest of my life. Don't you see, Mother, that would be like living in hell. I know what is inside me is wrong but it is something I must face, it will not be cured by running away. For your sake and for Philip's, as well as for my own, I have to defeat it, drive it out of my system for good and all. I won't do that by turning my back.'

And if he couldn't defeat it, couldn't wrest the thoughts from his mind, the desire from his heart, couldn't turn his back, what then?

Freeing her hands of his Naomi turned back to the task of making the afternoon meal. Did he think the village would turn a blind eye, that folk hereabout would accept such unnatural goings on? And then there was Archer Cranley. He wasn't one to stand by while a lad of his were . . .

Naomi's hand flexed tight around the home-made loaf as her mind turned from the word, but she could not stem the tide that carried the flotsam of her empty dreams, the debris of so many broken hopes.

Archer Cranley. The name broke in on her again. His was the influence of money and money wielded many axes. What would happen to Joshua should that man discover the feelings he harboured, just what would he do? Something, that was certain; and whatever it was could he truly be blamed, for what father would stand by while his son became wife to another man?

Her mouth tight against the hurt that burned like a brand on her heart, she ladled broth into a bowl. The Tarot had spoken of one who was honest and conscientious and that her son had always been. But where was his conscience now? He had owned to the wrongness of his association with Cranley's lad, yet refused to turn from it.

'*You fear a trap, a tempting that will be too strong.*'

Keziah's reading of the picture cards echoed loud in her mind. Did Philip Cranley know, was it an evil in his mind had turned his eyes to her son, had the snare that held Joshua been deliberately set?

'*a tempting that will be too strong.*'

Her son! Naomi's hand trembled and she wanted to cry out against the picture that formed in her mind's eye, the picture of her son lying with another man!

'Philip, there is something I feel I must say to you despite your father's saying you should not hear it.'

In the closeness of the carriage Edna Cranley's essence of rosewater had a cloying aroma.

'This is going to be hard to say.' As she fished a handkerchief from a beaded bag the movement wafted waves of the cheap scent around the carriage, the effect irritating Archer's nose so he sneezed several times. Reaching for his own handkerchief with one hand while guiding the carriage with the other, he answered testily, 'Then don't say it. Surely for once in your life you can hold your tongue.'

'Philip should be told, otherwise the shock . . .' Edna held the lace-edged linen to her mouth.

'Philippa's head turned towards the woman sniffing affectedly. Neither she nor her brother had ever had concern about anything they'd said before, so why the elaborate pretence, for pretence it must be.

'If there is anything you feel I should know then say it.'

Edna heard the coldness in the voice, felt the animosity in the way the words were spoken and inside she smiled. Philip Cranley was another with whom she would one day settle scores. Holding the handkerchief to the side of her mouth she went on, 'Today your mother was examined by a doctor brought in at my request. He is a physician specialising in . . . in diseases of the lungs—'

'Mother mentioned nothing of this when I saw her earlier,' Philippa said as she broke off.

'No.' It was Archer who answered. 'Your mother didn't want you told, she said the hurt would be sufficient when . . .'

'When what!' Philippa's hands tightened together, sudden fear a lump that filled her throat.

'The physician diagnosed Hannah's illness as advanced.' Edna resumed the telling. 'He . . . he warned she did not have many more weeks left to her.'

Lowering her head Edna Cranley pressed the handkerchief to her mouth, hiding nothing but a smile. Beside her she felt the tremble that shook the slight body.

'Turn the carriage around! I have to be with my mother!'

'And what good will that do?' Archer shook off the hand that reached for the rein. 'We already be doing what's best.'

'Best!' The word was an explosion. 'Best for who, for you, for Archer Cranley? Can't you forget your own desires even for this! My Mother is—'

'It be for your mother I be doing this,' Archer rasped. 'It be your mother's wish we go ahead with this meeting with the Lacys.'

'There will be no marriage!' Rage and bitterness biting deep, Philippa hit out in the only way available. 'I will not go through with any more of your dubious dealings.'

Pulling so sharply on the rein that the horse skidded in its tracks, Archer turned a furious look at the figure sat between himself and his sister.

'Then don't bloody well go through with 'em! Go back to the house, sit there and whine to your mother. That be all you've ever done all your useless life, ever since you killed her son. It be your doing her life's been spent in misery and it be your fault her be dying afore her time, and now you want her last days to be the same. I tell you this, and whether you believes it or not be of no matter to me: this meeting with the Lacys be going ahead not at my request but at your mother's. It's long been her dream to see her son married, it be the one thing her heart were set on. I thought that by settling things tonight, and by letting her see you wed then when her time comes she would go with her heart rested as we could make it. But that don't suit you, does it? The lad that dotes on his mother don't be so doting when it comes to the push!'

'It is true,' Edna put in. 'Hannah is at her happiest when daydreaming of the marriage of her remaining child. It would be a sin to deny her, Philip, to deny her the thing only you can give.'

How many sins had they committed against her, this woman and her brother? How many cruelties had Edna Cranley visited on her sister-in-law, how many nights had Archer Cranley's hand sent his wife crying into sleep? Philippa's heart cried out.

But this was not truly her wish . . . marriage to Joseph Lacy's daughter? It couldn't be. With teeth clamped together she remained silent as the carriage rolled forward.

Archer Cranley could rage all he liked.

There would be no marriage! The evil he planned would never be fulfilled.

# Chapter Seventeen

Philippa walked slowly across the open heath that separated Rowlay House from Phoenix Street. No marriage. That had been the silent promise made in the carriage. There could be no marriage to Davinia Lacy nor to any other woman, to do that would be a crime, it would bring misery to all involved. So why had the agreement been made, the date finalised?

Disturbed by the advancing footsteps a plover rose from the ground protesting loudly, but the cries were lost on her.

It could have been so easily done, all it would have taken to cancel the whole thing would have been those few words, 'I cannot marry your daughter.' But they had not been spoken.

Archer had apologised for his son's distant behaviour, explaining almost tearfully the sudden worsening of his wife's health. Another masterly performance! Philippa ignored the bird which circled before settling back to its nest. Edna too had played her part well, telling the shy young girl how very welcome she would be to the family, how they looked forward to having so pretty a daughter living at Rowlay House.

She was pretty, there was no disputing that. Fair hair curling softly to creamy shoulders, gentle blue eyes lowering shyly each time she answered a question. Yes, Davinia Lacy was pretty enough for any man to make his wife; any man except Philip Cranley!

But that was exactly what had been arranged. Why? Closing her eyes, Philippa stood for a moment, her face lifted to the sky. Why had that self-made promise not been kept, why once more had Archer Cranley's awful plans gone through?

Because there was no certainty that what he had said regarding his wife's wish was not true. She had not spoken of it in their moments together. Philippa walked on. If Hannah so badly wanted this marriage surely she would have discussed it with her own child, as it seemed she had with her sister-in-law. But had they told the truth? If so, why had Archer refused to let there be any discussion of it between Hannah and . . . ?

What was the use? She pushed the questions away. The risk was too great. To deny Archer Cranley was to place her mother in danger of being shut away regardless of how ill she was. To lose her to death was terrible enough, to lose her to death locked away from all she loved . . . to avoid that was something no crime was too terrible to commit.

It had been so easy. Archer Cranley smiled to himself as he drove towards West Bromwich. Oh, Philip had tried, had threatened, but then had accepted; as he would always accept. But only so long as Hannah lived! The thought wiped away the smile. He had charge of all Nathan Briant had left, Rowlay House, the Bottle and Glass, the daughter . . . but only while the daughter breathed. However, once that marriage ceremony was performed that restriction could be removed and Archer Cranley's life would become the one he deserved. And Philip? The smile returned. Like his mother, the restriction would be removed!

'Watch out there!'

A man's shout and the screams of several women brought Archer's attention to the present as the horse he was driving shied, backing the trap several yards.

'I've got 'im, mister.' The man had already sprung to the nervous horse, one hand on the bit strap.

Slightly confused by the suddenness of it all, Archer frowned at the several women, their dark skirts flapping like crows' wings as they hovered about a figure lying in the road.

'I seen it, mister.' The man glanced up at him. 'I seen it all, her stepped right into your road, walked off the footpath straight in front of your 'oss, never even looked, her d'ain't, I seen it all.'

In front of the horse. Christ, he'd run a woman down!

Jumping from the trap Archer elbowed the fluttering women aside.

'It be lucky 'er ain't dead!' Irate at being pushed aside a woman glared her annoyance.

'It be lucky a lot o' we folk ain't dead.' The answer rose over the hubbub. 'Drivin' traps at folk don't seem to matter to some, thinks cos they 'as money they owns the town!'

''E d'ain't drive it at 'er, nor at none o' you.' The man holding the horse soothed a hand over its nose as his shout startled it once more.

Tossing her head, setting the feathers of her black bonnet wobbling, the first woman turned her glare to him. 'You'd say anythin' if ya thought it'd bring ya a copper, swear black was white for a tanner would you!'

'Out of the way!'

'See, I tode ya, I tode ya! Folks wi' money thinks they owns the town, thinks they can do as they pleases wi' everybody else, thinks they can just push a body aside like . . . like . . .'

'Like throwin' shit in the midden! Well, that's all we be to the like of 'im.' One shrill voice answered the other.

Ignoring the remarks of the angry women Archer bent over the figure none of them had thought to help to her feet.

'I'm not 'urt.' Deep violet eyes lifted to him, the hint of an apologetic smile touching a beautifully shaped mouth.

'Ain't no fault of his'n if you ain't 'urt!'

Taking advantage of Archer's arm the woman rose to her feet, the faintly angelic smile encompassing the watching women.

'Please, you mustn't place blame where it isn't due, this

gentleman weren't at fault, it were me, I should 'ave looked where I were stepping.'

'That be right, I seen it all!'

'An' if you 'adn't then you'd put ya 'and on the Bible an' swear you 'ad, provided there were money in it!'

Her barb thrown, and realising there was to be no profit for her in championing the girl holding on to Archer's arm, the woman's interest faded and she turned away, followed quickly by the rest.

'T'weren't your fault, mister.'

Determined not to forgo his own reward so easily the man held on to the horse as Archer turned. Grabbing the half-crown held out to him he grinned and immediately disappeared along the busy street.

'I'm sorry.' Archer felt his insides lurch as he met those lovely violet eyes. 'Can I get you a doctor . . . the hospital?'

'No, thank you, I ain— I'm not 'urt.' Her smile widened, showing teeth well brushed. 'I'll just get me a cup of tea, that'll settle me nerves.'

'A glass of something will do a better job of that. I was about to take a meal, perhaps you'd join me.'

'I couldn't do that, I couldn't impose.'

She turned, Archer catching her arm as she swayed. 'You must take either one offer or the other, the meal or the hospital, which is it to be?'

Dark lashes fluttering kept Archer's attention from the cheap cotton gloves and well-worn coat. 'I'm afraid of hospitals,' she murmured.

His pulses faster than normal he helped her into the trap, glancing at the pretty face fondled by pale blonde hair peeping beneath a blue bonnet. First a meal, and then . . . ?

Setting the horse to a steady walk he resisted the desire to smile. But that was the only desire he would resist tonight.

✳     ✳     ✳

Edna Cranley took a last careful look about the room. Everything was in its place, everything as he had left it. She had come into her brother's bedroom as she often did after he left the house in the evening; as always she had searched but found nothing. He did have something to hide, of that she was sure, but what was it?

Twice now he had burned a newspaper he had scanned from end to end, thrown it into the fire before she had had chance to read it; and for what reason, what was it he wanted no one else to see? Her devious brother had more to hide than family secrets, instinct told her as much.

Closing the door she walked along the landing, thick carpet swallowing the sound of her steps. Archer was cunning, but even the most cunning of animals sometimes found themselves caught!

At Hannah's door she paused to listen, carrying on to her own room when she heard no sound.

Philip had taken that lie like a fish rises to the worm. She crossed to the fireplace, adding coals to the smouldering fire. Oh there had been another doctor called in, and he was a specialist in certain fields of medicine. Archer had been quick to see the sense of covering himself that way. But there had been no diagnosis of lung disease, that had been Edna Cranley's verdict; but Philip had believed it, would go on believing it to cover that lack of sense inherited from a useless mother.

Useless but pretty. Pretty in a way Edna Cranley had never been. Pretty enough to steal another woman's fiancé. As old memories tore at her Edna sank to a chair, staring at faces in the fire. A strong handsome face, blue eyes laughing, fair hair ruffling in the breeze as he took the hands of a young girl, a girl whose face glowed with love. Then the girl was gone, replaced by one whose pretty face captivated the man, blinding his eyes to all others until he could see only her . . . only her!

Bitter as gall the memories came faster. Hannah Briant was pretty. Edna had tried to reason. But there were far greater values than that of a pretty face. There was love, love he could never have from her brother's wife but which he could have in plenty from herself. She loved him, would devote herself to giving him a happy life. But in the dancing flames the handsome face turned from her.

And she was left with this. Lifting her eyes she stared across the dim sombre room. Left with an empty life and a cold bed. But the fires of vengeance burned hot and Edna Cranley had long warmed herself at them, and would again until the woman she hated lay cold as the man she had stolen.

'You be back then, Cranley!'

Cocooned in thought Philippa had not seen the figure step from shadows edging the wall that surrounded the glassworks. 'Couldn't stop long away from Fairley, you misses his kiss, does ya? Misses his touch on your pretty arse, does ya, or be it summat else you misses, summat as does more than touch that pretty arse? Be that the reason you returns to the cone?'

To one side of the gateway Ned Jukes stood, legs apart, hands on hips. Puzzled at the man's behaviour Philippa frowned.

'I have returned to the cone because it is time for my shift.'

'So it were at six o'clock last night but ya didn't work that one, how come? Your boyfriend waited for ya. Stood 'im up for another, did ya? Josh Fairley won't like that.'

'I had business with my father, not that I need explain to you.'

'No, no you needs do no explainin' to me.' Ned Jukes stepped forward, the dim light showing his unwashed face and unkempt hair. 'I don't be the one ya needs to keep sweet, I ain't the one 'olding ya like ya be a woman, spreadin' kisses over ya face; but then p'raps ya'd like me to do that.'

Watching the man's mouth twist in a sneer as he began to move, Philippa felt a flicker of trepidation. Ned Jukes was a thick-set man whose years of working in the cone had hardened muscles to steel. Once caught in them a body could be snapped like a twig.

'All I would like from you is for you to step aside and allow me to pass.'

She swallowed hard as the odious grin widened and bear-like arms lifted. It would be no use to turn away, if Jukes had waited of her coming, and it appeared he had, then he would follow. The thought of what could happen once they were on that lonely stretch of heath spurred Philippa.

'All you'd like is for me to step aside, eh!' As if reading the thought the thick-set figure moved, at the same instant catching Philippa close, the leering face pushed downwards. 'But 'ow can ya know that be all ya'd like 'til ya tries a bit o' summat else? A bit o' what Ned Jukes 'as in plenty . . . see for yaself.'

A low laugh gurgling somewhere in his throat he grabbed her hand, pushing it into his crotch and holding it pressed against hard flesh.

Breath fouled by the fumes of beer turned her stomach but the more she tried to break the man's hold the tighter it fastened.

'See.' Jukes laughed again, his mouth almost touching hers. 'See what Ned Jukes can give ya. That'll pleasure ya more than Josh Fairley bin pleasurin' ya.'

'Please!'

The fear locked in that one word acted like a stimulant, heightening the already hedonistic senses flooding Jukes's brain. Clutching the slight figure like some rag doll, lifting it clear off the ground, he carried it some way from the gate before dropping it face-down.

His laugh thicker now, throbbing with something more than a need for revenge, he slipped the buttons of his trousers then fell to his knees, powerful legs straddling the winded figure.

'Ya don't need to beg, an' ya won't need to pay neither, least not first time, Ned Jukes be a charitable man.'

'And a filthy one! I knew it was wrong letting you live, I should have killed you that first time!'

Feeling the weight lift, Philippa rolled clear in time to see the thick-set figure half floating, half staggering backwards, another taller, leaner one running after it.

'Joshua!' It was more a gasp of relief than a cry. Jumping up she caught a glimpse of a mouth set like steel, of eyes glinting like blue ice before Joshua Fairley threw himself on the other man.

Fists crunching against flesh, blow following blow they rolled and fought like snarling beasts. A stinging fist catching the side of the head sent Philippa sprawling, foiling the attempt to separate them. On his feet like lightning, Jukes sprang away.

'I ain't finished wi' you, Fairley!' he ground. 'Think on that while ya be kissin' ya pretty boy better.' Quick eyes flicking to Philippa he laughed, the threat contained in the sound thick and heavy. 'An' you! Old Cranley took unkind enough to you bein' carried into the 'ouse drunk, wait 'til he 'ears ya've been buggered, he won't snivel like Fairley's mother did; no he won't cry, he'll be like to break the back Fairley be so fond of mounting!'

Was that the reason his mother had kept to her bed when he got home from finishing the midnight shift? Jukes's words stunning him like a punch to the mouth, Josh stared after the figure running through the wide gateway into the glassworks. He had never known her not to be waiting for him, but he had thought her at last to be taking heed of his repeated request that she go to her bed and let him fend for himself in the dawn hour. But that was not the reason. Josh felt sick in his throat. What had that swine said to his mother, what lies had he told?

A few yards away Philippa saw the nuances of emotion chase across the tense face and felt an echo of them flicker across every nerve, the lancing pain of Jukes's blow forgotten as Joshua Fairley began to run.


The wench hadn't come across after all. Archer lay in bed, his mind dwelling on the events of the evening before. The wheel of the trap had knocked her down but she had made no fuss, unlike those harridans with their screeching and bobbing feathers. He should have had the lot of 'em run in, brought before the magistrate and charged with abuse. Ten years down the line would do 'em all a power of good, teach them to watch their tongues when speaking to their betters. But the girl, she had been different; not in her speech so much, for though she tried hard to hide it the Black Country dialect was still there; nor was it her clothes, for clean as they were no soap or water could disguise their cheap shabbiness. Yet despite all of that he had found her company very much to his liking.

She had refused Hemming's Dining Rooms as a place to take supper, her pretty face blushing as she said it was too grand, she would feel like a fish took from the water.

Right then he had felt relieved, he wouldn't want half the influential men of the town to see him escorting a common prostitute. But, common or not, the girl was pretty. Closing his eyes Archer watched the image of a small rosebud mouth pout slightly, deeply violet eyes gleaming their provocative smile. Yes, she was pretty but she had refused the money he had offered for her services and he had found himself apologising for his coarseness, him *apologising* to a wench he had picked up from the street!

Was she a prostitute? Opening his eyes he stared at the wooden canopy that topped his bed. Had refusing that ten shillings, a tidy sum for a night's work, been a crab set to catch an apple, a ruse played to draw him on?

'I couldn't be going in there.'

His mind skipped backwards, evoking again that earlier memory, showing him once more the blushing cheeks touched gently by pale blonde curls. She had made to turn away then but he had taken her arm and she had not withdrawn it as he had suggested they take supper in a tavern. She had led him from Tasker Street, the heels of her small boots clicking sharply on the setts. The Wheatsheaf Inn had proved a perfect choice, set in the quieter St Michael's Street. The landlord had furnished them with a private upstairs room, his wife serving a tasty meal.

'*Lilah.*' Her teeth uncommon white, the lovely eyes had gleamed jewel-like in the glow of candles as the girl had smiled her name. '*My special friends call me Lilah.*'

He had taken her hand, feeling its softness between his own. '*And those who would be more than friends, what do they call you?*'

She had laughed at that. A flesh-quickening husky laugh that Archer heard again in his mind. '*You,*' the whisper echoed softly across the hours, '*you too could call me Lilah.*'

Lilah or Delilah, prostitute or not, Archer knew he would be seeing his pretty temptress again.

# Chapter Eighteen

That look on Joshua's face, it was the look of a man ready to kill. Fear of what might happen should be catch up with Jukes added speed to pounding feet. Dashing into the huge cone, the heat from the bank of furnaces blasting against cool skin, the roar of air being sucked into the giant chimney deafening to ears soothed by the silence of the heath, Philippa stared in search of both men. The sounds of breaking glass and angry shouts rising even above the roar of air brought her stare to the alcove that housed Joshua Fairley's team, and had Philippa running again.

'Best stay back, Philip lad!'

A man with a neckerchief tied about his throat put out an arm to block the way, but Philippa dodged past.

'That be good advice.' Ben Harvey was quicker than his workmate. 'Stay clear of 'em.'

'They have to be stopped, Ben.' Dark with anxiety Philippa's eyes were unguarded. 'Joshua will listen to me.'

Looking for a moment at the anguish showing so clearly in those moist blue depths, Ben Harvey felt a coldness touch the base of his stomach. He had heard Ned Jukes's ravings, many of the others had heard them too as they had walked into the yard; but while they had commented, he had dismissed it as Jukes's bad blood reacting to Josh's action on that lock side. But was it all

# MEG HUTCHINSON

simply the rantings of a riled man? Looking now at the drawn face he felt the cold touch of doubt.

But it couldn't be! A glance calling Jake Speke to help hold the struggling figure he stepped in front of both. True or no what Jukes had said, it wouldn't do for others to see what he had seen, a fear in Philip Cranley's face that far outweighed that of one friend worried for another.

'I said I didn't be finished wi' you, Fairley, I said it that first time an' I've said it since. Now I be goin' to finish, an' when I am they'll 'ave to carry what's left of you back to that pig 'ole you calls home, back to bloody Churchyard Row where her you calls a mother can bury you!'

Pushing against Ben Harvey, Philippa tried to see past him as the gasps of watching men rose in a breathy chorus. 'Let go of me, Ben, I can make Joshua stop.'

'P'raps you could, but this 'as been brewin' a long time, better to get it over and done.' Holding on to the squirming shoulders Ben Harvey let his answer mask his thoughts. Maybe the lad could stay Josh's hand, but it would also destroy him. There wouldn't be a man Jack among the men of the Bottle and Glass who wouldn't believe the filth spewed by Ned Jukes if they caught so much as a hint of what showed in that white face; not one who wouldn't condemn.

'Christ Almighty . . . he's gone mad!'

Jake Speke's astounded cry had Ben turning to look to where Jukes had grabbed a rod, drawing it from the glory hole and swinging the blob of molten glass in an arc, sending several men stumbling from its reach.

'No!' As the cry dragged from a throat tightened with fear Philippa kicked sideways, bringing a heavy boot against Jake's ankle while at the same moment sinking teeth into Ben's wrist; then even as they shouted with pain she hurled bodily forwards, hands reaching for the rod.

'Philip . . . for Christ's sake keep away! Philip . . . !'

Hearing the shout that rose clear above the noise of the

210

chimney, Ned Jukes swung to face it. In his hands the rod swung, the blob of brilliant orange glass at its end glowing like a miniature sun. In the one instant it took for him to recognise the figure hurtling towards him, his mouth opened in a laugh of pure malice. Lifting the rod level with his chin he struck out.

Philip! The word silent on his lips, Joshua Fairley watched from the endless vacuum that seemed suddenly to surround him. There was no sound, no vision except for seeing one slight figure, arms outstretched, wheat-coloured hair seeming to spread in a pale halo about a face drawn with fear, a figure that fell slowly, so very slowly . . . Alone in that silent space there was no anger, no hatred, no pain, nothing but emptiness. As though caught in an invisible web that held every limb immobile he watched the figure settle to the ground, the head bounce like a pale ball, the hands wave as the arms jerked. Then, just his eyes moving, he followed the swing of that small fiery sun, the luminous arc that trailed a glittering rainbow, the beautiful orange star that hung in the void above his head.

It was all so peaceful . . . so calm. Like a string-worked puppet his arms lifted, hands reaching for the brilliant beauty, the exquisitely shining orb.

'Josh, watch out!'

The shout that was almost a scream touched the gentle peace, shattering it as a stone shattering glass, the shock jerking Josh from his waking dream. Hands already half-raised to grab the rod flexed stiff, the air ripping from his throat in one long agonised gasp as the molten glass was lunged into his shoulder.

'Get away from 'im, Josh, the bloody fool be gone mad! For Christ's sake get away from 'im!'

Ben Harvey's second shout acted on Joshua like cold water, washing everything from his mind except the fact that Ned Jukes had thrown that filth at his mother, and Philip Cranley lay possibly dead.

There was no peace this time, no silent isolation, no beautiful spangled rainbow. Only an ice-cold burning that seared every last blood vessel. Ignoring the calls of the others, paying no heed to the still glowing lump of glass at the tip of the rod aimed at his face, Joshua sprang forwards.

Shouting abuse, Ned Jukes lifted the heavy iron rod high above his head and, as the crouched body leapt for him, brought it hard down across its shoulders.

The force of it driving him almost to his knees, Joshua scrambled to regain his footing on the slippery setts while above his head the crazed shouts turned to screams of madness.

A blow from that rod hitting against his head and he would be done for. Closing itself off from the searing pain of burned flesh and stinging shoulder, Joshua's brain sought escape. Roll . . . he must roll clear . . . to stand now would be to catch that rod full on. Obeying the unspoken order, he let himself fall to the floor, rolling over several times before jumping to his feet.

Instinct keeping him crouched like some cornered animal he blinked droplets of sweat from his eyes as he sought for the figure wielding the rod like a flame-tipped spear. Watching Jukes's face contort with fury, the flecks of spittle tumble from the corners of his mouth, he realised that any control the man once had was gone, that in this state any of the watching men would do to vent his fury on.

Rising to his feet he called. His shout seeming to be the only one heard, Ned Jukes whirled to meet it. Eyes glazed, short stabbing breaths showering spittle into the hot air, he laughed, a long demented laugh.

'I said as I'd do for you, Fairley, and now I be goin' to.' Rushing forwards, the heavy rod lifted level with his face, Jukes swung with all his force. In the silence that suddenly fell, the iron bar cleaving the air sang like a siren.

Judging the swing of it, standing his ground, Joshua watched that arm of death are towards him. He would have just one chance and then Jukes would be on him. Around him the earth stopped turning. Wait . . . ! Wait . . . ! It seemed eternity passed as he watched the rod curve towards him, then at the last second he dropped to the ground. Finding no barrier the rod went on, the force of its momentum dragging Jukes with it. Feet scrabbling on the wet ground, hands still welded to the bar, he screamed as it swung him stumblingly towards the gap between the furnaces, opened now for coal to be fed to the gigantic fire.

The horror of the danger that gap posed acted like springs to Joshua's heels and in seconds he was racing towards the stumbling man.

'No, Josh, you can't . . . it be too late!'

Held by hands grabbing him from all sides he gasped at the sight that met his eyes.

Miraculously Ned Jukes regained his footing but not in time to cheat the hungry flames. Red-gold they reached for him, licking at greasy coat sleeves, sliding over trousers, swallowing them in greedy rapacious gulps to feed on the flesh beneath, flaring upwards to circle face and hair with a halo of bright incandescent flame.

For one long moment it seemed the eyes in that charring face lost their madness. Resting on Joshua they seemed to burn like ice. This was Jukes's victory, Joshua shuddered, he knew his own torment was ending but Joshua Fairley's horror of this moment would live with him for ever.

Above the roar of furnaces the clang of the iron rod falling rang like a bell, the blob of molten glass at one end greying as the fierceness of its heat was absorbed by the stone setts.

Still held by the others, Joshua blinked away the sweat clouding his vision. The rod was there and beside it a grotesque figure wreathed in flames danced the macabre dance of death.

'I don't mind telling ya, I thought as all three of 'em was done for.'

'Me an' all, 'specially the lad. The way his head bounced off the floor I would 'ave bet money 'e was a gonner.'

'Ar, well thank God he weren't, there be no tellin' what old Cranley would 'ave done 'ad his only lad been killed.'

'You ask me, old Cranley should have been the one 'ad his head bounced agen the floor, might 'ave knocked a bit o' sense into it!'

Seated at a table just feet from the bar Thad Grinley drew in his foot as the speaker spat contemptuously onto the sawdust-strewn floor.

'You should know better'n that, 'Arry, you of all folks should know you can't go growin' taters in concrete, you've been tryin' years enough!'

Over the burst of laughter that followed, Thad Grinley moved to the bar of the canal-side inn. Normally taking a lunch-time drink, he was no stranger to the Narrow Boat. He had heard of the fracas in that cone, of the fight between Jukes and Fairley and had tried to learn more, but that smart-mouthed Ginny Morton had made sure that hadn't happened. Fetching Platt the minute the first question were asked, the look on the charge-hand's face telling he'd been warned, there had been no more to gain from that quarter.

Bloody skinny-framed little bitch! She'd 'ave been sold long years since 'cept he couldn't see any man payin' two bob for her! But the conversation of these men . . . now that could prove enlightening as well as interesting, and Thad Grinley were interested . . . interested enough to pay for it.

'I've been hearing about that fight up at the Bottle and Glass, seems like it were a good one.' He shoved the pewter tankard across the beer-stained counter.

'It were no bloody cakewalk!' One man looked up.

' 'Arry be right,' another of them agreed, 'it were no pleasure ride, not the way them two went at it.'

'Been brewin', had it?' Grinley hid the fact he knew it had by holding up his freshly filled pot. 'Anybody join me in a tankard?'

Nodding at the chorused assent he laid a florin on the counter.

A swarthy man, tobacco-stained moustache speckled with flecks of foam from a tankard Bill Thomas set before him, looked at Grinley. 'Ar it has, for a few year now. But I reckon it'll brew no more.'

Waiting until each of the men had taken his pot and the change from the florin was in his pocket, Thad Grinley lifted his own tankard, watching the men's faces over the rim. Keeping his tone casual, he said, 'Do what I've been told be right, that a lad from Rowlay House 'ad summat to do with it?'

'Shouldn't be in the works, not 'im,' another of the men put in. 'That lad ain't strong enough to be workin' the glass, old Cranley should know that for hisself, shouldn't 'ave to be told!'

The back of one hand wiping beer froth from his mouth, the other placing a smoke-blackened clay pipe between his teeth, the man called Harry spoke again. 'The tellin' of that wouldn't 'ave no sway wi' Cranley, his bloody head don't be made of no concrete nor be it stuffed wi' sheep's wool; Cranley be no fool. Cut the clog that pinches an' you saves the foot!'

Signing to the landlord, Thad placed another silver coin on the counter, following it up with Harry's empty pot. This sort of information was worth the outlay. Nodding to Bill Thomas as each of the men hurriedly drained their own tankard and shoved it on the bar, he waited until they were refilled. Much as he wanted the answer to those last obscure words he knew it wouldn't do to be seen as over-interested.

' 'Ow do you reckon that?' A man who had not spoken before now added his own enquiry.

There it was! Thad sank his smile into the foaming pot. The question he so much wanted asked.

Harry inched the pipe to the opposite side of his mouth without removing it. 'Be my old woman as reckons it.'

'Same as her reckons 'ow many tankards you takes outta your tin afore you gives her any o' what you earns, eh 'Arry?'

'Ar, Sarah be like old Cranley,' another added. ' 'Er be no fool neither.'

Taking a long pull at his ale, Harry nodded good-naturedly as laughter once more filled the low-ceilinged, smoke-laden tap room. 'That 'er ain't, that be why I'm set to thinkin' what 'er reckons to the foot bein' saved by the cuttin' o' the clog be like carrying water in a bucket 'stead of a sieve . . . it makes sense. Think on it for yourselves –' the pipe travelled again, clinking on tobacco-stained teeth '– Cranley puts that lad in the glass, a lad even a man wi' no eyes could see ain't up to the job—'

'But 'e be doin' of it just the same.'

'Ar, 'e be a' doin' of it all right,' Harry turned towards the interrupter. 'But for how long, how long afore the silica does for 'im? P'raps what my Sarah reckons be right, p'raps that be the very reason Cranley put 'im to work the glass in the first place, so it *would* do forrim! Cut away the clog and the pinchin' be gone.'

''Is own flesh an' blood, the only lad 'e be like to 'ave! If you thinks that, 'Arry, then I reckons it be a pity you weren't a bit nearer the front of the queue when brains was dished out!'

'You think I'm stoopid if you like, that be your privilege.' Harry's pipe clicked again. 'But like my Sarah says, there be summat wrong as ain't right up at Rowley 'Ouse.'

His tobacco-stained moustache adorned with froth, the swarthy man swallowed loudly, eager to put his own point.

''Ow do yo're Sarah know what be goin' on in that 'ouse? Her would 'ave to 'ave the second sight, for there ain't nobody serves there to carry tittle-tattle back to Greets Green.'

'Obed be right in that, 'Arry,' another of the men nodded, 'there be no paid 'ands works in the 'ouse, unless it be that sister o' Cranley's.'

'Edna Cranley!' The swarthy man sniffed contemptuously. 'If women were convicted for bein' beautiful then that one would be judged innocent!'

''Er be no oil paintin', that's for sure.'

Listening to the to and fro of the conversation Thad Grinley remained silent. Listen a lot and say a little was a philosophy that had often served well in the past, it could serve equally well now.

'Neither do a lot o' women,' the conversation flowed on, 'but it don't follow as they be up to no good.'

'And I d'ain't say my Sarah said otherwise.' Harry drained his tankard, looking hopefully at Thad as he set it loudly on the bar counter.

Glancing at the tankard, Thad Grinley tried to estimate the worth of paying for yet another round. Could be there was nothing in the talk after all. But . . . taking out yet another coin he handed it to the landlord. You 'ave to speculate if you wants to accumulate, he told himself as Bill Thomas scooped up the coin; if a man don't sow then he don't reap.

Grabbing the foam-topped pot Harry took a long swallow, savouring what every instinct told him would be the last free ale. Wiping his mouth with his hand, replacing the clay pipe between his teeth, he surveyed the dirt-streaked faces of the men he worked with.

'My Sarah might be right an' there again 'er might not, I ain't sayin', but this I does say: old man Briant never 'eld no love for Cranley, there be men among us seen as much for us selves, an' I for one wouldn't put it past 'im not to 'ave left the Bottle an' Glass, no nor owt else as belonged of 'im, to a son-in-law 'e 'ad no time for but left it all, every last 'appenny to the grandson. If that be the case, an' I sees no other, then you has the reasons for that lad bein' put to the glass! And that be the reason Josh Fairley were sacked, not for savin' that lad from bein' killed by Jukes, but for not letting him *be* killed.'

'You wants to watch what you be sayin', 'Arry.' Bill Thomas slapped a cloth on the counter, mopping tiny puddles of ale. 'Men 'ave gone down the line for talkin' that way.'

'Ar, and there be others as should 'ave followed after 'em but never did! It ain't every wrongdoer be in gaol an' it be my bet that Archer Cranley be among 'em.'

His hand resting on the cloth the landlord paused in his mopping of the counter, a serious expression on his heavy-jowled face. 'Well, I don't 'ave the laying of bets in the Narrow Boat so if you 'ave any more talk like that then outside be the place to do it.'

'There could well be summat in what 'Arry says. We does all know Cranley for what he be; any man can walk behind the cart but 'e must drive the hoss. Likes to be the gaffer, do Cranley, an' I reckons 'e wouldn't be happy handing the Bottle and Glass to nobody, not even 'is own flesh an' blood.'

Leaving the cloth aside the landlord lifted the flap of the counter, coming to stand beside the group of men.

'You 'as the right to talk away your own livin', Obed Tonks, but you ain't talkin' away mine, so I says to you what I just said to 'Arry, do your reckonin' outside!'

Listening to the protestations, each of which the landlord brushed aside, Thad Grinley emptied his tankard. He would hear no more of the Cranley lad in this establishment. Wiping his mouth on the back of his hand he followed the others, the clear light after the smoke-filled semi-darkness of the tap room causing him to blink.

Standing for a moment, listening to the glassworkers call a greeting to a bargee securing his vessel to a post driven into the ground, he smiled to himself. So Cranley had put his own lad to the glass! Shut 'im away in that doll's house of an office. Now why do you suppose that was? Crossing the lock, the group of men well in front, he tried to sort out what he had seen and heard.

Seemed old Cranley had been cleaning the nest. The pretty-faced one he'd talked with in the yard of the glassworks, he'd bin throwed outta Rowlay House, why? Then Cranley's own lad put to skivvyin' in that poky office, for what reason? Could both reasons be connected, could it be they was joined . . . so to speak?

Reaching the cart he had left beside Ryder's Bridge he loosed the horse's tether, his smile widening as he climbed into the driving seat. Had the two young 'uns found they 'ad summat more in common than sharing the same 'ouse, summat like the same pleasures? Flicking the rein he set the horse to a walk, falling back immediately to his thoughts. Had Cranley come across 'em sharing the same bed? Some men would give their own lads anything . . . anything except their lovers. Was that the truth of it, had Cranley lost his plaything to his own son, and as recourse set 'em both to labouring, one in the cone and one in the office?

'*Cranley put 'im to work the glass so it* would *do forrim . . . Josh Fairley were sacked . . . for* not *letting him* be *killed.*'

It were a saying in Greets Green: there be no fury like that of a woman scorned. But then how many of them folk had seen the fury of a man who'd had another snatched from his arms?

# Chapter Nineteen

'I don't want Philip in the glassworks any more.' Hannah Cranley stared at her husband. 'Two accidents in as many days is too much, it seems like tempting fate.'

'Don't talk such rubbish!'

'Call it rubbish, call it anything you wish but I do not want Philip in that cone again.'

Hannah had changed. Archer turned towards the window of his wife's room. She seemed somehow different, answering him back, defiant where she had never been defiant before.

'How do you expect a man to learn his trade if he don't work in it? How will he run it?'

Calm as she often was since that visit to the church she looked with steady eyes at the straight-backed figure, hair cut well above the collar. How she wished she could turn back the clock, take her babies and disappear, leave Archer Cranley with his only real love. But it was too late for yesterday's dreams, too late for Hannah Cranley, but not for her child. Her hands folded, she answered quietly.

'You learned it without setting foot there more than half a dozen times a year, Philip will learn the same way. As for running it, your pattern again will suffice.'

Irritation like a saw edge against his spine, Archer turned, a cold stare directed at the woman sat in a velvet-covered chair. 'I've told you before, do not interfere!'

An almost imperceptible nod showing none of the fear she still had of him, Hannah replied, 'I should have interfered long ago, but that is in the past, while this is now, and I warn you, Archer, do not put our child back into that cone, or in any part of the glassworks!'

'Do not put him . . . you warn me, you warn me! How many bloody times 'ave I told you—'

'Too many, Archer.' Unflinching as the words hurled themselves at her, Hannah cut them short. 'But that tactic will not work any more. Despite what you yourself want so badly, and what that doctor might have warned of, I am not yet dead. That, Archer, should speak for itself. If you wish your plans to go through smoothly then you will take Philip away from the glass.'

'And if I don't, what the bloody hell can you do?'

'Perhaps nothing, but then perhaps a great deal. Maybe I can yet hit back at you; are you willing to take that risk, Archer?'

'There be no risk.' The small pointed beard jutted aggressively. 'You be talking horse droppings.'

The shadow of a smile flickering faintly over tired features showed for a moment and then was gone, but when she answered it held that same essence of warning.

'Many plants are nourished by manure, Archer, some of them grow tall enough to outgrow others, others that wither and die beneath their shadow. Think of that . . . think of it before you act.'

There was nothing she could do . . . nothing! Sat in his study Archer Cranley went over the scene of minutes ago. Hannah had threatened him, she had actually threatened him!

'Maybe I can yet hit back at you.'

The word burned like acid in his brain. Had she found some way to defy him, to take what he thought his? Rising to his feet he paced restlessly about the heavily furnished room. All she had was signed over to him, he had seen to that; the charity she was to name had been done according to his dictates and he had her Will safe in his keeping; the marriage to the Lacy girl was agreed, so there was nothing he had left undone. Hannah had simply tried to force his hand, to pull a fast one, as those men at the works would say. Poor fool! Didn't she know yet? Leaving the study he strode upstairs, the door of his bedroom slamming behind him.

Poor, stupid fool. Didn't she know . . . no one was fast enough to deceive Archer Cranley!

'Why you be here?'

Naomi Fairley stared at the figure stood on her doorstep.

'I told you when you come with them as carried my lad home that 'twould be in everybody's interests if you don't come again.'

'I had to come, Mrs Fairley.'

'Why?' Naomi's voice was harsh. 'Why do you have to come? Why do you play on a man's feelings, feelings that be friendship and no more? They be no more than that, they can never be more than that regardless of what you wants; my Josh be a man true-born, so you keep your handsome face and pretty-boy ways away from him!'

Why was she so angry? Her reaction when Joshua had been brought home with that dreadful burn to his shoulder was understandable, she had been distraught, as any mother would be seeing her son half-unconscious from pain, but that could not explain this outburst.

'I hadn't wanted to believe what my mind were tellin' me.' Naomi drew a trembling breath. 'I hadn't wanted to face such evil, but then Ned Jukes—'

Seeing the woman's mouth tremble as she fought for control, Philippa felt the blood in her veins suddenly run cold. Ned Jukes had shouted something of Joshua's mother, of her crying . . . what had he said, what lies had he told? Pretty-boy ways! That phrase was sometimes hurled at a lad who did not keep pace with the others of his chair, raising a good-natured laugh, but there was no good nature in the way this woman used it.

'Wait 'til he 'ears ya've been buggered.'

Was that what she thought, that Joshua was . . . ?

Staring at those angry features Philippa saw the heartbreak behind the anger, the misery behind the pain.

The shame of so terrible an accusation bringing colour to a face that moments before had been pale, the next words were little more than a murmur.

'I apologise for calling here uninvited, Mrs Fairley, I have no wish to cause distress. I wanted only to ask after Joshua's welfare and to—'

'My son be better for being left alone!'

The snap of it like a slap to the face, Philippa swallowed hard.

'Of course. I will not call again. I will have my mother write her thanks.'

'Your mother?' Naomi's brow furrowed.

'She would have preferred to come and thank Joshua herself for preventing my being injured by Ned Jukes in the works yesterday, but she is ill and so asked I bring her thanks for her.'

'I understands her feelings, a mother's heart beats for her children, one o' them be hurt or threatened and that beat be like to stop; tell your mother I thanks her kindly for her thinking.'

'Thank your mother from me also, I too take it kindly she asked after me . . .'

Already turned to leave, Philippa halted, Joshua's quiet tone restoring the heat to numbed veins.

'. . . just as I take your enquiry. My mother and I would be pleased if you would come into the house.'

Naomi Fairley would not be pleased. Every pore of her had exuded resentment, her eyes shouting animosity.

'Thank you, but I am already late for my shift and Samuel Platt does not go easy on those who do not report for work on time.'

'Samuel Platt!' Naomi's tone was bitter. 'Ar, he got his job given back to him, Ben 'Arvey and Jake Speke the same, all fetched back to the six o'clock shift; but not my lad, not my son.'

'Mother, you'll say no more.'

'I'll say my piece, Josh Fairley!' Naomi shook off the hand that reached for her arm, her eyes agleam with contempt as they rested on her visitor. 'Twice my lad saved you, once from certain drowning and once from being beaten to pulp with an iron bar, and what be his thanking? It be the sack, that be his thanking; given his tin for risking his own neck to save your'n! That be the thanks of the Cranleys!'

'I said that's enough!'

Wincing at the pain of his shoulder Joshua caught his mother's arm, drawing her away from the doorstep. Taking one look at his drawn face, Naomi ran sobbing into the house.

'Joshua, is what your mother said true, have you been dismissed from the works?'

'It be true enough; word was sent a couple of hours ago, I no longer had a place at Briant's.'

*'Had they left you to drown as your brother drowned then I'd have given twenty sovereigns apiece.'*

The words spat so viciously scudded again like missiles. Did Archer Cranley want vengeance so badly he would risk losing everything for the pleasure of it? Take away men's livings as revenge for being cheated of it? And why had there been no mention of Joshua Fairley being sacked when Hannah had asked her thanks be conveyed to him? Archer Cranley had stood in that room yet said no word of it!

'I did not know, my father said nothing of your being dismissed. I will speak to him.'

Glancing across Philippa's shoulder Joshua caught the inquisitive stare of a neighbour. Taking a step backwards he indicated for her to step inside. Cranley's sacking of him would be all over Greets Green by this time, there was no need to give gossipers more to talk of.

'My mother never set store by rudeness,' he smiled, 'she'll get herself all of a lather if you leave without giving her a chance to apologise.'

'Joshua be right in that.' Naomi appeared at her son's side. 'Speaking as I did were not called for and I says as I be sorry.'

Looking into eyes red-rimmed and still moist with tears, Philippa answered gently, 'There is no need for apology except my own. It was thoughtless of me to come knocking on your door, a letter would have been better.'

'It would like to have put me in me coffin, I ain't never had a letter not once in all me days . . . eh! The fright of it sends me heart fluttering and it best flutter where prying eyes don't have the seeing of it, so I puts my asking with that of Joshua, will you step inside?'

Inside a kitchen that seemed barely large enough to hold three people, Philippa stood hesitantly. Naomi Fairley's eyes still shouted the feelings her apology of a moment ago had not softened. She did not want any Cranley in this house, and she wanted Philip Cranley least of all. But given what Ned Jukes had been shouting it was not surprising. Glancing to Josh as he offered a chair, the same bewildering feeling that gripped whenever their eyes met clawed deep inside. Knowing it must show if this meeting went on, Philippa turned to the woman standing with hands folded across her middle.

'Mrs Fairley, I . . . I . . .' the words came falteringly, no softening of the woman's features to help them, 'I came here to thank Joshua again for saving me from Ned Jukes's temper, though I had no knowledge that it was he who prevented my falling into that lock until my mother spoke of it this morning. It must seem bad manners on my part not to have thanked Joshua for that sooner than I have, I can only ask you both forgive my ignorance.'

'You weren't told of that, and you weren't told of his being given his tin neither, hmmm!' Naomi snorted. 'Seems there be a lot that father o' your'n don't tell you of!'

'My father left the house quite early this morning while I was still with my mother or I am sure he would have discussed the matter with me.'

'There is nothing to discuss.' Joshua met the lie as though knowing it for what it was.

'Nothing to discuss.' Naomi turned angry eyes on her son. 'You being outta work be nothing to discuss! I say it be just the opposite, it be everything to discuss. Them three men all gets their jobs back while you be the one flung out on your backside and you say it be nothing to talk on!'

'Your mother is right, Joshua.' Glancing at the man, catching the look in those deep blue eyes, feeling a leap of the heart, a surge of blood that raced along every vein, bringing with it desire to go to him, to hold him close, Philippa could only turn quickly away. 'It is something I should have been informed of. I can only think my father has somehow been misinformed as to the truth of the situation. I shall speak to him as soon as I return home; you and your mother need have no worry, your position at the works will be waiting for you once you are well enough to return.'

Across the few feet which was all the space the tiny room allowed, Joshua Fairley had caught the emotions raging through that slight frame, emotions that so exactly matched his own. They were emotions that would not be fought off for ever and they were emotions he could not live with. He could not go on day after day meeting those eyes, hearing that voice as they worked, wanting with all his heart to hold that body close as they walked together across the heath. It must end now, end before the whole village got to know his shame, the shame of his love for another man.

'There'll be no return,' he said quietly, 'no need for you to discuss it with your father, I've done with Briant Bottle and Glass.'

'Josh!' Naomi Fairley's face paled visibly as she sank to a chair. 'Josh, what be you saying?'

Pain bringing a hand to the dressing strapped to one shoulder, Josh glanced at his mother's stricken face.

'I've been wanting to do this for some time, Mother, wanting to leave Briant's.'

A swift intake of break held the words from Naomi's tongue but her eyes said them all. Had he wanted to leave the glass for some time, or just that time since meeting Cranley's son?

'Joshua, if it is because of my father's——'

'Please, Philip, sit down,' Josh interrupted, not trusting himself to look at the face that haunted his sleep. 'Hear what I have to say. It has nothing to do with your father giving me my tin except that was the escape I had been looking for.'

'Escape? You sound as though you've been trapped!'

Reaching a hand to his mother's, Joshua held it tenderly. 'That's exactly how I've felt for years. There's no way for a man to express himself . . . his feelings for the glass . . . not at that place; all it be is bottles and more bottles, glass upon glass, 'til you feel you want to smash the whole lot.'

'But what did you expect, son? Bottles and glasses be what Briant's does.'

'I know, Mother, and as a lad I thought that were all I wanted, but as I grew so did the feeling of wanting more from the glass, of doing something with it that would express the beauty of it, something that would be treasured as a great painting were treasured.'

'Painting . . . beauty, I don't understand, a bottle be a bottle, summat as holds wine and such, there be no beauty in that!'

'I think I understand what Joshua means,' Philippa broke in quietly. 'A bottle is a bottle as you say, Mrs Fairley, and as such is useful in its own right; but I think Joshua feels that it could be so much more.'

Pulling her hand from her son's, Naomi stood up, all the worry of seeing her home torn from her if he refused the offer of reinstatement at the glassworks reflected in her eyes.

'I don't see how! No, I be sure I don't see how. As for it being treasured, who ever heard of such!'

'There have been many beautiful glass bottles made, Mrs Fairley, and I assure you they are very greatly treasured.'

'Well,' Naomi flashed, 'they ain't treasured here in Greets Green, Mr Cranley, nor be they made at Briant's and that be the only bottler we should be bothered about! Briant's be the roof over our heads and the bread in our mouths, if Josh turns his back on that where will we be?'

It was the very food in their mouths, Josh thought. But how long would it be there should Archer Cranley get the merest hint of his feeling for his son? How would they live then, how would his mother live with the shame of that hanging over her? At the moment it was just the ravings of a jealous-minded man, but what if those ravings were seen as truth?

'We won't starve, Mother.' His hand went again to his injured shoulder. 'I'll find work somewhere, there has to be something.'

'Oh ar, there always has to be something, but what, lad . . . and where? It won't be in Greets Green, that much I does know.'

Watching the woman's mouth tremble as she strove to hold back her tears, the fingers clutching and re-clutching the apron that covered her skirts, Philippa felt something of her desperation. 'Perhaps if I spoke to my father, told him of what Joshua feels, what could be done with the glass.'

'You'd be laughed at.' Joshua shook his head. 'You'd be laughed at, same as I was when I spoke of it years back. I showed Archer Cranley some pieces but he wanted to hear none of it. To put it in his own words, ' "There be too many folk with bloody fancy ideas as how to spend another man's money. Plain straightforward bottles be what you be paid to mek and if you don't be satisfied with that then take your tin and your fancy notions and bugger off." '

'I know what you feels, lad.' Naomi's tears spilled. 'I knows more'n you gives credit for. Your heart be in the glass but the sort you talks of be naught but notions, and all it can ever be is notions. I've felt the longing in you, read the dreams in your eyes and ached for them to come true. But like castles in the air they be sweet to look on, then reach for them and they melts away and you be left with nothing; so let them go, lad, let them dissolve like the fantasies they be and set your mind to reality. Let this lad speak for you—'

'No, Mother!' Josh cut in quickly. 'I'll have no man speak for me and I'll beg no charity.'

'It would not be charity . . .'

'To me that is exactly what it would be, and the same to every other man at Briant's; go whingeing to the gaffer's son, asking for your job to be given back . . . what else would it look like? Well, I won't be doing it, I want no more of Archer Cranley!'

Nor of me? Like a silent bell the thought tolled in Philippa's mind. Was Joshua really saying he wanted no more of Archer Cranley . . . or was what he truly meant that he wanted no more of Archer Cranley's son? Willing nothing of the thought to show in the glance directed to Naomi, but knowing it failed, Philippa tried to keep the next question light.

'The glassware spoken of just now, Mrs Fairley, that which Joshua showed to my father, do you still have it?'

'Them glasses and such was bought and paid for all proper like,' Naomi sniffed, her hackles rising. 'The receipts be in the drawer of that dresser and be all of 'em signed by Samuel Platt, my Josh d'ain't never taken nuthing as he d'ain't pay for!'

'Mrs Fairley, I'm sorry if I made you believe . . .' Philippa stumbled awkwardly, '. . . I did not think for a moment that Joshua would take anything from the works without paying for it.'

'Well, you'd have been wrong if you had!' Naomi flashed, protection of her son's reputation still a heat in her blood. 'Them bills also shows extra payment for the dribbling of them colours that be fused into the glass; Joshua paid for every last thing he used on 'em.'

Already at his mother's side Joshua placed an arm about her shoulders, but his eyes were on the face of the man who had called to see him.

'Philip never thought otherwise,' he said quietly, his heart twisting at what he saw in those liquid blue eyes.

'What other reason be there for the askin'?' Naomi refused to be mollified. If any man other than this had asked the same thing she would have thrown herself on him, clawing him like a cat for even thinking such, but much as she held the Cranleys in no special respect there was something about the lad that held the worst of her temper at bay.

'I asked because I thought if you still had some of the pieces then I might be allowed to see them.'

The smile accompanying the request gentle yet by no means condescending did more to soothe Naomi's ruffled feelings than any apology. Sniffing once more she nodded. 'There be one or two, one I has in my bedroom and there be a couple on the shelf in the scullery. I tells Joshua they be too pretty to be left out there but he says they best be left where none but him and me sees 'em.'

As gentle as before Philippa smiled again. 'May I see them, Mrs Fairley?'

Wiping her eyes on her apron Naomi hesitated, unwilling to go against her son's decision that none but she would see the glassware he had crafted.

'It's all right, Mother.' Joshua pressed the hand that draped her shoulder. 'I'll show them to Philip.'

Watching them walk together into the scullery, Joshua so tall and muscular beside the slender figure that reached only to his shoulder, the flood of her fears returned. Should her follow them, stand with them as they looked at them glass fripperies? Tears returning to her eyes she turned towards the teapot warming on the hob. Who would believe Joshua innocent of unholy love, who would believe in him if his own mother had no trust?

# Chapter Twenty

'Joshua, these are beautiful.' Philippa Cranley cradled the delicate wine glass, a spiral of milky whiteness twisting along the length of its stem. 'You showed these to my father and he refused to produce them?'

'Said they were of no value, that there was no place for such as that in Greets Green.'

'There is a place for beauty in any home.'

Eyes soft as skies after summer rain lifted to Joshua's. Gazing into them he felt his heart answer. Beauty was to be found in many places, in many things, the face of a woman . . . and the face of a man, this man! But that was beauty that could never grace Joshua Fairley's home. Taking the glass he lifted it back onto the shelf, revulsion as well as desire trembling along his fingers. How could he, Joshua Fairley, feel this way for a man . . . how could he have these longings? It was unnatural, a thing of evil, but each time that evil beckoned he found it harder to resist, harder to hold that secret in his heart. How long could he go on this way, how long could he resist that which called to him in the day and plagued him through the night; how long before evil called and he answered it in kind? But that would destroy Philip, destroy the very thing he loved.

His breath tight in his lungs, he answered, 'Your father

seemed to think otherwise, he wanted nothing more of what he called "useless rubbish".'

At his shoulder Philippa reached for a vase. Swirls of sea green and dusky sunset mauve swam in and out of each other around the balloon-shaped body, writhing up the slender neck to coil beneath the flare of a plain glass lip.

'No one could ever call such a lovely thing rubbish.'

Watching her carry the vase to the door open on to the yard and lifting it to the setting sun, Joshua watched the reflection of colour play over the pale face. It was like some beautiful painting, like the lovely gentle face of the Madonna in the stained glass of the church window; but in that other window, the one with a man and a woman stood beneath a tree, there was a serpent that beckoned, the same thing of evil that beckoned to him.

'We have nothing like this in Rowlay House.'

Joshua turned back to the shelf as Philippa looked at him. 'Sufficient unto the day' had been a saying of his father's. Feeling the hand touch his arm he snatched away. The saying was a true one, a man could only take so much!

'How did you make these, get the colour to fuse into the glass?'

There was hurt in the voice, confusion. Philippa had felt the emotion in the snatch of his arm. She must not face him, must not look into those soft blue eyes, see the pain she knew was in them.

'Different oxides give different colours. You don't necessarily have to fuse it into an article; you can if you wish thread it onto the surface, using it like a ribbon to create any design you want, like this one.' Joshua answered without turning, waiting for Philippa to take the next proffered piece of glass before handing back the vase. 'That is a flint batch with green oxide chrome and black copper oxide mixed in.' He touched a finger to the trail of soft, almost translucent, green slightly raised from the amber-coloured ground of a tall decanter.

'Is it terribly expensive this process?'

'Apart from the oxides then little more than a plain glass bottle. Of course there is the time . . .'

'Yes, of course.' Philippa held the decanter in both hands. 'That would have to be taken into consideration, but what of skills, would men need to be trained in its usage?'

'There be skills needed in every aspect of glassmaking, lads be trained constantly from their first day, be it shovelling silica into a wheelbarrow, collecting cullet or mixing a batch, the training never stops; not even when he gets to be in the cone itself whether as Bit Gatherer, Taker In, Foot Maker or eventually as the Servitor himself who is the leader or gaffer of a chair, the learning never stops.'

'And yours will never stop will it, Joshua? You love the glass, I hear it in your voice every time you speak of it, it throbs like some living thing.'

Was that all that was heard? Joshua swung away into the yard. Was it only the love of glass that was detected, or another throb, a deeper, more vibrant, more powerful throb, the throb of one man's love for another?

Stepping into the cool dark shadows of the small brewhouse he drew a deep breath, holding on to it, using the pressure of it to hold down the swell of emotion that threatened to break from his throat.

'This is where I etched a few pieces.' More in control he reached a bowl from a shelf, explaining, as Philippa stepped inside, 'The article is dipped in hot wax and once the wax hardens you can use things like this to scratch a pattern into it.' Selecting a pencil-like strip of wood he touched a finger to the sharp metal point set into one end. 'When you have the design you want then the article is put into a bowl of hydrochloric and sulphuric acids which set into the glass where the wax has been cut away, after that it is a simple matter of washing the piece to cleanse it of acids and wax and that is what you finish up with.'

Watching the slim-fingered hands holding the bowl Joshua felt the rush of longing return. Here in the dimness of the brewhouse, sheltered from any watching eyes, he could take those hands in his, kiss the roughness work in the cone had caused, touch that pale gentle face; here alone with Philip he could tell him . . . but he could never tell him, never speak the words that drummed with every beat of his heart, never say 'I love you'.

'It is too dark to see the bowl properly in here. Take it into the house and hold it under the lamp.'

He was already standing before the hearth as the scullery door closed behind Philippa.

'Will you tek a cup o' tea, lad?' Ashamed of her former show of hostility Naomi had brewed tea, telling herself that bad manners had never been part of her upbringing and that whatever fate had in store for Naomi Fairley and her lad, no amount of ignorance would alter it.

'I would very much like a cup of tea, Mrs Fairley.' Philippa answered the woman who only minutes ago she felt had wanted to sweep every semblance of a Cranley from her home.

Cups settling gently onto saucers as Naomi reached her beloved bone china bits and pieces from the cupboard of the dresser, Philippa glanced at the face, mouth drawn tight as Joshua held to his self-control.

'What did you say you called this process?' Philippa knew the question was feasible but unnecessary. Every word Joshua spoke, no matter where or when, was graven deep as the marks bitten by acids into the glass of the bowl.

The corner of his eye catching the movement of his mother's head as she turned towards him, Joshua forced down the lump in his throat.

'Etching,' he answered. 'It is a fairly simple process.'

'Ar, but them acids as he calls that stuff, I reckons they be dangerous, if it can bite into glass then what might it do to a man's 'ands? I says he shouldn't mess with such.'

'That is why I used it here rather than at the works.' Joshua smiled at his mother pouring tea. 'I wouldn't risk any of the folk at Briant's coming into contact with it.'

Taking the bowl to the window, Philippa held it beneath the lamp Naomi had lit against the rapidly lowering night. Blown thinner than the bottles produced at the works the delicate glass shimmered in the soft gleam, nuances of light and shadow seeming to imbue the figures etched into it with life and movement.

'You showed this also to my father?' At Joshua's quick nod Philippa went on, 'But he rejected all idea of producing such pieces?'

'You know what your father called them, there be no need to repeat it.' Naomi offered tea, a little of her previous tartness on her tongue.

'My father was wrong, Mrs Fairley.' The reply held no conciliation and no trace of pretence. Firm and polite as the words, the blue eyes met and held hers with quiet conviction. 'The pieces you have allowed me to see are most definitely not rubbish, they are beautiful, and this –' placing the bowl on the table she looked at it '– this is exquisite. I cannot imagine anyone not wishing to own something as elegant and beautifully crafted. Joshua is right when he says there is more to be made from glass than bottles.'

'Saying it be one thing, 'aving means to follow your own way be summat else again, and that be what 'e don't 'ave.'

'Then why not let me help?'

Naomi's glance followed that of Philippa then dropped to her own cup as she caught the effect of it in her son's eyes. Mebbe this lad could help, could get his father to take Josh back . . . but that wasn't the help either of 'em were really askin'. Nor the sort they truly wanted.

'I could speak to my father, get him to see the possibilities of work like this, let me—'

'No!' Joshua's reply was sharp. 'I have said it once and that be enough! I will not go crawling to Archer Cranley and no other man be going to do it for me. I will never work for that man again, let God be my witness, never again!'

'Then that be all there be to say.' Naomi looked at her visitor, the tears once more visible in her eyes. 'I thanks you for the offer you've made though it's been turned away. You speak to your mother on my behalf and tell her my gratitude her sought to thank my son.'

'I will, Mrs Fairley.' Philippa stood up, a glance going to Josh. 'I'm sorry for what has happened, Joshua, sorry that you feel you can no longer work for my father, it seems that neither of us will be returning to the cone.'

A frown creasing his brow Joshua gave a slight shake of the head. 'I'm not with you, Philip, you can't mean you've been given the sack as well as me.'

If only it were as simple as that. Meeting the blue eyes Philippa felt the world suddenly snatched away. This could be the last time they would talk together, the last time they might meet. Joshua Fairley had made the glassworks bearable, he had made life bearable!

'A man don't sack 'is own lad.'

Grateful for Naomi's intervention, Philippa glanced towards her, breaking the invisible tie that had become so strong that were it not broken now it would never be broken.

'No, my father has not ended my employment, Mrs Fairley, it is simply that once I am married . . .'

'Married! You be goin' to be wed? Eh lad, that be fine news. So when is it to be . . . if you don't think as a body be too forward for the askin'?'

The relief Philippa saw break across the lined face was unmistakable but it was the gasp which came from Joshua that struck the deepest. The question had been put by Naomi but the torment in Joshua's eyes said it was he who waited for the answer.

'I do not think it forward, Mrs Fairley.' The reply was given quietly but the eyes that held Joshua's screamed their torment, cried the silent words, 'But it's you I love!' Unable to break free of the deep soul-searching stare the rest was almost a murmur. 'I am to be married on Wednesday of next week.'

In an upstairs room of the Wheatsheaf Inn Lilah Cherrington slipped the bonnet from freshly washed pale blonde curls, her eyes smiling their violet promise to the man greedily swallowing every move of her sensuous body. It had become a regular occurrence coming here to this room, and each time she had felt him slide a little further beneath that particular spell. But tonight she had taken extra care over her toilette, taking time in choosing just the right gown, just the right undergarments. Not that he ever saw much of those, snatching them away in his haste to satisfy his lust. But that did not matter, Lilah Cherrington had more to gain than new underwear. Archer Cranley liked the things she did, the things she promised, liked them enough to pay well for them. True, he had already been generous, but he would pay higher yet, the true prize was yet to come and she intended it would be hers.

'No more.' Laying the prettily trimmed bonnet aside she allowed a tiny pout to tug the painted rosebud mouth. 'I won't give you any more!'

'Lilah.' Archer almost jumped forwards, disappointment leaping like a live thing across features already harsh with lust.

'No.' The pout more pronounced she thrust both hands, palms flat, against his chest. 'Not unless you let me do this first.'

Disappointment melting as quickly as it had formed, Archer Cranley's black eyes gleamed with the same anticipation that jerked his stomach. Standing motionless he smiled into the violet eyes as nimble fingers removed his clothes. Lilah enjoyed the things he enjoyed, she liked to see that which would pleasure her, liked to touch, to kiss, to taste . . . to do all the things Hannah had never wanted, not even in the earliest days of their marriage.

But now he had all of that and more. His desires were matched by ones as demanding as his own, sweet desires that ravished as well as satisfied, that stilled a hunger yet did not overcome it, alloweding it to return in all its turbulent passion to be quieted again by an enchantingly beautiful woman.

Reaching to his the painted lips pressed their promise, the delicate hands sliding over his naked flesh. Unresisting, he let himself be pushed backwards onto the bed, that beautiful body resting on top of him.

Kissing him again on the lips, Lilah slid slowly to her knees, trailing her mouth over chest and stomach towards the dark mound between his spread legs.

Yes! Archer's breath quickened. This was what he liked, what he wanted, this he would have, this girl to pleasure and to be pleasured whenever he desired.

Tapping a fingertip to the roused column she laughed softly. 'You are going to have to wait,' she murmured, 'but just so as you know Lilah ain't . . . isn't leaving you . . .'

Smiling down into dark excited eyes she touched her lips to the throbbing flesh, then stood up.

Keeping her look fastened on his she slipped the buttons of her jacket with slow enticing movements. Carefully selected petticoats following skirt and blouse in a rustle of silken lace, she took the ribbon of her chemise between long fingers.

'I don't want to tek this off.' The smile faded, leaving the lovely eyes smouldering pools of violet fire. 'I wants you to tek the rest.'

Every nerve tingling, every drop of blood crashing headlong through his veins, Archer took the narrow ribbon, the fragility of it heightening the intoxication, adding to the fervid, overwhelming passion flaring through him. He would take the chemise, take every last stitch until she stood as naked as he, then he would take her. Twisting the fingers of both hands about flimsy lace straps he snatched, then bending his head fastened his mouth over a taut pink nipple while tearing away the silken bloomers.

He would set this girl up in a quiet place somewhere away from the town, would make this girl his mistress. He would smooth the rough dialect, make her speech match her body. To the outside world she would appear a lady of perfection, but in the bedroom she would play the whore, his own beautiful, talented whore!

Held close to him, naked flesh throbbing against naked flesh driving the whirlwind that blasted his senses, fuelling the flames that consumed all but that one ravening urge, he spun the lovely figure around and to the bed. Unable to resist the desires tearing through him he thrust deep into her, the quiet laugh going unheard among the clamour of his brain.

# Chapter Twenty-One

Skirts brushing the tiny purple heads of ling that spread a carpet of heather over the heath, Edna Cranley was deep in thought. Her brother was absent more often from the house than he had ever been and it was not the Bottle and Glass he were visiting. So where did his afternoons take him, and what kept him from his bed until the early hours? It wasn't discussions with Lacy, of that she was certain.

That marriage! Edna's thoughts switched tracks. How would he proceed once that service were said, what did he intend then? She had tried to question him but always he cut her dead, refusing to answer anything other than that the ceremony would take place at Rowlay House.

Not in church! Edna held her skirts free of a mud patch. Was the self-confident Archer having doubts, was he afraid after all, afraid of his own greed being brought before the Lord? But afraid or not he had every intention of marrying Philip to the Lacy girl, a girl who had no idea of the kind of life she was about to take on.

But why should that worry Edna Cranley? Coming to where the edge of the heath gave on to St Michael Street she paused to allow a well-laden cart to rumble past. The truth was she wasn't worried, just the reverse. She crossed the street, quick eyes watching for the inevitable horse droppings. That girl would take her place and Edna Cranley would take the money so long promised, and that would be the last Archer and his family would see of her. There would be no more of his demands, no more drugging Hannah day and night to stop her tongue . . . But the longing would go on, every long night holding nothing but loneliness; though in those empty hours there would be one comfort, the comfort that would come of her at last saying what only she knew, of telling her brother the truth.

Ahead, where the small squat buildings reached to the church, a woman's laugh rang out as a man helped her from a closed hansom. Brows drawing together as she peered across the distance between them, Edna stared.

It was not the mauve and violet costume she stared at, with its deep-collared jacket, fitted bodice tight about the slender figure, the draped overskirt drawn upwards and finished with large bows of violet satin ribbon which trailed streamers to the hem, or the pert bonnet with matching silk flowers bunched above the brim. It was not even the woman, still laughing in that brassy, high-pitched tone that she noticed. It was the man.

Watching as the dark-haired figure turned to hand a coin to the driver of the hansom, she ran a quizzical eye over him. He was dressed in single-breasted grey jacket beneath which peeped a straight-cut waistcoat, the close-fitting grey trousers seeming to add height to an already tall man.

Could it be who it appeared to be? She had not seen Archer leave the house after lunch. But could the man she watched now be him? If so, he was dressed as she had never seen him.

The shrill laugh ringing out again, the figure turned full face and Edna lifted a hand to her mouth to shield her own. Light brown bowler hat, matching gloves and silk cravat . . . none of it was Archer Cranley's style, but the man wearing them was without doubt her brother.

The couple, the man's arm about the petite waist, passed into a building whose roughly painted sign proclaimed it as the Wheatsheaf Inn.

It was him. Edna lowered her hand. The clothes were different but the face, she could not mistake the face; those jet-black eyes, the tight mouth and sharp-pointed beard, they were all Archer Cranley; and the woman he drew so possessively against him, the woman was not Hannah Cranley!

A prostitute? Not some common one judging by the clothes. Edna stepped aside, allowing a heavily built woman carrying a large cloth-covered basket on one hip to pass. Ignoring the loudly observed comment concerning 'folk standin' gawpin' at nuthin' a' forcin' others to step into the 'oss road', she walked nearer to where the couple had passed from her view.

A mistress? Drawing level with the tavern she smiled inwardly. Had Archer taken himself a mistress? Casting a sideways glance at the bow windows jutting out over the narrow pavement, the open doorway through which tobacco smoke and beer fumes wafted, Edna's lip curled as much in disdain as in distaste. Any woman allowing herself to be taken into such a place could not be anything but common. A common prostitute! Edna wanted to laugh. And the clothes, paid for no doubt by Archer; and judging by what she had just witnessed that woman would not be satisfied with a new suit of clothes, it could well be she would go on taking . . . and Archer? Edna allowed the smile to touch her mouth. If she were right in her assumption then Archer would do the paying, and Edna Cranley would take more, far more than the sum agreed all those years ago!


Hannah had not wakened. Returned to Rowlay House Edna checked the sleeping figure. There had been no refusing to take the laudanum given in ever-increasing doses, no more argument and no further attempt to leave the house alone.

Why had she visited that church? Edna stared down at the waxen face, huge dark rings encircling the closed eyes. Was it an attempt to save Philip from that marriage? Did she really believe a prayer to a plaster saint would save her child? In the silence of the room Edna's laugh was harsh. A whole army of saints, real or plaster, would not turn her brother from his course; and Joseph Lacy? The little banker would know nothing until it was too late.

Outdoor clothes removed and hung away in the cupboard of her bedroom she set a match to the fire always kept laid. Settling in the chair beside it she gazed towards the bed, her eyes seeing only a thatch of softly curling hair, a strong handsome face turned towards her, brown eyes smiling.

'It's already too late, Richard,' she whispered, 'too late for all of them. I never told them, but you know, don't you, my darling? You know; and they will too when I'm ready. I'll see them suffer as Hannah Briant made me suffer, pay her back in full for what she did to us, for what she stole. The whole Cranley family will pay.'

The whisper fading, taking with it the image of the handsome face and smiling eyes, Edna turned her glance to the flames dancing headlong into the black reaches of the chimney. All of his life her brother had danced the same way, following a dark path of evil. Now it had led him into the arms of a prostitute, one who had more than a five-shilling hold on him; the way he had held her, pulled her close into him there on the open street, she was more than a one-night whore. And she, Edna, had seen him, watched them go into that tavern together; and she had also made certain he had not taken that woman into that establishment merely to drink a glass of wine. With her veil drawn over her face she had walked into the tavern, pretending her sister-in-law was near to fainting after the burial of her husband and was in need of a little brandy. The tavern keeper had gone in search of a small bottle in which to put the wine and she had used the moment, glancing in every part of the smoky room, but Archer and his jade were nowhere to be seen. They were in that tavern but not in the public room. To Edna Cranley, as to any she chose to tell, that spoke of more than simple friendship. And she would speak of it; unless Archer met her demands, then the whole town would hear, and that would put an end to Philip's so important marriage.

Leaning into the depths of the chair Edna closed her eyes, whispering softly to the image in her mind.

'Tomorrow, my love, tomorrow you and I will begin. We will know the true pleasure of revenge; tomorrow, my darling, I will give you vengeance.'

Listening to the footsteps pass her bedroom door Hannah opened her eyes. They had not paused as those earlier ones had paused, he had not looked in on her as Edna had done. It had been so hard keeping up the pretence of sleep, the pain arising from the withdrawal of laudanum almost forcing the sobs from her. But she had remained still, a heavy breathing saying all was normal, and at last Edna had left her.

Glancing sidewards, she looked at the glass stood beside the carafe of water, the last few dregs of laudanum gathered at the bottom. Edna had not suspected, she had no knowledge of the bottle hidden inside a boot. Now the bottle was almost full of the so-called medicine she left whenever she went to visit that grave. It had been a risk the thing she had done today, going down to the study and writing that letter, as big a risk as when she had visited the church. She had prayed there as she prayed lying in this bed, prayed the Holy Virgin protect Philip. But her prayers alone were not enough. She had had to find some other way, a way that would prevent the evil of Archer Cranley taking place. But would her child forgive? Would Philip understand, realise this was the only way she could help? Tears collecting in the corners of her eyes spilled onto sunken cheeks. 'Don't despise me, my darling,' she whispered, 'please . . . don't despise me.'

The settling of a coal in the grate her only answer, Hannah watched the flickering shadows glide their silent agitation about the room. Her life since marrying Archer had been so like the shadows cast by the glow of the fire, one moment bright, vital and alive, the next grey and hollow. She had seen marriage to the man she loved as being a paradise, and so it had become; except it had been a fool's paradise.

He had boasted of their first child's abilities, driven the boy to make those boasts a reality. His son must be the best, he must outshine the sons of every friend they had; Stephen must be the best horseman, jump the highest fence . . . the best, always the best. And what had being the best brought her son? He had tried to jump the river, and for what? To please his father. And that had brought the boy death. Yes, Archer Cranley had killed her son, killed him as surely as if he had thrown him into that river, as surely as holding him beneath the water with his own hands.

In his dressing room at Rowlay House, Archer Cranley stared into the mirror but the reflection he saw looking back at him was of a beautiful face, pale blonde curls peeping provocatively beneath a feathered bonnet, a pretty mouth that an hour ago had been closed over his throbbing flesh, curved in a laugh echoed in mocking violet eyes.

How could he have known . . . how could he possibly have guessed?

They had made love so many times, the deliciously sensuous body matching his every thrust, anticipating . . . satisfying, only to tease again, to arouse that craving need that had to be quenched. So many times and she had said not a word, not until tonight! Swearing beneath his breath he turned from the mirror. Tonight she had named her price. He had been prepared to set her up in a place of her own, give her all the appearance of a respectable woman, but the bitch had laughed. That was not what she wanted, she wanted only what she had set out to get.

It had been no accident that day in West Bromwich High Street, she had planned it all. She had watched him, waited until she was certain of who he was and then . . . and then he had fallen for it! Snatching off his cravat he threw it angrily to the floor. So many hours, so many times of being together and never once had he suspected, never once doubted. But he knew it now. Shirt following cravat, Archer's anger deepened.

'*I don't want no little 'ouse! I'll tek what you 'ave, all you 'ave! Lilah Cherrington don't intend to let 'erself be hid away by nobody.*'

The attempt to conceal the rough dialect had been forgotten as she had faced him, her rosebud mouth twisted in a sneer. '*I'll tek what you 'ave.*'

That had been her intention all along, as she had smiled and denied in those first meetings, teased and tormented, driving him almost out of his mind with desire, using all the skills of Eve until he was willing to give her almost anything, anything but give her his name!

She had gone to his head like wine, taken away his senses until all he could think of was her, how badly he wanted her, her body; and when she had lain beneath him, eager to take him, her soft flesh pressed close to his, his passion, her passion, there had been no real quenching of the fire; the flames of desire, of lust, had flared again in minutes leaving him wanting only their next meeting, their next delicious love-making.

Pulling off the rest of his clothes he slipped a freshly laundered nightshirt over his head. Walking into the bedroom he snatched open the heavy curtains and stared angrily across the moonlit garden.

He had been like a dog in heat. The whole of his mind centred so much on his own satisfaction he hadn't seen the wood for the trees!

'*I ain't in the market for being a mistress,*' she had laughed, '*I just wants what be due me, the five 'undred pounds you should 'ave paid to the man I was to marry . . . oh yes, 'e told me, told me the 'igh and mighty owner of the glassworks would be keepin' we in clover, that 'e was 'anding over five 'undred that same night and that it wouldn't be the last five 'undred we would see.*'

The laugh had died in her throat then, and those soft violet eyes had glinted knives. Seeing again the hate on that lovely face, Archer's fingers tightened, crumpling the rich velvet of the drapes.

'*Only you didn't give 'im no money!*' The words spat again in his mind. '*Oh, you paid 'im off all right, paid 'im once and for all cos you killed 'im! You pushed 'im into that lock. The bobbies reckoned as 'e was so drunk he tumbled into it but I knows better, Jim Baker were no drinking man nor never 'ad been; he were sober as a judge that night . . . No, Mr Archer Cranley, his death were no accident, it were murder, and lessen you wants to swing for it, you'll pay that money to me, and then you'll make me your wife!*'

The shock of that demand must have shown on his face, for her laugh had become the spitting of a dangerous cat.

'*You don't like the idea of that, do you . . . ? The oh-so-important Archer Cranley, the wealthy owner of the glassworks married to Lilah Cherrington! That don't go down too well, does it? But you'd best get used to it,*' she had laughed again, '*the only other choice be the gallows!*'

He had looked at her then, at the face that had so recently enchanted him with its pretty pouting mouth and sensuous velvet eyes, and in that moment the spell had broken, and behind the gaudy beauty he had seen the greed.

'*This country does not allow a man two wives,*' he had snapped contemptuously, '*but even should that dubious pleasure be granted, I would not marry a prostitute! As for your threat of the gallows, one more word and it will be you facing a court, facing a writ of libel and false accusation and all without a shred of evidence to support your claim; and remember, my pretty whore, after a few months in a rat-infested gaol, where not all of the rats are animal, those looks of yours will no longer have a man anxious to part with a shilling. And one more thing you might think on, the gallows hold no preference, they take a woman as willingly as they take a man!*'

He had thought that to drive the wind out of her sails, to end the matter completely, but the sneer had stayed on her lips.

'*That talk don't frighten me none cos I knows you would never risk the talk it would bring, and I knows you 'ave a wife, but that can be remedied; after all, you got rid of Jim Baker so you knows how it be done. Like it or lump it, you be lookin' at the future Mrs Archer Cranley.*'

The echo of shrill laughter clawing his brain Archer let the curtain fall back into place.

'*his death were no accident . . . you'll make me your wife.*'

Her lover had harboured the same idea, to make him pay and go on paying, just as he would even were he to marry that bitch! But Jim Baker had reckoned without the consequences, and look where it had got him. The first hint of pleasure since climbing off that soft body touched his thin lips with a smile. Turning, he looked towards the bed, his glance lifting to the wooden canopy.

Lilah Cherrington would not become wife to the owner of the Briant Bottle and Glass, but she would be paid her due, paid in the same coin as that other one who had tried a hand at blackmailing Archer Cranley.

Philip was to be married! Joshua stared at the shadows. He had watched them lengthen about his room but the passage of hours had brought no relief from the ache inside him. The news should have meant nothing to him, should have had no effect. But in truth the words had sent his brain reeling while his heart had dropped like a stone in his chest. He should be glad, he had told himself, relieved there would be no more midnight walks seeing the lad home across the heath, thankful there would be no more meeting of those eyes across the workfloor whenever the lad collected glassware to carry to the lehr, of reading the message held in them, a message he could never answer; he should thank his maker for that marriage, for it would rid him of this longing, this cry for the moon.

Yes, the longing would eventually be gone, but not before a lifetime had gone. The pain that ripped him would pass, but right now the sting of it was more than he could bear. Was this the retribution of heaven, the punishment of the evil of his longing?

Slipping from the bed, Josh reached for his clothes. 'Follow the way of evil and you pays the price of evil.' Those were his mother's words, and this was the price he would pay. This was no judgement of heaven, but the judgement of hell. This was the devil's own reward and Josh Fairley would reap its fruits through all the years left to him.

Easing shirt and jacket gingerly over his injured shoulder he let himself quietly from the house, threading his way through darkened streets, unmindful of where he was until the scream of a distant train whistle dragged him from the depths of thought. Whitehall Road. To his right the graceful chimneys of Cophall House rose black against the night sky, while on his left, setting line to the edge of the disused Eight Locks coal workings, the canal glittered silver in the moonlight.

Playing over every inch of the area in boyhood the spent coal mine held no fear for him. Walking slowly he crossed to the canal. Sitting beside the towpath he stared at the brilliant ribbon of water. A little further along was the lock that had almost taken Philip from him. He had swayed on his feet, a smile on his gentle mouth, then he had stepped onto the beam . . . The picture rising again in his mind Joshua caught his breath as the image of that slight figure began to slide away into the chasm of the lock. He had held that body in his arms; sending the others for help he had gathered Philip Cranley into his arms, felt the warm softness . . . A great wave of pain and longing almost tearing him in half Joshua dropped his head into his hands. He shouldn't have given way to those feelings, one man should not feel for another as he felt for that lad, it was against everything he held sacred, everything that marked him a true man. He knew he loved Philip, but that love could only be a cry against the wind.

But at least Philip would never know of the way he felt. He had heard the crazed shouts of Ned Jukes but would think that was all they were, just the rantings of a man half wild with temper. No, Philip would never find out, he would marry and be happy; and Joshua Fairley, what of him? Lifting his head he stared at the glistening water. What did it matter? Life for him had become purposeless from that first meeting; it would hold no meaning the day Philip Cranley took a wife.

Cart wheels rumbling in the silence caught his ear, and Joshua glanced towards the sound. Silhouetted dark against the sky a low-backed cart was crossing Ryder's Green Bridge.

Frowning, he watched it go, the driver flicking a whip above the head of a slow moving horse. Where could it be bound at this time? There were no pick ups from the brickworks at night, neither from Briant's and no bargee would load or unload at this hour.

His eyes following it, seeing it merge to become one with the darkness, Joshua let his head drop again. It would be easier for him to go on walking, to fade into the darkness as that cart had faded, to turn his back on Greets Green and never return. Easier for him! With his fingers clenched into tight balls, his eyes closed against the futility of the thought. His mother would never leave the village, and he would never leave his mother. He was trapped, meshed in a web of his own spinning, the strands like silken steel, too strong to break. But hunched there in the darkness, he recognised that beneath all the thoughts filling his mind lay a stronger one, one that told a truth he would not face . . . the bond that held his heart *was* strong as steel, but there was no steel that would not break; the truth was that he did not want it broken. He would rather live with the pain than lose all trace of Philip Cranley!

# Chapter Twenty-Two

It had been worth the wait, and Simeon Beasley would think so too when he saw what was in that cart. Walking beside the plodding horse, Thad Grinley led it the last few yards to the rear entrance of the large house. He had been forced to pay for more tankards of ale than he would 'ave preferred, but spending nothing bought nothing, and the talk he had 'eard in the Narrow Boat was going to bring him another fifteen quid.

He had waited for the lad coming to work, almost giving up as the time for signing on came and went, but then patience 'ad paid off. It 'ad bin a good ruse, slumping against a wheel of the cart, 'olding his stomach and groanin'. The lad 'ad come to his assistance, bending to help him to his feet. Grinley brought the horse to a halt. That was when he 'ad struck the blow, a sharp chop of the 'and to the base of the neck had laid his would-be good Samaritan out cold. It 'ad bin easy after that, with 'im trussed like a chicken, gagged so he could make no sound, it had been a matter of a few minutes to 'ave 'im in the cart and covered wi'' sacks.

'Special delivery for Mr Beasley.' His grin lost among the shadows he glanced at the man outlined by light spilling from an opened door. It were not the first such delivery he 'ad made, Thad thought, as the servant came to help lift the hooded figure from the cart and carry it to an upstairs room. There would be

no questions and no tittle-tattling later, Beasley paid his lackeys
too well for them to risk carryin' word of his doings beyond this
'ouse.

The servant returned downstairs, Grinley stared about the
room. He had been here on many occasions – Beasley was a man
with an appetite for the new – but always the house with its
beautiful furnishings held a fascination for him. This was the
way he would live given the means, he would 'ave fine furniture
and fine food, and he would 'ave new playthings on a regular
basis.

'You brought it?'

His thoughts disturbed, Thad turned to where Beasley had
stepped into the room, wondering as so often in the past how it
was possible for so much flesh to move with so little sound.
Nodding a reply he glanced at the still form laid face-down on
the elegantly draped bed.

'No one saw you?'

'None.'

'You be certain of that?'

It was the same old rigmarole every time he brought a new
catch in! Thad hid his irritation by crossing to the bed. Did
anybody see ya, ya be sure ya weren't seen? Beasley was nervous as
a hen in a vixen's sights; if he 'ain't got the constitution for this
game then he'd be best off not playin' it!

'I ain't been caught afore,' he replied, 'and I won't be now, the
roads I took were empty as the devil's charity, I weren't seen by
nobody.'

Joining Grinley at the bedside, Simeon Beasley ran an eye
over the unmoving figure. Even in rough moleskin trousers it was
a fetching sight, a soft rounded little bottom. Beneath a robe of
blue figured silk his roused flesh convulsed. Prettier than any he
had brought before, that was what Grinley had promised.
Leaning over the figure he ran a hand over the buttocks, the
soft feel stimulating a rapidly growing desire.

Watching the heavy-jowled features, Thad smiled inwardly.

The goods were as good as sold, the look on the man's face said he could already feel them sweet little cheeks clinging to his flesh, was already savouring the lad's own tender parts on his tongue.

A quick spasm at the base of his own stomach urging him towards a similar reward, Thad held out a hand. 'I'll be tekin' the rest o' the payment . . .'

Still half leaning across the bed, Beasley glanced up at the dirt-lined face, an echo of distaste sour in his mouth. The man was a sewer rat; but sometimes even rats must be allowed to run free, though only until different vermin entered the run. With a new source of supply, Thad Grinley would be dropped from the race, or perhaps 'eliminated' were a more aptly descriptive word to use.

'Never buy anything you haven't thoroughly examined, otherwise a man could finish up buying a pig in a poke, and that could be disastrous for the man who sold it.'

The fat lips smiled but amid the folds of flesh the sharp little eyes gleamed venomously and Thad felt the flurry in his trousers change direction to become a thud in his chest.

'I ain't never sold you nuthin' duff afore,' he swallowed nervously, 'the goods 'ave always come up to scratch.'

'So far –' Beasley blinked slowly, a serpent watching the twitching of its prey '– and for your own good that best be the way of all our transactions.'

'You'll like this one, I knows you will, he be the way inclined . . .'

'How do you know that?' Beasley shot upright. 'I buys nothing as has been tampered with!'

'This one ain't been touched, Mr Beasley, 'e be same as the day 'e were born, you 'ave my word on it.'

His button eyes withdrawing into folds of fat, sweat-filmed skin sallow beneath yellow gas light, Simeon Beasley stared. 'Then how come you know his inclinations?'

Trying to pass soiled merchandise to this man would be like

trying to roast snow in a furnace . . . a useless waste of time. The knowledge a clear warning, Thad tried to choose his words carefully.

'I only means I read the signs . . . I mean I 'eard things, 'eard 'em meself.'

'And just what was it you heard that makes you so sure this little bundle will be to my liking?'

Earlier confidence failing fast, Thad had a quick vision of the two five-pound notes in his pocket and the way they would be retrieved.

'I 'eard the talk as passed between 'em.' The glint in those small eyes turning to dagger thrusts, Thad realised his choice of words had not been careful enough. Christ, Beasley 'ad 'im sweatin' like a robber's 'oss!

'I'd seen that one a day or so afore you an' me spoke last.' Each word a straw clutched in haste, the explanation tumbled out. 'I seen his 'andsome looks, then I 'eard the men in the Narrow Boat tavern talkin' of 'im. What they said proved what I guessed, the lad would be pleased to meet up with such as yourself, somebody as would properly appreciate a pretty lad like 'im.'

'What of family?' Simeon's little eyes stroked the softly inviting buttocks.

Soundlessly breathing a sigh of relief, Thad nevertheless thought it wiser to twist the truth. 'I 'eard about them an' all. Seems there be no love lost between that lot, seems the old 'un would be more'n glad to be shot of the young 'un; won't be no wailin' nor a' weepin' over 'im going missing. So, what do you say, Mr Beasley, give me the reckonin' of our bargain and I'll be away to me bed.'

'Not your own, Grinley.' The heavy jowls shook with the laugh. 'Knowing you as I do it will be one that holds a similar dish to the one on *my* supper table. But you need have no worries as to payment, you'll get that whether I be pleased with your little offering or whether I don't! And I shan't be knowing which until at least seeing if the top be a pretty match for the bottom.'

Bending again, a podgy hand stretched to take the covering from the head, he paused, sniffing loudly.

'Drugged,' he snarled, ''ave you brought me a bloody addict?'

Forcing a smile, Thad tried to bolster his flagging spirit. 'Thad Grinley don't be that short of 'oss sense. It just be a drop of opium ya can smell. I needed to give him summat to keep 'im quiet while I was bringin' 'im here; he might 'ave kicked up a shindig if I 'adn't.'

True, the lad would not have taken kindly to being bundled into a cart whatever he was told; it was more than certain he would have made a fuss. Accepting the explanation, Beasley ran his hand once more over the rounded buttocks, the soft temptation agitating flesh already rigid beneath the cover of his robe. He would savour this a longer time, feel the ripeness in his hands, taste the sweetness with his lips before taking that first delectable bite of his forbidden fruit.

'I ain't expectin' 'im to be awake just yet.'

Mentally counting the money already as good as between his fingers, Thad felt his pulses skip when the hood was thrown in his face.

'What the bloody hell do you think you be playin' at?' The snarl, low and vicious as a savaging wolf, was flung after the hood. 'Why bring *him* here . . . 'ave you taken total leave of your senses! You'll pay for this, Grinley . . . my God, you'll pay!'

'I don't understand, Mr Beasley,' Thad grovelled as the fat hand moved to a tasselled bell pull. 'You likes 'em pretty an' that lad be pretty enough, look . . . look at the face . . .'

'I 'ave looked . . . I 'ave bloody looked, and so should you 'ave done. There'll be no weeping an' a' wailing over 'im goin' missin'!' he mocked. 'Not bloody likely, there won't! Do you know who that lad is . . . do you?'

Afraid more for his skin than the remainder of the promised pounds, Thad Grinley shook his head. To deny everything was his safest policy; admit to having heard the lad's name would be a sure way of signing his own death warrant. Beasley never joked about paying a man, especially when that payment carried no coin.

'Then I'll tell you!' Beasley pulled savagely on the bell rope. 'It be Archer Cranley's son, his *only* son! That lad goes missing and the whole of this town will be set alight. Now you get him out of this house and away from Harville's Hawthorne, take him back where you found him and pray, pray very hard nothing of this comes home to me.'

Slipping the hood back over the head of the sleeping figure as the manservant arrived, Thad felt his blood chill at the quiet threat that followed as, between them, they carried the limp form from the room.

'Remember our bargain, Grinley . . . Simeon Beasley always honours his debts.'

It would have been a nice little entertainment. He watched from a window as the cart rolled away. Cranley's lad was handsome, pretty, one could say, and Simeon Beasley liked his toys pretty; but to take that one would be to sacrifice the price of many others. Without his son reaching the age of majority Cranley would have no glassworks and he would have no more of those so-useful annuities. Yes, Archer's lad would have proved an amusing toy. He turned from the window. He always enjoyed a pretty new toy . . . and maybe after that business were signed to the father he might still have the son!

*'I'll tek the five 'undred in the alley alongside of the Wheatsheaf, after all who knows what might 'appen to a girl meeting with a man along of the canal? Then after you've paid me you can tek me inside and propose nicely over a drink.'*

The sound of the voice that had so recently been music to his heart now jarred against his senses as those words returned to his mind. The bitch would be paid all right but there would be no proposal. Archer Cranley wrapped the muffler about his neck, smiling as he pulled the flat cap low over his brow. He hated making proposals of any sort . . . especially ones he knew could not be kept! She had been smarter than her accomplice, but smart as Lilah Cherrington had been she was no match for Archer Cranley.

There had been no problem with leaving Hannah, she had spoken no word since asking Philip to convey her thanks to the Fairley woman, in fact since the business of slipping off to church that day she had rarely said anything at all, wanting only the company of her precious child, settling to her bed once he was gone. Well, that suited him down to the ground, no argument . . . no recourse! But Edna! Edna was a hound of a different colour, and her nose was everywhere. But she had not found Nathan Briant's gift, the one so carefully concealed in the canopy of the bed, the gift that was proving yet again to be so useful.

With his hands pushed deep into jacket pockets he walked quickly along the High Street, drawing little attention among similarly dressed men, most of whom were coming from the many coal workings and iron foundries that littered the land-scape of West Bromwich.

Turning the corner into St Michael's Street he glanced both ways before slipping into the narrow alleyway.

'Why so careful?'

Archer's veins tingled at the sound of that voice followed by a laugh that made no attempt to hide its mockery.

'Has the great Archer Cranley no taste for bein' seen with Lilah Cherrington any more?'

Shadows still wreathed like a dark veil, half hiding the figure that stepped forward. At their centre the face smiled but Archer felt no surge of desire, saw no beauty; the hold this woman had . . . could have gone on having . . . was broken.

'Well!' The mocking laugh came again. 'You 'ad better get used to it for we'll be seen often together once I be Mrs Archer Cranley! But first I'll tek that money. You 'ave brought it, I 'ope, I wouldn't want to lose you to the 'angman.'

'I've brought it, but I won't hand it over in that tavern, too many prying eyes.'

'You ain't minded 'ow many eyes seen you in there afore, you couldn't 'ave given a brass farthing who seen you with me or who knowed the reason for that private room, all you was moithered about—'

'Well, I'm not bothered about that now.' Archer glanced quickly into the darkness that swallowed the rest of the narrow alley running between the tavern and the church.

'Oh, so you ain't bothered!' Lilah swayed closer, her slim waist highlighted by the close fit of a wide-revered jacket with its huge leg-of-mutton sleeves, the glint of eyes taunting beneath a cheeky feathered bonnet. 'Do I tek it as that'll be a permanent feelin', even after we be married, you means you won't miss what you was gettin' in that tavern?'

He must keep a check on his tongue, he had said too much when they were together in that bedroom; he should not have told her he would marry no prostitute.

'I meant only that this was no place to give way to those pleasures, thought leads to deed and this alley is no private room, my dear. As to my not being bothered becoming permanent, let's get this business over and I'll give you the answer to that up there in our private little hideaway.'

Reaching to an inner pocket of his jacket, Archer took out an envelope. Holding it just clear of the gloved fingers he smiled.

'Don't I get a kiss first?'

Pressing her body close to his, Lilah lifted her face, eyes closed, painted lips parted expectantly. One arm circling the tiny waist, Archer swung her around. Her back against the wall, the front of her shielded by his own body, he lowered the envelope into the grasping fingers.

'Enjoy your money, my pretty whore.' A laugh soft in his throat, Archer reached again to his pocket. 'Ours will be a truly permanent arrangement.'

Covering her mouth with his he drove the slim blade of an ivory-handled knife up under her ribs.

'Damn an' bugger Simeon Beasley!' Thad Grinley swore beneath his breath. He'd never bothered before as to the identity of the goods he were brought, never refused the prospect of a new little body to warm his bed, a new tight little arse to probe, especially when one set of pretty cheeks was complemented by another. And the lad bundled in his cart was passin' 'andsome, there were no doubt of that. But Beasley 'ad refused . . . why? Reaching the point where Dial Lane edged on to the canal towpath, Thad turned the cart to the right, following Brickhouse Lane. Were it cos the lad were Cranley's son? Like bloody 'ell it were! It could be the devil's own an' Beasley wouldn't care tuppence, if 'e fancied it enough 'e would 'ave it. But 'e 'ad fancied the lad, that much 'ad been clear on his fat face as he'd stroked them tight little buttocks . . . so why turn away what 'e drooled over?

'Eh up, ya great daft happorth, you've 'eard a train afore!'

Thad quieted the horse that snorted in fright, coaxing it across the bridge that crossed the busy Great Western line. There would be little attention paid to a cart from here on, many carters took their loads from the goods' yard ready for an early morning start to a journey.

There were more to tonight's doings than could be seen. The animal reassured, Thad fell back to reasoning the other man's reaction when he had snatched away the hood to look at the sleeping face. It were no sense of wrong doin' 'ad Beasley act the way 'e 'ad; wrong doin'! Thad scoffed deprecatingly, the bloke were so crooked 'e couldn't lie straight in bed! No, there 'ad to be some other reason; 'e could think about it 'til the cows came 'ome but that wouldn't give the answer, neither would it stop Beasley 'avin' 'is guts. Losin' the remainder of the twenty-five quid were bad enough but he'd lose a damn sight more when Beasley sent his henchmen to collect.

That talk in the Boat, p'raps them men 'ad it wrong, p'raps Cranley wouldn't be glad to 'ave seen the last of the lad. Maybe the night's work needn't be a total write-off after all!

Climbing down from the cart he led the horse into the yard of the disused malthouse he rented in Charles Street. The effort of waylaying that lad on 'is way to the glass 'adn't been a loss after all, tomorrow 'e would sound Cranley out, and if he didn't want to pay? Thad glanced towards the loft where the figure he had kept drugged still lay. 'If 'e don't pay then 'e don't get,' he murmured. 'But not to moither, my pretty lad, old Thad can enjoy what Beasley 'as turned 'is nose up at, you an' me will warm each other's backside!'

# Chapter Twenty-Three

She had made hardly a sound, a quiet gasp beneath his lips and then she had slumped in his arms. He was surprised by that, to die so quietly.

His hands shaking slightly, Archer glanced at the huddled shape beside him in the carriage. That one sound, that was all it had been and then the lovely Lilah was dead, gone as quickly as her accomplice, both finished and not a single witness, not a penny paid.

He had thought to leave her there in that alley but they had been seen together in the tavern on several occasions which would mean the police would be certain to ask questions, and that was something he could not afford; the fewer people to come calling at Rowlay House the better, especially the police. It had been something of a risk leaving the carriage at the end of that alley but it being so close to the graveyard meant people were loth to walk there after dark. Superstitions! Archer's mean mouth twitched. The folk of West Bromwich were all of that, and tonight it had proved in his favour.

But the body! He glanced again at the still figure. He had to get rid of it. Not the canal. He had thought of using that way but it might not be so easily believed that she had been so drunk as to fall in to say nothing of a stab wound, and there would be the added question: prostitute or not, what brought a woman alone on the towpath at night? No, the canal as a solution was out. So where?

The last of the houses bordering Phoenix Street falling away behind, Archer looked across the expanse of empty heath, black beneath a cloud-filled sky. Virtually no one crossed that way since the last of the limestone quarrymen . . . of course, that was the answer! Turning the carriage onto the track that led to Rowlay House he drove for a few minutes then drew to a halt.

The chimney, a hole that let air into the underground limestone workings, was still open. The exact location was printed like a minutely detailed map on his mind's eye. He had visited the spot many times under cover of night, memorising the direction, the number of steps from the path, imprinting his brain with the route his sister's lonely burial would take. Now Edna would share her tomb with one more, with another woman who had tried to blackmail Archer Cranley!

Climbing from the carriage he drew the figure into his arms, a sudden shaft of moonlight illuminating the pale face. It was a pity she had tried to best him, they could have had quite an entertaining life together, now she had no life!

'Help me . . . help me . . . !'

The cry, though no more than a whisper, sounded like a cannon in his brain. She was alive! The bitch was still alive!

'Help . . .'

Lowering her feet to the ground, supporting her with one arm, Archer watched the pale eyelids flutter. She was so pretty. He could not throw her into that chimney like this, he must help her, of course he must help.

Setting her gently on the ground he looked at the knife still protruding from beneath her ribs, the ivory handle gleaming in the moonlight.

'It's all right, Lilah,' he murmured, 'everything is going to be all right.'

Bringing his lips to hers he pressed them gently, closing one hand over the knife.

'This will hurt only for a moment, my dear.' He smiled down at the closed eyes as he drew the knife free. 'Only a moment.' Taking her chin with his other hand he pulled her head backwards, slicing the blade across her white throat.

'What do you mean, he hasn't been home?'

'Try not to be so tiresome, Archer, you understand words very well. Philip has not been in this house since late afternoon yesterday, or if he has then neither I nor Hannah have seen him. He left for the glassworks as usual and has not returned since.'

Philip had not come home when his shift ended! Archer Cranley's ferret-sharp glance raked his sister's tightly drawn features. What was the sour bitch up to now, was this another way of trying to increase the money she hoped to get? Well, hope she could have in plenty, he would watch hell freeze over and the devil skate across it afore he would pay her one single penny.

'Did he say anything to his mother?'

With arms folded across her stomach Edna Cranley sniffed disdainfully. 'You know the answer to that already, you were in the room all of the time; it was your order he does not see Hannah unless you are there and that order is carried out.'

'It is when you are here, but what about when you are not, what about the times you go pithering off to mewl over your dead fiancé?'

Her eyes flashing like spear tips, Edna held on to the anger that bubbled like a hot geyser deep inside. There was an old saying in these parts, every dog has his day, and her day of triumph would come, she would see her brother fall and she would grind him underfoot like a dried leaf. Keeping her feelings hidden she answered calmly, 'If my being here does not suit you, Archer, then why not get someone else to take my place? Pay me what is due and I will leave, my mewling will have no effect on you then.'

'And none on Richard Stanton,' Archer returned acidly. 'It affects him as much in death as it would have done in life. He never wanted you; it was not him harboured thoughts of marriage; your fiancé . . . pah! When did he ever ask you to marry him, tell me when? But that were your idea, weren't it? The invention of your own pitiful desire. His suicide was a godsend for you, the perfect answer, for you knew no man ever looked twice at you, no man wanted your scrawny body.'

'Maybe not.' Drained of blood, Edna's pale lips were tight with rage she fought to hide. 'But at least I do not resort to going to bed with a woman of the streets, a common two-shilling prostitute . . . or did your pretty blonde whore take you for more than that, say a wardrobe of fancy clothes? You see, brother dear, I saw you in St Michael Street, saw you with your arm about her as you took her into the Wheatsheaf Inn. But you did not take a drink in the public bar . . . How do I know? Because I followed you in, and you were nowhere to be seen. Oh, you can check my story, how many better-class women go into a place like that even to purchase a measure of brandy for a fainting relative? The landlord will not have forgotten . . . and neither should you. Remember, my dear, your son is not yet married, maybe he should learn of your little amour.'

She could have the last word, for now. Archer recognised the warning. He would not put it past her to put a spoke in the wheel even if it meant she too would lose everything, but once Philip and the Lacy girl were wed . . .

'These Fairleys, the woman Hannah asked be thanked, where do they live?' He turned the argument about, though the bile of it rankled in his throat.

Triumph replacing the icicles in her eyes and about her mouth, Edna guessed the thoughts behind that narrow face. It had never been hard to read Archer, malice and greed always showed themselves to those who recognised the signs, showed themselves as clearly as the frustration and spite that filled that cold heart.

'I don't know,' she answered. 'But you should, the man did work for you after all.'

Sharpened by aggravation, Archer's retort spat out: 'So do a good many men, I can't be expected to remember every one!'

Having turned away towards the kitchen, Edna paused to look back at her brother.

'That's true enough, Archer, you can't, but I would have expected that even you would remember that one, the man you had dismissed for saving Philip's life. How would you have got around that, how would you have taken everything for yourself? Oh you would doubtless have had some answer, some contingency already worked out; but then you would not divulge any plan you have, you were never one to share a secret if you could carry it out by yourself. Have you ever asked yourself, Archer, would you have behaved towards your first child as you have towards the second? Rob him as you intend to rob Philip?'

His face dark as thunder clouds Archer glared. 'I haven't bloody heard you refuse a share! All I've heard from you is you want another thousand. Take a little advice, Edna, greed gives your face an ugly look . . . and you have more than a generous share of that already!'

'One more thing we have in common, Archer.' Edna smiled murderously. 'We both know how to use things to our own advantage. Your pretty blonde trollop is going to prove quite a valuable one . . . to me!'

Staring at her, Archer felt new fires blaze beneath old hatred. 'Lilah Cherrington'll do you no good, she'll do nobody any good!' Too late he realised the goading had driven him to make a mistake.

'Lilah Cherrington . . . a pretty name.' Edna's cold eyes gleamed their own victory. 'Her natural one, or one painted up to match a painted face? But why will the woman do me no good, Archer? Could it be because she is dead, is that it . . . have you killed your little prostitute?'

'Yes!' Thin lips curled back in a snarl, Archer let all the

passions of hate blaze forth. 'Yes the whore is dead, and take fair warning: where she is now is the place you will be if you think to breathe one word of this or of any other of my business. I make no threat, Edna, only a promise, speak one word to a living soul and you'll join Lilah Cherrington.'

It had been a mistake, a bad one. Archer stared at the door which had closed behind his sister, hearing the quiet laugh still ring in his mind. But she would say nothing so long as she thought to gain from her silence, and that silence would be eternal once Briant Bottle and Glass were his for good.

But for that he needed Philip. The thought subduing the turmoil he glanced at his pocket watch. Almost the end of the morning shift. Leaving the house he set off for the glassworks. He would find out for himself why Philip had not been home.

'I was goin' to speak to your father, goin' to see 'im today but it could serve my purpose more if I 'angs on to you for a day or two.' Thad Grinley held the chipped teacup to Philippa's lips. 'They says as 'ow absence meks the 'eart grow fonder, your father thinkin' you gone then finding you ain't might mek his pocket a bit looser.'

'A ransom?' She drew away from the cup. 'Is that what you are after . . . money?'

'It be useful.' Thad grinned, showing yellowed teeth.

'Then go ask for it now, my father will not be pleased by being kept waiting.'

'P'raps 'e won't be pleased by bein' told you be safe and sound; judging by what I've 'eard he would find the opposite much more to his liking. There be them at the glass as thinks 'e would be 'appier with you out of the way for good.'

It was true. Philippa's mouth clamped, refusing the strip of greasy meat held between grimy fingers. Archer Cranley would welcome nothing more, but not before that all-important Will was signed.

'If that is what you have heard then you have been listening to nonsense. I suggest you go to him now if you wish for him to be generous. Leave him to find out for himself where I am and I promise you things will go badly, you are more likely to find fetters about your wrists than money in your hands.'

'But 'e ain't likely to find out where you be.' Shrugging his shoulders as another strip of meat was refused, Thad slipped it into his own mouth, chewing as he talked. 'You see, there weren't not a soul seen me take you from that heath, ain't nobody knows where you be.'

'Folk will be searching for me . . .'

Thad smacked his lips noisily as he fished in the bowl for another piece of boiled mutton. 'I ain't disputing that, but they can look all they likes, they won't find hide nor hair of you, and ain't nobody gonna suspect Thad Grinley.'

The panic that had seized her on waking and realising feet and hands as well as mouth were bound, returned as the villain laid aside the empty bowl and, after wiping his fingers on the sides of his stained trousers, picked up a length of rag.

'Wait.' Philippa swallowed hard. 'I can pay you myself.'

The dirty rag halfway to her mouth was halted in mid-air. 'You can pay, what with . . . washers? You ain't got no money, you—'

'I will have,' Philippa put in quickly, 'in just a few days the glassworks comes to me, I shall own everything. I will pay you whatever you ask, I promise, only please let me go.'

'So you gonna be glassmaster!' Thad Grinley smiled. 'In a few days you'll own the lot. That be good, that be good for all concerned; and old Thad don't be ungenerous, he'll let you go . . . when them few days be up.'

Alter tying the rag about her mouth he turned away, clambering down a ladder to the ground below.

So that was it. Harnessing horse to wagon he sifted his thoughts. It were Cranley's lad not Cranley hisself was to get old man Briant's leavings. That would stick in Cranley's craw an' plague 'im 'til he got it out, either that or choke on it. Was that what the talk in the tavern 'ad been about? Was Cranley wantin' to be rid of his lad like 'e were a stone in the throat? Weren't impossible, if that were the only way a man could get summat 'e wanted real bad.

Leading the horse from the malthouse and closing the wide wooden doors, Thad climbed onto the cart.

Summat 'e wanted real bad; and what man wouldn't want that glassworks and all that went with it? The reins lying loose in one hand, picking threads of meat from between his teeth with a grimy fingernail of the other, Thad weighed the chances of making profit from loss. Beasley's twenty-five was a gonner an' a lot more besides, namely his hide once them henchmen got 'old of 'im. And the lad? Supposing 'e let 'im go what were to say 'e wouldn't set the bobbies onto 'im, a stretch along the line were not what Thad Grinley were lookin' to get. Seemed the best thing to do were to wait, see which way the wind blowed, meantime . . .

Running his tongue over his teeth, Thad sucked on the tiny bits of meat, his mind's eye running over the slight figure bound hand and foot in that loft. Meantime, the lad would be company in the night, the sort of company he liked, company 'e would make good use of. Beneath the soiled fabric of his trousers, hardened flesh jerked violently. It weren't only Beasley could take 'is pleasure, Thad Grinley also liked pretty playthings, and tonight – flesh jerking again Thad sucked harder on his teeth – tonight he would play.


'Where is he, where is my son?'

As he stood in Naomi Fairley's cramped kitchen, Archer Cranley's face was flushed with anger.

'Your son?'

'Yes, my bloody son.' Archer glared at the question. 'Philip Cranley, where is he, I know he came to this house!'

The question still in her eyes, Naomi nodded. 'Ar that be so. 'E called to bring the thanks of his mother for what my lad done . . . but that were yesterday evenin'—'

'I know when it was!' Archer snapped.

Holding her hands tight together across her apron, Naomi watched the brooding anger gathering on her visitor's face. She had heard folk from the glass talk of Archer Cranley's rages, it were not often he visited them works but whenever 'e did then even the strongest of them were feared, feared for the babbies their jobs fed. But her Joshua d'ain't work in the glass no more, this man had given 'im 'is tin, and all for saving a lad from serious 'urt, the same lad 'e were now showin' so much concern over. Drawing in a long breath she held the glinting black eyes with ones as calm as the others were angered.

'If you knows that then you should know your lad went on from 'ere to the work you set 'im in.'

'So Philip went on to the works, did he? Then tell me, why does Samuel Platt say otherwise?'

'I don't answer for Samuel Platt and I don't 'ave to answer to you. I tells you that lad left from this 'ouse to go to 'is employment an' that be an end of it!'

The surprise of being spoken to in that strain curled quickly into a snarl that settled on Archer's lips. His fingers already bunched into a fist he raised his hand. 'There'll be an end when I say there's an end. Now tell me, where is he?'

Slicing through the narrow space that separated him from the woman, his fist struck against her cheek.

'Tell me!' He stepped to where she had stumbled against a cupboard set into an alcove of the cast-iron range, his hand already raised for a second blow. 'Tell me, or by Christ I'll beat it out of you!'

'You've struck once, you bastard, and that be one more blow than any man strikes against my mother!'

His raised arm caught in an iron grip, Archer Cranley gasped as he was jerked backwards.

'Try beating a man, Cranley.' Rage twisting his features, Joshua slammed a fist into the narrow face. 'Or is it only women and young lads you can beat?' Grabbing the lapels of the other man's jacket and hauling him to his feet, he drove home another slamming fist. 'That be your style don't it, Cranley, vent your spite on them as can't fight back. Well, this be *my* style, I likes walloping men, especially the sort of contemptible blackguard you be.'

The fist crashing against Archer's mouth made him sprawl backwards across the table, sending crockery splintering on the stone-flagged floor. Dragging him to his feet Joshua breathed his rage. 'I should bloody kill you, Cranley!'

Twisting free, Archer scrambled for the door and climbed quickly into the carriage. Whip in hand he looked at the tall figure stood threateningly in the doorway.

'You should have done, Fairley,' he snarled. 'You should have given yourself that satisfaction, for the price you be going to pay is a high one; you be going to swing from the gallows for what you just did, and I'll still be there to watch!'

'I should never 'ave let you do it.' Naomi gathered the broken pieces of pottery. 'I should never 'ave let you larrup 'im the way you did, but truth to tell, lad, I wanted you to do it; yes, God forgive me, I wanted you to pummel 'is lights out.'

Dropping the fragments of her cups into the waste heap at the bottom of the yard, Naomi felt the first tinges of shame replace the heat of anger. She never ought to have allowed Joshua to strike Cranley. *Vengeance is mine.* The words of many a chapel meeting struck fear into her heart. The Lord might well take His vengeance, but Cranley would also take his. He would keep to what he had threatened, and even should Joshua escape the rope he would go along the line for many years, maybe even for the rest of his life; and it would be her fault, all because she had wanted to see that man suffer, suffer not for striking her but for the way he had treated her son.

But vengeance had a way of recoiling, of visiting itself on the one that used it. Naomi walked slowly into the house. Archer Cranley had always been a hard taskmaster, he would be no easier an enemy.

# Chapter Twenty-Four

Would that man go to Rowlay House . . . would he dare to admit kidnapping Archer Cranley's son? Wincing against the pain of cord biting into flesh, Philippa tried to ease cramped limbs. He had done it to obtain money, or so he said; but even should he have the courage to ask for it, would Archer pay?

With her wrists burning where the ties had bitten into them, she struggled to sit up.

It was only three days before that marriage was due to take place. Less than a week and Hannah Cranley would be safe, the wording of any document signed would clearly state that should she be locked away in any institution, or die of any unknown or unforeseen cause then that document would be rendered null and void. But that would not protect Davinia Lacy, keep her from a marriage that was nothing short of criminal. A marriage without love, a union brought about by two men each driven by their own selfish greed, was sin enough; but this was base and shameful, and Philippa Cranley was a part of it. It could have been cancelled, could still be cancelled, but then the full force of Archer Cranley's vicious depravity would descend on his wife.

But Davinia Lacy would not be made to suffer. That gentle girl must be spared a life of unhappiness. The agreement reached between Joseph Lacy and Archer Cranley would be short-lived. Philippa glanced upwards to where sunlight reached gleaming shafts between cracked roof tiles. Guilt at what Archer had forced to take place had plagued night and day, but at last the solution had come. There could never be a marriage with the one who held Philippa Cranley's heart, nor could love be spoken of between them. Joshua Fairley would never know, never hear the words that told of a love so deep that only death could end it; and that had been the solution, the answer the dark hours of night had brought. The marriage of Davinia Lacy and Philip Cranley would be solemnised, the business Archer Cranley so desperately coveted would be signed to him, and then Philip Cranley would commit suicide. Only the mother who was so very dear would grieve, but that could not be avoided, and forgiveness would fill her heart, leaving no room for condemnation. There would be little loss in forfeiting a life that held only the promise of pain, of heartbreak; but to live, knowing Joshua Fairley could never return that love, to watch him marry, would be a torture too cruel to survive.

Less than a week to that marriage. Yes, Archer Cranley would pay whatever that man asked. Philippa's eyes pressed shut. Less than a week and then this web of deceit could break.

'It be understandable Philip Cranley's father enquire at this 'ouse, but why not believe me when I told 'im the lad were certainly not 'ere now?'

Holding a cooling damp cloth to her bruised face Naomi watched her son pour the tea he had insisted on making.

'There's no accounting for Cranley's temper,' Joshua answered. 'But he'll think twice afore he comes displaying it in this house again.'

' 'E won't need to come again to do that, the bobbies and the magistrate will do it forrim. Eh lad! When I thinks of what that man can do to you my 'eart fair trembles.'

'I've said for you not to worry.' Placing the heavy platter teacup close to his mother's hand, Joshua dropped a kiss on her head before settling to a chair drawn to the opposite side of the fireplace. 'Give him time to cool off and chances be he'll see the folly of bringing any case to court; having to admit to being given a hiding will be embarrassment in itself, but having to admit it was the result of his beating a woman in her own home . . . well, whether the magistrate finds for or against him it won't go down well with his friends.'

'Friends!' Naomi sniffed her contempt. 'I d'ain't think 'is sort 'ad friends. I tell you, Joshua, 'e be a dark 'un, I wouldn't trust 'im no further than I could throw 'im! That man be bad, 'e were cast in a cracked mould and if 'e can do another man evil then it be my bet 'e would do it, ar, an' to the best of 'is ability an' all.'

'Well, worrying never improved any situation, isn't that what you always say?' Joshua smiled over the rim of his own cup.

Tears filling the back of her throat, Naomi made a pretence of swallowing tea as yet too hot to drink. 'Mebbe it is, but turning your back on it don't drive it away. I do be worried, Joshua, I admits as much; I says we should do a moonlight flit, pack what we can carry an' leave tonight as soon as it be dark.'

'We'll do no such thing!' Joshua banged his own cup down onto the table his mother's daily scrubbing had turned white. 'We run away from no man's spite. Let Archer Cranley do what he will, this is your home and you don't leave it for him or for any other man.'

'Could be we'll 'ave to, son. You might 'ave made a good friend of Cranley's son but you've made a bad enemy of the father. If 'e can do you 'arm then 'e will. I doubt you'll see work again in Greets Green.'

'Time will tell.' Joshua refilled his mother's cup. 'But we are not starving yet so Mr Cranley has a bit of a wait on his hands if he wants to see the Fairleys on the streets.'

Sipping her tea, the memory of the almost animal snarl and vicious eyes brought a shiver to Naomi's spine. Once an enemy always an enemy summed up her opinion of Archer Cranley, and instinct told her he was not one to treat lightly.

'You watch out forrim just the same, a fox be less sly than that one; it makes a body wonder 'ow such a man as that could 'ave so pleasant a lad as a son, for I 'ave to admit that all else aside young Cranley were pleasant mannered.'

Slipping to his haunches Joshua took an iron poker to the fire, clearing ash from its bed and hiding the emotion that swept through him. Pleasant mannered, yes that described Philip Cranley, but it didn't do him justice. Everything about him was pleasant, everything about him made it easy to love him . . . as Joshua Fairley loved him. But his was the wrong sort of love, the love that condemned him to a lifetime of misery, of wanting what never could be his. One time . . . just once to hold that slight body, to feel it respond to his, to feel those arms about him, those soft lips beneath his mouth, to hear those whispered words, I love you Joshua. But even once could never be.

'I say it be a blessing that lad be marryin', that way 'e don't 'ave to live with his father no more, for it strikes me there be no love lost atwixt the two.'

His mother's words broke in on his thoughts but chased away none of their pain. To look at her now would show it in all its rawness. Replacing the poker he walked through the scullery to the yard, taking more time than was needed to fill a bucket with coals.

'Where do you reckon that lad went after his visitin' of this 'ouse were done, where could 'e 'ave been all night, and where now?'

Questions meeting him as he came back to the kitchen, Joshua fed coal to the fire. He had wondered that, too; where had Philip gone . . . and why?

'Eh, Joshua . . . do you thinks the lad be run away?'

'I don't know what to think,' Joshua answered truthfully.

'If 'e has then it'll be nobody's fault 'cept that father of his, for in all honesty I can't bring meself to believe his mother be the same way inclined, surely her must 'ave love for her own child.'

'A strong love, Mother. It showed in her face when I—'

'When you what?' Naomi laid the cloth aside. 'What 'ave you done? No, don't go traipsing off to the scullery!' Her eyes shadowing with sudden anxiety, she stared at him. 'You can wash your 'ands later but right now you tell me, how come you knows that woman's feelin's, when did you see her face? What be it you 'ave done?'

'I went to Rowlay House.'

*'I have no potion that will rid your soul of the worm that be nibbling it.'*

The words of Keziah Silk, words that never left Naomi for long, repeated themselves like knife thrusts in her heart. This was that worm, the fear that feasted in the night, the dread of her son being so drawn to that lad as to follow after him.

'Oh my dear Lord! Oh Joshua, what brought you to do such a thing? There can never be anything there for you, going there can only add to what already be inside you.'

Every moment of pent-up fear, of hidden worries trembling in that one sentence, Naomi covered her face with her apron.

Did she know? Joshua stood like a statue. Had his mother seen the truth in his face, guessed the reason for the hurt he could not always keep from his eyes? Worse even than the reason for it all, did she think he had given free rein to that love, that he and Philip Cranley . . .

Dropping to his knees beside her, he pulled the apron gently away. Beneath the fast-purpling bruises her face was pallid, drawn with the haunting fear he recognised as his own, a fear of giving way to the demand of the heart. Faltering beneath the grief displayed behind tear-filled eyes he dropped his head into her lap.

'I won't lie to you, Mother,' he said softly, 'it is as I see you think, I do have feelings for Philip Cranley.'

Feeling the tremor those words sent through her limbs, Joshua paused. It sounded so wrong, but there had been no wrong done. Drawing a deep breath he went on. 'But I know those feelings can never be shown and as God be my witness there has been no talk of them between Philip and me. I would not bring pain or dishonour to either of you. Believe me, Mother, I will never bring shame to your door.'

Touching her hand to his head as she had so often done in the years of his childhood, Naomi heard the quiet words of the old herb woman.

*'There will be a parting . . . there be change, it stands close, change that will take that you cherish most . . .'*

Joshua would not bring shame to her door. Tears spilling silently she looked down at the fair hair so soft beneath her fingers. That could only mean he intended to leave, go away on his own. Your home, he had said a minute since; you don't leave it for any man. But he would leave it and she would lose the thing she cherished most, her son.

'You remember we talked of the sort of glass that could be made when Philip called,' Joshua went on quietly. 'It was after he left I thought of the pieces I had practised on. I took a bowl to Rowlay House as a gift for his wedding. His mother answered the door to me. She looked so ill I wondered how she could have been left alone . . . she thanked me for helping Philip that evening in the cone then said how beautiful the bowl was. Then as I was leaving she asked would I do something for her, something she could ask no one of her family to do.'

Trepidation holding the blood cold in her veins, Naomi sat silent as he lifted his head. What was so dreadful no woman could speak of it to her son? Only a love that broke all bounds, a love Keziah Silk had named profane! But Joshua had said no word of what he felt had been spoken to Philip Cranley, and Joshua's word was one to trust, so how could his mother know? Unless . . . Naomi's heart seemed to stand still . . . unless her lad held a similar love for Joshua!

'Mrs Cranley asked would I hold this safe.' Rising to his feet Joshua crossed to where his jacket hung from a peg behind the kitchen door. Taking out a sealed envelope he handed it to his mother. 'She made me swear an oath I would give it to none save Philip, and that I hand it to him on the eve of his wedding.'

Looking at the delicate tracery of writing Naomi could not help but feel despair. That woman's motherly intuition must have told her the same dreadful story, something too vile for her to speak openly of, so unnatural she could only write her horror of it; and what she knew Archer Cranley must know, and that could be the only reason the lad had run away.

'You ought never to 'ave gone to that 'ouse.' Naomi shook her head. 'An' you never ought to 'ave swore no oath; Cranley will not look upon it with kindness nor will 'e thank you for the doin' of it. I can't tell you to return that letter to where it came from nor yet to destroy it, for an oath be an oath an' good or bad it must be kept, but once it be 'onoured then turn your back on that place an' cut Philip Cranley from your heart, for to hanker after forbidden fruit can bring naught save an aching mind and a sorrowful soul.'

Cut Philip Cranley from his heart! Washing his hands beneath the pump in the yard, Joshua felt his own heart twist. It would be easier to take the moon from the sky than take Philip from his heart.

Edna was becoming careless. Hannah Cranley watched the dregs of laudanum settle to the bottom of the glass stood on the bedside table. She had been less attentive to her duty of seeing the drug safely swallowed since Hannah herself had made less objection to the taking of it; but these past few days had seen her leaving the bedroom almost before setting the dose down. It was clear her sister-in-law had things other than Hannah Cranley on her mind, even had the interest been there. And Archer, he had hardly shown his face in this room, but that too was a blessing, not to have to answer his questions, listen to his spite . . . his evil. It was only her child she missed, the child she loved so much. The usual afternoon visit to her room had not been made yesterday, nor again today. She had enquired the reason for his absence, but that had merely riled Archer and he had slammed out without answering.

Closing her eyes Hannah rested against the pillows, trying to close out the fear that clawed her heart. Where was Philip . . . had something happened she did not know of, something Archer and his sister were keeping from her?

He had called at the Fairley house, the man who had brought that beautiful bowl had said as much; then he had left for the glassworks. So Archer had not taken him out of there despite what she had said, but then had she honestly thought he would? He had never paid one second's notice to anything she had said, as ever he had followed his own path. 'You have always ridden a tall horse, Archer,' she murmured, 'but the higher the saddle, the further the drop to the ground.'

She had written that letter and smuggled it from the house without either Edna or Archer's knowledge, had dragged herself upstairs, natural exhaustion driving her into a deep sleep as soon as she lay on the bed. And the bowl, that lovely gift the Fairleys had sent to mark Philip's marriage, she had pushed it to the rear of the cabinet in the dining room and as yet Edna had made no mention of having noticed it. Perhaps that was an ungracious way of accepting a wedding gift but she could not risk the questions it would have brought.

Joshua Fairley had taken that letter, and now the bottle hidden inside one of her boots was full. It was enough. She had done what she had set out to do. Soon all of Archer Cranley's plans would be shattered, his evil ended, and his dreams no more than dust on the breeze.

'I put it down to the lad's father.' Samuel Platt lifted his flat cap with one finger, scratching his head with another. 'I simply thought as Cranley 'ad thought better of putting 'is son to the glass and 'ad teken 'im out of it again, that bein' so I made no more of it when the young 'un never showed for 'is shift; as for old Cranley showing up 'ere cursing cos I couldn't point to where his son be, well I tell you, you could 'ave knocked me over with a breath; I mean . . . 'ow could you tell a man summat as ain't known to yourself?'

'He came to our house too.' Joshua's glance ran around the yard of the works he had spent so much of his life in. 'He struck my mother when she told him Philip was not there.'

'He what!' The flat cap dropped into place as Samuel Platt's hand fell to his side. 'The bastard! Had I known as much when 'e stood 'ere in this yard I'd 'ave fetched one o' them crates across 'is 'ead and be buggered to the consequence!'

'He got as much and more.' Joshua smiled grimly. 'He won't be so handy with his fists another time.'

'The buggers should be cut off.' Samuel's rheumy eyes flashed. 'A man who teks 'is 'and to a woman don't deserve to 'ave no 'ands! I allis said Briant's son-in-law were no good, now I knows 'e ain't. The sooner that lad be master the better it be all round, be what I thinks.'

'I agree.' Joshua nodded. 'But Philip has to be found before that can happen.'

A finger creeping once more beneath the dust-covered cap, Samuel Platt frowned. 'Eh up, Josh lad! Can what I be thinkin' carry any truth, could old Cranley 'ave arranged all o' this to suit 'is own purpose?'

Catching the frown Joshua shook his head. 'I can't say I be with you, Samuel.'

'No, but you can't say you be far behind neither,' the chargehand returned quickly. 'You've 'eard the talk that's gone around this place, the askin' why Cranley should put 'is only son into a job that kills as it feeds. Mebbe's that talk ain't all just speculation, mebbe it ain't all just 'ot air blowin', mebbe there be more to it than we've give credit for. We all knows Cranley likes nuthin' more than to be the gaffer, we've lived with it for nigh on twenty years, and if every man be honest then he'll own up to thinkin' as 'ow that be summat that one won't give up easily, he'll 'old on to the reins for as long as 'e can, and mebbe 'e 'as found a way to 'old on to 'em for good.'

'You mean, he might have somehow—'

Samuel nodded while the answer was yet half given. 'Ar, I do means that. Could be that lad's been spirited away by the father who be goin' about pretendin' to search forrim just so as to mek things look good. It be right what folk says, a crooked stick throws a crooked shadow!'

If Archer Cranley did want rid of his son then it could be Philip was no longer even in this country! Perhaps what Samuel Platt had said may be true, perhaps Philip's father might hold no love for him, but what of his mother? For a brief instant Joshua saw that pale face as it begged him to take that letter, to let no one but her son know of its existence; it had been no act, the love and the pain behind those gentle eyes was no pretence: Hannah Cranley loved her son and in no way would she be an accessory to doing him harm. Joshua knew then that he must continue looking for Philip, he must try to find him, if not for himself then for that frail gentle woman who loved the boy as deeply as he did.

'Have you any objection to my speaking to the men?'

Seeing his own doubts reflected in Joshua's eyes the charge-hand shook his head briefly. 'No, lad, you go on in, but keep a north eye open for Cranley, could be we ain't seen the last of 'im for today an' could be we won't know 'e be comin' afore 'e lands, for birds o' prey don't sing!'

Leaving the cone some half hour later Josh stood for a moment. The clear sunlight filling the yard was brilliant after the furnace-lit gloom of the huge circular building, but the years of serving in it had accustomed his eyes to rapid change and he stared at the assortment of low dirt-blackened structures without blinking. Not one of the men or the lads working in the cone had seen Philip, and that being so it would serve no purpose to enquire at the office or the packing shed, for what one man at Briant Glass knew the rest knew in five minutes; news of any sort shot through the place with the speed of forked lightning.

So where to look next? Drawn to the rumble of wheels, he

glanced towards the wide gates fastened back to leave the works' entrance clear.

'Eh up, Josh lad, 'ow be you, an' 'ow be that mother o' yourn?'

'We are both well, Mr Boswell, as we hope you be.' Joshua walked beside the cart with its covering of powdery white dust, to the rear of the cone. Waiting until the horse was brought to a standstill and the heavy wooden-block brake applied to one wheel he asked, 'Have you seen a young man, a lad of about twenty, slight build, vivid blue eyes and wheat-coloured hair, might have been alone or might not?'

Flat cap and the top half of his face filmed by the same white powdery substance gave a clownish look as the cloth wrapped about the nose and mouth was removed, but the brown eyes were sharp. 'Eh lad, if that description be only 'alf ackurat then I'd remember, but the fact be I ain't clapped eyes on none such. I ain't seen nobody 'alf as 'andsome as you be describin', not every step from the lime kilns at Dudley. Who be it as you be askin' after?'

It would do no good to lie, this man would hear all there was to be heard before the afternoon was over. 'It be Mr Cranley's lad,' Joshua answered reluctantly. 'He was set on in the glass, but not being used to the area he seems to have taken the wrong path, it's easily done in the dark.'

Shaking powdered lime dust from the cloth still held in his hand Boswell wiped the cloth over his face. 'It be easily done as you says, Josh lad, but the whole of Greets Green be undermined with coal shafts, tumble down one o' them and the devil hisself wouldn't find the body!'

The thought had plagued Joshua's own mind. Born and reared to the heath a man must still watch every step when crossing it; for a lad like Philip, who had never spent any time on it, the danger of pit shafts left unfilled or uncapped increased a thousandfold. Thanking the man now folding sacks that had covered the cart's cargo of powdered limestone, Joshua turned back at his call.

'Have you enquired of the Rowley raggers? Could be they've seen summat o' the lad.'

His glance going to the canal running a few yards from the cone's rear entrance Josh felt a thread of hope. It was a slim chance, but any chance was worth the following and one of the raggers was moored just a few yards along the towpath.

Nearing the narrow boat, one of many that carried stone quarried from Rowley Hills and nicknamed raggers by Black Country folk, Joshua nodded to the man watching from beside the flower-painted hatch, a black-and-white mongrel dog at his feet.

'Ain't seen nobody as answers to that.' The bargee shook his head on hearing the description. Touching a finger politely to his brow Joshua thanked him. There was no point in staying around the cone, Philip Cranley was not here, and if his father truly wanted him out of the way then he was probably not even alive. The thought hitting like a fist, Josh turned away.

# Chapter Twenty-Five

'I tell you, Beasley, I've looked every place I can think of and there be no sign of him.'

Across the table Simeon Beasley's corpulent body filmed with perspiration. Did Cranley have any suspicion the lad had been brought to Harville's Hawthorne, was that the reason he had asked for this meeting? Touching a hand to thinning hair carefully brushed to one side, he felt the flurry of nerves jar inside him. He and this man had been friends for years; but that was not the word, accomplices was a more apt description of their association, one which for years had systematically robbed Briant Bottle and Glass, diverting funds to their own pockets. To be an accomplice of Archer Cranley was running a fine line, to be his enemy was downright bloody dangerous!

'Did you have words wi' the lad? You know what youngsters be like, speak a word of sense to 'em and they goes off like dynamite. Give him time and he'll be back.' Touching a napkin to his mouth Simeon Beasley tried to hide the nervous twitch.

'Words!' Archer slapped a hand to the table, sending his half-filled glass of wine swaying precariously. 'We 'ave words every time we meet!' He steadied the glass. 'If that were the cause of his going missing he'd have gone long since.'

Studying the meal placed before him, Simeon Beasley felt his appetite slip away. Glancing at the waiter he ordered brandy to be sent to the table.

'It be more than twenty hours since we last had sight of him.' Archer pushed his own meal away. 'His mother be fair frantic and his Aunt Edna the same.'

Grabbing the brandy glass as it arrived, Beasley threw half of the contents into his throat. Frantic, Edna Cranley? Then it would be panic over more than the safety of her brother's child!

'I went to the Fairley place.' If Archer noticed the shaking hand he ignored it. 'The son worked a chair at the glass. Hannah asked Philip to call and give her thanks for some hullabaloo or other the son put paid to. He had been there but stayed only a few minutes before leaving to go to the works, at least so they said.'

Some hullabaloo or other! Beasley tossed back the rest of the brandy, signalling for another. Was that how Cranley had got the bruises colouring his face . . . had the Fairley lad settled some other hullabaloo?

'And he didn't go there?' Beasley took the second goblet of brandy, holding it to steady nervous hands.

Throwing up his head impatiently, Archer loosed an impatient breath. 'That were what I said! Samuel Platt vowed and declared Philip hadn't shown for work. Said he thought as how I'd done a bit of re-thinking about setting him in the glass and had decided enough was enough as far as learning that side of the trade, so had taken him out; that being so he'd sent no word to Rowlay House regarding his absence.'

He had shown no obvious sign he knew of that bundle delivered to Harville's Hawthorne. Filling his mouth with liquor Simeon Beasley swirled it over his tongue. But looks were no guarantee so far as Archer Cranley was concerned; snakes always struck when least expected. Swallowing slowly, his eyes lowered to the glass, he tried to sound light.

'Then there be your answer. Like I said, the lad were annoyed, you say yourself there were words between you, so he's taken himself off in a huff, but given time . . .'

'Given time!' Archer's voice rose then dropped as several heads turned his way. There had been a veritable buzz of conversation following him as he had walked to the table in an alcove of Hemming's Dining Rooms, speculation as to the heavy bruising he could not disguise. That was something the future would take care of; bruises faded but vengeance did not, and Fairley would suffer more than a bruised face, much, much more!

'Time!' he snarled. 'That be the only thing we haven't got. That wedding be almost on top of us and if Philip isn't there, if that marriage don't take place as scheduled, then you and I stand to lose a lot more than the wearing of a buttonhole! In case that brandy-sodden brain has forgotten there is the little matter of a twenty-first birthday; if that marriage don't take place before that then no amount of signatures on whatever papers be going to keep that business in my hands. Do you understand what I am saying?'

'There was the making over of the proceeds to a charity of your choosing.' Beasley met the ferret-sharp eyes at last. 'You did get Hannah to—'

'Of course I did!' Archer cut in testily. 'But it ain't the running of any charity I be interested in, and it ain't no charity will pay you a lump sum every year; I lose the Bottle and Glass and you lose your nice little stipend. And that is exactly what will happen unless Philip is brought home, and soon!'

The loss of money that had supported his particular preference over the years would be a nuisance. New toys, especially the kind he liked, could be expensive. Simeon Beasley swirled the amber liquid around the glass, staring into the colourful depths. But much as he valued his particular hobby he valued his life more. Far better to lose one than the other and there could be no doubting Cranley's actions should he learn the truth; and should it be that Thaddeus Grinley contacted Cranley, there was no proof of any complicity . . . no proof of anything!

'If there is anything I can do . . .' The brandy having steadied his nerves he looked blandly at his companion, leaving the sentence to hang unfinished in the air.

'I don't see as there is, unless you can suggest some other place to look.'

'No.' Dropping his glance once more, Beasley shook his head. 'I wish I could but I honestly have no idea as to where he could have taken himself to. What will you say to Lacy?'

Pushing away from the table Archer glared at the waiter who stepped forward to hold his chair.

'Leave it!' he snapped, then as the man stepped quickly away looked at Beasley, anger unmistakable in his dark animal eyes. 'Damn and bugger Lacy,' he snarled, 'it's not Lacy I be bothered about . . . it's me!'


Edna Cranley stared at the still figure in the bed. Eyelids lowered, the dark lashes seemed to touch the deep hollows that circled the sunken eyes. Hannah Cranley had cheated her, after all these years the woman had cheated her! Her glance switching from the marble-pale face to the hand resting on the bedcover, she snatched the glass bottle still held between cold fingers. There was no need to ask how it had been done, that was obvious; but how had she managed to get hold of enough laudanum to kill herself? She had swallowed every dose set for her, the glass had always been empty when it was collected for washing.

Always empty! Edna turned the bottle in her hand. Hannah had taken every dose set for her, but had she swallowed it all, or had she somehow managed to save a little from each glass? Edna remembered the carelessness of the past few days. She had not stayed with Hannah to see the drug swallowed down, she had left it there on the table, left it for her sister-in-law to take . . . or, as it could only be, to drink half and hide half away; and now she was dead and the revenge Edna Cranley had for so long promised herself was dead with her.

Her promise to make that woman pay was gone, but Archer

would want to know how come his wife had died so suddenly. True, the town would accept the speed of her passing, the doctor's certificate would certify the fragility of her health, but that would not do for Archer, he had seen his wife earlier in the day, he would know her sudden passing was not natural. But he would not be able to say how long since that passing. Edna's mind clicked into rapid motion. She must remove that bottle, without the evidence it offered Archer could not confidently lay the blame at her door. She had given the correct dosage and at the appropriate times specified by the physician, she had stood beside Hannah as she swallowed it, what more could she have done? The sudden onset of death could not be laid at her door.

Seeing the boot lying at the door to the open wardrobe, Edna realised how the laudanum, kept a little at a time, had been hidden from her. Slipping the bottle into her pocket she scooped up the small medicine glass, dropping that into the same pocket of her dark skirts. Then moving quickly and decisively she replaced the boot beside its fellow. Rapidly searching each shoe and garment but finding no other hidden bottle she closed the wardrobe door. Turning she glanced swiftly about the room, coming finally back to the figure lying on the bed. Hannah could not be found like that! Dressed in day clothes it would be obvious to Archer she had been alone since the afternoon. Snatching at buttons and laces, her fingers trembling with fear of being caught in the middle of her task, she dragged the clothing from stiffening limbs. Hannah had to be in her nightgown, it must look as if she had died since being prepared for the night.

Pulling a fresh white gown over the head she struggled to push the lifeless arms into the sleeves. Archer could arrive at any minute, Hannah must be dressed and everything as normal before that. The gown at last in place, narrow ribbons tied at throat and wrist, she drew the covers over the still body, her own chest heaving with the effort it had taken. It was done, no finger could point at her. Gathering the dress and shoes she placed them in the wardrobe, then picked up petticoats and bloomers. They would go as usual into the wash-house until laundry day. Holding the underwear in one hand she walked to the window and stood a brief moment looking out across the moonlit garden. Hannah had loved the garden, but not every-thing a woman loved could she keep for ever; sometimes it was snatched away as Richard Stanton had been snatched away. Raising her free hand she pulled at the heavy curtains, drawing them together, shutting out the darkness. Everything was neat and in place. She turned for the door, the light seeping into the room from the landing causing her veins to run cold. The lamp! She had forgotten to light the lamp, it was always left beside the bed, with enough paraffin to last the night.

Setting the underclothes on the bed she hurriedly put a match to the wick, replacing the tall glass funnel as it caught alight. That was it, she had thought of everything. Glancing once more at the waxen face, at the eyelids closed on life, she laughed pitilessly.

'You escaped,' she murmured. 'You escaped, Hannah Cran-ley, but your husband will not. He will long to be where you are now; long for the agony that comes from what he hears to be taken from him. But Archer does not have your courage, Hannah, he will live with the torment, live as I have lived these many years, longing for that one thing he can never have; and that will be my true reward, Hannah, that will give me more pleasure than any amount of your father's money.'

Taking up the underwear once more she left the room. Closing the door she walked quickly to the kitchen. She would wait for Archer's return before taking the next dose of laudanum upstairs.

Hannah's death would have no marked effect upon her plans, and the only grief she had was that of being unable to take the revenge she had nurtured for so many years. But there was Archer! Sat upright on her chair beside the range Edna stared at the gently steaming kettle hanging from a well-polished bracket. She would yet have the satisfaction; the heart-warming joy, the ecstasy of seeing his face when she delivered her blow. She would see him reel, watch the colour drain from his face, what little pleasure he had in life ebb from his eyes. The death of his wife would cause Archer Cranley no pain, but the vengeance of his sister would. Lifting her gaze, she smiled at the handsome face watching from her memory.

'I will make him suffer, my dearest,' she whispered, 'I will make him suffer as they made us suffer.'


'Psst . . . psst, Mr Josh . . .'

At the corner of the packing shed a hushed calling of his name drew Joshua's attention to a pale little face peeping from its open doorway.

'. . . I can't come out to you, Mr Josh, I can't let old Platty see me canting in the yard lessen I gets me tin.'

'Should Mr Platt hear you calling him by that name he won't wait to catch you gossiping in the yard to give you your tin.'

'I knows it.' The worn little face crumpled into a grin. 'But it be a 'abit.'

His own mouth curving into a smile Joshua wagged an admonishing finger. 'Then it be a habit you best get rid of, young woman, afore you be the one be gotten rid of.'

'Me mother tells me the same thing but I never remembers the warnin' 'til it be too late.'

'Too late will be an apt enough description if Samuel catches you.'

'Me mother tells me that an' all, her says my 'ead be like the walls o' that cone, made of brick, but it ain't nowheres near as thick an' I ain't so dumb I can't put one thought to another an' mek them fit. An' that be what I've been doin'.'

Seeing the cheeky grin give way to a solemnity that took the spark from the brown eyes, Joshua's own smile faded. Ginny Morton was ever on the lookout for a moment of mischief to break the monotony of life in the shed but there seemed no mischief behind the look she gave him now.

'I can't come out there, Mr Josh, I could be copped any minute, but if you was to pop in 'ere to say "how do" then I couldn't rightly be 'spected not to answer; it wouldn't be actin' polite, would it?'

'No, Ginny, it wouldn't be acting polite, nor would it show politeness on my part not to ask after your family.' The look on the thin little face so serious he could not allow the smile rearing again inside him to show, he stepped into the damp shadowy coolness of the packing shed.

'I 'eard what you said to Platty . . . to Mr Platt.'

Joshua did not doubt the truth of that but said nothing, letting the girl continue in that hushed, conspiratorial whisper.

'I 'eard what the both of you said about old Cranley and I ain't sayin' there don't be truth in it, but I don't reckon as Samuel Platt has it all right . . . not this time, I don't.'

'What does he not have right?' Joshua put the answer gently but the girl caught the half-hidden smile behind his eyes and her quick temper flared.

'Seems *I* don't 'ave it all right neither!' Dashing a dirty hand across her cheek she smudged away a silver tear. 'I knowed it were no use to speak of it to Platt nor to none of the others, but I thought that you at least would listen wi'out laughing, I thought as you liked Mr Philip as much as I does! But I see I was wrong, I be sorry I 'eld you up, so best you goes your way.'

'I'm sorry too, Ginny.' Joshua lost the smile, reluctant to hurt the girl's feelings. 'Sorry to have given the impression of laughing at you. I would be pleased to listen to anything you have to say.'

Life returning to Ginny's grin, it flashed quickly. 'Eh up! You sounds just like Mr Philip when you talks like that, I wish I could use big words like you does but me mother says that would be all mouth an' no bloomers!'

Difficult as it was now to prevent his own smile, Joshua kept it at bay by swallowing hard. 'Supposing you had the words, Ginny, what is it you would say?'

'Well, I ain't got 'em, so what I tells must be in me own way.'

Glancing first towards the open doorway, she went on. 'An' it be this. Philip Cranley ain't the first, nor be 'e the only one gone missin' from these parts, an' all of 'em wi' a face a mother could be proud of . . . so I 'eard tell anyways . . . seein' as 'ow they all 'ad jobs and 'omes to live in then it stands to reason they d'ain't all of 'em do a moonlight flit.'

Wanting to ask where all this was leading but not wishing to hurt the child by seeming disinterested, Joshua stood quiet.

'An' I don't think as Philip Cranley done one neither, not without 'elp that is . . .' Lowering her voice the girl leaned closer. 'What's more, Mr Josh, I thinks—'

'You don't think at all, wench, that be your trouble, but you've 'ad the last warning, so now you get across the yard and collect your tin, an' there'll be no arguin' this time!'

Crestfallen, the girl looked once at the frowning face of the chargehand then ran out of the shed.


She had hoped that learning of that coming marriage would take the worm from his soul, that her son would find peace from the unnatural longings that had taken him, but on hearing of the Cranley lad not reaching his work he had gone from the house like summer lightning.

The fire banked, Naomi swept the hearth. Her wouldn't have Joshua sit on his backside and lift not a finger to 'elp search for the lad, no o' course her wouldn't; but the look on his face as he left the house told her that for her son this was more than a search for just any lost lad.

Sitting back on her heels Naomi stared blankly at the grate she polished every week with Zebo polish, but the glistening blackness of it was lost on her.

It were goin' to tek more than word of any marriage to 'elp her lad. Why couldn't it 'ave been a wench he'd set 'is cap at . . . why another man? Her 'ad watched her son grow. From child to man 'e had never shown no fallin' away afore, never had he been given towards unholy love; not 'til the meetin' up wi' Philip Cranley. But this feelin', which any eyes could see were ripping 'im apart, it were wrong, it were sinful love, one the Lord would not forgive and man would not sanction.

'Why?' The word sobbed from her lips as she pushed to her feet, carrying the empty bucket through the scullery into the yard. But there was no one to tell her why, no one to answer as there was no answer to her prayers.

'. . . *take your heartbreak to the Lord* . . .' Keziah Silk's words spoke softly in her mind. '*He'll not turn His back to you . . . He will keep evil from your door.*'

But the Lord had not kept the evil from her door. It had come looking for Joshua, taken him to Rowlay House and now out onto the heath searching for his own damnation!

Returned to the tiny living room she had strived so hard to make cosy, she looked from the pocket-handkerchief-sized window of the house, identical in every shape and detail down to the last brick to the others in Churchyard Row, out over the fields that gave on to the heath with its disused coal shafts. This had been her home from her marriage day, Joshua had been born here and so had the two that had followed and now lay in the same grave as their father. Her home for so long. Tears thick and choking congealed in Naomi's throat. But for how much longer would she live in it, how long would she be able to lie in the night and feel in her heart the presence beside her of the man she had loved with all her heart, how long before the gossip and back-biting would drive both her and Joshua away? Oh, it had already begun, the spiteful innuendo, the mutterings behind a shawl, the looks of disgust as she passed. They had heard the shouts and callings of that man Jukes, the women of Churchyard Row missed nothing and that included an opportunity to pass the latest titbits to any other whose ears were willing to flap!

'*Ask 'im . . . ask your precious son why it is 'e walks another man 'ome . . . what it be they plays at on the 'eath?*'

The shame of those remembered shouts from outside her

window bringing blood hot and stinging to her cheeks, Naomi turned away; but even as she set about the several little tasks that needed no doing, the plaguing voice continued to hammer in her brain.

'*I knows the games they play, so does every other bloke at Briant's, so it be only right 'is mother know it an' all. It be called buggery!*'

Her breath escaping in a gasp, Naomi clasped her hands over her ears. 'It weren't true . . . it weren't true!' But even as the sobbed denial wrenched itself from her quivering lips, the question followed. If her were so certain there were only innocent friendship between her son and the Cranley lad why 'ad her paid that call on Keziah Silk?

Taking a cup from the dresser she held it, her eyes not seeing the pretty floral pattern.

The gossip that had started the day of Ned Jukes's visit would grow. She had told Joshua nothing of it but it could only be a matter of time afore somebody threw it in his face, and once it were out that would be the finish of her life here in Greets Green. But Joshua! Lowering the cup to the table she stared at the chair in which her husband had always sat.

'What'll our lad do?' she whispered to its vacant silence. 'He be finished at the glass an' he'll be finished in Greets Green, but will 'e leave it, an' will 'e leave Cranley's son . . . even after that one be wedded, will our Josh turn away from 'im?'

Across the room a coal slid further into the crimson bed of the fire, a bevy of blue-tipped flame enveloping its dark shape.

The flames of hell! Naomi shivered. The legacy of the damned! And her son was running full tilt towards it.

# Chapter Twenty-Six

What *would* he say to Lacy? He could hardly tell him that sooner than marry his daughter the lad had run off, but if that weren't the reason then what was? There could be no other. It wasn't as if there had been another girl. Huh! Archer Cranley's tight laugh was scornful. Philip would run like a hare! There had been no association of that sort with any woman, in fact there had been no association of any sort with anybody, he had seen to that. The couple of weeks or so at the glassworks, they had been the only time away from the house and Philip would have struck up with no wench there, not without his being informed of it, Samuel Platt knew his job would have rested on his telling of it.

So where the bloody hell was he? Jerking irritably on the rein he set the horse to a canter, the wheels of the carriage bumping over the rough road. He had called at the Fairleys. Touching a hand to the bruises he swore vehemently. That one would pay the price of striking him, he'd never work again, not in Greets Green or anywhere else, Archer Cranley could pull the strings. So if Philip had left, as the woman vowed, then where had he gone? Platt said he had not turned up for his shift, so what had he done? He could not have left the area, a man needed money to do that and Hannah had no money, and Edna? She wouldn't give a blind man a light! The only alternative was to walk . . . or hitch a ride on a carter's wagon. To where . . . and then what? Playing the thought over in his mind Archer rejected the possibility. Philip was spineless, he would have thought of all the consequences, especially the living rough. No, he was hiding out somewhere, hoping to get various agreements as to his mother, no doubt, by staying away to the last minute; but Philip Cranley's last minute would follow very soon after his marriage.

'You too, Philip,' he murmured, 'you think as they think, Edna and Beasley. They too think to better Archer Cranley, but like you they be in for quite a shock. Beasley be going to find his source of revenue cut off, his little playthings taken away. He won't like that, Philip, he won't like that at all; and your Aunt Edna, she thinks she be on top, that her little nest will be feathered in comfort once you be wed, but there'll be no feathering and her only nest will be that chimney in the limestone. Edna will lie in the comfort she has earned but her eternity will not be shared by her all-time love, it will not be Richard Stanton who lies beside her in her stony bed, she will have a prettier companion to rot with.'

Turning the carriage onto the track that led to Rowlay House he allowed his thoughts to continue running free.

Edna had guessed what had happened, guessed he had killed Lilah Charrington, but without proof, without evidence of any kind she could do nothing. True, she could produce that tavern keeper to uphold her statement of his being with the woman, but that would be to no effect; what man, given the circumstances of a bed-ridden wife, would not keep a mistress? No, that line of attack would hold no ground, and as for any other evidence there was none. Cap, muffler, jacket and ivory-handled knife had been his dowry to Lilah, a gift to mark the marriage she had hoped to force on him: they had followed her into those obsolete workings. And the powder bought from that long-ago chemist? That too had gone from its hiding place, so should his sister discover that hidden panel she would find nothing in it.

They thought they had been so clever, Lilah and her lover. Archer smiled in the darkness. But like her, Jim Baker had underestimated the man he had tried to blackmail, and like her he too had paid the price; and so would Edna.

Halting the carriage outside the stable to the rear of Rowlay House, he laughed softly.

Yes . . . so would Edna!

The girl had been more helpful than the rest of them put together. Joshua Fairley stood in the shadow of the buildings that edged William Street. He had watched from just beyond the glassworks, changing position only when the later hour told there would be no pickup of glass before morning.

'*I seen 'im often, Mr Josh, he be livin' in the old malthouse, you knows the one, where William Street joins to Charles Street.*'

There was no guarantee that what young Ginny had said would lead to Philip Cranley, but he had nothing else left to try.

It had been difficult to understand what she said at first, her throat crackling with tears, panic at her mother's fury in every word. But at last he had soothed her, telling her if she could help in the finding of the lad then old Cranley would give back her job and a raise in wages to go with it.

'*It mebbe as I be wrong,*' she had said at last, calming her storm of tears, '*but I listens; ar, I knows what folk thinks, that I listens where I shouldn't, but sometimes listenin' pays off.*'

Standing beyond the gate, in the shadow of that massive cone, Joshua had willed there be something in what the child had to tell.

'*It be this way, Mr Josh –*' she had sniffed hard '*– like I said there in the shed, I've 'eard me mother and the other women talk of lads goin' missin' from these parts and not a one of 'em showin' up again. Well, it ain't natural, not for all of 'em to stay away, it ain't; and though I be thought brainless, I ain't, I can put two and two together and when I seen the same thing again—*'

He had wanted to be away, to carry on the search for Philip, but something in the girl's pale work-weary face had held him.

'*What was it you saw again?*'

She had glanced around then, a sort of fear in the movement, and only when she was satisfied they were not overheard had she answered.

'It were summat 'appened the day Mr Philip started at the glass. Thad Grinley was collectin' bottles, like he do regular. Well, he'd nigh on finished loadin' of his wagon when he spotted Mr Philip sittin' on the bench alongside of the packin' shed. Kept on askin' questions he did, questions such as where did 'e live and was it what 'e d'ain't do 'ad Cranley pack 'im off to work in the glass. It were obvious Mr Philip wanted to mek no answer but Grinley kept on. But when he said it were probably games that old Cranley wanted to play and Philip wouldn't join, then I poked me nose in; I told 'im to mind 'is own business. Well, that caused a stink, the upshot bein' as Platt said to get me tin.'

'But Philip prevented your being sacked?'

Moving limbs numbed by standing so long in one position Joshua glanced along the empty street, the memory of the girl's answer echoing in his mind.

'Ar 'e did, an' there were more than meself looked to his every word. You 'ave to be quick on the uptake in our 'ouse, Mr Josh, them as blinks twice gets the bread pinched from under their nose; well, Ginny don't blink twice and 'er don't miss nuthin'. I seen Thad Grinley pretendin' to see to that hoss's 'arness, I seen the way he tried to 'ear what Samuel Platt and Mr Philip talked of, but more than that I seen the way his eyes wandered all over Mr Philip, like 'e was buyin' summat new and wanted to mek certain it were up to standard.'

From a distance the rumble of cart wheels touched the silent darkness, but Joshua's thoughts ran undisturbed.

'Ginny, I don't . . .'

'I knows, Mr Josh.' The brightness of her eyes enhanced by the wash of tears, the girl had looked up quickly. 'You don't know where all this be leadin'. Well, could be it won't lead nowheres but then the 'earing of it won't cost you nuthin'. What I be sayin' is this. I seen Thad Grinley wi' that same look on 'is face once afore. It were close to where we lives in William Street. He stopped that cart of his to talk to Salome Paget's lad, 'e were about ten years at the time; you remember he was supposed to 'elp shovel silica into the wheelbarrows but 'e kept runnin' off; ninepence short of a shillin' 'e was, but cos *he d'ain't 'ave all his marbles folk took no notice. Then when one day he never come back everybody put it down to his fallin' into some old coal shaft.'*

Joshua remembered the lad and his sudden disappearance but, with his mind on Philip, the girl's words had made little impression.

*'But the other day, when I seen that same look as had been on Grinley's face when he'd talked to Davy Paget, then summat inside seemed to tell me there was more to them looks than just bein' friendly.'*

The rumble of cart wheels growing stronger it seemed the voice in his mind grew louder, forcing itself into his brain, insisting he listen.

*'Don't you see!'* The girl had pulled at his sleeve. *'Don't you see the connection? Both lads were 'andsome, both of 'em had Grinley looking them over as though they was prime cuts o' beef and both of 'em went missin' nobbut weeks later. Tell me I be imaginin', Mr Josh, tell me I 'ave nuthin' in me 'ead but fancies same as me mother would should I try to tell her what I've bin tellin' to you, but I feels there be that as ain't right about Grinley.'*

She had been so positive. Joshua stretched his limbs, the returning blood sending prickles like the touch of needles along arms and legs. Her small face looking up at him had begged to be believed.

*'Where can I find him?'*

Stood in the darkness of the shadowed buildings, Joshua even now did not quite understand why he had asked the question, except those bright eyes, which held a power all their own, seemed to bore into him, sending their own message straight to his heart.

*'I ain't sayin' as I sees 'im every night.'* Ginny's reply was filled with relief that he showed an interest albeit not a strong one. *'But I reckon 'e comes back to that malthouse, the one that stands on the joining of William Street to Charles Street, wouldn't pay to stable that hoss nowheres else while he be payin' for that. I say if you be wanting words wi' Grinley then that be the surest place of nabbin' him.'*

It had taken half an hour and more to persuade Samuel Platt to take the girl back. Agreeing with the chargehand that yes the works could only have one gaffer, and yes Ginny had stepped out of line too many times already, he had played his one card. If what the girl had told him should lead to Philip's whereabouts becoming known then the man that set the search in motion was going to be well thought of, and that man could be Samuel Platt.

It had been a form of blackmail. Joshua saw again the grin on the girl's face as he had beckoned her back to the yard, heard the quick, 'I won't, Mr Josh, I promise, honest I does,' as he had warned her against adding her words where they weren't asked. But the blackmail had worked, Samuel Platt was ageing fast, how soon before Cranley decided he was past working in the glass? The chargehand had been swift to reckon that any favour owed him by the glassmaster could only be to his benefit.

The rumble of cart wheels so close as to drive the rest of the thought from his mind, Joshua pressed further into the shadows. If this were not Thad Grinley's wagon then it were better not to be seen, and if it was . . . then surprise were still best on his side.

Waiting until it passed along the road he stepped forward, watching from the lee of a large warehouse as it stopped in front of a pair of wide wooden gates. It was Grinley's cart. Seeing the hunched figure climb from the driver's seat, hearing the grumbles as it swung the heavy gates back on rusting hinges, he waited, darting forwards only when the cart began to move into the darkness beyond.

The slight sound of his steps lost beneath the crunch of heavy wheels and the grumbling of its driver, he slid into the yard. Taking advantage of the deep shadows he followed into the barn, all the time listening to the drunken rumblings of the voice he recognised as Grinley's.

'Beasley said no, said he d'ain't want that one. Well, that be 'is loss . . .'

His eyes well accustomed to darkness after his long wait, Joshua watched the other man fumble with a lantern. Slurred words mixing with the slap of leather and jingle of brass Grinley settled the horse into its stable then, taking the lantern from a nail hammered into a post, weaved his way falteringly to a ladder leading to an overhead loft.

'. . . but Beasley's loss be old Thad's gain. Twenty-five quid . . . that'll 'ave to be written off, but not altogether . . . we can find another willin' to pay as much . . .'

Wrapped in shadow Joshua listened to the drunken rambling. Who was Beasley, what was it the man had refused? Whatever it was he wasn't interested, he wanted only to talk to Grinley about Philip, find out if the man knew anything that might say where the lad was. He could have halted the cart out there in the street, but then Grinley might have refused to answer; as young Ginny Morton had proclaimed, the man weren't backward in coming forward when it were questions he were asking, but he be tight-mouthed as a mute when it be his turn to answer. If the girl's fears had ground, if Grinley did know something of Philip's not turning up for his shift, then it was more than possible he wouldn't want to admit to it, therefore it could be better to wait of his finishing up in the barn and face him as he came out.

His feet missing a tread on the ladder Thad Grinley swore volubly, the lantern swinging madly in his hand as he clung on to the sides. Watching from below, Joshua could have smiled had he been here on any other business. Slipping and swearing in turn the figure pulled its way to the top of the ladder, heaving itself onto the floor above. Standing for a few minutes, the swaying lantern casting yellow pools of light into the shadows then scooping them back to throw to the other side, it seemed to Joshua he was looking for something on the floor of the loft.

'. . . there'll be another willin' to dig into 'is pocket –' the drunken rambling reached to where Joshua waited '– Beasley don't be the only bloke as likes new things . . .'

Hanging the lantern from a beam the figure lurched forwards then dropped to its knees. With Grinley lost from his sight Joshua moved restlessly. A few minutes, he'd give Grinley a few minutes to find what it was he was looking for.

'You still be sleeping?' Grinley's slurred words drifted through the silent blackness. 'The little drop of opium I give to you at dinner time 'as you still asleep. Well that be no matter to bother on, asleep or awake the pleasure be the same of old Thad.'

Asleep or awake . . . the pleasure be the same? A frown settling on his forehead Joshua peered through the pitch darkness towards the ladder. What on earth was Grinley mumbling about?

'Ask at the 'ouse you said, the money'll be paid . . . but what if it ain't? Thad Grinley be no fool, 'e looses you and he be paid wi' a stretch along the line.'

Mumblings indistinct between heavy breaths were accompanied by sounds of shuffling. His restlessness increasing, Joshua stepped forwards. What the hell was taking Grinley so long? A muffled cry stinging his senses he stood motionless, his own breathing silent and controlled.

Overhead Thad Grinley smiled drunkenly at the figure lying face-down on a heap of straw. Legs stretched wide, each ankle tied with twine to posts supporting a rickety roof, arms drawn together over the head, wrists secured to an iron ring set into the rear wall. As he took a knife from his pocket the blade shone in the light of the lantern.

'You'll pay Thad yourself,' he muttered, head swaying up and down on his chest. 'You'll pay Thad once you be glassmaster . . . but what if you be like Beasley, what if you changes your mind? Then Grinley be left wi' nothing 'ceptin' a clear view of the gallows . . . no, no, I told you afore, I be no fool. I be going to tek my pleasures, then I'll find another who'll pay 'andsome to do the same.'

The light of the lantern licking against the steel blade he brought the knife weaving uncertainly towards the figure, a cry squeezing beneath its gagged lips as it tried to twist free of the securing bonds.

'So you don't be sleepin',' he slurred, the knife hovering

above the spine, 'you thought to fool old Thad, but that would mek no difference, sleepin' or wakin' you'll still give what I wants . . .'

One hand throwing the jacket up over the head of the bound figure, the other brought the knife glinting downwards. Slashing through trousers and underpants he dropped the knife, using his hands to rip the cloth apart.

Mouth drooling, flesh jerking with anticipation, he leaned forwards and snatched the gag, the fierceness of pulling it free dragging the head cruelly backwards.

'I wants you to talk to me,' he grunted. 'Thad likes to 'ear a bit o' appreciation when 'e be pleasurin' a lad . . .'

Fingers hindered by the effect of drink fumbled awkwardly with the buttons of dirt-caked trousers, a lewd laugh drowning the strangled words coming from the straw.

'. . . I wants to 'ear you say you likes what I be goin' to push into you, the delight it gives you when you feels them sweet little cheeks close about this . . . but we don't need to 'urry, it be greedy to suck on all the sweets at once, one bite at a time –' he laughed again '– one bite at a time be the way Thad Grinley likes it.'

'Please . . . please let me go, I promise you will be paid whatever you ask . . .'

Terrified and filled with pain, the cry that came rang around the darkened barn.

'Philip!' Joshua's gasp was left behind as he raced for the ladder. Unsure of where his feet landed, missing rung after rung, he dragged himself to the top.

Lit by the sallow gleam of the lantern Thad Grinley knelt between spread legs, his mouth pressed to the tight rounded cheeks of a bare bottom, but it was the head of the bound victim that drew Joshua's gaze. Collar-length hair, wheaten colour clear in the yellow gleam: Philip!

Fear that over the past hours had been building inside him burst suddenly, sweeping through him like a tidal wave, dashing against his brain, smashing away all sense of restraint.

'You filthy bastard! You dirty filthy swine!'

Grabbing the collar of the kneeling man's jacket, Joshua hauled him to his feet. Holding him easily as a rag doll he stared into the bemused face.

'You've buggered your last, Grinley,' he ground. 'You'll take no more innocent lads off the streets.'

Bringing up one knee he jammed it into the soft flesh between Grinley's legs, and as the man folded Joshua brought a closed fist hard to his face before allowing him to crumple to the floor.

'I'm going to put paid to your sordid little games.' In the shadows Joshua's face was a mask of hate and rage. 'I'm going to rip off that which you like to push into boys but I won't shove it back up your own arse cos you'd enjoy that, I'm going to make you eat it, Grinley, you hear me . . . I'm going to make you eat your own balls!'

Drunk as he was, fear cleared Grinley's brain and lent speed to his limbs. Scrambling to his feet he scurried backwards, his eyes on that hate-filled face.

'Listen to me, Fairley, I d'ain't know who the lad was, listen to me, I'll—'

But whatever it was he intended it was left to trail into a scream as Grinley fell over the edge of the loft.

# Chapter Twenty-seven

'Is he back?' Archer Cranley glared at the woman come into the hall from the kitchen.

'No,' Edna Cranley answered abruptly.

'Damn him.' Halfway to the stairs Archer came to a halt. 'What the hell does he hope to gain by playing bloody silly games?'

'Well, if it's time he's hoping to gain then I'd say he's winning!'

'You'd say . . . you'd say!' Rounding on the sarcastic remark, Archer's eyes flashed the anger that had been with him since leaving Beasley. 'If that be all you can think to say then you best keep your mouth shut, it be no handsome sight at any time but it be more bearable when it be closed!'

A look of disdain masking her true feelings, Edna turned away. It would almost be worth losing the money promised her to see him lose everything, as he surely would if Philip did not return, to see him cheated by the child he intended to cheat, the child he had detested for so long. The idea had its appeal.

'Has his mother asked for him?'

The question halting her, Edna turned again to face her brother. She must take care how she answered, must give no clue to what she knew.

'She asked this afternoon, she wanted to know the reason he had not been in to sit with her.'

'What did you tell her?'

He was nervous. Edna gloated at the tense brusqueness of the question. Archer was never gentle but the times his nerves were gaining an upper hand his voice held a razor edge, and tonight Archer was nervous.

'I told her what you wanted her told, that Philip was taking his midday meal and afternoon break along with the men at the works.'

'And?' Feral eyes flashed. There was no telling how much of the truth Edna Cranley told, how much her spite kept hidden.

Watching his face, a surge of near joy swept through the thin spinster-dry body and Edna almost smiled. He was deeply concerned now, but wait until he saw what awaited him in that bedroom. Keeping her pleasure buried deep she answered with her usual indifference.

'It upset her, she seemed to think you were keeping Philip from her.'

'And you no doubt told her that was nonsense!'

Drawn as if sucking on a mouthful of acid drops, Edna's lips tightened but still she held to the cold calm of hate.

'How well you know me, brother. What else *would* I say?'

Yes, how well he knew her, the waspish tongue that was merely a veil drawn across the canker that was her soul, the sly viperish ways which served only to highlight the venomous poison of her heart. What else *would* she say? Anything that would give pain to her sister-in-law and bring about the downfall of her own brother. But he had played against Edna Cranley for too many years, he knew her stroke too well to be deceived by her. Glaring at her now he spat his next words.

'You are an evil-minded, spiteful woman, Edna, but even given those attributes you have one more: you know how to safeguard your own interests. Filled with hate as you are you would say nothing that might adversely affect them.'

Across from him Edna inclined her head. 'As you say, Archer, I know how to protect that which is rightfully mine, and how to fight for it if I have to.'

'Has she asked for him since?'

Keeping her eyes on his face as he glanced towards the stairs, Edna let the answer slip easily from her tongue. 'Yes. She asked for him when I went in to give her the evening dose of laudanum. I reminded her his next shift would not be over until midnight and that she would see him in the morning.'

'You stayed with her, saw her swallow it?'

'Yes, I stayed.' One lie slid after the other with the smoothness of satin. 'I stayed until she was asleep, but she fretted for some time. It was obvious she thought things were not altogether what she was being told.'

Taking the watch from his waistcoat pocket, Archer glanced at the dial then back to where his sister stood, hands folded over her skirts.

'Where do you keep the laudanum?'

A quick frown pulling her brows together Edna stared in silence until the question barked again.

'In the small cupboard beside the dresser in the kitchen, it's quite safe there.'

'Get it!' Archer turned for the stairs. 'Bring it to her room. If she has woken then she will need a little more.'

Bottle and glass in her hands Edna Cranley walked steadily up the staircase she had cleaned for years. A little more! She glanced at the bottle, the deep green of its glass burnished to brilliant emerald by the light of the overhead gasolier. Hannah Cranley would be needing no more laudanum . . . ever!

'Will I pour a dose?' Hiding what she knew she set bottle and glass on the small night table.

'When were you last in this room?'

The question hissed across the bed and Archer's face as he

looked up was white with passion. Tread carefully! Edna warned herself. This was not the moment, the full savouring of that was yet to come.

'An hour,' she answered glibly, 'maybe a little more.'

'Then you haven't seen . . . you don't know?'

'Know what . . . what are you talking about?' Keeping her eyes from the figure in the bed Edna laced her answer with her usual acerbity.

'She's dead!' Archer's eyes glowed with animal brightness. 'Hannah is dead!'

Her reaction near perfect after the silent rehearsals in the kitchen she turned to pick up the bottle. Holding it against the glow of the lamp she snapped irritably, 'Nonsense, of course she isn't dead.'

'Don't bloody argue with me!' One hand streaking across the bed he swiped the bottle from her hand, sending it flying across the room. 'I tell you she's dead!'

Her eyes widening with all the dramatic skill of Lillie Langtry, Edna stared. 'She . . . she can't be, I . . . I spoke to her only an hour ago.'

'How much of that stuff did you give her?'

'The same as I give her every evening after supper.' Edna held on to the drama, letting her lips quiver. 'One glassful, I measured it exactly, I gave her only what you ordered.'

'Then how?'

How had she died? Edna kept the satisfaction from her eyes. She was not about to reveal that. Archer Cranley must think the whole thing his doing.

'I warned you,' she said quietly, 'I warned you she was having too much, that the effect of it was building in her 'til she slept more hours than she had minutes of waking, I warned you of what might happen but you would take no telling.'

Bead-bright eyes darting from her to the silent figure in the bed he stared for several moments at the eyes closed for ever amid their shadowed circles.

*In the event of the death of his wife Hannah Cranley . . .*

The words of Nathan Briant's Will danced feverishly in his brain. Well, he had worked around that clause, Hannah had willed everything to a charity of his naming; but what bloody good were that, he wanted no charity to administer and he would have none! That glassworks were his, he'd worked for it and none save Archer Cranley would have the owning of it.

'This means the house and the works must be sold—'

'It don't mean no such!' Rounding like a cornered fox he snarled savagely. 'Save the burying of Archer Cranley 'til he be dead as that one in the bed.'

'But with Hannah's death and no marriage . . .'

'There'll be a marriage, all I need is time.'

'A marriage with nobbut a bride?' Edna allowed her sarcasm full rein, but for once Archer did not retaliate. Drawn deep into his own thoughts he seemed to forget she was there. So let him forget . . . for the moment. Deep inside she smiled; the rest of his life would be long enough to remember.

'Get her a wrap.' He spoke suddenly, anger replaced by a brisk, efficient note. 'Get her a cloak . . . something with a hood.'

Edna stared blankly. Why a cloak? Hannah was dead. Opening her mouth to ask, she closed it as he snapped again.

'Get a cloak, now!'

Whipping away the bedcovers he took the dead body by the shoulders, dragging it from the bed.

'Put it on her,' he ordered, holding Hannah upright, 'cover her head with the hood.'

Doing as she was bid Edna fastened the toggles braided on to the midnight-blue cloak, stepping aside as he swept his dead wife into his arms and carried her to the carriage in the stable.

'Where are you taking her? Archer, you can't just dispose of her! What of Philip! He's bound to ask where his mother is.'

The horse harnessed to the carriage, Archer swung himself into the driver's seat.

'Archer!' Edna laid a hand on the rear of the horse. 'What of Philip . . . what do I say?'

Looking down at the woman half hidden by the night shadows, Archer gathered the reins into both hands. 'If he returns before I do you can tell him his mother could not stand the strain of his taking himself off, that she suffered a serious relapse, so much so that I have taken her to the sanatorium.'

Was that where he was taking Hannah? Edna listened to the crunch of carriage wheels fade into the distance. Or was he taking her to some convenient pit shaft? Would the coffin that would eventually bear the name of Hannah Cranley really hold that woman's remains, or would it be empty as Archer Cranley's heart?

Falling into the well of darkness, Thad Grinley's body hit the floor with a sickening thud, but Joshua paid no heed. Keen and incisive as a knife, the rage that had twisted in him plashed afresh as he turned to look at the figure lying on the straw.

Bound hand and foot, trussed like a chicken, trousers ripped away to expose soft buttocks, there could be no mistaking what Grinley had intended. Pulling off his jacket he dropped it over the pale flesh then, his fingers shaking, he bent to loose the twine that held wrists and ankles.

'Philip.' He spoke the name softly, gentle as to a frightened child, but the only response was a sobbing buried deep in the straw. There was no shame in the lad's tears. Beneath his anger Joshua felt the strength of pity. Why shouldn't a man cry . . . why must he never show his fear to the world?

'It's all right, Philip.' He touched a hand to the heaving shoulder. 'He won't touch you any more.'

Feeling the hand against one shoulder Philippa's trembling body curved in on itself, the sobbed answer hushed to a whisper. 'I want to die . . . I want to die.'

'Don't say that! Don't ever say that!' Grasping both shoulders

Joshua twisted the slight figure into his arms, holding it tight against his chest.

'That man . . . I . . . I feel so dirty.'

'You needn't,' Joshua answered quickly. 'You've done nothing wrong, what happened was not your fault.'

'But that man, he . . . he . . .'

Held against him Joshua felt the shudder that wracked the small frame. The lad was terrified, and who could blame him? Snatched from the heath, subjected to God knew what ordeal. But Grinley would pay and so would any other man found to be involved.

'If it's rape you be feared of then your body would tell you had that happened. Does your body hurt, Philip, is there pain below the waist?'

It was put as carefully as he knew how. The lad was sensitive and already half out of his mind with fear and humiliation; Joshua feared adding to it with questions no man wanted to hear. Relief tumbling in his veins at the shake of Philippa's head, his own breath trembling from his lungs, Joshua offered a silent prayer of thanks. That lad had suffered too much already, carrying the knowledge of his own violation would be the straw that broke him.

'Then there has been no rape.' He touched a hand to hair that glistened like pale silk beneath the lantern's gleam. 'Be assured of that, lad. Whatever else Grinley did to you he did not do that.'

But he would have done. Joshua's anger re-surfaced, lodging itself in his throat. Signs of that swine's intentions couldn't have been more clear. Five more minutes and . . . Unable to bear the thought, he forced it away but he knew it would live for ever in the recesses of his mind, haunt him in the dark hours as that other pain haunted.

'Why? Why did that man abduct me, why would he not go to my father or let me go? I promised him I wouldn't tell what had happened . . . I promised to pay him but he still did this . . .'

Fingers already tense where they gripped his shirt tightened and the sobs intensified as the figure pressed closer. Without thinking, Joshua's head lowered until his mouth rested against the wet cheek.

'Why, Joshua . . . why?'

As he knelt there, the shadows seemed to echo the cry. But Joshua had no answer. His body the only comfort he could give he held the lad close, murmuring softly as to a frightened child.

Drawing slightly apart, her head tilting backwards, Philippa looked up and Joshua felt the whole of his insides twist together. Gleams of saffron yellow bathed the blanched face in a film of light, gilding the pale skin to golden ivory, glinting like blue diamonds from the tear-wet eyes, sheathing the wheat-blonde hair with soft aureate gold.

A beautiful golden child! Holding his breath in his throat, Joshua stared. Just below his own the lips parted, the eyelids closing to rest thick lashes on the soft cheek. A beautiful golden child!

Held as if in the bonds of sleep, invisible unbreakable bonds, he gazed at the face he dreamed of touching. Then despite his will, despite all of his strength, his mouth touched the softly parted lips.

He had gone from this house as though the devil whipped his back. But wasn't that exactly what were happening to her son?

The fire stoked for the third time that night, Naomi swung the bracket holding the steaming kettle back over its quiet heat.

The devil was riding Joshua and the destination was hell; her lad were plunging head first into the bottomless pit, throwing himself into the fire of eternal torment, and his mother could do nothing to prevent it.

She had tried. Naomi moved restlessly about the cramped room. Hadn't she said he ought not to have taken that bowl to Rowlay House, hadn't she said he never should 'ave swore, no oath! The fire of eternal torment! Naomi turned to the grate,

staring at the black coals. Her son had been burning in that for
weeks.

'*You will know pain.*'

It seemed in the hush of the quiet room that Keziah Silk's
words spoke aloud. Listening to the silence Naomi smiled
ruefully. She had known the pain the herb woman had meant
and she knew it still; like a phantom that never left her it walked
beside her every day, lay beside her every night. She had told
herself it would be over once the Cranley lad were married, that
the demon tearing at Joshua's soul would be gone. But that was
cold comfort. The truth of it had shown clear on his face as he
had rushed from the house. No wedding ring could banish that
which was locked fast to his heart, no marriage vow exorcise the
demon that held his soul; Philip Cranley was the scourge that
would follow throughout his life and bed with him in his grave.
A dry sob rattling in her chest Naomi reached for the teapot.
Her son was beyond the help of this world, God grant he did not
step beyond the help of the next.


They had taken her into that sanatorium. Holding the reins of
the horse Archer Cranley smiled, but it was not a satisfactory
smile that said all had gone as he would have wished. To the
contrary, the fee he had thought would be more than sufficient
had been almost doubled when that quack of a doctor had
touched a stethoscope to Hannah's breast. But money spent
meant money gained. The consolation lent humour to the smile.
Spend a little now and be master of it all in just a day or so.

No one at that hospital had suspected apart from the doctor,
and he cared far more for his fee than his medical ethics; and he,
Archer, had played his part to perfection.

He had carried that dead body bundled in a blanket. Holding
it close he had kicked at the door, crying out for help as it was
opened. Real tears – that had been the most difficult part – had
spilled to his cheeks as he refused to give up his burden,

murmuring broken words of love and reassurance against the shrouded face as he carried Hannah to an upstairs room. Telling him gently that he must lay her down if his wife was to be helped, the man had dispatched the nurse to fetch injection needles and medicine, though his glance as the woman left said he knew Hannah to be well beyond the need of them.

Speaking quietly, their voices hushed, the bargain had been struck. Hannah would be certified as having died a few hours after arrival at the sanatorium and the necessary papers signed and dated to that effect, and in exchange a large sum of money would be handed over. But it was worth it! Archer flicked the rein, urging the animal to a trot. Expensive but worth it. He would have what he wanted, and that was no directorship of any bloody charity! He would have what he had worked years for, what was due to him more than to any child born of Hannah Cranley!

*In the event of the death of his wife Hannah Cranley . . . a male child, born of her body, shall reach the age of twenty-one years . . .*

The carefully worded phrases echoing in his ears he laughed softly. 'So many wasted words, Nathan, so much time and thought, and now it is of no use, no use at all. I've taken it all, you hear me, Nathan? I've taken it all, every last penny you tried so hard to keep from me. Archer Cranley, the man you despised, the son-in-law you kept beneath your finger since writing that Will, has bitten that finger off and now spits it in your face. I've beaten you, Nathan, I've beaten you, think on that as you rot in hell!'

The smile still on his lips after stabling the horse for the night, he stood a moment in the yard looking at the rear of the house. It was acceptable enough as houses in Greets Green or even Swan Village went, but Rowlay House would not be acceptable to Archer Cranley once he was truly glassmaster; no, not acceptable at all! Striding inside he slammed the heavy door behind him, the smile fading as Edna hurried into the hall. He would be happy to see the finish of life here, but happier still to see the end of his sister's life!

'What have you done with her . . . where have you left Hannah?'

Meeting the demand with a look of sheer derision he turned away, placing hat and gloves on the elaborately carved coat stand that dominated the hall.

'Quite the actress.' He turned about, facing her with a look of cold distaste. 'Anyone who didn't know better would think you cared.'

The tension built over the past couple of hours reached its breaking point. As beacons of anger flashed from half-closed feline eyes, Edna's mouth tightened and her voice became a low threatening snarl.

'Stop the clever talk, Archer! You were never as smart as you thought even when you were a child, and you are no smarter as a man. I could always run rings around you as far as common sense went and I still can. Getting rid of Hannah's body solves no problems, it will simply create more. You can't expect Philip to believe her to be in a sanatorium if he can't see her there!'

She could always run rings around him so far as common sense went? His clever sister . . . his so very clever sister! Jubilation curving his mouth, though it left his eyes gleaming like black ice, he walked across the hall, stopping on the first tread of the stairs to look back at her.

'But he *can* see her, as you yourself can see her; I wouldn't want to deny a grieving sister-in-law the privilege of saying goodbye to the woman she nursed so devotedly. You may both pay your respects, you and Philip. When he returns you can go together to the sanatorium, you will find Hannah . . . or should I say you will find Hannah's body . . . there; and before you ask, let me tell you that your not very smart brother, the child you could so easily outwit, the man whose brain is so inferior to your own, has it so arranged that she passed away *after* she was admitted to the care of the nursing staff there.'

'So, you have everything neatly wrapped up.'

Across the hall his eyes flashed their cold triumph. 'All wrapped,' he smirked, 'and tied with a mourning ribbon!'

'But that ribbon has a knot in it . . .'

The quietness of it halting him in mid-step Archer froze. This was how it had always been and always would be. Edna forever treading down his success, playing checkmate to every small victory. This was how it would be until *he* played checkmate, until he played that final move, the move that would finish the game for good.

'. . . the knot of seeing through a marriage without a bridegroom.' Edna laughed harshly. 'How will you untie that, Archer? You can hardly take a pair of scissors to it.'

Every movement of his body, every nuance of emotion that sped across his narrow features exhibiting the hatred brewing like poison inside him, Archer looked to where his sister still stood, hands folded in that oh-so-familiar position across her skirts.

'There'll be a bridegroom,' he ground. 'Philip will be back in time.'

'In time perhaps, but in time for what, brother? In time for the taking of a wife or the reading of a Will, a Will that snatches away the prize you yearn for, that will take away Nathan Briant's leavings for good and all! What will you do then, Archer, what will my smart little brother do then?'

Laughing, Edna followed slowly up the stairs to her room.

'What will you do, Archer?' she whispered, her laugh dying as she stared at the empty bed. 'What will you do when I finally tell you?'

# Chapter Twenty-Eight

God Almighty, what had he done!

Stripping off his shirt Joshua handed it to the figure still sat hunched on the floor of the loft, before turning his back.

The very thing he had vowed never to do, to show his true feelings for Philip Cranley, to let him know what he had strived to keep hidden from him, to keep hidden from himself. But as he had held him in his arms, looking down into those tear-drenched eyes, all the strength of that vow had faded, every atom of his will melting beneath the look he saw reflected there. But that had been a look which existed only among his own imaginings, it had no reality outside of his dreams, no substance except in his own desires. Yet the kiss had been returned, he had felt the soft pressure of it against his mouth, the arm that had lifted to his neck . . . But that too was imagination, it could be no other. Philip Cranley would have no liking for such thoughts.

Turning his back as Philip pulled on the shirt, Joshua stared into the shadows pressing in on the fragile pool of the lantern's light. A man could want a thing so badly he could tell himself it had happened when it hadn't. And that had not happened. There had been no return of that kiss, no arm lifted in response to his own emotion. The hand that touched his shoulder had lifted to push him away, the pressure beneath his mouth was the tightening of lips closing against the abhorrence of another man's kiss. He had committed the unforgivable, taken advantage of a lad caught so deep in a net of fear he could not defend himself. He had prevented Grinley further abusing that young body, only to abuse it himself.

'Philip,' it choked out, 'Philip, I'm sorry, I never meant to touch you . . . I've never touched any man that way, I—'

'There is no need for apology, Joshua, we were both over-wrought. If there is blame then it is mine.'

'No!' Joshua whirled, shame and guilt etched deep on his face. 'It was not your fault. I'm no child, I should have known better!'

Touching a hand to his arm Philippa answered gently, 'I'm no child either, Joshua, I realise the things worry can cause a man to do. We have both been under a great deal of strain and in the face of that what happened just now was simply a reaction. I behaved like a child, breaking into tears, you gave the natural comfort any adult would have given; we are equally to blame, if blame there must be. But no one knows of it apart from us, so let us just forget it, put it out of our minds completely.'

How could he do that? Reaching for the jacket held out to him Joshua buttoned it across his bare chest. The touch of those soft lips burned yet against his mouth. Not if the devil claimed him would he forget the feel of that small body held close to his; he would never *want* to forget.

'Are you recovered enough to leave?' Forcing himself to be practical Joshua reached for the lantern but, as the glow showed, the lad's fingers trembled as they fastened coat buttons. 'We can stay here 'til morning . . .'

'No!' Philippa's cry held traces of the fear which had filled it minutes before. 'Let's get out of this place before that man—'

'Grinley won't ever touch you again, in fact he won't come within a mile of you if he wishes to go on living!' Stepping to the ladder he stretched out a hand, the heart inside him shrivelling as the other man pulled back. That kiss was the result of stress, holding him in his arms was purely a means of giving comfort. That was what Philip Cranley had said. Joshua moved mindlessly down the rickety ladder, standing away from it as Philippa followed. He did not blame him, but it was obvious from his pulling away that he did not trust him either, did not trust he would not be touched again.

Holding the lantern high he caught the gasp that came from behind.

'Look.' Philippa pointed as he turned.

Grinley! Handing the lantern to a shaking Philippa he knelt beside the figure spread-eagled on the dirt-packed floor.

'Is he dead?'

'No.' Joshua touched a hand to the side of Grinley's neck. 'There's a pulse, he's alive.'

'Thank God!' No more than a murmur, the relief of it trembled on the silence.

'It's more than he deserves.' Needing no lantern to see among the shadows Joshua strode to the doors of the malthouse, leaving Philippa to follow.

Outside the moon had risen, bathing the street in silver.

'Leave the lantern,' Joshua spoke tersely, 'we won't need it.'

'Joshua, wait!' Blowing out the small flame she set the lantern on the ground beside the still open doors. 'We can't leave that man, he might be injured, we . . . we have to help him.'

'Help him!' Joshua exploded. 'Help that swine! After what he's done to you, I'd rather kill him!'

'I know how you feel.'

Looking at the face lifted to his, moonlight turning the smooth skin to palest alabaster, the eyes to dark mysteries, Joshua felt the full force of love and longing strike his stomach like a battering ram.

'No.' He lifted a finger but, remembering the drawing back

from him, dropped it before stroking that gentle face. 'No, Philip, you don't know how I feel, and God willing you will never know.'

Standing so close as to touch, so near as to almost hear the beat of that heart, the effort of denial dragged silent sobs of misery from the deepest reaches of Joshua's being. Why did the lad stand there looking at him with eyes that branded his soul, why didn't he draw back as he had in that loft?

Lips barely moving, the answer a murmur that scarce impressed the silvery hush, a smile of sweet sadness touched Philippa's mouth. 'I do know, Joshua,' she whispered, 'believe me when I tell you, I know exactly how you feel, for I feel the same.'

Thank heaven it hadn't been her son had done this. Naomi glanced at the trousers and long-legged underpants, the back seam split almost to the crotch. It had taken the very breath from her body seeing that lad walk into her kitchen, Joshua's shirt reaching to his knees beneath a torn jacket.

'*He was in the loft of the old malthouse that stands near the junction of William Street and Charles Street.*' Joshua had met her eyes. Reading the horror that bred in their depths, he had allowed no anger, no reproof to show in his own as he continued, '*Grinley had him, he abducted him.*'

Motherly instinct overcoming all other feeling as the lad stumbled forwards, she had gone to him, her own strong hands lowering him to a chair. Catching the quick shake of her son's head she had asked no more questions, leaving the rest of what Joshua had to tell until they were alone. She had first bathed wrists and ankles rubbed and cut by the savage bite of twine, thinking how small the bones were as she creamed them with soothing Indian Cereate and bound them with strips torn from old sheeting boiled to a pure white. Then insisting they both take a bowl of hot broth she had laid trousers and undergarments from Joshua's cupboard on to her own bed saying that to see her son come home dressed as he was could do a woman in Hannah Cranley's state of health no good at all.

She had wanted the lad to stay here for the rest of the night, fearing from the paleness of his face and the dark circles around his eyes that he wouldn't find the strength to walk the distance to Swan Village, but he had insisted he must go home; his mother, he had said, would be fretting at his being gone so long.

There had been no crying, no giving in to the feelings that must have been wracking every nerve, and definitely no play acting. She had admired the lad for that, it took a kind of strength many men might have a hard time finding yet here he was, just a strip of a lad, behaving like a Trojan. A body would have expected him to play for sympathy but he had changed his clothes, ate a little broth, then thanking her for her kindness had left.

Gathering up the trousers streaked with dried mud she touched a finger to the torn seam, shuddering at the thought it invoked. Wrists and ankles bound so tight as to cut deep into the flesh, clothes ripped apart! It could mean one thing and one thing only, that lad had been taken from the heath, snatched as others in the past had been snatched, and for what? Her fingers tracing the line of slashed cloth Naomi closed her eyes, pressing the lids hard down against the awful truth in her mind. Philip Cranley had been taken to satisfy a man's evil, to feed a foul licentious appetite, to be used in ways nature never intended a man be used.

In the quiet of her tiny living room lit by the glow of her one lamp, Naomi slid to her knees on the hearth rug she had pegged herself.

'Oh Lord,' she whispered, 'I give thanks it weren't my lad following the ways of evil, I give thanks it weren't him running to catch the devil's coat-tails; and I says thank you on behalf of

Hannah Cranley for the safekeeping of her son for I doubt her'll be told the all of what happened this night.'

Her eyes still closed, Naomi crossed her breast devoutly before rising. The thanks due to the Lord had not been fully paid, nor would they ever be; a lifetime was not enough for her to repay the Almighty for His goodness in keeping Joshua free of that wickedness, nor long enough to pray that as it had been tonight it would go on being. Joshua had feelings for the Cranley lad, she could draw a veil over what her mind told and her own eyes showed, but she could not hide what was in her heart, and them feelings were not the sort no man should have for another. There was love between father and son and love of brother for brother, but the love of a man for a woman was different and the two should not be crossed; that love, the sort that flamed to desire, was not meant for a man to share with a man, yet it was that kind of love that her son carried in his heart.

But given time he would overcome them feelings, drive out the worm that nibbled his soul; Joshua would never give in to unnatural love.

Folding the garments she laid them aside. Tomorrow she would mend and return them to the Cranley lad. Tomorrow this nightmare would all be over.

But as she glanced towards the window, pearl-washed with the light of the new day, something deep inside brought back coldness to her blood and Keziah Silk's words warned fresh in her mind.

'*There be change, it stands close, change that will take that you cherish most.*'

And in the silence that followed their fading, Naomi knew with certainty that the nightmare was far from over.


'Grinley! You say it was Grinley abducted you?'

Archer Cranley stared at the figure dressed in trousers several sizes too big. 'For what reason . . . money? Did he hope to get paid for bringing you back?'

'I don't think it was ransom he had in mind, Father.' Philippa gave a brief shake of the head, refusing the glass of wine Edna placed beside her.

'Then if it were not money what the hell *did* he hope for?'

There was anger on Archer Cranley's face, anger and a certain confusion, but where was the thankfulness for the safe return of a missing child, where was the relief . . . where the love? She had seen more of each on the face of Naomi Fairley; a woman who was virtually a stranger had shown feelings Archer Cranley had never held.

'I think this might explain more clearly.' Lifting the sleeves of the shirt Philippa displayed the bandaged wrists, then hoisting trouser legs showed the same about both ankles.

'How?' The one word seemed to take an age to leave the man's throat.

'Twine,' she answered. 'There was a blow to the back of my neck. I don't remember any more until we reached a disused malthouse. I was three-parts asleep, opium I think he called the drug he gave me, but whatever it was it had me helpless and I finished up tied hands and feet in a loft.'

'So why didn't he come here, or at least send a note stating what he wanted in return for your safety . . . but what else if it wasn't money?' Edna too seemed confused.

'It was money he had hoped for when he kidnapped me, and after discovering that particular money was not forthcoming he did consider approaching Father, but then—'

'Then *what?*' Archer barked as the explanation halted.

'I . . .' Philippa faltered, glancing at the woman who, like her brother, had never shown love for the child who had spent so long under her less than tender hand. 'I think perhaps the rest might be better said to my father alone.'

Her beady eyes half closing, Edna Cranley breathed her fury.

Why should she not hear . . . what could be so private as to require her absence?

'I don't see . . .' But she got no further, her brother's sharp order to leave showing he would brook no argument. Glaring at them both she stamped from the room. But the display of chagrin was for their benefit only, a sharp ear pressed to a door missed little.

'Now,' Archer's voice came clearly through the panelled door. 'What is it you couldn't bring yourself to tell in front of your aunt, just what was it Grinley expected to get?'

'From what I heard him muttering to himself in that loft it appears I had been taken to be sold.'

'Sold! What the hell are you talking about, do you take me for a fool?'

Strangely calm after the horror of these past hours Philippa answered, 'No, Father, I do not. Whatever else you may be thought, no one could think you a fool; but if it seems I am lying—'

'Stay where you are.' Archer shot out a hand as if to hold her to the chair. 'You say Grinley thought to sell you, so who was to be the buyer?'

'Someone you know rather well, Father . . .'

Beyond the door Edna listened.

'. . . The name that man spoke was Beasley, Simeon Beasley.'

'Beasley! So that's his game!'

It was satisfaction not anger that coloured the reply. Hearing it, Edna smiled. So her brother's partner in robbing the business was not the upright citizen he liked folk to think, not that she had ever thought of him as such; of course she had no proof that he took bribes from Archer, but she would stake her life on the surety of being right.

'It could be that Beasley recognised me, but whether it was that or not he reneged on the agreement; that was how come I finished up in that loft. I begged Grinley to come to you, told him you would pay whatever reward he asked. It appeared at first that he was agreeable, at least to considering the proposal, but when later he returned drunk, he . . . he . . .'

Her mouth trembling, Philippa gripped shaking hands together, trying desperately to fight back the returning nightmare.

But though her father watched the emotions ebb and flow across the colourless face, the fear registered on it made no impression upon him. Utterly without feeling for the effect that abduction must have had or the further trauma of answering questions so soon after it, he demanded coldly, 'Well, out with it. When Grinley came back drunk, what then?'

'Please, Father . . . no more. I can't—'

'Now!' The reply whipped out. 'You'll tell me now, and make sure I hear it all.'

Teeth sunk into lower lip, fingers white from gripping together, she blinked against rising tears.

'I said tell me!' Quick as a striking snake Archer grabbed the lapels of Philippa's jacket, snatching it forward with a force that rocked the slight figure. 'Tell me, or by Christ I'll knock it out of you!'

Thrown back against the chair as the jacket was released Philippa raised a shaking hand, expecting a blow to follow the outburst.

Fighting rapidly thickening sobs she knew the answer must be given. 'He . . . he decided he would take what Beasley had refused. He slashed my clothes with a knife.' Eyes lifting to Archer pleaded not to have to give voice to the rest, but the face that stared back remained impassive. Resigned to the awfulness of telling the rest, Philippa lowered her head. 'I felt the touch of him against my buttocks, I know he would have raped me.'

'Would have?'

Her ear pressed against the door, Edna drew a sharp breath. She had known all her life that her brother put his own needs and interests before any other, but the callousness of his questions, of this latest treatment of his one remaining child caused even her to catch her breath.

'Had it not been for Joshua Fairley . . . he arrived just in time.'

Fairley again! Archer turned away, his brow creasing. How come he always turned up in the nick of time, was there something between him and Philip . . . had Philip told him? But no, he would not dare, not while his mother remained beneath the threat of that institution! And he must not know the threat had been removed, that it was no longer viable . . . not yet, not until the marriage had taken place and the glassworks signed over . . . then, and only then would he be told of Hannah's death.

She had wondered at the oversized clothing her nephew had returned wearing. Fairley! Having heard all she wished, Edna walked up the stairs to her room. What part was that man playing in all of this?

Staring into the fire Edna had kept alive through the night, Archer pressed the next question ruthlessly. 'Just in time for what, to finish what Grinley had begun? Do them clothes you be wearing belong to him, lent you in place of the ones he ripped off you?'

'I told you! It was Grinley, he slashed my trousers with a knife then ripped them apart. Joshua never touched me.'

Too much protection! Archer continued staring at the prancing flames. Philip had been too quick in denial. Whatever the relationship between the two it would bear looking into, looking into and ending!

'He gave me his shirt to cover my torn clothing, then took me to his home where his mother bathed my wrists and ankles.'

Rising from the chair Philippa stared at the man stood with his back turned.

'The Fairleys were very kind, I found more help and under-standing in that house than ever I found in you or in your sister;

and now that you have heard all there is to hear I am going upstairs to see my mother, and soon, like it or not, you will no longer be in a position to make her life the misery you have made it for so long. My grandfather could not prevent your cruelty but his money can, and I, Father, intend to see that it does!'

# Chapter Twenty-Nine

'*Your mother be in the sanatorium and it be your fault!*'

Closing her eyes against the venom behind those words flung at her as she left the sitting room, Philippa lay in the bath but there was little comfort in the warm water.

'*She couldn't take any more,*' Archer had bellowed, following up the stairs, '*couldn't stand the strain of you not coming home, of you preferring to take your midday meal and afternoon rest with the men from the glass, or should I say with Fairley? Is it his company you prefers to that of your mother?*'

The accusations had followed along the landing, not ceasing even on reaching the bedroom that had proved empty.

'*You see what you've done!*' The voice had gone on, strident and condemning. '*You and your bloody selfish ways . . . couldn't be bothered with coming home, too far for you to bother! Well, this be the result, this!*' Archer had jabbed a hand towards the empty bed. '*Worry were the doing of it, your mother collapsed from worrying about you, now she be in the sanatorium.*'

She remembered the shock of hearing it. Though deep down knew the reason given was a lie, that the accusations were merely a club to beat her with, yet still the shock of finding her mother gone had struck like a hammer.

But why else would she have been taken from Rowlay House . . . was her mother truly in the sanatorium? Archer Cranley told so many lies, twisted things to suit his own purpose. But not in this . . . surely even he would not go so far as to say she was being cared for in a hospital if she were not, he would be bound to realise how easily that could be ascertained. Hearing just that Archer had laughed.

'*I am still the master here . . .*'

The words spoken in her mother's room returned, battering Philippa's mind like a sledgehammer.

'*. . . and master of my own wife . . . nobody sees her without my say so, and you'll see no more of her 'til after that marriage.*'

Keeping his wife locked away, refusing to allow even her own child to see her was Archer Cranley's trump card and he had played it.

Scooping water across eyes bright from crying she tried to wash the tears away, but fast as she did so they returned.

Archer was giving no chance of refusal, letting no possible avenue of escape remain open; and for the sake of her mother's safety Philippa knew that those dictates must be followed.

What Archer Cranley demanded would be done. Her eyes closed against the thought. His demands would be satisfied, though Davinia Lacy would suffer. At least she would not spend a whole lifetime in suffering as she, Philippa, had done; the shock would be sharp and bitter but, like having a tooth extracted, it would be over and done in one go. Only the grief which the death of her remaining child would bring to Hannah Cranley had stayed Philippa's hand this long, but now the evil of her father had stretched too far; he had ruined one young life, he must not be allowed to ruin another. Her mother would understand, understand and forgive.

Beyond the small window the light of morning was already strong. Staring at it Philippa again felt the urge that had driven through her in that bedroom, the urge to go at once to that sanatorium, to apologise, to hold that dear form close, to be with the only person who had ever loved Philippa Cranley . . . but not the only person loved by her.

Admission, if made only in the privacy of the mind, brought

colour stinging swiftly, a brisk rub with soap refusing to wash it away. That kiss in the loft, the gentle yet fierce pressure of those lips, the arms that held firm yet tender. It would be so easy to think that was more than an effort to comfort, to construe it as more than it was meant to be, to match Joshua's kindness to the feelings that had pulled so deep inside, and which still did pull; feelings of love. Yes, it was love, love so strong as to choke each time the memory of that kiss brought the feel of it once more. The nightmare of Grinley's abuse was not forgotten, but it was Joshua Fairley's arms, Joshua Fairley's mouth that was the strongest memory. But that was all it must be, a wonderful heartbreaking memory.

They had walked to Swan Village together. Thanking Naomi for her kindness and concern and refusing the offer of company crossing the heath, she had turned to leave. But her refusal had been brushed aside, Joshua leading the way from the house. They had walked most of the way without speaking, the early morning song of larks and thrushes the only physical sounds, but mentally the shouts of emotion had drummed against her brain until the desire to step into those strong arms had been almost overpowering. Yet not once had Joshua looked at her; there had been no smile, no touch and no word of affection. But then Joshua could never truly feel more than friendship for another man, there could be no question of love between them; that kiss and the way he had held him in his arms had been no more than simple pity, the sympathy any adult would show a frightened child.

Except Philippa Cranley was no child! And these feelings for Joshua Fairley were not the feelings of a child.

Sliding lower in the warm water she rested against the cast-iron rim of the white enamelled bath.

Why was life so cruel, what did fate find so amusing in tearing the heart from a body, of condemning the soul to a never-ending torment? Why had it not been herself who had died in that mill-race . . . why?

The questions smarting now had been asked many times before but the fates, if they had ever listened, kept their counsel, their laughter silent though the echo of it cut deep; yet this time it cut deeper still. The agony of one-sided love, a love destined to remain for ever unfulfilled, was the deepest pain of all. But for all the heartache it had brought, all the misery of longing, it was the one thing, apart from a loving mother, the one treasured love that life had given, the one brief moment that would remain for all eternity locked deep inside a broken heart.

'. . . *you don't know how I feel, and God willing you will never know.*'

Those had been Joshua's words. If only they could have been a reflection of the feelings in her own heart, a semblance of that same love instead of the anger felt against Grinley. They had been almost the last words that had passed between them. With her eyes pressed hard shut, breath binding tight about the throat, she saw again the tall figure turn away as they had come within sight of Rowlay House, felt the same scorching twist at the finality of it. Joshua Fairley had not said goodbye but the meaning of it was clear. He wished not to see or meet with Philip Cranley again.

And then, yards away, silhouetted dark against the flush of the rising sun, he had turned.

Teeth biting into her lips, she found it hard to breathe as the rest of the memory flooded back. It had seemed for a moment that every angel in heaven sang, that the very earth trembled in the sweetness of it as Joshua walked back.

But it had not been the promise of love his outstretched hand had offered, not the same crazy happy smile that touched his lips.

'*I almost forgot,*' he had said, '*your mother asked me to give you this.*'

The envelope had been offered, but afraid of what must follow Philippa had held back, just to have Joshua there with her was enough, to have him turn away again . . . But not meeting her eyes Joshua had thrust the letter at her.

Against closed lids Philippa saw the figure turn away and in her mind heard the muttered words.

*'Be happy, Philip . . . for God's sake be happy!'*

'I'm sorry, Mr Cranley, but I must observe your father's instructions. I cannot allow you to see your mother without his presence or his written permission.'

'Then at least tell me, is my mother recovering, was it stress brought on her relapse?'

'Please understand my dilemma.' The doctor had smiled blandly. 'I must honour my word to your father.'

There had been no more to be gained. Philippa had turned away then. The doctor would say no more, give no assurance of wellbeing, but then there had been no need; for all the blandness of a well-practised smile there had still been a furtiveness in the eyes, a look that said as much as any words.

The letter had remained forgotten in a pocket, forgotten until those thoughts during bathing had brought remembrance of it rushing back. The turmoil of emotion ripping apart every vein as Joshua had almost thrown it had taken away all thought of asking how come Hannah Cranley had entrusted a letter to Joshua Fairley, how they had met and where? Only there in the bathroom had they made themselves heard.

Read twice, the letter had been dropped to the bed, Philippa staring at the tiny pool of white against the deep blue of the cover.

Carved as if in stone the words returned now, filling her mind, blocking all sight of the buildings flanking West Bromwich High Street, of the figures hurrying about their various business as the hansom returning to Rowlay House bowled past.

*My dearest child,*

Philippa's heart swelled with pain.

*My one dear love, by the time you read this letter life for me will have ceased. Forgive me, my dearest, forgive your mother the pain and sorrow she has caused you, for the misery of your own life. You see, my love, I knew! All these years I have known of your father's lies, known what he told you concerning my illness. What he told of those so-called 'turns' was no more than a web of deceit spun to ensure that which he coveted above all else would be safeguarded, kept until one day it could in every sense belong to him. I knew the truth behind the masquerade but did not have the courage to face the evil of it. I could not bear the thought of what his madness promised, what the snatching away of the business would drive Archer Cranley to, the killing of you, my dearest child. I love you, my darling, love you too much to lose you and too much to let you go on being the instrument of Archer Cranley's foul iniquity. This is the only way I can see to put an end to it.*

*I ask you again to forgive and beg you always to remember that I never stopped loving you, my dearest. May God in His mercy give you the happiness your mother could not.*

Tears edging a crystal line along heavy lashes, Philippa leaned forwards, giving fresh instruction to the cabby.

'My son were brought to you at Harville's Hawthorne, brought by Thad Grinley, but you never spoke of it when we met in them dining rooms.'

Stood in the private office Archer glared at the corpulent figure sat behind a pretentious walnut desk.

'You said no word, though you knew of his whereabouts.'

'My dear fellow.' Fat hands spread wide on the desk, gold rings glinting in the morning sunlight blazing in at the tall window. 'What gives you to think your lad would be brought to my house?'

'Don't you come your bloody fancy talk with me, Beasley!' Archer's temper flared to the edge of eruption. 'I knows he was fetched to you same as I knows what he were fetched for. You've always had a liking for lads, especially young, pretty lads; they be what satisfies your appetite.'

Simeon Beasley's smile was thin, barely concealing his disdain. Cranley could bluster all he liked, he had no proof his son had been brought to Harville's Hawthorne.

'I don't be the only one plays with what they shouldn't,' he said, a quiet venom lacing the tone, 'you also has a liking for playing away from the nest.'

'That be true,' Archer conceded, the poison of his tone matching that of the man watching him with careful eyes, 'I takes my pleasures where I wish. But them pleasures don't be with any lad, unlike you I don't go poking a boy's arse.'

Ferret eyes gleamed across the desk, fat fingers closing and opening as Beasley caught his breath. 'Take care, Cranley . . .'

'It don't be me needs to take care,' Archer flashed, 'a man taking a prostitute be one thing, a man engaged in white slaving be summat else again.'

'For Christ's sake keep your voice down!' Jowls wobbling, his face turned a dull red, Simeon Beasley was on his feet.

'Why?' Archer's smile was icy. 'So your little secret can remain secret, so no one will hear of your particular preference, your penchant for having a boy in your bed? Such a pity you turned one away, that was a mistake, Beasley.'

Leaning both hands on the desk, his head jutting forwards on his thick neck, Simeon Beasley glared his contempt.

'A mistake, was it?' He glowered. 'The mistake of turning away the offer of your son, or of not keeping him, of passing him along the line, getting rid of him and so leaving you a clear field? No body, no death certificate, eh Cranley! That way you would still be master of all Nathan Briant left behind.'

'Put on it whatever interpretation suits you, the mistake be still yours.' Smooth as oil on water the smile spread on Archer's mouth. 'Take as many pretty boys as you will but there'll be no more Briant money pays for them. You've been paid the last you will get from me, and before you make any threats let me inform you of this: Philip saw the man that abducted him, heard him talking to himself of carting him to Harville's Hawthorne.'

'Talking to himself . . . *himself*, Cranley,' Beasley looked jubilant, 'where be the proof in that?'

Glancing at the tall hat held in his hands Archer flicked a non-existent dust speck. 'None at all, taken in itself. But you see, Beasley, not only did my son speak to Grinley of being in your house, so also did the man who rescued Philip from Grinley's malthouse. The constabulary would be interested in hearing of my son's disappearance, I understand that for some time now they've been attempting to discover who is behind the taking of lads from the streets. Now you see where your mistake lies!'

'And you, Cranley?' As anger deepened the glow suffusing his face, Simeon Beasley's harsh intake of breath sounded loud on the quiet air. 'Do you see where *your* mistake lies? Constabulary be interested in more than one basket of eggs, and you be like to break yours. I don't be the only man in this room with secrets to hide, what if I tells of the years you've taken money from that business to use to your own purpose . . . what if *I* tells?'

'It will be unpleasant.' Archer shrugged, pretending the threat was of no consequence. 'But more so for you than for me. To compound a felony by dishonouring the trust Nathan Briant placed in you by naming you executor of his Will would add greatly to your guilt in the eyes of any jury, a jury already considerably impressed by the crime of abusing young men, of selling them on once you tire of their particular charm. You can't prove my misuse of Briant money whereas I have proof, trustworthy proof, of your doings. Say what you must but before you let your tongue run away without your brain, think of this: murder isn't the only crime a man can hang for. White slaving be an offence in the eyes of any man and that jury will prove no exception; they'll hang you, Beasley, as surely as I stand here, they'll hang you!'

✻    ✻    ✻

*I love you . . . too much to let you go on being the instrument of Archer Cranley's foul iniquity.*

Philippa touched a hand to the pocket which held the letter given to Joshua Fairley. Hannah had asked that he take it. But when had she asked . . . how had those two met, and for what reason?

Following along Sheepwash Lane the hansom turned left into Tinsley Street but, deep in thought, Philippa was oblivious of the carts rumbling past on their way to and from the wharf and basin of the canal or the several brickworks that had arisen in the area.

She must have planned it all so carefully . . . planned it God knew how many weeks or months ago, lived with the knowledge of it . . .

Philippa's hands curled into tight balls, her teeth clamped hard against the pain that twisted like a live thing. When had her mother decided, what could have driven her to take such a step?

But that question had been answered. It was there in her letter: *This is the only way I can see to put an end to it.* Hannah Cranley had sacrificed her life in order to end her husband's evil. She had died in order to prevent any more of his cruelty.

But why could she not have spoken of what she knew, talked of it in their times together? Why not try to sort things out between them? Because she knew the outcome of that as surely as she had known of Archer Cranley's deceit. In the privacy of the hansom Philippa's head dropped. Hannah had not told of what she felt she must do because she would have guessed Philippa would have beaten her to it, taken her life to save her mother's; and now it was too late. Stress, Archer had said, the strain of not seeing Philip during the afternoon break. But there had been no word of the stress caused by his own demands, the strain of living under the hand of constant oppression, for that was what her life had been; Hannah Cranley had lived a life made miserable by the hatred of a sister-in-law and the tyranny of a husband.

Drawing a ragged breath Philippa leaned back against the leather upholstery. The letter had come too late to save Hannah but it had come in time to destroy the dreams of Archer Cranley and repay the spite of his sister.

# Chapter Thirty

'I ask you again, Father, is my mother recovering?'

Returned to Rowlay House, Philippa had sat in the sitting room waiting for Archer's return. Now, with eyes cold as ice she stared at her father.

'I've just come from the sanatorium.' The lie came readily. 'Your mother was resting easy.'

Resting easy! Philippa felt nerves stretch to near breaking. Yes, she was resting easy, no doubt for the first time since coming to this house.

'Then there is no reason why I should not visit her . . . is there, Father?'

The tone of voice had altered with the question, just a shade but nevertheless it had changed, become almost a challenge. Hannah's child was growing up, rapidly shaking off the youthfulness that could be controlled, dominated. The sooner that marriage were consecrated the better. Once the business were completely in his hands this excuse of a child could be written off, but for the moment he must tread with caution. Short of being trussed like a chicken and locked away until the vicar stood ready nothing could be certain.

Hiding the thoughts behind what he hoped was a concerned look, Archer gave a slight shake of the head.

'The doctor advised she should not be disturbed. Complete

rest was what she needed for at least another twenty-four hours. Tomorrow will be soon enough, a half-hour in the evening perhaps, your mother should not be overtired.'

How very considerate! Philippa swallowed hard on the contempt. Since when had Archer Cranley been so solicitous of his wife's welfare?

'Of course, mother should not be overtaxed, but a peep in at her door should not be too much.'

'We must abide by what the doctors advise,' Archer returned quickly. 'I will not risk your mother suffering another attack. Tomorrow you may visit her but not before.'

Not before that marriage was finalised. Not before every card was safe in Archer Cranley's hand! Suppressing the thought with difficulty, Philippa went on.

'But you saw her, father, you actually saw for yourself that mother is recovering?'

Lies making no impression on his voice, Archer nodded. 'Yes, I spoke with her just for a few moments while the doctor's back were turned. I gave her your love and said you would be visiting tomorrow.'

Given her love! Disgust burned like acid in Philippa's throat. Archer Cranley was incapable of giving love, either his own or that of anyone else. This man was capable of nothing but greed.

'Thank you, father.' Knowing contempt could not be hidden much longer she turned from the room.

'Best you don't leave the house.' Archer smiled triumphantly as he flung the directive. 'You should rest, get some colour back in your cheeks ready for the wedding tonight. You turn up looking pale as a virgin and that wench of Lacy's might think as you don't want to marry her.'

Wincing at the low laughter that followed, Philippa continued on up the stairs then paused as Archer came into the hall, laughter interjecting his shouted command.

'You make sure you be ready! Eight o'clock on the dot.'

Her fingers tightening about the banister rail, Philippa turned, and at that moment all the childhood dismay of knowing the father she loved did not love her, the unhappiness of a growing realisation that she was looked upon as a failure, a disappointment, the inner contention of youth having to accept what she knew was wrong, all coalesced, shooting wild fire flames of anger through every vein.

'Oh, I'll be ready, father.' Spoken quietly the answer belied the fire. 'I will most certainly be ready!'

'You couldn't 'elp what happened, lad, there were nothing you could 'ave done, nothing any of us could 'ave done, the furnace had him afore we could get to him.' Samuel Platt glanced at the man sat opposite. 'The fault don't lie with you, Josh.'

'If I hadn't lost my temper . . .'

'Ned Jukes would cause a saint to lose his temper, and there ain't none of us be saints, lad. What spewed from his mouth were foul, no man could hear of such being said to his mother and still call hisself a man in the doing nothing about it. You done only what any other in Greets Green would 'ave done, you tackled him.'

'Yes, I tackled him.' Joshua stared at the grate his mother kept polished to silver. 'But I could have chosen a more suitable place to fight.'

'Choosin' don't always be left for a man to make.' Samuel held his stained clay pipe, looking to Naomi for permission to light it. 'Sometimes the devil takes a hand, and it be the devil's hand has lain on Ned Jukes's shoulder from being in short trousers; even afore he could properly toddle that lad had a demon in him, a bad streak that nobody could wipe away; I says he made his own end.'

'But it were a terrible end, even for one as ill-minded as Ned Jukes.' Naomi's hand trembled as she lifted the teapot.

'Everybody be in accord with that, Naomi,' Samuel nodded,

'same as every man who seen what happened in that cone be of accord that it were no doing of Joshua's. Ned Jukes swung that rod with a force meant to kill, and kill it did. It pulled him off balance, dragged him straight into that feeder hole.'

Having poured tea in the cups, Naomi sat the pot on the table, covering it with a cosy she had stitched and stuffed from a dress long ago worn out. 'What be bothering me most, though p'raps I shouldn't say it in the light of a man's dying, be that feeder hole, why were it open? Archer Cranley be sure to ask the question.'

Replacing the spill he had held to the bowl of the pipe, Samuel Platt blinked through the tiny cloud of lavender-grey smoke.

'Oh, the question'll be asked right enough,' he said, sucking on the stem, 'and the answer'll be given. Gates have to be raised from the feeder holes every few hours for coal to be fed to the furnace . . . you knows that for yourself, Naomi, your man and son both worked the glass.'

Handing cups to both men before sitting at the table with her own, Naomi answered, 'Ar, I knows that, but I still don't see . . .'

'You also knows that come the time for them gates to be lifted there be a hooter sounded, six short blasts which warns the Bit Gatherers and the Carriers In to have special care in their comings and goings. They was already lifted and Joby Birch were shovelling coal into that particular hole when the men's shouts warned summat were amiss. Ned Jukes were already staggering towards the open feeder when Joby turned. He tried to lower the gate but them iron plates be heavy, they don't move easy as a babby's toy, needless to tell the furnace got Jukes.'

'His poor mother.' Naomi dabbed her eyes with her apron.

'Ar, Mary be the one we all feels for, but like the rest her knowed that son of hers would reach a bad end. The pity of it be as Joshua be shouldering the blame.'

Glancing at the works' chargehand sat with pipe in one hand and teacup in the other, Joshua knew the man had called to bring comfort to him and his mother, but guilt for what had happened lent a tenseness to his answer.

'Somebody has to!'

'Ain't nobody has to!' Naomi's own tension snapped like a spring. 'It be as Samuel says it be, an accident pure and simple, and you playing the martyr won't alter not one single bit of it! There be no fault on anybody's part.'

Turning to look at his mother, Joshua's eyes were gentle. Her outburst was due only to the love she held for him, the result of hours of worry for him.

'Archer Cranley will not think that, Mother,' he said quietly. 'A man's death occurring in his works is not something he can dismiss out of hand, there will be enquiries. I won't have any of the men held responsible for something they had no part in.'

'They won't be, lad.'

Returning his glance to the man handing back his empty cup, Joshua frowned.

'You know Cranley better than that, Mr Platt, he'll have no shadow cast over what's his; no matter from where, he'll come up with a scapegoat.'

Tapping the pipe against the inside of the grate, the older man rose to his feet. Flat cap in hand he met the frightened look in Naomi's eyes.

'Try not to dwell on it too much, wench,' he said, pity gruff in every word, 'the Lord be always on the side of the innocent and your lad be innocent.'

But as she followed the stooped figure to the door, watched him fit the cap to his greying head, Naomi heard only the words, *'you'll look into the very face of fear . . . it stands close . . .'*

Did she have to wear that, didn't she own a dress with a bit of colour in it? This was to be a wedding not a funeral; but then what did it matter what she wore, she would still look like a dried stick. Turning his critical glance from his sister to the clock stood on the mantle, Archer Cranley felt a warm rush of satisfaction. Ten minutes, that was all the time left to wait; in ten minutes the bride and the priest would stand here in this room and the end would begin. He had waited many long years, waited for the time when all of his carefully nurtured plans would come to fruition, and now that time was here. Before the next hour was past the whole of Nathan Briant's wealth would be his.

There had been those who sought to share it, thought one way or another to take part of what was to be his. A hint of a smile touching the mouth edged by a neatly trimmed beard he walked across the room to where glasses and decanter stood ready to toast the bride and groom.

Touching a finger to the heavy glass stopper he allowed the smile to widen. But their hopes had come to nothing, they had chosen the wrong man when they chose to blackmail Archer Cranley, and they had paid for that mistake; only poor little Sally Povey had died for no reason. Memory of that night in her room across from the churchyard took the smile from his face. Sally Povey had been no more than a common prostitute doing the job he had paid her to do . . . no, he had not meant to kill her. But the others! He breathed deeply, tasting the dregs of anger. They had intended to rob him. Five hundred pounds . . . that slimy little toad of a man had asked for five hundred pounds! But that would have simply been the first of a string of demands, it would have gone on and on; but he, Archer, had taken care of Jim Baker, then the lovely Lilah had tried her hand at the game.

His fingers tightening about the stopper, the angles of its cut pressing deeply against soft flesh, he stared at the vision rising before his inner eyes; a small brightly painted rosebud mouth smiled provocatively, deeply violet eyes beckoned with that special seduction while light danced golden soft among blonde curls. Lilah Cherrington had been beautiful, but with that beauty had gone avarice. Lilah had wanted the money her lover had failed to get, but she had wanted more beside, she had thought to win a bigger prize, thought to become Mrs Archer Cranley.

How stupid! That earlier glow of satisfaction deepening as the lovely vision faded, he walked back to stand before the hearth. How very stupid of them both to have thought to blackmail him; now they would never think of anything again!

It had all gone so smoothly. The newspapers had reported the finding of a prostitute who had presumably hanged herself, and a man so far gone in drink he walked over the edge of a lock and drowned, and as for Lilah, she would never be found. There had been no mention of foul play and certainly no member of the constabulary had even glanced his way. Yes, everything had gone so smoothly, even Hannah was no longer in his way.

Only Philip remained, Philip and Edna. He glanced again at his sister sat straight-backed on the edge of her chair. Neither posed any problem. Philip had swallowed whole the tripe told of Hannah's supposed illness, believed she was recovering in that private sanatorium; and Edna, who cared what that sour-faced bitch believed! Plans for the dispatch of Philip and the blushing bride were already in hand, and that of Edna would follow soon after. There would be no obstacle in the way of his new life, life enhanced by the prospect of no longer having Beasley eat into the profits.

Thought of that last meeting added fuel to the flame of satisfaction warming Archer's veins. How the man had squirmed, how he had denied having any knowledge of the missing Philip, and how that bluster had evaporated when he heard of a third party, of someone else hearing what Grinley had let drop; and Grinley too would squirm, like kettle calling pot black he would try to place all blame for his filthy trade on Beasley. But it would be worse for him, for unlike his white-slaving partner he had no private income and with the threat of being exposed to every manufacturer and every mine owner from here to the next county he would no longer have a living; Briant Bottle and Glass would bring limestone in its own cart and supply Grinley's erstwhile customers direct. That canker-ridden Judas was finished in West Bromwich and Simeon Beasley had been paid his last bribe.

On the mantelpiece the clock chimed the hour. Taking his pocket watch from his waistcoat, Archer checked the time. What was keeping the Lacys, and the vicar, why was he not here?

About to voice the question, he paused as the doorbell rang. Without a word, her face its usual vinegary self, Edna rose to answer it.

Philip . . . where the hell was Philip? Archer's smug satisfaction drained away. If he thought to stall, to refuse to go through with this wedding then he was in for a disappointment. He would do as he was told even if it meant being dragged downstairs!

'I don't think Philip be quite ready, my dear.' Archer handed the girl to a chair after greeting her and her father. 'I always thought it the privilege of the bride to be late.'

His attempt at a joke brought no smile to either face. Archer felt a touch of unease. It could be understood the wench not smiling . . . wedding nerves and all . . . but Joseph Lacy had a face as long as a fiddle. Christ, his girl marrying had him about as cheerful as a pall-bearer!

'Edna, my dear.' Archer turned to his sister. 'Would you be so good as to give Philip a call.'

'There will be no need, Aunt.' Dressed in moleskin trousers and rough jacket, a muffler tied about the throat, Philippa stood in the doorway. 'As you see, father, I am quite ready.'

'What the hell do you think you be playing at!' Archer exploded. 'Get out of them clothes at once, they don't be suitable for a wedding.'

Coming into the room Philippa smiled at the girl dressed

demurely in plain blue coat and bonnet, her gloved hands empty of flowers, then extended a hand to Joseph Lacy before looking again at Archer.

'Not suitable? I thought them a perfect choice, eminently suitable for the dirty work you have in mind.'

'Watch what you say—'

Interrupted by a second ringing of the bell Archer paused, his glare carrying the rest of the threat.

'It be about time you got here,' he snapped at the flustered cleric, whose long black gown flapped like the wings of some gigantic crow as he hurried into the room.

'I beg everyone's forgiveness, I was delayed . . .'

'Well, you be here now, so get on with it.'

Opening the prayer book clutched in his hand the priest looked over the top of horn-rimmed glasses perched precariously on his hooked nose.

'Dearly—'

One word only clearing his lips he looked up again as Philippa interrupted. 'Before you begin there is something I wish my father to hear.'


Philip would be wed by now. Stood on the heath Joshua stared at a sky strewn with stars. Married to banker Lacy's daughter. The pain of it had cut deep all day but now here on the heath where they had walked together it bit even harder. By all the rules he should feel nothing unless it were a feeling of congratulation for Philip, but there was none of that, nothing in his heart but dejection, nothing in his soul but misery. His mother had seen it; try as he might, he had not managed to keep that misery from her perceptive gaze, and though she had said no word her face had reflected what was in her mind. It was enough for him to suffer, he would not have her do the same; but so long as he was here in Greets Green, so close to Rowlay House with even the chance of coming face to face with Philip, that unhappiness would continue. He may make promises and keep them, but Naomi would not know complete peace of mind; each time he was gone from the house she would wonder. She was not of a suspicious mind, he knew she trusted his word, but trust did not always erase worry. The only way he could do that was to leave the Green, to find a job far from Briant Bottle and Glass, to leave his mother, let her live out her life without the shadow of shame.

She had lived in this village the whole of her life, she visited his father's grave in the tiny churchyard cemetery every Sunday and Wednesday, placing a bunch of wild flowers against the headstone that carried his name. Everything she had known and loved was here, the neighbours who were her friends . . . he would not ask her to leave all that, to start over again in some strange place.

Overhead a shooting star traced across the sky. Joshua watched its fleeting brilliance, watched as it extinguished itself in the darkness that was the far horizon. His mother would argue against each point he made, say her place was with her son, but he knew her place was here in the Green, here was her peace, here her solace.

The hardest bit of all would be watching the tears form in her eyes, the unhappiness adding more creases to her face, and knowing he was the cause of it. How long would that unhappiness last, how many weeks before she no longer cried in the night? Cried as she had all those weeks following his father's death.

Christ, oh Christ, why did this have to happen?

Smashing a fist into his palm Joshua lifted his face to the sky, the words bursting onto the darkness, a cry that carried with it all the bewilderment, all the perplexity, all of the soul sickness that was tearing his life apart.

'Why . . . why? Why should I fall in love with a man?'

Spreading themselves on the shadows the words melted into

the velvet blackness, their only reply a sighing of the breeze, the half-heard whispers of the night.

But who could tell where the heart led or why? Starlight touching his face Joshua turned towards home, a whisper he had spoken once before on his lips.

'Be happy, Philip, for God's sake be happy.'

# Chapter Thirty-One

'Please, would you be seated, this will not take very long.'

Glancing at Philippa's unsmiling face then at Archer's scowl the priest hovered for a moment, then perched nervously on the edge of a chair.

'Father, I—'

'There'll be no talk 'til you be changed into clothes appropriate to the occasion!' Archer Cranley snapped, glaring at the moleskin trousers. 'They be an insult to the girl you be marrying.'

Opposite him Philippa answered, contempt in every syllable, 'And what you have engineered is not an insult to Davinia?'

Above the pointed beard brilliant black eyes narrowed, threat spitting from them.

'I've warned you once already, watch what you say. You don't be twenty-one 'til that clock chimes midnight, until then I be master—'

'You be master in this house, Cranley, and master of what be yours.' Silent until now, Joseph Lacy interrupted. 'That includes your child, but not mine, Cranley. You don't be master of mine.'

Swivelling his glare to the bank manager, Archer frowned.

'There be no question of that. Your wench will be answerable to one man only, her husband.'

'Yes, her husband.' The other man nodded. 'But he will not be found in Rowlay House!'

'What the bloody hell be you blethering about?'

The prayer book still open on his knee the priest coughed, shuffling on the chair, his discomfort at the use of strong language obvious on his face.

'I tell you what I be blethering about, it be about deceit, *your* deceit, Cranley. You be a liar and a cheat and were it not for the sake of my daughter I would have had the constable here with me, I would have had you answer for your lies and connivance. You have her to thank that you don't already be behind bars. Take a little advice, Cranley, ask forgiveness while that priest be here, for he be the only one might bring himself to give it.'

'One moment please, father.' Davinia Lacy looked to Philippa as her father rose to stand at her side. 'I want to say I realise the courage it took to call on me earlier in the day, the heartache you must have felt telling me what you did. I admire you for that and though I refuse to marry you, Phil–' she smiled as the abbreviation slipped from her lips '– I hope we may remain friends.'

'Refuse to marry him . . .!'

'You heard my daughter, Cranley.' Joseph Lacy's own threat was heavy in his answer. 'I thank heaven she took the decision she did, for as true as God's above, had this marriage gone through I would never have been able to face myself again, or her.'

'If there is to be no marriage—'

'Sit down!'

Archer's bark taking him by surprise, the priest almost fell back to the chair, his nervous glance to Edna evoking no response.

'She can't refuse!' Archer glared at the bank manager. 'We have a bargain, Lacy, you get to handle the business of the Bottle and Glass and my lad gets to wed your daughter.'

'Yes, we had a bargain.' Joseph Lacy reached for his daughter's hand, holding it gently in his. 'My greed matched yours, I was blinded by your offer, and had it not been that Philip . . .'

'That Philip what?' More of a hiss than a growl the words slithered ominously into the silence left as the rest fell away.

'That I told Davinia everything.' Philippa answered for Lacy. 'Of the lies you have persisted in telling for so long; of the desire to be sole owner of my grandfather's business that burns inside you, a desire so strong you sacrificed your own marriage to it and are willing to sacrifice anyone else's on that same altar.'

'It's only your courage prevented my girl treading that path.' Turning to face Philippa, Joseph Lacy held out his hand. 'Like my daughter I admire you for that. It is as much respect for you as it is love for her holds me back from what I would only see as justice in having your father arrested. You have my thanks, and if he has any decency left in him then you should have his too.'

'Lacy!' Archer's face was livid. 'Call this agreement off and I guarantee that bank will have not one client come Monday, you hear . . . not one client!'

'Agreement.' The banker's head swung slowly as if even now he could not quite comprehend the other man. 'That is all this union meant to you, isn't it? An agreement that suited Archer Cranley, his purpose and his purpose only and be damned to these two young people; as for the bank suffering because this contract fell through, then that is the chance I must take. But there is one thing I know will not be chance, it will be a certain fact. Raise your hand against me in that or any other way and I will expose you for the liar you are. There will be no place for you in this town after that, nor in any other for many a mile around.'

'If this evening is not convenient would you like me to arrange some other date for the nuptials?' Twittering nervously the little priest glanced at Archer as Philippa followed the Lacys from the room.

His features dark as thunder Archer swung a foot and kicked the book from the man's hands.

'Get out!' he snarled. 'Get out and take your bloody prayer book with you!'


'So you went running to the Lacys . . .'

Venom filling his feral eyes, Archer glared as Philippa returned to the room.

'. . . you told them everything.'

Strange, the fear this man's anger had always instilled, the trepidation whenever that frown crossed his brow. How often had it caused a trembling inside; but there was no trembling now, only a calmness that was equally strange. Her eyes holding those spilling vengeance, Philippa answered quietly.

'No, father. Not everything.'

'So what was it you didn't tell 'em?' Archer smiled, a vicious evil smile. 'Could it have been you couldn't marry the banker's daughter cos you be in love with a man . . . that you lusts after a common glass-blower? Could you not bring yourself to take her after you had been taken by a penniless nobody, taken by that Fairley lout?'

Her lips white from listening to the latest display of temper, Philippa let the disgust for it show in a quiet reply. 'No, father. It was neither of those things. What I did not tell the Lacys was your treatment of my mother, yours and the sister you brought to this house to take care of her, a woman who abused both her and myself.'

'I took care—'

Turning towards her aunt's quick angry words, Philippa cut them off.

'You took care my mother was always too heavily drugged to talk of what you two put her through, but the marks you left on her face did the telling for her. I knew the lying you did concerning those bruises, I knew she did not suffer the "turns" you claimed, just as I knew it was lies when I asked earlier if my mother was recovering and was told yes. You see, I already knew she was not, that she would never recover, I already knew my mother was dead.'

'That lie be your'n and not mine!' Edna screamed at her brother.

'Is it, father?' Philippa swung round. 'Is it a lie? Then tell me, is my mother dead or alive?'

'You claims to know the answer to that so why ask it?'

'Yes, I know the answer, but perhaps you will tell me what I do not know, was my mother dead before you left that sanatorium?'

His eyes acid-bright with the fury that still rode high in him, Archer Cranley laughed, a short scorn-filled laugh.

'What bloody difference does it make!'

'A great deal of difference, father.' Philippa glanced from one face to the other. 'To both you and your sister, but before we go further I must tell you of the letter mother wrote to me, a letter speaking of her own death.'

'Letter . . .?'

'This letter, father, one which I have already shown to Lawyer Bettem of Paradise Street, this being a copy.'

Snatching the letter Philippa had drawn from an inner pocket, Archer Cranley's face slowly lost all trace of colour, only his eyes smouldered like boiling pitch as he flung the sheet of paper at his sister.

'This be your fault, you stupid bitch! You and your bloody maundering after a corpse that be long rotted. You left her alone when I gave strict orders not to, left her so you could go snivel on a dead man's grave!'

'You gave orders!' Edna Cranley's mouth was tight as a trap as she glared at her brother. 'That's all you ever did. Do this . . . do that . . . while you were off playing with your whores. Nobody was entitled to life except Archer Cranley, his sister should have no interests other than running his household and nursing a wife he had no time for. But I did have interests, and I had love . . .'

'You had love.' Archer laughed again, the same scorn giving it a cruel, biting sound. 'You Edna, you had love but where was Richard Stanton's love? Not with you, sister, not with you. That man never loved you, all you had was the figment of your own imagination, you've spent the years drooling over a man who loved only one woman, Hannah Briant!'

As her fingers curled about the sheet of paper, Edna's eyes took on a glow of madness. 'That's a lie . . .'

The laugh faded, Archer met his sister's stare with icy calm. 'Another lie? Not this time, Edna, not this time. I have simply spoken what you have always known, Richard Stanton was in love with Hannah and had he lived he would never have married you.'

Breath easing long and hard into her lungs, Edna Cranley rose slowly to her feet. For one terrible moment she looked at the man who mocked her; then, eyes still glowing with the light of insanity, she turned to face Philippa.

'Your mother were dead!' she breathed. 'She were dead when I got back from the cemetery, I made it seem she had died no more than a few minutes before he returned to the house. I should have told him she were sleeping, left her for you to find as they found my Richard, dead by her own hand! But he took her body to that infirmary, paid handsome to have that doctor say she passed away while in their care, and all this so he can get what he was never intended to get . . . your grandfather's money.'

'That will no longer be possible.' Philippa's glance swung to Archer. 'You see, father, it was not just the letter. Whilst I was with Lawyer Bettem I drew up a Will revoking the one you had me make while my mother was still living; and once I knew you had lost that yardstick I had no need to abide by what was extortion on your part. So, for all of your greed, you have finished up with nothing.'

It seemed in the moment of silence that followed that Archer would have no more words, that Philippa's news ended all conversation. But then he laughed. Not short and scornful like before but a long howl of pure triumph.

'You made a Will!' he choked. 'You made a new Will revoking the old one. You fool! You made a Will before you came of age to inherit, you can't dictate what is to be done with what don't be yours. That lawyer be as daft as you if he led you to believe any such Will would stand in a court of law.'

'You are probably right,' she answered quietly. 'But in three hours from now I will be of legal age . . .'

'But still you'll be able to claim nothing.' Edna's laugh erupted. 'Remember the terms laid down by Nathan Briant? You should do, Archer, you've dwelt on them times enough. Should his daughter die before—'

'That's enough!' Sharp as a knife blade Archer cut through the rest. 'No more, sister . . . no more, unless—'

'Unless I go the same way as your pretty golden whore?'

'I said enough!' One hand slicing sidewards caught across her mouth.

Wiping the thin red trickle from the corner of her lips Edna looked at him.

'You've lost,' she laughed again, 'after all your tricks you've still lost.'

'No, no I've not lost. But you have, Edna, I had it in mind whether to pay the money we agreed on, now I don't have to think on it any more. You won't get a brass farthing!'

'But I got something more valuable by far, worth more to me than as much again as the money you promised.'

Lit by the maniacal light of madness, the terrible enjoyment of vengeance, Edna Cranley's eyes glistened with the revenge she had held hidden for so many years.

'I was given retribution. The Lord provided me with the chance to pay back what Hannah Briant did to me, to take an eye for an eye. It was her took my Richard's life so I took one in return; it were not Philip killed your son, it were me, Archer, me!' Swinging the wild look to Philippa she laughed again. 'It were not as my brother had you believe, what your mother was forced to let you go on thinking. You were not the first born, not the older child jealous of a younger one replacing him in a mother's affections; it were Stephen was first born, Stephen the apple of his father's eye. But as I was robbed so I robbed in return. Your mother took my Richard from me and I vowed they would both pay the price. It's too late for her to hear, that loss of pleasure I must bear, but it is not too late for Archer, not too late for him to hear.'

The terrible laugh erupting again she turned back to the man staring in disbelief. 'I told you the boy fell from his horse while trying to jump the brook, that part is true enough, as is the fact that the fall left him dizzy. But telling you that before I could reach him Philip ran up behind and pushed him into the water? Lies, Archer, all lies. It were me reached Stephen first. I picked him up and held him, held him several moments. Then I threw him into the mill-race, watched his body taken down by the wheel, watched it go around and around, again and again. That is my payment, brother, my reward. I destroyed his life as Hannah destroyed mine.'

Stunned by what Edna had told them, Philippa stood held in the nightmare of the words, watched, from somewhere in an endless distance, Archer's body sway, his head go back on his neck, his mouth open in a long howling scream; watched, transfixed, the arms suddenly reach out, the hands fasten about the throat of the still-laughing woman.

'. . . *it were not Philip killed your son . . . it were not Philip killed your son . . .*'

Over and over the words drummed in Philippa's brain, drowning all other thoughts, clouding the reality of what was happening a few feet away.

Knocked to the floor by her brother's weight, Edna Cranley's fingers clawed the face just inches from her own, but caught deep in a frenzy of pain and madness Archer pressed both thumbs tighter on her throat.

'I told you, Edna . . .'

Somehow the half laugh reached through the haze that clouded Philippa's mind.

'. . . I warned you . . . I said one day I'd kill you!'

Full awareness flooding back, Philippa rushed to the struggling figures, catching Archer's shoulder in an effort to pull him off the choking woman.

'Father, no . . . Father, please, you'll kill her . . . Father this isn't the way . . .'

As if the strength in him were suddenly switched off, Archer's hands released their grip, but the eyes that looked at Philippa as he got to his feet still held the wild manic gleam.

'She killed my son,' he breathed slowly, 'that bitch killed my son . . . killed the boy I loved . . . she killed my son and left me with *you!*'

The last word rising on a scream he brought a closed fist crashing with all his strength to Philippa's temple.

'Left me with you.' Laughter bubbling quietly in his throat Archer Cranley kicked the figure fallen unconscious at his feet. 'Edna thought taking Stephen would be taking the Bottle and Glass, but her were wrong, as you were wrong by thinking to better me. In three hours you'll be of legal age . . .'

'Yes, Philip will be of legal age' – holding a hand to her throat Edna croaked the words –' and I'll testify to your cruelty.'

Turning the crazed gleam to his sister struggling to sit up, Archer smiled as he leaned forwards delivering a half-stunning blow to the thin mouth.

Reaching to an inner pocket of his coat he drew out a small packet.

'A woman as well as a man needs to be alive to testify, Edna.'

As laughter curdled again in his throat he forced the bleeding lips apart, tipping a small heap of white powder onto his sister's tongue.

'You never knew about the powder did you, Edna?' Holding her lips closed, Archer pinched the narrow nostrils, smiling into terrified eyes as she was forced to swallow. 'You never did find it, nor that cap and muffler, though you searched my room often enough; but you'll see them in a short while, they be waiting for you along of Lilah Cherrington. Oh yes, Edna, you were right about the pretty Lilah, I killed her after I killed her accomplice, killed him same way I've killed you!'

'Archer . . .' His hand withdrawn from her mouth and nose Edna clutched at him, fear adding its own special mark to features already drawn hard by the spite of years.

'No, Edna.' He slapped the hand away. 'There be no time for talking, Lilah grows lonely waiting for her companion.'

Hauling her to her feet, dragging her to the stable, Archer bundled her easily into the carriage, terror and poison feeding greedily on her strength. It would take only minutes to drive to that chimney, drop her into the vent that fed air to the old underground limestone workings and then . . . then he would deal with Hannah's daughter!

'You thought you were being so clever!' A wild laugh rising into the night he slashed the heavy whip across the horse's flank. 'So clever making a Will . . . to cheat me of everything . . . but you were not as clever as Archer Cranley.' Whistling through the air the whip rose and fell, cutting into the animal's flesh as it galloped frenziedly across the heath. 'A charity of my daughter's choosing, that were the dictate of Nathan Briant, but the charity her named were of Archer Cranley's choosing, you hear, Nathan? Of *my* choosing. You and your Will be of no matter, what were once yours be mine now, all mine, and the child left to your daughter will lie with Edna. The woman who took the child I loved, and the child I had no love for will be together . . .' The whip fell again, the horse screaming its agony as Archer laughed. '. . . together Nathan! Together for all eternity!'

# Chapter Thirty-Two

'I tell you that be what were said.' Naomi Fairley looked at her son across the table. 'Betsy Clarke who has the grocer shop along of Sheepwash Lane got it from Annie Beasley, you know the one, lives in Cophall Street, has a lad with a twisted leg . . .'

'I know Mrs Beasley, Mother.' Joshua tried not to show his lack of interest in what would simply be more gossip. It was his mother's way of trying to alleviate his unhappiness and he felt guilty for showing such little enthusiasm, but it would be easier for him were he left alone to deal with his emotions, to come to terms in his own way with what had happened these last weeks. He had fallen in love with another man, that at least he had come to recognise honestly, and now he must find a way to forget . . . no, he would never be able to forget . . . to close it from his mind, to go on living, to live without love.

'It were while Annie Beasley were taking back the clean linen, her washes and irons for the Lacys . . .'

His mother's voice went on, droning over his own thoughts. He should at least make an effort, try to show some interest in what she was saying; he could make some excuse to leave the house once the meal was finished, he could say he needed to collect his tools from the works, after all that wouldn't be a lie.

'. . . well, it were after her set the linen in the kitchen and were waitin' of her coppers, the daughter always pays seein' her father be at the bank 'til evenin', that Annie hears voices coming from the front room. Says her couldn't help but overhear, but like Betsy Clarke says, the way that woman's ears have been trained over the years her wouldn't miss a whisper in the next world let alone in this one.'

Pausing in her story Naomi poured tea into both cups then rose from the table to set the pot to keeping warm on the hob.

'It were while her were stood there that the door opened and out from that room came the banker's daughter and another wench Annie didn't rightly recognise. But her vows that the words her heard next were, "Philip and I both decided we would rather not marry" . . . says her heard them clear as a bell . . .'

Philip had not married! Fingers gripping the spoon bent the cheap metal. Philip had *not* married. Had he heard correctly, was that what his mother had said? Of course not, he had not been listening properly and as a consequence had misheard.

'Why be that do you reckon?'

Trying to hide the feelings those imagined words had stirred, Joshua deliberately dropped the spoon, pretending to set his boot on it as she shuffled to retrieve it.

'Sorry, mother.' He set the damaged spoon on the table. 'I wasn't really listening; what do I reckon to what?'

'To Philip Cranley and the banker's wench not weddin' each other after all.'

He could not pretend any more, not tell himself the words had existed only in his mind.

'Not marrying?'

It must have sounded suitably vague, for his mother drew one of the breaths that always said her patience was nearing its limit. Grateful for the mercy that set her turning to swing the bubbling kettle back from the fire, he clenched his teeth hard, the pressure of it forcing his mind back to his control.

'You be just like your father!' Naomi fussed with the kettle. 'He were the same, God rest him, talk to him of anything other than the glass an' he never heard. I often thinks he only said "I do" thinking the vicar had said "Do you take this glass", instead of "Do you take this woman"; I been telling you for the last five minutes . . .'

Facing the table once more Naomi rested both hands on her hips.

'. . . I been saying as Annie Beasley vows and declares her heard Davinia Lacy say quite plain and open that there had been no marriage atwixt her and the Cranley lad.'

First taking a drink from his cup, moistening the dryness of his tongue, Joshua managed to ask, 'But why?'

'D'ain't say why.' Naomi swung her head from side to side.

'But if what Mrs Beasley claims she heard . . .'

'If Annie Beasley says her heard a thing then you can rest assured it were heard!' Naomi said emphatically. 'Her says them words was spoke and I for one believes 'em said . . . Annie Beasley has ears only the Lord Hisself can better.'

'I wouldn't question they weren't said.' Joshua knew better than to argue when his mother's hands went to her hips. 'But it seems hard to understand.'

'I finds it that way an' all.' Mollified by the attention her son now showed, Naomi slipped back into her chair.

'Why?' Joshua frowned. 'Philip himself told us he was to be married, why the change of heart?'

Stirring sugar into her own cup Naomi buried her gaze in the swirling liquid. Why the change of heart? She had asked herself that. Could it be the Cranley lad's heart had not been in that match from the beginning, had he refused that wench cos his heart were given elsewhere? The thought pulled at her, stretching nerves she had thought to be loosened by that marriage; but there had been no such, Philip Cranley had taken no bride, did this mean he would turn again to Joshua, take her son from her?

*There be change . . . change that will take that you cherish most.*

Amid the freezing dread that suddenly gripped her, Naomi felt the words of Keziah Silk stab like icicles in her heart. The feelings of her son had not changed, the shadows in his eyes showed as much, the pacing in the long hours of night. But he would have got over them, he would have broken the spell that lad had cast; given time Joshua would have turned away, refused the devil and his temptations, cast away all thoughts of profane love. Now that chance had been snatched away, the devil beckoned again; would Joshua follow? Silent as her thoughts Naomi's prayer followed. Keep him safe, Lord, protect my son from evil.

Her gaze lifting she caught the look that crossed her son's strong face, the perplexity in his normally clear eyes, and knew not all of her fears were groundless.

'I don't understand,' Joshua was saying quietly, 'why call off a marriage, was it one or both took the decision . . . or could it be the parents, did something not live up to their expectations?'

'Who can tell?' Naomi sipped at her tea. 'Annie Beasley heard no more than I've told you, says them wenches must have heard her in that kitchen, for they closed their mouths tight as mussel shells, Davinia Lacy payin' what were due and seeing her out of the door and it shut firm behind her. But if it be as the marriage be off for good and not just set back a mite then there be a reason, and a good few folk around Greets Green will be wondering why.'

'I wouldn't have thought anybody other than us to have known of Philip's proposed marriage,' Joshua answered. 'I can't see Archer Cranley announcing the fact in the *Express and Star*.'

'And they won't have heard it from me –' Naomi set down her cup '– whatever I feels for Archer Cranley I knows his lad told us of that marriage in confidence and that I respects.'

No, his mother would not betray a confidence. Though, like many women, she listened to the gossip of others she did not offer any of her own. *Naomi Fairley's lips be tighter than the strings of a miser's purse!* How often as a lad he had heard those words said of her. The village would get news of Philip Cranley's marriage not taking place, but that news would not be given by Naomi Fairley.

'As for the father, what he don't have said don't have to be taken back.' Her tea finished Naomi set about clearing the dishes from the table, stubbornly refusing any help from Joshua. 'That'll be welcomed by Archer Cranley for it be hard enough for him to hold his head up in the Green as it be without having to face the withdrawing of a wench from marrying his son; that be a smack in the face for any man let alone one with the bob that one has on him!'

Archer Cranley was a haughty man. Joshua understood the meaning of his mother's words. He could never abide losing face with the men of the glassworks, the ridicule of fellow industrialists would be unbearable. But had it been the girl had done the refusing? The thought returning, he rose from the table.

'You best get along to the works and collect what be your'n, no sense in leaving 'em when you holds no intention of going back.' It had needed no flash of insight, no motherly intuition to tell Naomi of his need to be free of the house, the same as it needed none to tell her that trying to hold him close, to shut him away from hurt was of no use; Joshua was no longer a child to hide his face in her apron, he was a man grown, a man she could pray for but could not order: what would be would be and she must make the best of it.

'That don't be the all of it, Josh.' Having recounted the story already told by Naomi, Samuel Platt pushed the dust-sodden flat cap back from his forehead, scratching a finger through greying hair. 'There be talk of the Cranleys bein' found on the 'eath.'

'Found?'

'Ar, lad . . .'

Joshua watched the cap being lifted and lowered several times before its owner was satisfied it sat in exactly the same position as before.

' . . . up along this end of Swan Village, close to where the limestone were once worked.'

The Cranleys, Samuel had said, not Archer alone but the Cranleys. Swallowing the alarm hammering in his throat he looked at the man who, head turned, called a sharp order to the young girl whose face peered from the doorway of the packing shed.

'You said found, Mr Platt,' Joshua said as the older man turned again to him, 'what did you mean by that?'

Warmed by the respect Joshua never failed to show whenever they talked together, the chargehand ignored for a moment the pale face that had bobbed again at the door the instant young Ginny thought he no longer saw her there.

'I sees your meanin' lad.' Silica-blackened fingers fastened on the peak of the cap, tugging it yet more firmly into place. 'The Cranleys could hardly get lost in a place they've known for years, though the 'eath don't rightly let itself be known to many folk, not proper it don't . . .'

'Mr Platt, which Cranleys, and what happened that they were found on the heath?' He had almost said Philip . . . was it Philip found on the heath? Not caring now what showed in his eyes he asked again, 'Which Cranleys?'

'It were old Cranley and his sister.'

Relief tingling through to the very tips of his fingers, Joshua breathed slowly. 'Philip was not with them?'

Glancing again towards the packing shed Samuel Platt called a warning that even Ginny could place no misinterpretation on. The look on Joshua Fairley's face at this moment were not for inquisitive eyes. This lad had always shown him respect and if in return he could shield him from gossip and slander then he would.

'No, lad,' he answered, giving the other man time to hide what he had already seen. 'Thanks be to God, that lad were not with 'em.'

Silently echoing the sentiment Joshua glanced at the tools held in his hands, the specially sharpened parrot-nosed shears which would cut a rod of glass and not destroy the roundness of it, an iron compass for measuring the depth of a bowl and the pucellas whose prongs allowed a variety of uses, and all of which had belonged to his father.

'The coach were spotted by a couple of men on the way to their employment at the Phoenix Enamel works.' Samuel Platt resumed his telling. 'Seems like Cranley might have dozed and that hoss of his'n wandered from the track, going too close up against the limestone, them rocks be lethal sharp. Any road up, they found the carriage tipped onto one side and Cranley lying under its wheel, his top half crushed.'

'His sister?'

The chargehand's head moved slowly, a side-to-side movement like a flag in a half-hearted breeze. 'Dead as he was, the bobby them men fetched seemed to think the fright of that carriage going arse over must have caused her to have one of them heart attacks, for her weren't cut nowheres as could be seen right off; but then there'll be a doctor looks at both I supposes.'

Archer Cranley and his sister dead! The news still difficult to absorb, Joshua lifted his glance.

'That carriage must have been travelling at a pace to have overturned.'

'Ar, lad.' The older man nodded agreement. 'It must have been going at a fair old lick as you says, for running slow it wouldn't have tipped over, not even after banging a wheel agen them rocks; which causes me wonder!'

It had him wondering too but Joshua kept his own thoughts quiet, allowing the other man to voice the uncertainty they both felt.

As a finger crept beneath the dust-heavy cap, the faded eyes took on a quizzical look. 'You see, Josh lad, if that carriage were movin' fast, as seems probable, then it would have had Cranley and that sister of his'n bouncing like dried peas in a tin; that way I can't see as either of 'em would be dozing, an' if it be as that be the case how come that carriage finished up lying on its side wi' Cranley beneath it?'

'It's hard to say, Mr Platt.'

The finger still jiggling beneath the cap, Samuel Platt gave a final shake of his head. 'Ar lad, it be hard to say but not so hard to think. It be my opinion as Cranley were going somewheres special and driving hell for leather to get there, but why across the heath? For it don't lead nowheres 'cept to his own house. It be altogether a mystery to me, Josh, but talkin' don't get the glass blowed. I'll have to be leaving you, lad, give your mother me regards.'

'I will, Mr Platt, and ours to you.'

'Thank you, lad.' Leaving the cap to lie once more down over his brow Samuel Platt winked as he called over his shoulder, 'Josh be on his way now, young Ginny Morton, and lessen you wants to be on your'n you'll keep your nose inside of that packing shed.'

Cranley dead. Walking from the yard with its tall bottle-shaped cone, Joshua stared unseeingly ahead. An accident? It had to be, there could be no other explanation. But why drive at so great a speed as to turn the carriage onto its side? And of all Sam Platt's speculation that at least was most likely. Then there was Edna Cranley, why had she been in that carriage and not Philip or his mother? Where were those two in all of this?

A sudden icy clutch at his stomach causing him to almost stumble, Joshua gripped the tools tighter in his hands. Where *was* Philip in all of this . . . had Archer Cranley been driving *towards* somewhere or something . . . or had he been driving *away* . . . away from something he had done?

'It be none of our business!' Naomi's face wore a troubled look. She had listened to Joshua recount what Samuel Platt had told him, but now that he said he must go to Rowlay House she let her old anxiety show. 'You have no call to go showing yourself at that house, it ain't as if you be hired help there, let alone family!'

'But that woman, Mrs Cranley, she looked so ill that day she gave me the letter, it could be Archer was going to fetch a doctor.'

'Could be, but it ain't!' Naomi returned flatly. 'I be willing to bet my Sunday bloomers that don't be no reason. Were it as you says then common sense tells that Edna Cranley would have stayed with her in that house, and not gone swanning off with her brother. No, Josh, it were no doctor the man were seeking, but whatever it were it be no cause for you to take yourself to that house.'

'But Mrs Cranley could need help—'

'Ar, and Mrs Cranley has a son that be capable of getting it for her!' Naomi cut the protest short. 'Whatever Philip Cranley might or might not be, he ain't no fool. He be well able to get help to his mother should her stand in need of it, and however you feels you haven't been asked to give that help. It speaks for itself, Josh, you don't be wanted up there.'

His mother's words were blunt but they held a deal of sense. Joshua carried his glass-maker's tools to the tiny outhouse, hanging them from nails his father had long ago driven into one wall. Philip knew he could call on him for help, the fact he hadn't was proof he didn't want it. That kiss! Swift as lightning, the feel of it burned again on his mouth. Philip had resented it, resented being treated as not a man in every sense, and the way he chose to show it was to turn his back on the friendship they had shared. His mother was right, Joshua Fairley was not wanted.

'We don't be family to the Cranleys but that don't mean we can't mark our sympathy for that woman and her lad.' Naomi looked up from the potatoes she was peeling into a chipped enamel bowl as Joshua re-entered the kitchen. 'That much I'd do for any woman. But it should be me as does the calling, you understands that, don't you Joshua? It wouldn't be seen as proper for you . . .'

'I understand, mother.' Joshua smiled wryly. 'Give them my regards and if I can do anything . . .'

'I'll tell 'em, lad,' Naomi answered softly. 'I'll tell 'em both what you says.'

# Chapter Thirty-Three

He had promised his mother he would not come here. Joshua stared at the house, its brickwork glowing orange-gold in the sun. She had been thanked for her consideration and offer of help which had been refused. Simeon Beasley it was had kept Naomi standing like some beggar woman at the door. Simeon Beasley, pointed out among the mourners at the funeral a week later, a funeral that stunned the whole of Greets Green when it became known that three people were being taken from Rowlay House, that Hannah Cranley too had died.

There had been no word from Philip. The pain of that had been almost worse than the pain that burn to his shoulder had given, a pain that never stopped night or day but drove on, cutting and slicing at his heart 'til it must stop beating. But that too never stopped even though he prayed it would; prayed nightly for the relief that would bring. Philip Cranley held no feeling for him, no friendship. That at least had been driven home. So why was he here now? Joshua drew a long breath. Why was he breaking the promise he had given to his mother?

They had talked long and hard the evening she had returned from taking their sympathies to Rowlay House. Philip was in no state to receive visitors, he was resting after being given a strong sedative, so Beasley had said. It would be better if no one from the village or the works called again, as a long-standing friend of

377

the family he would take care of everything . . . 'And that included the lad, though deep down I feels Philip Cranley would be best served by tipping that one from his house!' Naomi had added, the look which followed heavy with distaste.

Stood with his mother on the edge of the assembled villagers beside the lych gate as the funeral procession arrived at the church, Joshua had felt the same dislike for the corpulent figure who held so closely to Philip, with an attention that seemed in some way possessive. He had watched as they alighted from a carriage drawn by horses whose sable coats were gleaming, black feathers bobbing on their heads; watched for some sign from Philip, some nod of recognition, but none had come. He had passed into the church, his head bent low on his chest.

That silence and withdrawal had not been broken in the days that had followed, no word had come, no recognition of Naomi's visit from Philip Cranley.

It had been hard to endure. Using every pretext not to do as he had decided, he put off for no real reason his decision to leave the Green. But it had not been for the leaving of Naomi that he stayed on; she would have to be left behind sooner or later, for he would not tolerate the upheaval that moving away would cause her. Face it, he had told himself each night, face the truth, it is Philip Cranley you cannot bear to part from, him that holds you to Greets Green.

But now the decision was made. Tomorrow, he had told his mother and this time with an air of quiet finality, tomorrow would see him gone. She had wept and tried to argue when he had said he was going alone but in the end had accepted it as it was meant, the best for both of them. She had seemed to recognise that without a mother to watch his pain, to see his suffering, then it could be brought out the quicker. To leave him to handle his hurt alone might hasten the process of healing.

He had spent the night awake, looking at stars he and Philip had shared, listening to the silence of the heath that had wrapped them close in the same warm dark veil, remembering eyes that had seemed to smile only for him, the voice soft, gentle and husky as summer breeze; but most of all remembering the feel of that slight body held tight against his own, that warm sweet mouth.

But Philip Cranley was no longer the lad who carried glasses and bottles to the lehr; with his father dead he was the owner of Briant Bottle and Glass, he was glassmaster and as such was above friendship with a common employee. Somehow he had never thought that of Philip, never thought he would turn away from the men who had befriended him. But actions could take the place of words and Philip's action had spoken volumes.

In the face of that, ought he to go on to that house? The question chewing at his brain, Joshua continued to stare at the house. Ought he not to turn away now, leave things as they were? Maybe Philip would refuse to see him . . .

The thought cold in his mind he half turned. That would mean more pain but his heart would ache the worse for not wishing Philip happiness in life. Sucking air deep into his lungs he swung around, his steps firm and sure as he walked on to Rowlay House.

Did that trap belong to Simeon Beasley? Reaching the heavy front door he glanced at the trim black-painted governess cart thinking a man with such bulk would have difficulty fitting into it. Pulling on the iron ring set into the wall beside the door he glanced again at the cart. That pony didn't look big enough to pull Beasley.

The sound of the doorbell faded, leaving in its wake a silence that seemed even more jarring. What was it he had decided upon saying when he met Philip?

*I just wanted to say I'm sorry for the loss of your parents and to wish you . . .*

But as the door opened the well-rehearsed words stayed silent on his tongue, his breath catching awkwardly in his throat as the pretty golden-haired figure smiled a welcome.

\* \* \*

'I . . . I just wanted to . . . to offer . . .'

'Well, whatever it is you want to offer it would best be done inside.'

As blue eyes added their own smile, the slight figure stepped aside, silk gown rustling softly with each movement.

The village women had often commented on there being no paid help at Rowlay House so who had he expected to answer his ring? He had not thought of who it might be, but then not once had he expected this!

'In here.' Eyes bright as glass beads smiled again, a slender white hand ushering him forwards into a room whose heavy curtains were drawn across the windows closing out the day, as was the custom in a house of mourning.

Used as he was to rapid changes of light Joshua had no difficulty adjusting from the brilliance of sunlight to the shadowed room.

'I'm sorry, how foolish of me, I forgot to ask your name.' The pretty mouth parted in a giggle, but it was the other slight figure held Joshua's stare.

'It's all right, Davinia, Joshua and I are friends.'

'Philip!' More a gasp than a whisper the name dragged from Joshua's throat. 'Philip!'

Lamplight dancing like yellow diamonds among pale golden hair, the figure dressed in deepest black stepped forward. It was then Joshua saw the glass bowl he had delivered to this house, his wedding present to Philip.

'Allow me to introduce Miss Davinia Lacy.'

'I was just admiring your beautiful gift, you are Joshua Fairley, are you not?'

Not moving his glance from the figure enhanced by the glow of the lamp, Joshua nodded.

'I was hoping you would call, Joshua.'

The voice was the same, the eyes as gentle, the face as appealing, but the enchantment was gone, whatever had existed in his heart for Philip Cranley was dead as ashes.

'I could not return your mother's visit, not until the period of mourning is—'

His voice lifeless as the heart inside him Joshua looked from one figure to the other, shaking his head as he cut the words short.

'Don't say any more. I understand, Philip, I understand everything, and it disgusts me, *you* disgust me, I never want to see you again!'

'Joshua, wait . . . please . . . Joshua!'

The call fading behind him Joshua was gone from the house, the feeling that had risen like acid as he had looked at Philip still raging like a volcano as he strode across the heath.

I understand everything! Those were the words he had flung at Philip. The long period of mourning some people felt they must observe before returning calls, he understood that. The fact of Davinia Lacy, the girl Philip had been set to marry, maybe was still to marry, being with him to give what comfort she could, that too he could understand. But the rest . . . the dress, the ribbons . . . no, he would never understand that!


Something dreadful had happened. But what, what could it be had brought that terrible look to Joshua's face, the deadness to his eyes? Naomi cleared the dishes from the table, carrying away the meal her son had refused to eat. She had called to him from the kitchen but, shut away in the brewhouse, he had made no answer. But where was it he had been? She returned the bread to the wooden locker. Who, if anybody, had he talked to? Lifting the kettle from the bracket above the fire she turned with it towards the scullery. She poured a stream of hot water over the cups she had placed in the chipped enamel bowl, then she paused. For a second she thought she'd heard a knock on the door. Lord! Joshua's mood had her jumpy as a cat with its tail in the fire; o' course there'd been no knock, folk in Churchyard Row called out as they put foot through the door, they didn't stand waiting for it to be opened.

Putting the kettle aside to be filled from the pump in the yard once the dishes were washed, Naomi's nerves flared again. That *was* a knock to her door, and knocks brought naught but ill tidings. Wiping her hands on her apron she walked hesitantly across the tiny kitchen. First Joshua returns home looking as though he had fought with the devil, and now a knock to her door!

With her heart beating rapidly she opened it, apprehension building further as she stared at the man dressed neatly in black suit, the stiffly starched collar of a white shirt pressing beneath his jaw.

'Good day.' The man removed his tall hat. 'Do I have the home of Mr Joshua Fairley?'

Was this summat to do with Joshua's being in such a tizzy? Naomi thought as the man asked his question. Had her son caused some mischief? If so, where was the bobbies? They be the ones had to arrest a man.

'Ar, this be his home, and I be his mother!' Hands going to her hips, Naomi stood squarely in the doorway. This one would have to knock her down to get to her lad! 'Is there summat I can be doing for you?'

'My name is Caddick, solicitor at law.'

Every nerve dancing, Naomi glanced at the doors already ajar, neighbours openly gawping at this man stood on her step. He was from the law, mercy! What had the lad been up to?

'Perhaps you could tell me where I might find Mr Fairley?'

Her couldn't do that. Her couldn't hand her own son over to the law! No matter what he'd done blood was still thicker than water.

'Perhaps I might. But that would depend on what it is you be wanting him for.'

Aware of watching eyes, aware listening ears would miss little, if anything, of what was said, Naomi nevertheless stood firm. The law might have sent him but it would take more than that to get him inside her house.

Clearing his throat the black-suited figure shuffled. Clearly disconcerted he answered, 'My business is with Mr Fairley, it cannot be discussed with anyone else.'

'Then you'd best go look for him elsewhere, for he ain't here!'

Putting out a hand as the door began to close, he withdrew it quickly as Naomi glared. 'You get yourself gone, mister, afore I throws you from my doorstep. I tells you my lad ain't home, and that be a' telling I won't give twice!'

'You didn't hear me, mother, I came in through the scullery.' Behind her Joshua's glance travelled to the stranger. 'I heard you ask for Joshua Fairley, I am the one you wish to speak with. Please come inside.'

'Caddick, Edward Caddick.' Shaking Joshua's hand the man accepted the chair offered. 'I have solicitors' chambers in West Bromwich New Street.'

'I best leave you.' Face pale with worry, Naomi glanced at her son.

Catching her arm Joshua smiled as he pressed her to another of the rough wooden chairs set at the table. 'There is nothing I would hide from you, mother, anything that is to be said will be said in front of you.'

If only that were the whole truth. Resting a hand on her shoulder he felt the twist inside him. There was nothing he would want hidden from his mother . . . except what he had seen at that house!

'As you wish.' Touching a hand to the Gladstone bag set on his knees the solicitor cleared his throat again. 'I am acting in accordance of a document lodged with me by Mrs Hannah Cranley.'

Hannah Cranley, Philip's mother! What on earth could she have to do with him? He had only ever seen the woman once.

'I think you must be mistaken.'

'In my business we cannot afford to make mistakes.' The jaw seemed to settle further onto the stiff collar. 'You *are* Mr Joshua Fairley, employed as glass-blower at the works known as Briant Bottle and Glass?'

His mother's hand lifting to his where it rested on her shoulder, Joshua gave a brief shake of the head. 'Not any more; Archer Cranley saw fit to give me my tin.'

'But you were employed there?'

'Until a couple of weeks ago, yes.'

'Then you are the Joshua Fairley with whom I wish to speak.'

'Look, Mr Caddick, without wishing to appear rude or to be telling you your business, I say you have made some sort of mistake. Whatever the cause of Mrs Cranley consulting you it can have no bearing on me, I have only ever spoken to the woman one time and then just for a few minutes.'

Both hands resting on the Gladstone bag the man allowed himself a thin smile. 'Mr Fairley, whilst I do not accept that a mistake has been made I will concede that my wording may have proved slightly misleading, but then only because I was not given time to render a full explanation of exactly what brings me here.'

'Then you'd best do it now so as you can be on your way!' Irritated and afraid Naomi snapped, then glanced up at her son, her eyes apologetic.

His smile fading the solicitor's nostrils flared as he drew an indignant breath. 'As I have already informed you —' he released the air from his lungs in a long slow breath designed to convey displeasure, but receiving no apology from a tight-lipped Naomi, went on '— I am a solicitor and specialising as I do in taking acknowledgements of deeds by married women I took one from Mrs Hannah Cranley. It is in accordance with her wishes and on behalf of Phil—'

'That's enough!' His face livid Joshua stormed to the door, pulling it wide on its hinges. 'Whatever else you have been told to say, I don't want to hear. I have finished with the Cranleys, I owe them nothing. You take that document, Caddick, take it to Rowlay House where it belongs.'

\* \* \*

'But why would he not listen?' Davinia Lacy frowned, sending a tracery of fine lines across her smooth brow.

Edward Caddick glanced again at the pretty face that had captivated him from first entering Rowlay House. 'I really have no idea, Miss Lacy, all I can tell you is the man seemed about to explode with anger when I tried to tell him the reason for my visit.'

'Did you not tell him you were there on behalf of Phil?'

'I made an attempt but the man simply would not listen,' Caddick answered, trying hard to keep his mind on the business in hand and not so much on the girl's pretty face.

'That does not sound like the Joshua Fairley you told me of, Phil, he sounds positively bad-tempered.'

'No, you are wrong in that assumption, Davinia, Joshua is not at all bad-tempered, he is the most patient and helpful man I ever met.'

'I hope it is not my visit you find the reason for the change in Mr Fairley's attitude, I assure you . . .'

'You do not have to assure anything, Mr Caddick,' Davinia Lacy smiled, her bright blue gaze resting on his face. 'Phil does not blame you, we are both quite sure you did your very best. If the man refused to hear what you had to say then he must suffer the loss.'

'Perhaps if I called again tomorrow Mr Fairley would be better disposed to listen.'

'That will not be necessary, Mr Caddick . . .'

Rising to his feet the solicitor took the hand held out to him.

'You have my sincere thanks for all you have done, and for the help you gave my mother.'

Hearing the break in the soft voice Davinia Lacy stood up quickly. 'Allow me to see Mr Caddick out, Phil.' She turned to the door, giving no chance of refusal. 'I am sure Mr Caddick will not mind just this once.'

His eyes saying he would not mind her escorting him anywhere and for all time, the solicitor followed from the room.

'Why do you think Joshua would not listen?' she asked the moment she returned. Then a shrug her only answer, she went on, 'But if he is not told he will never know the chance you are giving him, never know what your mother did. It's what you want, Phil, I know it is and like it or not that man is going to listen.'

Snatching up her gloves she pulled them on, a determined set to her mouth.

'Your mother's solicitor could not get him to do so but I will. I am going to see him right now.'

'No, Davinia . . .'

In the limp gleam of lamplight Davinia Lacy looked at the pale face.

'. . . Joshua is hurt and angry and I know why. I am the one must go to him.'

# Chapter Thirty-Four

'*It disgusts me . . . you disgust me . . .*'

The words he had flung at Philip battering remorselessly against his mind Joshua stood staring into the black oily waters of the lock. He should not have said those words. Whatever Philip Cranley chose to do or however he chose to behave he was not answerable to Joshua Fairley. But this . . .! Staring into the smooth mirror-like blackness it seemed the image of that face he had loved so much laughed back at him.

Why? And in front of Davinia Lacy. Yet she had shown no revulsion; could that be because she herself was part of it, the motivating force behind it? But that could be no excuse, Philip was of an age to dictate his own moves, his own behaviour . . . and choose his own friends!

The last thought was strangely calming, the anger and bitterness if not the hurt drained away, taking with it the laughing image pictured in the depths of the lock. Yes, Philip was his own master in all things, free to behave in whatever way he wished, free to make new friendships, free to break old ones, and that was what he had done. There had been no words between them, no spoken goodbyes; but some silences spoke louder than any words and Philip Cranley's silence had shouted loudest of all.

It had been a shock seeing him like that, and it would stay a long time in the mind, but it would not kill . . . Still staring into the depths of the lock Joshua drew a deep breath; no, that shock would not kill nor would he let it destroy. He could exist without that friendship . . . without Philip Cranley.

'Eh up, Josh lad, you don't want to think of going for a swim in there.'

Deep in his own thoughts Joshua had heard no sound of the approaching men, now as Ben Harvey called to him he glanced up.

'Ben be right.' Jake Speke negotiated the beam spanning the lock with cavalier assurance. 'You don't know what you might go finding in it but I'll lay a pound to a penny it won't be no mermaid!'

'And *you* won't find no pound, neither in that water nor in your pockets, for your missis'll 'ave been through them wi' a fine-toothed comb!' Crossing the beam with the same impudent ease a third man added his own flippant remark.

The laughter that followed gave Joshua the chance to pull his emotions more into order as the men drew level with him on the towpath.

'What do you reckon, Ben?' he smiled. 'Has Jake ever had a pound in his pocket?'

'Well, if'n he did then it were never paid by Cranley!' Removing the clay pipe clamped between his teeth Ben Harvey spat on the ground.

'Ar well, that bugger be finished payin' anybody 'cept the devil, and he'll go on payin' his dues there for eternity, and serve him right.'

'Blaspheming the dead don't right no wrongs, Ned.' Ben resettled the pipe between smoke-yellowed teeth. 'Leave 'em lie in what peace they can find.'

'I be wi' Smith on this one.' Jake Speke shook his head. 'To my way o' thinking Cranley don't deserve no peace.'

'Then it be a good thing that such matters be left to the Lord's deciding. Me, I be deciding to go for my tankard afore it be time to set off back to work. Come wi' we, Josh lad, you looks as though a pint of Bill Thomas's finest be what you needs.'

'Ar lad, come wi' we,' Jake added his invitation to Ben's, 'Bill Thomas's ale be better for you than any doctor's brew, get a couple o' them on your chest an' you'll 'ave no worries.'

No worries! Walking with the three of them into the tavern, Joshua felt the pang of returning bitterness. The landlord's ale might ease those for the moment but what would ease the misery, what would cure the pain?

'You found yourself a job yet, Josh?' Tom Smith wiped a line of froth from his mouth with the back of his hand.

'Not yet.' The answer did not include the fact he had not looked for one. Joshua lifted his tankard, taking a swallow of the cool beer. That would bring all sorts of questions, questions he did not want to answer.

'Strikes me there'll be more than Josh searching out a new employment.' Ben tapped the bowl of his pipe into his palm then tipped the ash into a brass spittoon set alongside the brick-built fireplace. 'There's bound to be layings off at the glass if'n that lad of Cranley's don't stop actin' so half-baked.'

Over his tankard Joshua's eyes held a mixture of confusion and accusation.

'What leads you to think Philip Cranley is stupid?'

'The lad don't be stupid, Josh,' Ned Smith put in, 'We all knows that well enough, but you 'as to face it, he don't be exactly acting like no bum baillif in an empty 'ouse.'

'That be the truth an' all!' Jake nodded. 'The lad *don't* seem bothered, he ain't been nigh the works since that accident.'

'That can be understood!'

'Ar Josh, it can,' Ben answered. 'But the lad needs to understand glass don't be made wi'out limestone and there's been none o' that brought in these few weeks. I tell you there'll be work for a lot less men in Greets Green if that lad don't move hisself.'

'But surely Samuel Platt could have reordered limestone, he

knows as well as any the price Thad Grinley charges to bring it in.'

Emptying his tankard with a noisy gulp Ben set it on the tap-room counter, signalling the landlord for a refill.

'None knows it better,' he continued, setting down two copper coins. 'And given the circumstances I don't doubt Platt would 'ave done just that, but fact is there's been no hide nor hair of Grinley in that time, he ain't been to the glass not once, nor has he been seen coming or going in the village. He be clear gone an' that's the top and bottom of it, clear gone and nobody knowin' why.'

Grinley *had* left the Green. Josh lifted his tankard, letting it hide the knowledge in his eyes. He had gone back to that malthouse several times since rescuing Philip from that man's filthy intentions, but each time he had found no cart and no Grinley. He had guessed what had happened. Archer Cranley had found out what had been done to his son and as a result Grinley was gone, left the village or left life, either way he was gone. But why no replacement? Cranley knew as they did that the works could not continue production without limestone.

'Somebody has to go talk wi' the lad, Josh, afore matters be gone too far, we 'oped you . . .'

'That be Samuel Platt's responsibility!' Realising the answer had been too sharp Joshua tried to soften it. 'I won't be the man to steal it from him.'

'It wouldn't be stealing, in fact it could well be the very favour Sam Platt be lookin' for.' Refilling his pipe with Shag tobacco sliced thinly from a block, Ben lit it with a taper held in the ever-burning fire. Puffing hard, his features lost for a moment behind a veil of grey smoke, he stayed silent.

'Sam did go see the lad.' Jake Speke took up where Ben had left off. 'Yesterday he went and come back lookin' like he'd seen a sight that had fair turned his stummick. White as milk he were and would speak a word to nobody 'cept to say as Philip Cranley had a visitor, a young woman visitor.'

His fingers tightening about the handle of the tankard, Joshua felt his own stomach lurch. A young woman visitor . . . Davinia Lacy? That was more than probable, but she was no sight to turn a man's stomach or bleach his face white; there was more to it than a pretty visitor . . . so what had Samuel Platt witnessed at that house . . . was it the same thing Joshua Fairely had seen?

'There don't be nobody else'll go to Rowlay 'Ouse.' Ben Harvey resumed the telling. 'The men at the glass feels it be none of their place to speak to the lad about what be his own business, and you can't go sendin' a woman; an' what wi' you and Philip Cranley bein' on such good terms . . . I means . . . Well, the lad seemed to take a shine to you, that be why we 'oped as you might speak with 'im, tell 'im what be the situation.'

No! No, he could not go to Rowlay House again, could not face the possibility of seeing what Samuel Platt had seen, what he himself would never forget. They would have to find another way. But what way? Looking into the faces watching his own, Joshua read the hope in the eyes of all three men, he knew that for them there was no other way. Unless someone told Philip of the situation the production of bottles and glasses would come to an abrupt end and with it the living of each man at Briant's together with that of their families. But they were not his concern, not his responsibility. Joshua sought desperately for the reason not to do what Ben Harvey asked, what each man at the glassworks would have asked; but as he saw hope turn to resignation he knew he could not refuse. What happened to those women and children were of concern to him, how could he live with the knowledge he had lifted no hand to help them?

Every nerve stretched tight as a trip-wire he set the tankard on the bar. 'Tell Samuel Platt I will go to Rowlay House.'

Why had he said he would come here, why had he not left the men of the glassworks to fend for themselves, why cause himself more pain? Joshua stared for the second time in a few hours at the tall red-brick house. Yes, he cared about those families, but was that all of the reason for his coming? He had felt every emotion drain from him as he had looked at that slight figure, the glass bowl which had been a wedding gift held in his hands, seen the look that had passed between him and the smiling Davinia Lacy. That had been the moment he thought his heart had died, the moment he had thought love for Philip Cranley had died. But now, stood a little way from the house, he knew he was wrong. Shock and disgust had made their play and it seemed then they had succeeded; but shock fades, leaving the nerves raw and exposed . . . the heart injured but alive. Joshua drew a deep breath, trying to find in it the will to go on. Could he go through that again, see Philip as he had been earlier and not turn from him, hold back the revulsion he would feel? And most of all, could he talk to him and not show the love recovering in the ashes of his soul?

Almost glad of the carriage stood in front of the house Joshua walked on. At least with Davinia Lacy here his own business with Philip would be kept short. But that was not the same vehicle, not the small light trap he had seen earlier; this was heavier, more solid-looking, not the carriage you would expect a young woman to drive.

Perhaps he should come back later. But would the resolve live on until later? Chances were less than even it would not; he spoke with the lad now or not at all!

Moments after his ring Joshua felt a wave of emotion wash over him as the figure of Philip Cranley, familiar in dark jacket and trousers, opened the door.

Had his name breaking from that shapely mouth been a cry of something other than welcome, had the look that leapt to those blue eyes been more an expression of relief than of courtesy?

The question unresolved in his mind, he followed to a room filled with heavy ornate furniture, its sombreness unrelieved by thick drapes still fully closed across the windows.

Simeon Beasley! Hackles rising Joshua forced a brief nod as he was introduced to the corpulent man who hardly gave time to look in his direction. Dislike thick in his throat he spoke quickly, wanting to be out of this house, away from Philip and all he stood for.

'So you see,' he ended, 'unless you bring in limestone, and soon, the works be going to go to the wall.'

'I had no idea.' Philippa frowned. 'Mr Beasley, you said you would see to the works.'

His jowls wobbling, the man nodded. 'And so I have.'

'But the limestone! Joshua says the need for it is very pressing.'

'There will be no more limestone!' Simeon Beasley looked across to where Joshua stood beside the chair he had refused. 'The works are to be sold.'

It struck like a blow and as Joshua looked at the pale drawn face of Archer Cranley's son his mind still reeled.

'Sold!' It was quiet, almost unbelieving. 'Philip . . . you can't!'

'I'm afraid matters do not lie with Philip.' Beasley's beady eyes smiled humourlessly.

'There is nothing I can do, Joshua.'

Staring for a moment into sad eyes Joshua felt the birth pangs of new anger. Was every man, woman and child labouring in that works to be written off, put on the street or into the workhouse because one man said there was nothing he could do?

'Nothing you can do!' he rasped. 'Nothing you can do . . . or nothing you want to do! Is that it, Philip, doesn't it matter to you the folk you worked with, the folk that befriended you will have no living? *You* are glassmaster now, Philip, that works is your responsibility, those men who work in it are your responsibility; or are you another Archer Cranley? A man who puts his own pleasures before the needs of others.'

Looking back at him, eyes already shadowed with suffering darkened to deep pools of anguish.

'You can't believe that, Joshua, I would not . . .'

'The running of those works is none of your business, Mr Fairley.' Beasley's slack smile remained fixed. 'But seeing as you are here it will do no harm to tell you. As Philip says, there is nothing he can do.'

'Then if not Philip, who . . .? Who is in charge of the works?'

Beady eyes lifting to his gleamed with satisfaction. 'I am, Mr Fairley, and I say they will be sold.'

'Archer Cranley did that!' Joshua shook his head, trying hard to come to terms with what was being said. 'Archer Cranley left the Bottle and Glass to you?'

'Not Archer Cranley.' The fixed smile slid expansively across the fleshy face. 'But his father-in-law. As Nathan Briant's executor *I*, and not Philip, am glassmaster, and I say that property will be sold. You see, Fairley, the old man's Will stated, among other clauses, that in order to inherit then Hannah Cranley's son must be married by the time of reaching his twenty-first birthday; Philip, sadly, was not.'

'I have asked the works continue as normal, that it not be sold, but other than that . . .' Philippa broke off, a dark glance pleading for understanding. '. . . it was taken out of my hands.'

'And straight into yours.' Anger tracing every line of his strong body Joshua faced the fatuous smile. 'That must suit you very well, Beasley . . . better, shall we say, than a certain delivery made to you by Thad Grinley!'

It was a shot in the dark. Climbing that ladder in the malthouse he had heard the name muttered and until now had paid no real mind to the reason, but as he saw the instant death of that smile, fear replacing the glint of satisfaction, he knew the barb had found a target.

'You know what I'm talking about,' he went on, 'the same thing I told Archer Cranley of. I told him, told what Thad Grinley couldn't spit out fast enough once I got hold of him, told of your taking young lads for your own filthy game, then selling them off once you tired of them!' It was a lie, he had not spoken to Archer Cranley, and as for Grinley, no search had shown so much as a footprint of the man. But Beasley did not know that, the look on that fat face said as much. Confident he was on the right track Joshua flung the rest, watching each word hit like a kick to the stomach. 'Thad Grinley told me everything, but knowing you would deny it I made him write down every word, every transaction that had taken place between the two of you, especially that involving Archer Cranley's son.'

More lies, but watching that florid face blanch as every drop of blood drained away, Joshua felt no guilt. He was fighting for each man in that works and how he did it was of little consequence.

Lips working uncontrollably, Beasley stared. 'You're lying!' he managed at last. 'And you'll pay . . . you'll pay with every day left to you.'

Ignoring the gasp from Philippa, Joshua continued to stare calmly at the spluttering Beasley.

'Am I?' he asked. 'Maybe. But then you won't know until it be proven in a court of law and by that time everyone for miles around will know of it, of what you are. There won't be a man in West Bromwich will speak to you, no man will deal with you for fear of being marked by the same brand of evil. Yes, I might spend the rest of my days paying, but then so will you, Beasley. I don't know what you hope to get by taking the glass out of Cranley hands but you should think first, is it worth the price?'

With the question hanging between them the bright animal eyes suddenly held a crafty look. Moving slowly to Philippa they played over the pallid face.

'And what about you, Philip?' he asked silkily. 'What will the town think of the man Fairley seems so anxious to protect? They won't have to think very hard before coming up with an answer; now you must ask yourself, will it be worth it, will destroying my name be worth destroying your own? You see, while people are asking questions they are bound to ask this one: why, with Archer Cranley knowing the ins and outs of his son's abduction, didn't he take revenge? And the reason they'll come up with is this: he did nothing cos his son enjoyed it, enjoyed the games that were played, games it seems he'd played before . . . with a glass rat!'

'Beasley, I . . .'

'No, Joshua!' Moving quickly Philippa stepped between the two men as Joshua made to grab the seated Beasley. 'The question was asked of me, I'll be the one to answer it.'

Turning to Beasley the sadness that had clouded her eyes became a bright defiance.

Contempt adding strength to a voice which had shook, it now become firm. 'Mr Beasley, Archer Cranley long ago destroyed any respect I had for the Cranley name, there is nothing more you can do to add to that. Whatever lies you might tell of me I will not deny except for the one involving Joshua Fairley; but I too will have something to tell, like the fact you have received regular payments from the estate you were entrusted to oversee . . .'

'Your father saw fit to pay for my advice!'

'You may of course claim so, but how a court may view your taking money which, as executor, you must have known was not Archer Cranley's to give—' Philippa broke off, leaving the rest to speak for itself, then as Beasley opened his mouth to reply, she added quickly, 'I kept the books for several years and as you no doubt were about to remark there is no record in any of them regarding those payments; but since my father's death I have had access to his private papers, papers that list each date, each amount. They add up to quite an impressive total . . . but then perhaps I should show you the private account book, let you see the truth of what I say.'

'There be no need!' Simeon Beasley pushed to his feet, jowls reddening as much from temper as from exertion. 'Take the bloody glassworks, follow the ridiculous terms set for it by that mother o' yours, you'll have my letter stating my wish to have no more dealings with the Briant estate by morning.'

Watching the corpulent figure heave itself into the waiting

carriage then drive away, Joshua felt a sudden emptiness where anger had been. There would be no more of Beasley's meddling in the glass, but then there was no more reason for him to stay here, no reason for him to see Philip Cranley again.

Glancing at the slight figure which still barely reached to his shoulder, he tried to smile and when it failed said quietly, 'With Beasley resigning as your grandfather's executor the Bottle and Glass must belong to you, it's yours to . . .'

'No, Joshua,' Philip answered. 'I can't run the Bottle and Glass . . .'

So he did not want the works, did not want it to carry on, he had no feelings for the folk who depended on it.

'So that's it!' Anger returning to fill the gap it had left, Joshua gave a contemptuous half-laugh. 'And I thought you were different, but you're not. You are no better than he was, Cranley through and through, to hell with everybody so long as you're all right. Cranley would be proud of you, proud of his son!'

Already several yards from the house Joshua halted, stunned by the quietly spoken words.

'The glassworks are not mine to manage. I am not Archer Cranley's son!'

# Chapter Thirty-Five

'Eh, me wench! I can 'ardly believe what you've been saying.'

Her head swinging slowly from side to side Naomi Fairley stared at the young woman sat in her kitchen.

'I know what you mean . . . I could not believe it either.' Davinia Lacy smiled, showing small white teeth.

'But how can you be sure? It be such a tale as takes some swallowin'; I don't mean as you be lying but I 'as to ask again, how can you be sure?'

'I had the proof of my own eyes, Mrs Fairley.' The girl smiled again as Naomi gasped.

'You . . . you seen for yourself?'

'There was no other way I could have accepted it. The whole story was just too unbelievable. I thought it a complete and utter fabrication, a way of breaking an agreement.'

'Well, the word you uses be out of my understanding, but if it should mean as you thought the tale to be naught but a wicked lie then that would have been my thinking; but you says you seen proof, then I takes your word, but the reasoning behind it all . . . that be beyond me. How could a body do such a thing and still face the world? The shock of hearing it 'as me all of a dither.'

'Let me make you a cup of tea.'

Looking at the young woman, pretty as a rose in dusky pink velvet, Naomi shook her head. 'Nay, wench, best I do that, it'll give my hands summat to do other than pull my apron to bits.'

Watching the older woman busy herself with teapot and cups Davinia Lacy felt again the twinge of guilt she had felt on resolving to visit this house. What had been told had been told in confidence; but she had seen the hurt in Joshua Fairley's eyes, the pain as he strode away from Rowlay House. A confidence was a confidence and she should keep it, but secrets could destroy as well as protect. 'Mrs Fairley,' she said, watching tea pour from the pot. 'What was said to me . . . I do not normally repeat what I am told in confidence, but your son's anger yesterday, I . . . I would not want him to place all of the blame at Phil's door.'

She had seen it too. Naomi's hands trembled as she set the teapot back on the hob. Seen what her own nightly prayer asked might never be seen by eyes other than her own, the love that showed in her son's face, love for another man!

'I takes it kindly you felt enough for me and mine to 'ave come here, to say what you 'ave. It ain't been easy for you, wench, that much I can see, and I appreciates the friendship you keeps wi' the other one; it don't be many given what you was put through would see things in the same light, as for that father o' your'n . . . it be a wonder he didn't break Cranley's neck!'

'I thought at first he would!' The smile returning lent a mischievous curve to the pretty mouth. 'You should have seen his face when I told him, I truly thought he was about to burst.'

'After a shock such as it would give then it only be surprisin' he didn't.' Naomi reached into a cupboard, bringing a small unlabelled bottle to the table. 'I never thought to see the moment I would take a sup of Methodist Cream but after listening to what you've told I reckon tea be needing more than a spoon of sugar to settle a body's nerves.'

'Methodist Cream? I don't believe I've ever heard of it.'

'Mebbe not by that name, that be what folk in the glass and the mines knows it by, but it be rum. A spoonful of it often 'as to serve as medicine in these parts, for it comes a damn sight cheaper than the doctor's bill.'

'And is, I would guess, more palatable.' Davinia Lacy's eyes twinkled.

Carefully measuring the strong-smelling liquid into a small spoon Naomi stirred it into her cup.

'It don't be right for me to go offering you the same though the shock you suffered be deep as my own. It be nobody's place to give medicine to a child 'cept its own parent.'

'Especially not Methodist Cream.' Davinia chuckled.

'Ar, wench, 'specially not when it be that. No doubt your father would rather pay a doctor his fee.'

The bottle returned to the cupboard, Naomi resumed her seat at the table.

Sitting silent both women sipped their tea. She had been right to come here, hadn't she? Davinia Lacy returned her cup to the saucer. Would Joshua Fairley think so . . . would Phil think so? Or would this breaking of confidence end the friendship she had come to enjoy, to value? But Phil must be told, must hear of it from her and no one else.

'Mrs Fairley.' All trace of amusement gone from her face she looked candidly at Naomi. 'I will understand should you wish your son not to know of what has been said, but I hope in turn you can understand that I must tell Phil, it has to come from me.'

'That be only right an' all.' Naomi nodded. 'You be a brave wench and a true one, Cranley should be proud to own you as such.'

And Joshua Fairley? Climbing into the small black-painted trap Davinia Lacy hid the query behind a smile. Would Joshua Fairley be proud to own a friend who betrayed another?


'*I am not Archer Cranley's son.*' The words seemed to ricochet around his brain, bouncing in his mind, in his ears. '*I am not Archer Cranley's son.*'

Turning slowly Joshua looked back at the dark-suited figure, black mourning band circling the left arm. Not Cranley's son, could that be the reason for the dislike, the animosity that had been so obvious on the older man's part?

'If you will come back into the house I will explain.'

Still stunned by the statement and by the sincerity in the voice when it was made, Joshua followed back to the dimly lit room.

'Under the terms of my grandfather's Will,' Philippa began as they were seated, 'should the beneficiary not marry before attaining the age of twenty-one then all of the property was to be sold and the money given to a charity of my mother's choosing. In order to avoid this and thereby losing control of the business, Archer Cranley forced her to sign everything to a charity he named, one that would benefit only him.'

'But you were to be married, you told my mother and me yourself.'

'So I was, and I would have gone through with it had it not been for my mother's letter, the letter she entrusted to you. It is a long story, Joshua, but I will try to be brief. When I was a very small child my brother was killed, we always believed that due to my childish jealousy I pushed Stephen into the brook where he drowned.'

'Believed?'

'We were out with my aunt.' The words shook in the telling. 'Stephen was thrown from the horse he was riding and our aunt picked him up. He was only dazed, but instead of bringing him home she threw him into the mill-race.'

'God Almighty!' Joshua breathed. 'Why?'

'Revenge.' Blue eyes reflecting the light of the lamp seemed to fill with tears. 'It seems she held my mother responsible for the death of the man she loved, an eye for an eye.'

'And she blamed you for the drowning!'

'I had no reason to disbelieve it, it was not until Edna told of it the night of the accident in which she and her brother died that

I had any idea; she kept it hidden for all those years, I just thank God my mother never heard the truth, for the truth she already carried in her heart was a burden heavy enough.'

The burden of a bastard son? A child born not of Archer Cranley but given his name to hide a woman's shame. A shame Nathan Briant had known of? Joshua's thoughts raced ahead.

'With Stephen's death my father saw his dreams of owning the glassworks fade, without his son—'

'But you are Hannah Cranley's child, Nathan Briant's grand-child!' Joshua interrupted. 'What difference should it make to him that Archer Cranley was not your father? If Cranley accepted your mother's . . . accepted you as his own flesh and blood, then why not Briant?'

'It seems my mother's father was a man of stubborn will, Joshua, he had no love for the man his daughter married.'

'But why carry it over to you, why name one grandson as his beneficiary but not the other?'

With fair hair gleaming like pale silk in the citrus glow of lamplight, Philippa's head lifted. 'The answer to that is simple, I am not Nathan Briant's grandson.' Ignoring the gasp, the softly spoken explanation continued. 'That is the reason my mother made a new Will, the one she placed with Edward Caddick. She knew I could not inherit any part of her father's estate so, unknown to anyone, she declared the document held by her husband to be null and void. She named a different charity. That is the reason Lawyer Caddick paid a visit to your house.'

Patience ebbing away Joshua pushed to his feet. 'I don't see the connection, what can your mother's Will have to do with me?'

'She wanted the making of glassware to grow, Joshua. Like you, she believed in the beauty of it, knew that the Briant works could produce beautiful things along with bottles and glasses. I think she must have known she was dying when she wrote that letter telling me she knew of the lie my father had perpetrated for so long, one she saw could only be ended by her death.'

Watching the shadows of pain and sorrow chase across those pale features Joshua's anger melted. What twist of fate had landed such suffering on a lad's shoulders, why did he have to pay for his mother's mistake? If he could just hold him, comfort him as he could a child. But Philip Cranley was not a child and giving comfort was not the full reason for the desire to hold him. Self-disgust thickening in his throat Joshua turned his back. He had shamed this lad once by holding him, by touching those soft lips with his own; he would never do it again, never take that slight body in his arms, never tell this pain of the heart.

'Her death released me also –' a little more than a whisper now the explanation went on – 'released me from a sin that is almost too terrible to speak of but one I was prepared to commit in order to save my mother from being locked away in an insane asylum as her husband threatened, one I would have paid for by ending my own life as soon as it was done. But her letter prevented the terrible act, I went to see Davinia Lacy, I broke off the marriage.'

Glancing at that powerful back, the shape of the head outlined against the weak lemony light of the lamp, Philippa twisted her fingers into each other like knots. It was taking every ounce of strength, every atom of will not to beg to be taken into those strong arms, not to have that mouth press . . .

'Huh!'

The scorn in that one sound cutting as sharply into the heart as it did into the thought, she glanced downwards as Joshua turned.

'Is that what all this is really about? Was that what you call sin? Your marrying Davinia Lacy knowing yourself to be Hannah Cranley's bastard, or was it not being Archer Cranley's son mattered so much?'

He had not meant it to sound so hard, so condemning. Pressing his hands close to his sides, Joshua struggled against the urge to take the small unhappy figure, to hold it close, to whisper his love, to say he would shield Philip Cranley from the world.

'It was neither of those things.'

There was no reproof in the quiet answer, no anger in the words, just a gentleness that in itself was punishment. Knowing he could not hold his secret of love much longer, Joshua crossed the dimly lit room.

'There is no need for you to tell me of matters private to your family.' He reached for the door. 'I came here to inform you of the situation at the works, that I have done.'

'Please, Joshua!' Philippa looked up quickly. 'I should not have embarrassed you by speaking as I have when it was only the glassworks I should have spoken of. The Will my mother lodged with Edward Caddick stated the proceeds of the sale of this house together with the works should not exceed one sovereign, it also stated the buyer who should be chosen by myself should undertake to house, educate and train in the skills of glass-making, three apprentice boys each year. I choose you, Joshua. Will you undertake my mother's charity?'

'Me!' Astounded by what Philip had said, Joshua could hardly speak. 'I couldn't . . . it wouldn't be fair . . . I . . .'

'Would it be more fair to let it go to Simeon Beasley?'

The simple question steadying him, Joshua shook his head. 'You are the one should have what Nathan Briant left, what your mother would have wanted you to have even though you are . . .'

'Hannah Cranley's bastard?' Philippa smiled gently. 'No, Joshua, I am not my mother's bastard.'

'Not a child born out of wedlock, yet not a child born of Archer Cranley? Philip, I don't understand . . . why can't you be given the glassworks?'

Lamplight soft on her sad smile Philippa waited a moment, seeming to gather enough courage to answer.

'You asked a few minutes ago was it the fact that I am not Archer Cranley's son which mattered so much. The answer, Joshua, is no; my not being his son did not matter, but then I am not Archer Cranley's son, I am his daughter.'

For one wild moment the earth seemed to spin around Joshua, a great burst of sound crashing in his mind, deafening him to everything as the barrier that had imprisoned his soul crumbled into nothingness.

'*I am his daughter.*'

The words laughed and sang in his brain.

'*I am his daughter.*'

They rang on, their sound like the notes of the purest bells, their taste sweeter than wild honey.

'Philip . . .'

'No, not Philip, not ever again. My name is Philippa.'

The very sound a pleasure that tingled along every vein, Joshua took a step forward then checked himself. He had not loved a man after all, but the woman . . . what right did he have to love her?

'Was it being a girl caused Cranley to do the things he did?' He needed no more explanation, the question was asked only to relieve the emotion tearing through him.

'Yes.' The answer came quietly. 'My grandfather could not conceive of a woman owning his beloved works therefore my father passed me off to the world as a boy, that is the reason for these clothes.'

'But when I saw you with Davinia Lacy . . .'

'The dress? I had wanted so many times to wear a woman's clothes, to be what I am, to end the lie, to let you see the truth, but when I caught the look on your face, the disgust in your eyes, I knew I could not, that I would rather live that lie for the rest of my life than face that look again.'

'Why?' His whisper seeming to fill the room, Joshua looked at the face he loved with all his heart. 'Why?'

'So many questions, Joshua . . .'

'Why?' This time it was a shout, a cry that held all the yearning, all the pain.

Lamplight reflecting blue-washed tears Philippa Cranley looked at the man stood a few feet from her, the man she had loved from the moment their eyes had met across the floor of that heat-filled cone.

'Because,' she faltered, 'because I love you, because . . .'

But the rest was lost as Joshua caught her to him, brought his mouth down on hers, whispered the words he never thought to say.

A lifetime later, a gentle love-filled lifetime later she pushed a little from the hold that never wanted to loose her. Looking into his face she asked, 'Will you undertake my mother's charity, Joshua, will you take the glassworks?'

Brushing her lips with his own, Joshua smiled.

'Only if you come with it.'